Sue MacKay lives with her h
beautiful Marlborough Sound
doorstep and the birds and the
It is the perfect setting to indulge her passions of
entertaining friends by cooking them sumptuous meals,
drinking fabulous wine, going for hill walks or kayaking
around the bay—and, of course, writing stories.

Traci Douglass is a *USA TODAY* bestselling author
of contemporary and paranormal romance. Her stories
feature sizzling heroes full of dark humour, quick
wit and major attitude, and heroines who are smart,
tenacious and always give as good as they get. She holds
an MFA in Writing Popular Fiction from Seton Hill
University, and she loves animals, chocolate, coffee, hot
British actors and sarcasm—not necessarily in that order.

THE NURSE'S TWIN SURPRISE

SUE MacKAY

A WEEKEND WITH HER FAKE FIANCÉ

TRACI DOUGLASS

MILLS & BOON

First Published in Great Britain 2019
by Mills & Boon, an imprint of HarperCollins*Publishers*
1 London Bridge Street, London, SE1 9GF

The Nurse's Twin Surprise © 2019 by Sue MacKay

A Weekend with Her Fake Fiancé © 2019 by Traci Douglass

ISBN: 978-0-263-27958-0

MIX
Paper from
responsible sources
FSC® C007454

This book is produced from independently certified FSC™ paper
to ensure responsible forest management.
For more information visit www.harpercollins.co.uk/green.

Printed and bound in Spain
by CPI, Barcelona

THE NURSE'S TWIN SURPRISE

SUE MacKAY

MILLS & BOON

CHAPTER ONE

FAKE IT TILL you make it.

Yes, sure. So easy. She did it all the time.

Try harder. Remember yesterday's courier delivery.

The final lock had been undone. She was free. Single again. Two years of waiting for the legal process to finally be over. Today was the first day of the rest of her life, and it was going to be a doozy.

That was once she worked out how to proceed with a newer, wiser, not so damned cautious version of herself that yesterday's delivery must shut the door on. Those baby steps she'd been making were fine, but the time had come to stride out, head high, wearing a 'don't mess with me' attitude. Starting now.

Molly O'Keefe pasted on a facsimile of a smile and turned to glare into Mr Nathan Lupton's eyes. And gasped. Those burnt-coffee eyes were spitting tacks. At her?

'What's wrong?'

That's your idea of don't mess with me? Try again.

'That phone call. Something I need to know?'

'I've just spent valuable time ringing round to put specialists on alert at five-thirty in the morning for a patient who's now been taken to another ED.' His hands gripped his hips.

'The man found lying by the train tracks?' Surely not even he was blaming *her*? They weren't friends, but this was ridiculous. The thumping starting up in her chest was deafening. No, he wouldn't be, but he was angry.

Not at me. I can handle this.

Really?

Absolutely. *Fake it till—*

Yeah, yeah, she knew that line back to front. Still needed some practice, that was all. Beginning right now.

'I wonder why the ambulance was redirected to another hospital when we're closest.'

Nathan was staring at her, though she wasn't certain he was actually seeing her. 'That's something I intend finding out. It's not happening again.' He was still angry. Who could blame him when they'd been flat out busy when the initial call had come through? So much for the patients tapering off in the early hours. 'Shouldn't you be keeping an eye on Archie Banks?' he barked.

Odd how on her first day in Sydney General's emergency department when he'd growled at her to get the defib, which she'd already been in the process of wheeling towards the Resus unit, she hadn't been afraid of him. Mightn't like him much, though to be fair she didn't know him except as a doctor, but she was never on guard around him or ever felt threatened by his grumpiness. Which said a lot. She'd think about that later. Right now an answer was required to placate him, because placating kept everyone happy—except maybe her—but it was an old habit she'd still not managed to dump. *Game face, girl.* Duh. Two seconds and her promise to herself had flown the coop.

'I was coming to see if you'd take another look at him. His pain level is increasing, not decreasing.' Nathan had administered a strong dose of painkiller forty minutes ago.

The anger softened. Of course it did. From what she'd seen around here Nathan adored children. 'Anything from the lab yet?'

'No, and I've only just checked,' she added hastily, raising one of her grandmother's glares in case he found fault with her. Another sign she might be getting her act together.

Dark eyebrows rose in that annoying manner of his that inexplicably riled her beyond reason. Then he swallowed and pulled up a smile. 'Sorry. It wasn't your fault the man was taken elsewhere after I've been chasing my tail preparing for his arrival.'

It wasn't the greatest of apologies, but he had tried, and that was unexpected. 'No problem.' None he need know about. She had a list of them, but nothing to do with work. This was her safe place. 'Archie?'

'On my way.' He strode off, his back ramrod straight, his jaw jutting out, yet she'd swear some of his tension had eased.

'Good girl, not letting him rile you.' Vicki nudged her, and brought her back to focusing on anything other than *Mr* Lupton.

'You think?' she asked around a tight laugh, her eyes still taking in the sight of Nathan despite trying to concentrate on what Vicki had to say.

'I do.' Her fellow nurse was also watching Nathan, now heading into a cubicle, and there was a thoughtful tone to her next question that unsettled Molly. 'Still coming to breakfast?'

'Wouldn't miss it for anything.' She meant every word, even after struggling with a strong reluctance to socialise and get too comfortable when she half expected to be nudged out of the way by people who wanted more from her than she was prepared to share. She had initially hesitated about accepting the invitation, then decided to give it a go. After all, Vicki had been friendly and helpful since she'd begun working in here two months ago.

A flicker of excitement warmed her. Look where *faking it* got her. Right into the middle of her colleagues, whose good intentions had brought her close to tears on occasion, even when she didn't trust them enough to give back anything of herself. Getting out and about with this crowd might go some way to fixing the loneliness that filled her days and nights. Not being a team player had come at a price, one that needed to be dealt with if she was to be happy again.

'Molly? Can you come here, please?' Nathan had reappeared in the cubicle doorway, back to being calm and efficient.

Molly looked at the man and, hiding the uncertainty he created in her belly, nodded. 'Need the phlebotomy kit?' Her voice had returned to non-confrontational, Gran's glare long gone. Situation normal. Previous normal. Lifting her shoulders, she reached for the bag of needles and tubes.

Nathan's smile might be reluctant, but it actually seemed genuine. Meaning it was further unsettling. 'Yes. I want liver functions done while we wait for the orderly to collect him.'

The boy, recovering from an appendicectomy last week, was back with pains in his gut and chest. Nathan suspected septicaemia and had started him on an array of intravenous antibiotics. They were now waiting for the children's ward to collect him.

In the cubicle, she said, 'Hey, Archie, I'm going to find you some dry pyjamas after I've cleaned you up.'

With the fever drenching him continually, the boy needed regular wiping down.

Archie was eyeing the kit with trepidation. No hiding what was coming from this kid. 'I don't want another needle.'

'It's annoying, isn't it?' Nathan said as he slid the tourniquet up the boy's thin arm. 'You'll be able to tell all your friends how brave you are.'

Molly sponged Archie's legs, in an attempt to distract him. 'I hope you're not ticklish.' Not that she intended tickling him when Nathan was about to slide a needle into a vein. That would be taking distraction to the next level.

'Mum tickles me.' Archie's eyes were on Nathan, apprehension blinking out of his big eyes.

'There, all done.' Moments later Nathan handed her the tube of blood to name and date. 'Mark it urgent.'

'Right.' She headed for the hub to call for an orderly to take the blood sample to the lab.

Nathan had followed her. 'How're you settling in with us?'

'Fine.' I hope. 'I really like the job, and the people I work with.' Had she done something wrong he was about to mention? Wasn't she good enough at her work? The usual worry over making herself stand out began chugging through her mind.

'Good. We don't like swapping staff too often.' Then, 'So what do you do when you're not here?' Nathan was being friendly? Abnormally friendly, since he wasn't known for idle chitchat.

How to answer without giving herself away? 'There's always heaps of things needing attention where I live and people to check up on and shopping at the mall.' Drivel spilled over her lips. 'And I like going for walks.' Definitely faking it. She rarely left the apartment other than to come to work.

He was regarding her like he was sorry he'd asked. Good, then he wouldn't find any more questions for her. *Wrong.* 'Sounds like your evenings are free so you'll have time to come to our midwinter Christmas barbecue.' Nathan was talking about the out of season party some Aussies celebrated that had come about because of English people living in Australia who missed a cold Christmas. He tapped a sheet of paper lying on the desk. 'I don't see your name here.'

That was because she had no intention of going. She wasn't ready for that level of integration. An hour over breakfast was one thing, a full-on party quite another. *Thought I was starting over, now that I'm free.* 'I haven't thought about it.' What excuse could she come up with? She tried to read the shift roster behind Nathan, but he was blocking her line of vision.

'It's a fortnight away but I like to know who's coming well in advance. Bring a plate and your own alcohol. Meat provided.' He was pointing a pen over his shoulder. 'You're not working that night.'

There went that excuse for not going. Little did he know about how hard it was for her to go anywhere that was attended by lots of people.

He hadn't finished. 'I encourage all the staff to join in. It's good for morale, amongst other things.'

New beginnings, remember? Deep breath. Go for it. Taking the pen from his fingers, mindful of not touching him, Molly scrawled her name beneath Vicki's and added *Dessert* next to it. 'There. Done.' And she hadn't stopped too long to think about it. *Definitely* a first.

'Good.' His tone didn't back his reply. Those toast-coloured eyes were focused on her as though she was a mystery he was trying to unravel. She'd probably surprised him by giving in so quickly when it was well known she didn't go out with any of the staff to movies or breakfasts.

Amazed at how easily she'd signed up, she stood absorbing the slow wave of excitement rolling through her. She could do this. She really, really could. 'Where's the barbecue being held?'

'At my place out in Coogee.' He picked up a patient file and began reading the notes. Dark blond hair fell over his brow, making her itch to push it back in place.

'Oh.' The heavy pounding in her chest had returned, and her mouth began drying up like an overbaked sponge. Why hadn't she noticed before that Nathan was disgustingly good looking? Probably her massive hang-up about getting close to men had kept the blinkers on until today, when she'd made the promise to move on, get a life. Did that mean finding love? Thump, thump, thump. It couldn't. That'd be going too far, too soon. Molly had learned Paul's lessons well. An absolute charmer, he'd sworn his undying love for her and wooed her completely. One year into their marriage the real Paul had come to light when he'd started hitting her whenever she'd disagreed with him, which was a sure-fire way of making her keep her mouth shut. Suddenly noticing Nathan as more than a doctor was scary. Wasn't it?

'Problem with that?' Nathan asked without looking up.

'Hell, yes.' She wasn't ready. It was too soon—wasn't part of the plan to move on.

Puzzlement blinked out at her. 'Why? It's usual to go to someone's house for a party.'

Embarrassment rose. She'd answered her question to herself out loud. This man was rattling her, which made no sense when, because of his self-assurance, she'd pretty much ignored him in the two months she'd worked here, unless it was to discuss a patient or argue over small things, like where the order for more syringes had got to. It'd been years since desire had lit her up, but if this tightness in her stomach and heat in her veins were any indication, she might be making up for lost time right now, in the middle of the ED. 'Um, of course. I didn't mean that. It's fine. I'll be there.'

The alarm sounded. Code one. Relief had her racing to Resus and the man sprawled on the floor, unconscious.

'Cardiac arrest,' Vicki said, her clasped hands pushing down regularly on the exposed chest.

Molly grabbed the electro pads, handed them to Nathan, who was right behind her. Next she snatched up the ventilator in preparation of a good outcome before kneeling down next to him.

'Fill us in on the details,' Nathan said as he prepared to administer a shock.

'Geoff Baxter, forty-eight, chest pains, readings show a minor cardiac arrest an hour ago,' Vicki intoned. 'He was getting stroppy and didn't want to stay on the bed. Started getting up and collapsed on the floor.'

'Clear.'

On Nathan's command everyone moved away from the patient. The lifeless body jerked. The line on the monitor remained flat. Vicki started back on the compressions and Molly squeezed the oxygen bottle when she reached thirty.

'Clear.' Nathan gave a second shock.

The line blipped, rose, then fell into an erratic pattern.

'That's better,' Molly nodded. 'Not perfect, but we're getting there.' She put the ventilator aside and got up to get the scoop stretcher so they could lift the man off the floor and back onto the bed.

Another nurse, Hank, attached an oxygen mask, then began wiping a bleeding abrasion on Geoff's forehead. 'He hit the floor hard.'

Nathan leaned close to the man. 'Geoff, can you hear me?'

Geoff opened his eyes briefly.

'You've had a cardiac arrest. We're going to keep you in here for a while, then you'll be admitted to the intensive care unit.'

Geoff shook his head once. 'No.'

'That'll be a yes, then.' Nathan gave one of his megawatt smiles.

Molly's stomach stirred, and he hadn't even been looking in her direction. He'd often smiled at her, particularly whenever he'd wanted something unpleasant dealt with, but not in that full-on, cramp-her-stomach way he saved for others. Not that she'd given him reason to. Unless working hard and caring deeply about their patients counted, and apparently it didn't. That was expected of her, no reward given—or required.

Would a man ever again look at her and think, *She's lovely*? One without hard fists? Did she want a man to notice her, get to know her? This new idea had to be part of moving forward, didn't it? It was funny how in a previous, happy-go-lucky life she'd had her pick of gorgeous men, never had a problem finding a date for the glamorous occasions that came with being her entrepreneurial mother's daughter. Not funny, really. Glancing over her shoulder, she saw no one to frighten her. Not that she expected to, but there were still times she just had to check, even though Paul would be in jail for many years to come. She'd lost a lot, but she was free.

Hold on to that. And, yes, think about maybe one day falling love.

Vicki nudged her. 'Time to knock off, day shift's here.'

Another night done and survived without too much drama amongst the patients. She could relax, except her muscles weren't playing the game. The old tension tightened her stomach and neck, while her shoulder blades tried to meet in the middle of her back. Because of the past? Or did she put this down to the rare heat in her veins, stirred up by Nathan Lupton? Yeah, like that'd be a blast. *It might be.* As if. He'd have to get a lot friendlier first, though he had made an effort earlier. Were things looking up all round? Smiling at Vicki, she asked, 'Which shoes are you wearing this morning?'

'Those orange, thin-strapped ones you were green about last week.' Vicki was a shoeaholic, with an incredible collection that made Molly envious—and that was only over the shoes she'd seen at work.

Molly laughed. Twice in one morning? *Go for it.* 'Clothes are my go to when the urge to have some R and R in the malls beckons. Shoes always come second. Maybe I should try the shoe shops first next time because those ones are amazing. When you're sick of them you know which locker's mine,' she said. 'Let's go change.' As well as her trousers and blouse, she needed to put her game face on.

Nathan turned from the specialist taking over Geoff's case. 'You all right?'

'Why wouldn't I be?' There were a million reasons, but he knew none of them, and never would.

'Because you look ready to bolt.'

Make that one million minus one reasons. Except this morning that had been the last thing on her mind. Disconcerting. She'd been laughing and he'd thought that? She hated that nearly as much as she'd hate him to see the truth. 'Actually, I'm working on how to nab Vicki's shoes without her noticing.'

His expression softened. 'Good luck with that.'

'I reckon.' Unbelievable. They were having a normal conversation for once.

'By the way, you were good with Geoff.'

Surprise stole the retort off her tongue. She hadn't done anything out of the ordinary, and yet he was saying that in front of the other nurses? She looked around at Vicki, then Hank, before locking eyes back on Nathan.

He got the message fast. 'So were you two.' He nodded. 'Right, get out of here while you can.' This time he was talking directly to Vicki.

Molly knew she could relax now that Nathan was no longer focused on her, but it wasn't happening. Instead her body was winding up tighter than a ball of twine, and just as rough. Why did this man in particular make her feel a little lighter in the chest, as though hope was knocking? Hope for love one day? Sadly, never for family. That dream had been smothered as a wet sack would a flame by a fist in her belly that had stolen her baby and quite likely any chance of another.

She looked at Nathan as he laughed with Vicki over something, and her heart dropped. If only she had the courage to let a strong, confident man close enough to trust. Until now it never occurred to her to want the things Paul had stolen. But it couldn't be this man waking her up. They were mostly civil with each other, but it took more than civility for a relationship to succeed. Or maybe it didn't. There hadn't been any of that going on in her now defunct marriage.

Flip-flop went her heart. Her stomach softened as the tension started backing off. As though her body was telling her it was ready to have fun. Had certain parts of her anatomy forgotten the pain of the past? It wasn't wise. Or safe. But very tempting. And eye-opening. One thing this newer version of herself had in common with the last one was that it needed a man who had his own world sussed and wasn't afraid to stand up and be counted. As long as he didn't hurt her.

Nathan knew he'd overreacted to Molly O'Keefe's false smile about the barbecue, but he'd had enough of those. Two months and not once had she joined the staff for a meal, let alone anything else, despite everyone trying to persuade her. Whether she thought she was too good for them, or she believed she wasn't good enough, the jury was still out.

Yet she'd been quick to sign up for the barbecue. Part of him questioned whether she'd actually show up; another suggested maybe Molly didn't back down once she'd taken a stance. Despite working alongside her, often in trying circumstances, he didn't know her at all, which was unusual given the work they did. She didn't fall over backwards to get on with him. That might make him egotistical, but nothing added up. He got on well with most folk, and socialised enough not to return to being the hermit he'd become after Rosie's death.

Molly's a challenge.

He stumbled, righted himself, his eyes seeking out the woman doing this to him. Did he want her to like him? Now, *that* sounded needy. Hardly true when he had his pick of friends, even women. His gaze cruised across the department to the locker-room door from where a burst of laughter came. Vicki was doing her best to be happy on her thirtieth birthday, but her heart was sad because Cole was supposedly deployed offshore with the army.

He couldn't wait to see her face when he dropped his

best friend off at their apartment this afternoon. It would be a big surprise, one he couldn't justify when he saw the sadness lurking in the back of Vicki's eyes. He'd prefer to tell her the truth, and have her meet Cole, but he'd given his friend his word, and promises were not to be broken.

Molly appeared in the doorway, a rare genuine smile lighting up her face and causing those emerald eyes to sparkle, though she'd glared at him earlier. He shouldn't have pushed her buttons but, hell, it'd been impossible not to when he was exhausted after eight hours dealing with what felt like half of Sydney coming through the ED's doors.

Molly rattled him in ways he couldn't believe. He was not used to having his libido captivated by a woman who wasn't interested in him. What libido? Since Rosie's death there'd been little going on in that department, and when there was it was for relief, not involvement. He couldn't imagine being lucky enough to find love for a second time, hadn't been ready to consider it because who got that lucky? Yet today Molly had him questioning that.

Nathan shrugged. So there might be more nous behind Nurse O'Keefe's non-confrontational looks and that beautiful, heart-stopping face than he thought. He should've wound her up weeks ago if the flaring temper in her expression was the result. Far more interesting than quiet and mousy, as he'd believed. A shiver ripped down his spine, but not because her haughty glare daunted him. Not a bit. Instead it gave him a sharp awareness of the woman behind the glare.

Molly was waking up his body, which he preferred to leave in sleep mode until *he* decided otherwise. The sense of being slightly off balance had come out of left field the day she'd started in the department, and now he'd had enough of feeling out of whack. This morning it'd been time to push her boundaries over not joining in staff events so he could get relief from these frustrating sensations. This reaction confused him, and made him feel more than annoyed. Yeah, frustrated. But as in sexually or more? He didn't have a clue.

'You all going to spend the day in there?' he called out. No way did he intend heading to the café without making sure Molly didn't do a runner, because, say what she liked, she had looked edgy for a moment. Vicki liked her a lot, so Molly doing an about-face wasn't happening.

'Pretty much. How come you waited?' Molly's enticing shoulders had returned to their normal, slightly sloped position and her chin had softened back to quiet and mousy.

Except he no longer trusted his interpretation of that look. There was more to Nurse O'Keefe than met the eye. Deep down, had he always suspected so? And reacted accordingly by keeping his barriers in place to protect himself? For better or worse, there was a need ticking inside him making it impossible to look away, or deny how she intrigued him, or pretend he did not want her in his bed, underneath him. Or on top if she preferred. Jeez. He scrubbed his hands down his face. What was wrong with him?

'You run out of words?'

Something like that. 'I'm making sure no one gets lost.'

Her smile didn't slip a notch. 'I told Vicki I'd be there, and I never go back on my word.' Then doubt—or was it guilt?—slid through her sharp gaze and she looked away.

'Glad to hear it.' What was that about? Had she let someone down? In a big way that had come back to haunt her? Behind his ribs a sense of confusion lurched and an unreal feeling of protectiveness crept over him. For Molly? Hardly. There was definitely far more to this woman than he'd realised, but why spend time wondering what made her tick when it was obvious she wouldn't have a bar of him? She was a challenge. And causing a pool of desire to settle in his gut.

Could be hunger for food doing a number on him. Not Molly. He'd missed snack breaks throughout the night—always a bad thing. But nothing was dispelling that softening sensation in his belly as he watched her. Without even trying, she was doing a number on him. Bet he was the last person she wanted to spend time with, even if only over coffee. Was it time for a change? On both their parts? Could be it was time for him to step outside his secure bubble and poke at life, see where it took him.

As long as it wasn't more than he was prepared to give. More than he was *able* to give. He'd given his heart to Rosie, and she'd taken it to the grave with her. Or so he'd believed, until—until now and the thin ray of hope beginning to pierce his long-held belief that he couldn't be that lucky.

He and Rosie had been childhood sweethearts and so in love it had been unreal at times. Except reality had got in the way of their plans for a house and babies in the form of leukaemia. From the first day Rosie had complained of lethargy and swollen, sore glands they had been on a one-way road to hell. It had been a short trip, lasting little more than three months. He'd been glad for her sake it was over quickly, but for himself he'd only wanted her never to leave him, taking his dreams away for ever.

The disease that had taken Rosie's life had a lot to answer for. He used to picture them together, raising their kids, having a great life. The past four years had been long, and lonely in a way he wouldn't have believed before she'd died.

'Nathan?'

He pulled out of his reverie to find Vicki watching him with amusement forming crinkles at the corners of her eyes. 'Yes?'

'Lead on. We're all good to go.' Her wink was slow, and downright mischievous, reminding him how she and Cole thought it was time he came out of his cave. Grabbing his elbow, Vicki strode ahead of the group, tugging him along with her.

'I'm hangry,' he warned around a smile. His friends cared about him so he let them off their interfering ways.

Vicki only laughed. 'I heard you giving Molly a bit of a roasting this morning about the winter party. One she didn't deserve, by the way.'

'Someone had to tell her to get over staying on the fringe around us.'

Vicki jabbed him with an elbow. 'Others have told you they'll be there and not signed the list. Who needs a list anyway?'

'I do.' He huffed a breath. 'Why did she do that pen-snatching thing and scrawl her name across the page large enough to suggest I might be blind?'

'To rile you? It worked, by the way.'

I know that. Damn her. 'Right.' A spurt of resentment soured his mouth. He swallowed it away, and managed to laugh at himself. So Miss Mousy had got one over him. Game on, Molly O'Keefe.

Vicki hadn't finished. 'I'm glad you nudged her about joining in. It's good for her.' Another jab from that blasted elbow. 'She needs to get out more.'

Nathan stared at his friend. 'Since when has she talked about anything that's not to do with patients?' He'd never heard Molly say something as simple as she'd been to the hair salon. And, yes, he knew when she went because those short, red curls would be quiet, in place, for a few days before returning to their riot of crazy colour. He preferred the wild to the tamed.

A tingling itch sometimes crept over his palms as he wondered about pushing his fingers through her hair. Then he'd remember he didn't have a heart any more and would go and see a patient. See? Early on she *had* disturbed him in ways only Rosie had ever done, yet they were opposites. Rosie had mostly been calm, with little that would upset her. On the other hand, Miss Quiet and Mousy, red head contrasting with her temperament and all, managed to upset his orderly existence without even trying, especially when he was overtired or pressured by a particularly ill child. As of now he was going to delete mousy from the nickname.

Vicki tapped him none too gently on the shoulder to bring his attention back to her. 'Molly lives in an apartment on the third floor of a block in Bondi Junction, takes the train to work, has a regular car that doesn't stand out at the lights, and likes to watch comedy shows on TV. Oh, and she has lots of amazing clothes that suggest a previous life that wasn't so lean.'

'You two are close.'

'Sarcasm is the lowest form of wit.' Vicki grinned. 'But you're forgiven since you're in need of food.'

Nathan shook his head. He'd learned more in two minutes than he had in the past weeks. More than Molly being a superb nurse with a special way with the younger patients that came their way so they all fell in love with her, even when she was cleaning a wound that stung or sliding a needle into their arm. He could also admit to seeing her wearing stunning—and expensive—figure-enhancing outfits when she strode onto the ward heading for the staff changing room at the beginning of her shifts. Not that her figure needed enhancing; it did a damned good job of filling out her uniform and her day clothes all by itself.

Bondi Junction, eh? And here he'd been thinking she probably lived in one of the upmarket suburbs near or on Sydney Harbour's waterfront.

Expensive clothes, average address. Once had money, now getting by? Throw in not mixing with people, the loneliness that sometimes blitzed her eyes, and he had to wonder if she'd been let down big-time. That protective instinct raised its head again. Guess he'd never know what was behind Molly's attitude since she wasn't likely to spill her guts over breakfast. Especially not to him. 'Let's hope she enjoys herself.'

'We'll do our best to make sure she does.' Another wink came his way.

'Stop that. Whatever that wicked mind of yours is coming up with, it's not happening. You have a birthday to focus on, not someone else's problems.' Suddenly Nathan was more than pleased Molly was here. He understood loneliness, knew how it could drag a person down deep. After Rosie had died he'd holed up in their home, only coming out to attend lectures or work a shift at the hospital, doing what was required to qualify—no more, no less. None of his friends or family had been able to prise him out into the real world to become involved with people and life other than what was required for patients and qualifying as an emergency specialist.

To get past the pain of losing Rosie he'd focused entirely on those things and it had worked for the first couple of years. Then he'd begun to understand he wasn't any use to the people who needed his medical skills if he didn't get out and about, and that he owed the people he loved for sticking around.

'We're having champagne this morning.' Vicki laughed.

'Already sorted,' he agreed, his mood lightening further in anticipation of spending time with this group of chatterboxes.

And Molly. No, forget that. She wouldn't start yabbering on to him. Maybe by the end of breakfast they'd be a little further ahead in knowing each other, but that was all. Bet she'd still have his hands tingling and his gut tightening, though. 'Shows we're in need of a life when this is as exciting as it gets.'

Nathan hated admitting it, but he'd been looking forward to breakfast. His heart felt lighter, and the blood seemed to move faster in his veins. Molly had nothing to do with the happy sensations in his chest, or the sudden urge to be on his best, most charming behaviour. *That* needed a bit of practice anyway, and she'd see straight through him and ignore his attempts.

CHAPTER TWO

As THE GROUP approached the café entrance, Molly smoothed down her trousers and jacket, hauled her shoulders back so that she looked and felt confident, before following everyone inside to the reserved table where Nathan was pulling out a chair on the far side.

Why did she seek him out? Because his mood had improved? Out of doctor mode and into something friendlier, less gruff than usual. Still handsome and mouth-watering. He didn't often come across as too confident and charming, even though he could enchant a screaming patient into quietly accepting an injection and his medical knowledge was second to none. Experience had taught her to look behind a man's character traits to find out what really made him tick.

'Vicki?' Nathan indicated the chair he'd pulled out.

'The birthday girl gets to sit at the top of the table.' Hank pulled out another chair.

'You're right.' Vicki grinned and sat down on Hank's chair. 'Molly, why don't you take that chair Nathan's holding?'

Because Nathan had already slung his jacket over the one next to it. Looking around the table, Molly saw seats were filling rapidly, leaving her little choice. *Fake it...* Forcing a smile on her mouth and lifting her chin like nothing was wrong in her world—because it wasn't any more—she strolled around to plonk down on the chair Nathan was holding out. 'Thanks.'

'You want a coffee?' he asked, surprise and something else she couldn't interpret flitting across his face.

Thoughtlessly putting a hand on his arm, she said, 'I'll get it.' She jerked away. She never touched a man. Showed how safe she felt around Nathan, despite his attitude.

He said in his I'm-here-to-help-you voice usually reserved for patients, 'I'm going to check the champagne I've ordered to toast Vicki's birthday is coming out soon. I'll put our coffee orders in at the same time.' His gaze was intent, his eyes searching for something in her expression.

Okay, lighten up. 'That'd be great. A flat white, thanks.' Her tongue felt far too big for her mouth. Just another way he tipped her world off its new axis. 'Are we all putting in for the champagne?' But he was gone, slipping through the crowd building around other tables, aiming for the counter, head and shoulders above everyone he passed.

Since she'd run away from Paul she hadn't gone out with a man, never let one in her home or talked about her past to anyone. At first she'd struggled facing the world as most people she knew had blamed her for Paul's arrest. He was so charismatic they'd believed him until the truth had come out in court and those same people had begun fawning over her, wanting to get back onside. She'd struggled not to turn bitter. At the time, dating men had been an impossibility.

Until now. Looking at Nathan, she thought he'd be protective of those he loved. He always stood up for a patient whenever a family member tried to force proceedings in the department that were wrong. No doubt he'd protect anybody who got into danger if he was close by.

Downright crazy to believe that without proof. Look what happened the last time I trusted a man.

Paul hadn't been kind and gentle with those less fortunate than himself, instead he'd enjoyed showing how much better than others he was. Something she hadn't seen until it had been too late. Hadn't known to look. Paul had been the catch every woman wanted, and with her mother actively encouraging her, she'd gone for him and won. Then lost. The first year of her marriage had been bliss, then the cracks had started appearing. She was a lousy hostess, a simpleton, useless at any damned thing. Then she'd fallen pregnant and it was all over.

Molly shook her head. *Stop right now.* She was out with a bunch of great people. She needed to forget the self-pity and enjoy herself, not turn in on herself and repeat the mistake she'd made with the Roos, the basketball team she'd been a member of. The regret she felt every weekend when she looked up the team's results from the Saturday game made her ache, made her wish she'd stopped worrying about letting anyone close for fear of being hurt and got on with enjoying being a part of a great bunch of women. If only she hadn't given in and quit, she might've moved on with getting a life sooner.

So, get cracking and enjoy this morning.

Straightening her spine and breathing deeply, she then fell into another old habit, checking out the latest suits to walk into the café, swinging briefcases and checking their phones. But today she wasn't looking for trouble, instead comparing the men with Nathan. He came out top every time. Something to think about once she was back in her apartment.

'Here you go. Coffee's on the way.' A glass of water appeared before her. 'As is the champagne,' Nathan told Vicki.

'Great.' Molly sat up straighter. Today she might even celebrate her divorce. One sip of champagne for that, and no one at the table would be any the wiser.

Her gaze returned to Nathan, and instantly her heart forgot that memo about not thumping too hard. Crazy. He was just another male she worked with—one who happened to be bone-meltingly good looking, and currently making her aware of him in ways she'd hadn't known around men for a long time. Yet there was something about him that had her wondering what it would be like to curl up against his chest, be held in those strong arms and just relax, be happy. No, it wasn't happening. She wasn't ready. Could she give it a go? Probably not.

Nathan handed her a menu. 'Here, take a look. Most of us know this off by heart. There are some great choices.'

'Suddenly I'm starving.' Molly began scanning the page.

Nathan grunted. 'I'm past hungry. Could eat a whole sirloin.'

She laughed. 'How about tofu and grains?'

His eyes widened. He hadn't thought she'd tease him? Last week she wouldn't have. 'You can't pull that one. Like I said, I've been here before.'

'Okay, so one whole sirloin, and what?' The whole steak wasn't on offer, but he could order two helpings. 'Chips or hash browns, as well as eggs and bacon?'

'Stop right there.' He was smiling directly at her, and it was making her stomach feel like hot chocolate dropped into cream, swirling, warming, tempting. 'Don't mention food like that when I'm this hungry.'

'But you're smiling.' When she was starving she couldn't smile.

'Don't trust it.'

Sorry, Nathan, but I do believe you. Gazing at him, and especially at his smile, Molly felt no qualms. No fear of him erupting into a rage because he needed to eat now, not in ten minutes. Again, she felt that rare sense of safety around him. Needing to put mental space between them, she'd join in the conversations going on around her and enjoy the birthday celebration. After she told the hovering waitress she'd like the eggs Benedict, that was.

The room was crowded, with a queue waiting at the counter for take-out coffees and pastries. In their corner her group was out of the way and could talk without yelling. The champagne arrived and glasses were filled.

Nathan stood up. 'Happy birthday, Vicki. May all your wishes come true.'

Vicki blinked. 'Thanks. I only have one, and it's not happening.' Another blink, and she raised her glass. 'Cheers, everyone, and thank you for joining me today.'

Molly wanted to hug Vicki and wipe away that sadness. Spontaneous hugs not being her thing any more, the best she could manage was to have fun, and not bring her past into the room. Suddenly she was very glad she'd come. Today she'd started to live, not just exist. It was a tiny step in the right direction, but it was a bigger step than usual. There'd be plenty more. Yes, there would.

Nathan sat down and picked up his glass of water. 'Anyone want to start singing "Happy Birthday"? Not me, I'd empty the place.'

'That'd make it a memorable day for Vicki,' someone joked.

Without a thought, Molly began singing 'Happy Birthday'. Instead of everyone joining in, they stared at her. She faltered to a stop. 'What's wrong?'

'Nothing,' everyone cried. 'Carry on.'

Embarrassed, she shook her head and sipped her water. 'Someone else can have a turn.'

'Not after that, they can't,' Nathan muttered. 'You sing like an angel.'

For a moment she forgot everything except the memories of singing, especially with Gran, and how happy it had made her. 'I inherited my grandmother's singing gene.' Gran had paid for her lessons until she'd decided she didn't want music as a career but rather a happy go-to place. 'She sang for the national opera company.' She'd also been the only one to question her love for Paul before the wedding.

Not now, Moll. Having fun, okay?

She turned to Nathan. 'That's some car you've got. I saw you arrive at work last Wednesday when I drove in for a change.'

Again he was watching her intently, but at least there was no tension lurking behind his gaze this time. *And* he went with her change of subject. 'Not bad, eh? I only bought it a month ago and haven't had time to take it for a spin out on the highway. But it has to happen soon, or else I might as well sell it.'

'That'd be a waste.' She couldn't think of anything more exciting than speeding along the road in that amazing car, forgetting everything and enjoying the moment.

Wrong, Moll. Being with Nathan would be more exciting.

Molly spluttered into her coffee.

Nathan held out a serviette. 'Here, wipe your face.'

Trying to snatch the paper serviette from his fingers only caused her to touch him, and she pulled back. Heat that had nothing to do with stopping the spluttering and everything to do with longing began unfurling deep inside her. It came with a growing awareness of herself as a woman, and of the man beside her. 'You a dad, by any chance? You have a thing about goo on faces?'

The serviette was scrunched into a ball and dropped back on the table. 'No kids,' he muttered and looked away.

Back to upsetting him. She didn't know what to say for fear of further annoying him. Time to talk to someone else. Leaning forward, she eyeballed Emma across the table. 'When do you head over to Queenstown?' The intern was going to New Zealand's winter festival.

'Thursday. I can't wait. Have you been?'

'Years ago. It's an amazing event in an extraordinary location.'

Nathan wasn't going to be ignored. 'Did you go on the jet boat?'

'Of course.'

'You're obviously into speed.' When he smiled his whole face lit up in a way she rarely saw.

'I guess I am. Not that I've done anything extreme. Nor will I be. Safe and sensible is me.'

'Nothing wrong with that.' Nathan was watching her in a way that suggested he wanted to know more about what made her tick outside work. But he waited, didn't push.

Which had her opening up a little. 'I liked my sports, sailing on large yachts, going to rock concerts, things like that.'

'Liked?' he asked quietly. 'Not any more?'

Thump. Reality check. Hurrying to deflect him, she spluttered, 'Still like, but I don't seem to find the time any more. Neither do I know anyone in Sydney with a yacht the size I'm used to.' Actually, she did, but that family was part of the past, so she wasn't paying them a visit any time soon. In fact, never.

'I don't suppose a three-metre Paper Tiger would suffice?' Nathan wasn't laughing at her, just keeping the conversation going on a comfortable level, like he was trying to stop her tripping into the black hole that was her past. He couldn't be. He knew nothing about it. 'My brother-in-law's got one.'

A laugh huffed across her lips, surprising her. 'Me? Actually sail a small yacht? I don't think so. I'd probably fall off or drop the sail at the wrong moment.'

'All part of learning to sail.' He grinned, then told her about his misadventures on his surfboard.

Nearly an hour later people had finished eating, and were beginning to gather their gear together.

'Guess it's time to head away,' Molly said reluctantly. It had been fun talking and laughing with everyone, but especially with Nathan. He was different away from work, more at ease with her somehow, talking about Queenstown, his car, and other things. He even laughed and smiled often. He was a man she liked and wanted to spend more time learning more about.

Nathan leaned closer, said quietly, 'Feel like a ride in my car?' There was a cheeky smile on that divine mouth, and something in his eyes that asked if she was up to it. 'I can drop you home.'

Molly's mouth dropped open. She snapped it closed. Then spluttered, 'That's not necessary. I'm fine with the train.'

Across the table Vicki rolled her hand from side to side. 'Train or top-of-the-range sports car. I know which I'd prefer.'

So did she. Except the car meant being squashed into a confined space with a man. Not just any man. Nathan. Standing up, she said, oh, so casually, 'It's a long way to Bondi Junction.'

'It's on my way. I live in Coogee.' When she raised her eyebrows, he continued in a voice that suggested he was determined she'd go with him, 'I didn't even finish one glass of champagne so you don't have to worry about my driving.'

'I wasn't.'

Nathan shrugged. 'Let's fix our bills and get the car.'

'Nathan, you don't have to do this.' At least he hadn't offered to pay for her meal. Thank goodness for something, because she'd have argued hotly. Paying her own way meant never owing anyone anything. Her stomach was doing a squeeze and release thing, while her head spun with the thought she'd be crammed into a car with a male she didn't know very well. With Nathan Lupton, sex on legs, kindness in his heart and, don't forget, someone who was quick to get grumpy with her, but who she trusted not to hurt her.

'You said you like fast cars.'

True. She couldn't contain the smile splitting her face. Her first car had been a racy little number bought by her mother for her eighteenth birthday. She'd loved it. 'But you can't get up any speed between here and my apartment.'

'Now, there's a challenge.' He smiled back and flipped a coin in the air, caught it and laughed.

Nathan watched the conflicting emotions zipping across Molly's face and damned if they didn't make him want to spend more time with her, not to prove he could win her over but because he just might like her. The challenge was heating up. Though not in the way he'd intended. The offer of a ride home was because on and off throughout breakfast he'd warmed to her more and more, therefore he didn't want the morning to end.

Today Molly intrigued him. He was not walking away. Nope. The genuine happiness lightening her gaze throughout breakfast had stirred him in places usually unaffected by other people, and had him wishing for more, had him remembering he'd once had a heart and thinking he just might like to get it back—if he could find the courage. She'd be a keeper, if he wanted to get involved, and that was the problem. He didn't. Here was the rub. He might be ready to start dating on a regular basis but the thought of anything permanent still freaked him out. To fall in love and have his heart torn out of his chest a second time was unimaginable.

'Ready when you are.' The smile lifting the enticing corners of Molly's soft mouth was real, and not that strained, 'smile if I absolutely have to' version she was so good at. Seemed she'd quite quickly got over trying to talk him out of giving her a lift.

Because he wanted to believe Molly's smile had been for him, he'd risk being hit over the head by teasing her. 'You could seem more excited.'

'Sure.' She leaned in to give Vicki a hug. 'Happy birthday. If you need some company later, give me a call.'

Vicki's eyes lit up. 'I might just do that. Shoe shopping comes to mind.'

Molly was looking surprised about something. It wouldn't be shoes. Everyone knew of Vicki's fetish for footwear. Something else had put the stunned look on her face.

'You could do worse than hanging out with Vicki.'

She glanced down at her high-heeled, black-with-a-bow shoes. 'I reckon.' Then she looked back at him and shrugged, said with caution in her voice, 'No time like now to get back into it.'

Get back into friendships? Again that protective need nudged, stronger this time. He felt certain something had gone amiss with Molly, something that kept her on edge and wary around her colleagues. 'Vicki, you right for getting home?'

That cheeky grin flicked from him to Molly, then disappeared, unhappiness replacing it. 'I'm fine.'

Only because his car was a two-seater, he nodded. 'See you around three.'

'You don't have to coddle me because it's my birthday. Anyway, I'm going shopping with Molly.'

'Yes, I do.' Or Cole would have his guts for guitar strings. 'Shop as much as you like but be home when I get there.'

Molly eyed first him then Vicki, who gave her a big smile before heading out the door. 'You two are close.' Something strangely like envy darkened her voice.

'Her husband's been my best mate from years back when we were into surfing. We continued our friendship into med school, and never stopped since.' Cole had been there for him in the darkest days. Taking Molly's elbow, he kept his touch light when he longed to pull her closer and breathe in that rich fragrance that was her. Funny but he hadn't realised how often he'd smelled it until now. She really was doing a number on him, and didn't have a clue. Which was something to be grateful for. That, and not how he was spending time with her, breaking down the barrier she kept between them.

'You don't surf now?' When she tilted her head back to stare up at him it was almost impossible not to reach across to tuck some wayward curls behind her ear.

Resisting required effort, so it took time to answer. 'Occasionally I chase a wave out where I live but not as often as I used to. Cole joined the army and I broke an ankle. That didn't prevent me getting back on the board once the bones mended, but around that time specialised study began taking up all my spare hours.'

What was left had been for Rosie. Rosie. His heart wavered. The love of his life. Nothing like Molly. Would he have taken a second look if she had been? It would be too strange.

Hang on. *Second* look? There'd been a third, fourth and more. He shivered, suddenly afraid of where this might lead. All the moisture in Nathan's mouth dried up. He might be getting closer to stepping off the edge in the hope of finding that deep, loving happiness he'd once known, but what if it all went sour? Turned to dislike instead? Or worse, what if he fell in love with a woman he couldn't make happy because of his past?

They reached his car. 'What's your address in Bondi Junction?'

'I'll put it in the GPS.' Molly settled into the seat and buckled in. 'I know the way, but let's play it safe.' Seemed she wanted to get there as soon as possible.

They didn't talk on the way, but when he pulled up outside the apartment block Molly indicated, he said, 'I'll walk you to the entrance.' The sooner the better. He needed to breathe air not laden with Molly's scent, and to put space between them. Then drive away, windows lowered and music on loud. He needed to stop, think about what he was doing getting to know Molly, before it got out of hand.

'That's not necessary.' She grabbed her bag from the floor and elbowed the door open, snatching up the hairbrush that had fallen out of her bag.

The door shut with a soft click, but Nathan was already moving around to join her on the pavement. 'When I see someone home I go all the way.'

Her emerald eyes widened as something akin to laughter sparkled out at him. 'We don't know each other well enough for that.'

'You know what I meant.'

That was not disappointment blinking out at him. It couldn't be. Then Molly proved it wasn't. 'That's a relief. I wasn't a hundred percent sure what you were saying.' Her eyes cleared, but there was a little twitching going on at the corners of her mouth.

Hell, he'd love to kiss that mouth. He needed to know if those lips were as soft and inviting as they looked. His upper body leaned forward without any input from his brain, but as he began to lift his arms, common sense stepped in. Molly would kick him where no man wanted a shoe if he followed through.

Stepping back, he looked around the area. The entrance was accessed immediately off the footpath where a bus stop was outlined. Nothing wrong in that, but it was so ordinary and Molly was anything but. He sighed, long and slow. It had nothing to do with him where she chose to live. This was getting out of hand. He was making up stuff without Molly saying a word. But he had to ask, 'How long have you lived here?'

She was focused on a pebble, rolling it round on the pavement with the toe of one classy shoe, then, raising her head, she eyeballed him. 'Since I moved to Sydney a year ago. I worked in a medical centre down the road while looking for a job in an emergency department anywhere in the city.'

'I'd have thought there'd be plenty of opportunities in

that time. You picky, or something?' He added a smile to take the heat out of his question.

'I got a job within weeks of starting at the medical centre, but a nurse I worked with came down with leptospirosis and when the manager asked me to stay on until she was back up to speed I didn't feel I could let them down. They'd been nothing but good to me from day one.'

How many questions could he get away with? Pushing her wasn't being fair, but he needed to learn more. Maybe the answers would dampen the ardour taking hold of him. 'I'd have thought you'd move closer to the city, where the shops and nightclubs are.'

'I like it out here.' For the first time he heard doubt in her voice. 'Neither do I mind the train trip. It doesn't take long. Judging by the traffic the few times I've driven in, I think the train probably gets me there in less time than it takes you in that fancy car.'

True. 'Where did you move from?' So much for shutting up.

'Adelaide. Before that, Perth.' The pebble flicked across the path as she turned away. 'I'm heading inside for some sleep. Thanks for bringing me home.'

His heart skittered. What was wrong with his last question? 'Wait.' What the hell for? Despite the tightening in his belly and groin brought on by those curves outlining her jacket and trousers, he had to let her go. He wasn't ready for this. He'd bet Molly wasn't either.

She paused to look over her shoulder. 'Go home, Nathan. Get some sleep too. Being Friday, tonight's bound to be hectic.'

Ignoring that, he said, 'You want to come with me sometime when I take this…' he waved at his car '…for a blast along the highway?' What happened to not ready, and thinking things through? Damned if he knew, other than he wasn't giving up that easily now that he'd started.

She stared at him as if he'd just asked her to fly to the moon in a toy box.

He waited, breath stalled between his lungs and his nostrils, hands tightening and loosening. What was the problem? He'd asked Molly to go for a spin, which meant sharing the small space and breathing her scent some more. No big deal. Yet it felt huge. It was a date. So what? *About damned time.* There'd been the occasional romp in the sack with women who understood that was all he was offering.

He knew instinctively that Molly would not want that with him. Then again, maybe she would, and he could have fun and walk away afterwards. Shock hit him in the gut. He didn't want that with this woman. All or nothing. No half-measures. *All* had to be out of the question. She wasn't his type. So it had to be nothing. About to withdraw his offer of a ride, he got a second shock.

Molly was grinning at him, and it was the most amazing sight. Beautiful became stunning, quiet became gorgeous and cheeky. 'Only if I get a turn at the wheel.'

His heart must've stopped. Nothing was going on behind his ribs. His lungs had seized. It didn't surprise him when his knees suddenly turned rubbery. How could he refuse her? Leaning back against the car to prevent landing in a heap on the damp asphalt, he asked, 'You like driving fast?' Fast and dangerous? He hadn't thought dangerous would come into anything Molly did. She appeared too cautious. Appeared, right? Not necessarily correct.

'Strictly safe and sensible, that's me.' The grin dipped.

Phew. He could get back on track, be the colleague who'd brought her home—and ignore the challenge he'd set himself. If only Molly's mouth hadn't flattened, because that got him wanting to make her smile again. 'I promise I'll be so safe you'll want to poke me with needles.' He straightened, took a tentative step and, when he didn't fall over, began walking up to the main door, making sure Molly was with him.

He got no further than the entrance.

'Thanks, again.' Molly punched a set of numbers into the keypad.

'I'll see you to your apartment.'

'I'm on the third floor. Think I can manage,' she muttered. 'See you tonight.' The lock clicked and she nudged the wide door open. 'I'm glad I went to breakfast. It was fun.'

Warmth stole across his skin and he had to refrain from reaching out to touch her. 'Glad you came. Now, I'd better get going. I've got things to do before I pick Cole up from the airport.'

A frown appeared between those fall-into-them eyes. 'I thought he wasn't going to be around for her birthday.'

'It's a surprise. He managed to wangle a weekend's leave. The rest of his contingent is on the way home via Darwin, while he's coming direct from KL.'

'There goes the shopping.' Molly smiled. 'She can't work tonight.'

'I organised that without letting slip what's going on. I'll tell her when I drop Cole off.'

'Good on you. It'd be awful if she had to waste this opportunity of having time out with her man.' Though filled with longing—for what, he had no idea—at least Molly's sigh was better than her quiet, mousy look.

Not mousy. Not any more. Sauntering towards his car, he called over his shoulder, 'See you tonight.' Time to put distance between them before he did something silly, like ask why it had taken weeks for her to front up and socialise with the people she worked with. That would put a stop to getting closer.

Nathan remained beside his car until Molly went inside and the door had closed behind her. Then he got in and drove on to Coogee and his small piece of paradise, his mind busy with all things Molly. She'd tipped him sideways by wanting little to do with him.

Except go for a spin in this beast.

No matter what else came up, he'd find time to follow through on that. Hopefully this weekend, so he could get to spend time unravelling the façade Molly showed the world.

Don't think that's going to happen in a hurry.

Better remember to get her number tonight.

Pulling up at traffic lights, Nathan tapped the steering wheel in time to the rock number playing on the radio. A strident ringing from the passenger side of the car intruded. Leaning over, he fossicked around until his fingers closed over a phone. Had to be Molly's. His finger hovered over the green circle, but of course he couldn't answer it. If for no other reason than she'd kill him.

A smile slowly spread across his face. Now he had a reason to return to her apartment and speak to her, and get her phone number at the same time.

CHAPTER THREE

'HOT DAMN.'

Molly leaned back against her apartment door as it clicked shut and tried not to think about Nathan. Like that was going to happen.

A grin spread across her face. What a morning. They'd gone from grumping to talking to smiling and then he'd driven her home and insisted on walking to the entrance with her. He'd have come up here if she'd let him.

She looked around the tiny space, smaller than Gran's chicken coop, and sighed, glad he wasn't seeing this. The shoddy apartment block would've already given him reason to wonder why a nurse on a reasonable wage would choose to live here. But it was ordinary, wouldn't attract attention.

She kept the apartment simply furnished with the bare basics in an attempt to make the rooms feel larger. The polished wood furniture came from her grandmother's cottage after Gran died. The furniture had lain in storage until Molly had moved to Adelaide and set up house on her own. The only good thing about Gran's passing was that she didn't get to hear she had been right about Paul. She would've gone after him with her sewing scissors.

No one came to the apartment. Lizzie, her best friend back in Perth, kept saying she'd visit but never managed to make it happen with her job taking her offshore for weeks at a time. Molly missed her more than anyone from her previous life. They'd done so much together, shared a lot of laughs and tears, always been there for one another. But, more important, Lizzie had believed her right from the beginning when she'd said Paul hit her, and she hated him almost as much as Molly did.

Paul Bollard. Nathan Lupton. They were nothing alike. One evil. The other caring. Both could be charming, strong, over-confident. That spooked her. Paul had wooed her as though she had been a princess, at first making her feel like one. Nathan confused her, sometimes making her cross and occasionally, especially this morning, all soft on the inside.

She huffed the air out of her lungs. Nathan wasn't wooing her and, by the expressions that crossed his face at times, had no intention of doing so. Fine. With a hideous marriage behind her, the wedding ring long gone in the bin, as of this week she was single and wanting to trust and love again, but she was very, very cautious.

Going out to breakfast had been the best thing to happen to her in a long while. She worked with a great bunch, and from now on she'd attend every get-together anyone proposed. She'd also get involved with more than the charity shop. Fake it till she made it. This latest and final version of herself would not be the socialite of the past, or the cowering abused woman. Married two years, separated for two, now alone. If nothing else, she'd become more caring and understanding of other people. Mrs Molly Bollard was gone for ever.

In the kitchenette she filled the kettle for a cup of tea. Sleep would be elusive while her mind was going over the morning. Pride lifted her chest. She'd managed to fit in with her workmates to the point she'd relaxed enough to forget everything that had brought her to that point. So much so, she'd even managed to sing 'Happy Birthday'. Now, there was a step in the right direction, and she mustn't stop at that. There was a city out there to get to know, and if she was careful not to keep her distrust to the fore, she didn't have to carry on being alone, could make friends in all facets of her life.

Did Nathan go to the meals every time the staff got together? She chuckled. He wouldn't do the shopping expeditions. She mightn't be fully ready for a partner or even a lover, but spending time over a meal with a man who laughed, grumped, looked out for others, could not be time wasted.

The doorbell chimed. Molly spun around. No one visited her. Bang went her heart. Crunch went her stomach.

Knock, knock. 'Molly, it's Nathan. I've got your phone.'

Relief prodded her towards the door. How had he managed to get inside and up to her floor without knowing the apartment number? Peering through the peephole, she got a grainy view of the man who'd driven her home.

'Molly?' That familiar irritation was back.

She opened the door. 'Sorry to be a pain. It must've fallen out of my bag with my hairbrush.'

Nathan was watching her with that intensity that was more familiar than his smiles. 'You had a call. That's how I found it.'

'A call?' she asked. 'Who from?'

He shrugged. 'I didn't look. Figured you'd be cross if I did.'

'You bet,' Molly admitted sheepishly as she checked out the caller ID. An unknown number. Her smile snapped off.

'Problem?'

'What?' She shook her head and glanced up at Nathan to soak up the warmth in his gaze. 'No. Wrong number probably.' As far as she knew, Paul only had access to the prison phone and that number was definitely in her contacts file so she could ignore it if he tried to get in touch. Anyway, he'd stopped calling her after his guilty verdict. Though who knew what receiving the divorce notice might've done to his narcissistic brain. He hated losing control over her more than anything.

The kettle whistled. Molly glanced toward the kitchenette. 'Thanks for this.'

Nathan stepped through the door. 'You into minimalist?'

Closing her eyes, she counted to four. Nathan should have left, not come inside. Yet it didn't feel wrong. More like it was okay for this man to be inside her home; as if she wanted him here. Which was so far out of left field she had to stop and look at him again. All she saw was the good-looking man who'd brought her home gazing around her apartment as if it was a normal thing to do. It probably was, for most people. That had to be in his favour. She was not thinking about the pool of heat in her stomach. Not, not, not. 'I'm making tea. Do you want one?' Ah, okay, maybe that heat was getting the upper hand.

He hesitated, his gaze still cruising her living room.

He was going to say no. She got in first. 'It's okay. You've got things to do before picking up Cole.' She wanted to feel relieved, but it was disappointment settling over her.

'Thought you'd never ask.' His gaze had landed back on her. His hands were in his pockets, his stance relaxed, yet there was something uncertain about him, like he didn't know if he was welcome. Nothing to make her afraid, more the opposite. If such a strong, confident man could feel unsure then he was more real, human—flawed in a good way. 'White with one.'

Her disappointment was gone in a flash. Replaced by a sudden longing for another chance at love. Truly? Yes, truly. Still had to go slowly, though. Turning her back on him before she fell completely under his spell and screwed up big-time, she said, 'Would you mind shutting the door? I don't like leaving it open. Never know who might wander in.'

'No problem.' A moment later, 'In case you're wondering, it was the old lady three doors down who told me which door to knock on after I described you.'

'I guess that goes with the territory.' She'd have to talk to Mrs Porter about telling strangers which apartment was hers. Except Nathan stood in the middle of her tiny one-bed home, waiting for a mug of tea. Not a stranger. 'Take a pew.' She nodded at the pair of wooden chairs at her tiny, gleaming wooden dining table. Her mouth dried as he sat and stretched those endless legs half across the kitchenette.

'Not a lot of space for a party, is there?' He smiled.

She could get to like those smiles far too much. They warmed her in places that had been cold for a long time, places she'd held in lockdown for fear of making another hideous mistake. Reaching for the two mugs on the tiny shelf above the bench, she answered, 'As partying wasn't on my agenda when I needed a roof over my head, I'm not complaining. This suits me fine in that respect.'

He looked around again. 'You're not happy with your neighbour telling people where you live.'

'I'm a bit circumspect about giving out personal info to any old body.' Shut up. Too much information. She was not telling Nathan why she felt that way. Anyway, she needed to move on from all that. Paul was locked up. No one else wanted to hurt her.

Nathan was watching her, apparently casually, yet she'd swear he wasn't missing a thing going on in her head. 'I suppose you wouldn't want just anyone turning up unannounced.'

She needed to be on guard around him. Always. 'Exactly.' Glancing around the room that had gone from tiny to minuscule the moment he'd entered, a flicker of yearning rose. Everything about her lifestyle since moving to Sydney had been average. Average suburb, average apartment, average car. Her job was a lot better than that, but the one at the medical centre had been on a par with the other things in her life. Nobody noticed average, which had been the intention. Except now she was restless.

'I like it here, but it might be time to move somewhere more spacious, a place I can feel more connected. I come and go every day, along with everyone else in the apartment block, and all we ever do is nod and smile at each other.' Once, that had been perfect. Now it seemed to roll out in front of her like an endless dark mat leading to a door going nowhere.

'Where would you like to live?'

The phone rang, saving her from having to find an answer. The idea was new, and using Nathan as a sounding board would be stretching their new relationship a bit far. But then, this morning she'd have laughed if anyone had told her he'd be sitting in her apartment drinking tea right now.

There was no caller ID on her phone, only the same unknown number as previously. It wouldn't be anything untoward, would it? 'Hello?' Molly said, hearing the caution in her voice and forcing a smile on her face. 'Molly

O'Keefe speaking.' Easier to be brave when Nathan was sitting opposite her.

'Hi, Molly. It's Jean from the charity shop. The shop phone's playing up so I'm using my personal one.'

Relief threaded through the tension that had begun tightening her body. 'What can I do for you?'

'You said to call if we got stuck for staff. One of the ladies who works Mondays has been called away to look after her sick mother. Is it possible you could help out?'

'I'd love to. I have to be at the ED by three. Does that work for you?'

'Perfect. Thank you so much. See you then.' A dial tone replaced Jean's voice. Just like that?

She dropped the phone on the table. 'That takes care of Monday morning.'

Nathan was looking at her as though expecting more from her.

'I put in a few hours at a charity shop that supports the women's refuge. Fill shelves, run up sales. That sort of thing.' The shop raised quite a lot of money for abused women and their kids, and it gave Molly a sense of satisfaction to contribute to people she understood all too well without having to explain herself. Though sometimes she suspected Jean had figured out why she turned up.

'Go, you,' Nathan said. Then a frown appeared. 'You must get to hear some horror stories. I don't think I could cope with those.'

She hesitated, torn between dodging the bullet and being honest. 'Most of the people I meet come in to spend money and support the charity. Rarely are they the women who've survived abuse. Those who have don't usually talk about it.' *Stop.* This man wasn't stupid. He'd see behind her words if she wasn't careful.

'You're probably right. The rare exceptions being

those brave women who go public about their ordeals in order to raise awareness.' Awe shaded his voice, his face and that steady gaze. 'I don't know how they do it.'

'Neither do I,' she muttered truthfully.

Draining his mug, Nathan stood up. 'I'd better get cracking, get things done before heading to the airport. Sleep being one of them. You look like you're in need of some too.'

She might look tired and messy, but for once she felt more alive and awake than a toddler after a nap. Ready for fun, not sleep. Was Nathan responsible for that? Away from work she didn't get so wound up around him, took his comments on the chin. 'I might go for a run first. That always helps clear my mind.' *Anything to shake you out of my head.*

'Running doesn't wake you up?'

'Not often. I'm usually exhausted and a hot shower finishes me off.'

His eyes widened briefly. 'Right,' was all he said, but he managed one of those devastating smiles.

When she could breathe properly, she growled, 'I thought you were leaving?'

'Can't a guy change his mind?'

The smile was still going on and now her legs were starting to protest about keeping her upright. Legs that were supposed to take her for a run. The couch was looking mighty good right about now. With or without Nathan? She wanted *Nathan*? Hell, when she finally woke up she didn't do it in half-measures. There hadn't been any sex in her life for a long time and now every last cell in her body was sitting up, fighting to be noticed.

'No,' she muttered around the need clogging her throat. Not sure if the 'no' had been directed at Nathan or herself. This was not going anywhere. They worked to-

gether. He was confident, she wasn't. That was a work in
progress. He'd have a woman in his life. What gorgeous-
looking man didn't? She'd get over this lust as soon as
he left. Or in the next hour while she was out jogging.
Or while she was in bed sleeping. Or on the train going
into work tonight. She would. It was only an aberration
in her carefully controlled world. A damned distracting
aberration, but it would pass. No choice.

'Can I have your phone number?' Nathan pulled his
phone from his pocket.

So much for passing. He'd raised the ante. 'Why?'

His dark eyebrows rose. 'So I can call when I'm going
to take the car for that spin. Is that all right?'

If she was supposed to be getting over her reaction to
him, then why was the thought of going for a ride with
Nathan winding her belly tighter than ever? Rattling off
the number, she hoped she'd got it right. She could've
given him the number for the zoo for all she knew. 'I'll
look forward to it.' She headed for the door and hauled
it open, needing to get him out of her small space where
he took up all the air and made her feel tiny and fragile,
and so, so alive.

Guess this was what getting a life meant. She had
to pause, evaluate what was happening, figure out why
she felt like this with Nathan when no one else brought
on these feelings. No, no more pausing, hanging around
waiting to see what the universe threw at her next. Try
taking control instead. Slowly.

Nathan stepped past her, leaving a faint trail of out-
doorsy aftershave scent behind him.

She gulped. Were need, desire, hope rising because
she truly was attracted to him? Or was this all about getting a new life and he was merely a stepping stone? It
was something else to figure out.

'See you tonight.' Quickly closing the door, she leaned against it and tipped her head back to stare at the ceiling as though the answers to her questions were written there. The excitement tripping through her veins, warming her long-frozen heart, was real. There'd been nothing slow about this debilitating sensation rocking her. Oh, no. Wham, bam, Nathan Lupton had stormed in and turned up the thermostat, taking her by surprise, and she didn't want to back off. Even if she should.

'Hell and damnation.' Nathan shook his head as he pulled into the drive and parked at the back of his large, sprawling house. Towards the end of last night's shift, quiet Molly had shown another side to herself, had become interesting. Except, having spent time with her dressed in a figure defining, classy blouse and trousers, sexy kept coming to mind, raising more questions than answers about what made her tick than anything had during the previous two months they'd worked together. From now on her stereotype uniform was not going to negate those images.

And the short time he'd spent in her apartment had him wanting to know more about where she came from, the life she'd led before moving to Sydney.

Hah. Know more? Or feel more? Touch more? Enjoy more? Learning all about her had become important. He had no idea why, except his hormones got wound up whenever she was near. Hot, alluring, *tempting* came to mind.

Temptation? The groan that spilled out of his mouth tasted of shock and disbelief. Sure, Molly was beautiful, had his hormones in a dither, but tempting? Yes, damn it all to hell and back. Because this was starting to feel like he was seriously back in the real world, where dating might happen. He'd thought for a while he might be ready, but reality was scary.

Slamming the car door harder than necessary, he strode around the house and out to the fence lining the front lawn to stare across the public green space on the other side of a wide walking path to the Tasman Sea beyond. The light breeze meant no windsurfers doing their number on the waves. Which was a shame because right now he couldn't think of anything he'd rather do than get up on a board—and no doubt fall off just as quickly, since it had been a while since he'd last surfed. At least that would occupy his mind and put these damned fool ideas to bed.

Bed? Nathan groaned. He was exhausted, and needed sleep more than anything before signing on again that night. More than thinking about Molly.

But the idea of sprawling over his couch in front of the television and trying to doze off turned his blood to thick soup. There'd be no sleep while she rampaged through his mind. The hell of it was he didn't know why she was doing this to him when up until today he'd been more likely to get annoyed with her and wish she'd pester someone else. Sure, he was annoyed with her right now, but for all the wrong reasons. So much for getting her to put that cold shoulder to rest. Instead she'd been winding him up tighter than ever. At least she didn't have a clue how badly she was rattling his cage.

You sure about that?

Good question. He'd been determined not to let her see his reactions to her, to the scent of limes from her fruit basket, to relaxing and laughing in her company.

Yeah, and what was that doubt in her face when she'd picked up her phone and seen no ID displayed? Because something *had* darkened her eyes and tightened her face.

Certainly more reaction than called for by someone wanting to ask why she hadn't paid the power bill or had she forgotten she was meant to be at the dentist. One thing he knew for certain—she'd never tell him.

The apartment had been a shock. 'Poky' had the place sounding larger than it was. It was tastefully decorated, though. Was that Molly's taste? Or had she rented the place fully furnished? The late morning sun had shone through the large, sparkling windows to brighten the atmosphere. The place was spotless, her few possessions gleamed. The two mugs on the shelf, the two glasses and dinner plates, said lonely.

Turning back towards his house, Nathan hesitated. Molly had mentioned maybe looking for somewhere else to live with more space, a place that was connected to the outside world. There was a twist to her story. Maybe she came from a tight community and was missing that easy friendship with all the neighbours, except she didn't like the way the old woman had told him which apartment was hers. He looked left, right and back to his house. He knew his neighbours. While they didn't live in each other's pockets, they were there for each other if the need arose.

Don't even think it.

This place was further from work than her apartment, which meant a bus or car to the train station.

He strode towards the back, stopped and studied his house. Slowly that familiar sense of belonging, of having found his new place in the world right here, rose, pushing other annoying emotions aside. With each front room opening out onto the veranda that ran the full width of the house with an overhanging roof, it was a haven in summer and winter.

He'd said, 'I'm buying it,' the moment the real estate salesman had pulled up outside. An impulsive purchase, made two years after Rosie's death, yet nothing had caused him to regret his decision. At the time he'd been stuck in the past, so he'd gone looking for a new home that didn't echo with Rosie's laughter.

Coogee might be a little way out of the city for travelling to work, but the vista at the end of his lawn cancelled out any annoyance about that. He'd weathered storms that had wrecked the cliffs, baked in unrelenting sun, and surfed the waves, and had finally known a quiet within himself that had been missing for far too long. The large house and sprawling, uncontained grounds were his sanctuary.

It couldn't be more different from the small, cosy, modern home he and Rosie had shared. That one had been like her; everything had had its place and the colour schemes had been perfect, the neat gardens with their carefully spaced plants drawing passers-by to lean over the fence in admiration. While this place—it was more like him. Out of sync.

No. Molly doesn't need something like this.

He didn't need Molly in his space. It wouldn't remain a tranquil place to go when the world got on top of him if temptation came to live in the attached flat.

Occasionally he had tenants for short periods, usually medical personnel moving to Sydney General from out of town who needed temporary accommodation while they got somewhere more permanent sorted. He liked it when people moved in, and he was equally happy when they left again. Easy come, easy go. It was a waste having the flat going empty, and occasionally he'd thought of asking around work to see if anyone wanted to rent it permanently, but then he'd got cold feet. What if they didn't get on? Or if the noise level increased? Or if he plain wanted his whole house to himself?

The flat's more spacious than Molly's apartment.

Molly wouldn't be noisy or intrusive. They did argue quite often. But today he'd learned they could get along just fine.

But he'd find it very difficult to ask her to leave if the day came where he wanted to be alone.

Far safer for him to leave things as they stood.

CHAPTER FOUR

'YOU ALL RIGHT?' Nathan asked from the other side of the counter in the department's central hub where Molly was *supposed* to be writing up patient notes. Her head was so messed up with this new awareness of Nathan and wondering what he was doing that she hadn't seen him approaching.

'Couldn't be better,' she lied. 'I managed some sleep after my run.' It was true, though her kip had been filled with dreams of being held in Nathan's arms while she drove his car. Why were dreams so ridiculous? On all counts? 'What about you?'

He grimaced. 'I managed an hour before going to the airport, and then a couple more after an early dinner.'

That explained the shadows beneath his eyes. 'It goes with the territory.' Night shifts played havoc with sleep patterns.

'At least next week I'm on three to eleven. Back to...' he flicked his fingers in the air '...normal.'

'Me, too.' She glanced at the clipboard in his hand. 'You seeing Colin Montgomery next?'

His thick, brown-blond hair tumbled over his forehead as he nodded. 'I see he's got history of arrhythmia and is presenting with palpitations and chest pain.'

Molly followed him to their seventy-one-year-old patient and immediately noted down Colin's pulse and other obs. 'Did anyone come with you to the hospital?'

Colin shook his head. 'I've lived alone since my wife died two years ago.'

'I'm sorry to hear that. What about other family?' There was nothing in the notes about relatives to contact.

He blinked, and his mouth drooped. 'My son and I haven't spoken in years. Last I heard he lives somewhere in Brisbane.'

'How long have you had arrhythmia?' Nathan read the heart-monitor printout and asked pertinent questions.

'Twelve months, give or take.'

'When did the pain start?'

'Around eleven. When it didn't ease off I phoned for an ambulance. I hope I'm not wasting everyone's time. It's very busy in here.'

'A typical Friday night,' Molly assured him.

'Never think you're wasting our time. With your known condition, it's always best we check you out.' Nathan listened to his chest through a stethoscope. 'You're on warfarin. How steady are your test results?'

'Usually my bleeding times stay within the allowable range. Prothrombin, isn't it?' He didn't wait for an answer. 'But last week the test ran really high and I had to have the test every day until the results returned to normal.'

'Although that's not normal for people not on the drug, it is within the required range for someone taking the anticoagulant drug,' Nathan explained.

Colin looked worried. 'Isn't that dangerous?'

'It's what's preventing you having a stroke. That must've been explained when you first started taking it.'

Colin looked sheepish. 'It probably was, but at the time I was too worried about everything, and not being medically minded just accepted that I needed to take the warfarin to stay alive. I could've gone on the internet to find out more but I'd have confused myself further.'

'Relax. You're not the first to react that way, and you won't be the last.' Nathan locked a steady gaze on his patient. 'I'm referring you to Cardiology so they can run more tests to find out what's going on with this pain and that spike in your prothrombin results.'

'Better safe than sorry?' Colin enquired, his worry-filled eyes glued on his doctor.

Nathan calmed him with his straightforward manner. 'I don't believe there's a major problem but I'd prefer you spent at least the rest of tonight in the hospital, where you can be monitored and not at home alone, worrying about what might or might not be going on inside your chest.' He was good. 'That'd only raise your blood pressure, which we don't want happening.'

Colin relaxed more with every sentence.

While Nathan called Cardiology, Molly went to check on eight-year-old Ollie Brown, who'd fallen out of his bunk and broken an arm. 'Hey, young man, how's that head?' There was concern he'd got a concussion as well and a scan had been ordered.

'Hurts like stink.' Ollie grinned.

The grin vanished as his grandfather snapped, 'You're not on the farm now, lad.'

Molly chuckled. 'So you're a country guy? What are you doing in the middle of Sydney, then?' She wanted to observe Ollie for signs of confusion or amnesia.

'It's the school holidays,' Ollie said, as though she was the dumbest woman out. 'Granddad always lets us come to stay so we can do townie things, like go on the ferries and eat take-out food and stuff.' There was nothing wrong with his coherence.

'You forgot to mention that fighting with your brother was why you fell out of the blasted bunk in the first place.' The granddad scowled, but there was a load of love in his rheumy eyes.

'Connor started it.'

'You know better than to let him rile you, lad.'

Molly clapped her hands. 'Okay, guys, the orderly is on his way down to take you for the scan, Ollie. Mr Brown, you can go with him, if you'd like.'

Mr Brown nodded. 'Someone's got to keep an eye on the young pup.'

Before Ollie could say anything, Molly cut in, 'I'll be here when you get back. Then the doctor will decide if you can leave.'

Suddenly the bright, brave eight-year-old slumped and looked at his grandfather. 'I don't want to stay here. I want to go home.'

'Aw, shucks, lad. You'll have a grand time. The nurses will spoil you rotten.'

Leaving them to it, Molly headed for Kath Burgess's cubicle, only to have Hazel, the only female doctor on duty, call from the hub, 'Molly, I want you with me when I examine Kath. She's spent time with you already, and I think it's important not to bring in too many new faces since you managed to calm her down.'

'I agree.' The woman had been distraught when she'd arrived, clutching her stomach like it was going to split open, howling that she might be losing her baby. It had taken ages to quieten her enough to get some obs done.

'We all heard the commotion and our first instinct was to crowd in to see what we could do, until it quickly became obvious that the screeching was lowering to sobs and you had the situation under control. Nathan and I decided not to interfere unless you called for help. We didn't want to fire her up again.' Hazel was reading the triage notes.

'Thank goodness you did. She refuses to be seen by a male doctor.' That'd immediately put Molly on notice, wondering if Kath had been abused by a man, but when she'd tried to find out she had been told she'd fallen down the stairs at the back of her house. Molly had gone straight to Hazel to explain her concerns, but as Hazel had been about to suture a deep wound in a young male's thigh, she'd flagged Kath's notes instead and kept an eye out for whoever might be going into the cubicle.

'That doesn't sound good,' Hazel commented as she led the way into the small space where Kath lay curled up on the bed, a bunch of tissues clasped in her hand.

Closing the curtains, Molly watched Kath closely as Hazel asked questions about what had brought her to hospital.

'I fell down the steps.'

'You're complaining of abdominal pain. How did that happen?'

'There was a toolbox there, all right?' Kath's voice was rising. 'I must've landed on that.'

'You don't know for sure?'

'I did.' Tears streamed down the woman's face.

Molly's heart went out to her. If only she could hug her and say, 'Tell us everything, and we'll get you help'—but she knew where that'd lead. The police would have to be informed, and social services would send someone to help. Kath had to be ready for what that involved. It wasn't as easy as someone who hadn't been abused would believe. Of course, Molly could be wrong, but she doubted it. It was like looking into her own eyes from the past.

When Molly had removed the sheet covering Kath and

lowered her jeans and panties, she stepped aside for Hazel's examination, talking softly to Kath about anything that didn't broach the subject of her husband.

Finally Hazel straightened and pulled up Kath's clothes. 'You're not miscarrying. But I want you to remain in bed for the next few days, at least until the pain subsides. There's still a risk of miscarriage.'

'He won't be happy,' their patient said in a dead voice.

'About you staying in bed, or about not losing the baby?' Molly asked softly.

'What do you think?'

Both, if she was on the right page. But she kept quiet. Kath was getting wound up again. Better to keep her calm and only mention help was available if she was receptive.

Molly opened the curtains so they could keep an eye on her from the hub.

'Hey, you can't come in here without permission,' Hank said loudly from the other end of the department.

'Try and stop me,' came the angry voice of an unknown male.

'Come here,' Hank demanded.

'Where is she?'

Kath gasped, 'No,' and curled in on herself.

Molly asked, 'Someone you know?'

'My man. He's been drinking since early afternoon.'

Great. Just what they needed. The sound of curtains being jerked open and sliding doors rammed back made her skin crawl. He was getting closer, and it wouldn't be long before he found who he was looking for.

'Stop right there,' Hank ordered.

'This is going to be fun,' Hazel muttered.

'Stop. You are disturbing our patients.' Nathan stood at the central counter, hands tense at his sides, his feet planted slightly apart. 'Tell me who you've come to see and I'll check if you can visit.'

'You've got my wife hiding in here. I'm going to find her. Now,' the man shouted.

Kath buried her head under the pillow.

Then her husband stormed into the cubicle, the rage in his face terrifying. 'Get out of my way,' he yelled at Hazel, raising a fist.

It was instinctive. Molly saw movement out of the corner of her eye. One step closed the gap. Her arm came up, locked with the assailant's. Using his forward motion she hauled him toward her, dropped her weight forward and swung her upper body around, taking him with her, dropping him to the floor before landing on top of him, her knees pressing into his shoulders, her hand still tight around his lower arm.

Silence fell over the department.

Then the man began swearing. He struggled beneath her, trying to push her off, getting madder by the second.

She was about to be tossed aside by a raging man who had no brakes on his temper. Then Nathan planted a foot firmly in the small of the man's back. 'Stay still.' Under his breath he added, 'Or, hell, you're going to regret it.'

She was probably the only person to hear that. Certainly the man underneath her either hadn't or didn't believe Nathan because he was still trying to get up.

Then Hank grabbed the man's flailing arms and slammed them down on the floor. 'Shut up, buster.'

Nathan tapped her lightly. 'You can get off now. We've got him.'

She did, fast, not taking her eyes off her opponent until she'd stepped away. 'Has someone called Security?' Where had they been when this guy had got into the department? Taking a break? At least one security guard had to remain at the main entrance at all times.

'Right here.' Two uniformed men raced towards them and took over.

'You okay?' Nathan asked, his hand on her elbow.

'Sure.' She nodded.

'Molly, he was going to hit me.' Hazel nudged Nathan aside to throw her arms around her and hold tight. 'I froze when I saw his arm come up.'

Molly squeezed back, a trembling starting up in her belly and spreading throughout her body. 'Glad *I* didn't.'

Hazel stepped back and wiped her eyes. 'Seriously, you saved me. He was aiming for my face.'

'You reacted so fast, it had to be instinctive. I'm impressed.' There was something akin to awe in Nathan's voice as his hand moved from her elbow to her shoulder. 'Come and sit down. You look like you've been hit by a bus.'

Now that the adrenaline was ebbing, that was exactly how she felt. Flattened. Shocked. 'I can't believe I did that.'

'How'd you know what to do?' Nathan asked after he had her seated and parked his butt on the counter. 'One second that man was attacking Hazel and the next you threw him on the floor and sat on him.'

'Not quite. I had my knees on his shoulders.' She gulped. That had been so close. Not once had she thought about what she was doing. When she'd caught sight of that swinging arm out of the corner of her eye the rest had followed naturally. As she'd been taught to do in her judo classes. If only she'd done martial arts when she'd been with Paul, she might have stopped him in his tracks permanently. 'I saw a movement and instantly went into defence mode. I've got an orange belt in judo,' she added when she saw the confusion enter Nathan's eyes.

'That explains it.' Maybe, but that confusion remained.

Molly hastened to divert him. 'I've always wondered how I'd react if I needed to. Now I know.'

'Why did you learn judo?' Straight to the point.

'Nathan, not now. I need to get back to Kath. The attack proved what I suspected—she's being abused. She'll need reassuring her husband's not going to get near her while she's in here. We'll also have to convince her to stay in hospital for the rest of the night.'

You're talking too much. He's going to see right through you.

Molly clamped her mouth shut and tried to stand up to pull away from those warm fingers still on her shoulder, but Nathan only tightened his hold.

'Sit down. You're as pale as the walls, and shaking like a leaf in a breeze. I'm getting you a strong coffee.'

Actually, she was damned pleased with herself. Who'd have believed she could take a man down? She opened her mouth to argue, but nothing came out when she locked her eyes with Nathan's and found compassion there, and something else. Something hinting at him beginning to understand what made her tick. Her bout of verbal diarrhoea might bring unwelcome questions.

Then a shudder ripped through her. Sinking deeper onto the chair, she looked away, fidgeting with the hem of her top as nausea crept up her throat. That had been too close. What if he'd hit Hazel? Or her? The guy had been off the scale with rage. Not cold and calculating but hot and loose. Was that how he treated Kath all the time?

Molly's heart pounded. She was safe, but Kath wasn't. Seeing that man come charging through the department as though he had the right to do as he pleased with his wife had turned her blood to ice. And brought back memories of a fist hitting her stomach, slamming against her ribs, under her chin.

Nathan was crouched in front of her, his hands now covering hers. 'Your reaction's normal.'

She nodded, afraid that if she opened her mouth she'd never shut up.

'There's more to this, isn't there?'

Another nod, sharp and uncontrollable.

'Hank,' Nathan called over his shoulder. 'Molly and Hazel could do with coffee, please. Make them sweet.'

'Onto it.'

Molly glanced around, away from those all-seeing eyes in front of her. 'Hazel?'

'I'm right here, and, like you, I've got the shakes. I'm also angry and would love a chance to tell that creep what I think of him, coming in here and trying to hurt people who want to help his wife.' Hazel pulled a chair near to Molly's. 'How're you doing?'

'I'm good.' She wanted to laugh and rejoice in being strong. She wanted to cry and hide, and go home. She wanted to bury her head against Nathan's broad shoulder, breathe him in, and feel those warm muscles under his top against her face. She wanted to be comforted by this man she knew without a doubt would never hurt her. But it wasn't happening.

One, they were in the hub of the ED, surrounded by staff and patients, and there was work to do. Two, what she wanted and what she'd get might be two different things, and right now she couldn't handle the disappointment if she'd misinterpreted that look in Nathan's eyes and he put her aside. So she'd toughen up, drink her coffee and get back to work. It was the only way to go. Once the shaking stopped, and some sense of equilibrium returned to her brain. 'I'll be right in a minute.'

Nathan said, 'Don't rush. We've got you both covered until you're ready. Even if it takes the rest of the shift.' He might be talking to them both but it was her hands he was gently squeezing.

Her bottom lip trembled. 'Thanks.'

'Take pride in what you did.' His return smile slowed her stewing stomach. 'I'd rather have you on my side than against me.'

'Then you're glad we're getting on?' No trembling in her smile now. Pride was appearing. She'd been strong, had helped Hazel. Did this mean that no man would ever again hit her? Not without a fight, anyway. Her chin lifted, and she eyeballed Nathan. 'Seems things are looking up for me.' Her new life was well and truly under way.

'Here, coffee for two.' Hank placed two mugs on the counter. 'I pinched some chocolate biscuits out of the fridge as well. Thought they might be better than sugar in your drinks.'

Nathan stood up. 'I'd better see to some patients. Don't rush, either of you.'

Molly reached for her mug, paused. 'Can I suggest only female staff work with Kath? She was leery of Hazel examining her. She's not going to like any male staff approaching her.'

Nathan nodded. 'I'll ask Myra to take over.' Myra had taken Vicki's place for the night and was a midwife and nurse who did extra shifts in ED for the money.

As Nathan passed Molly to pick up a file, his hand brushed her upper arm, and when she looked at him he gave her another soft, heart-melting smile, but sorrow darkened his eyes.

Damn it, he knew. Without being told, he'd put the pieces together and come up with the correct picture. He would want to know more. Would demand to be told everything. No, he wouldn't. They worked together, they weren't best buddies or in a relationship. He might like to know but he wasn't going to ask her for details. He was a gentleman. Wasn't he? Guess she'd find out soon enough.

For the remainder of the shift Nathan had trouble remaining calm whenever he glanced around to check on Molly. Anger at an unknown man boiled up. Given half the chance he'd like to tear out of the department to go and find him, beat him to a pulp. Not that he'd ever hit anyone before, but sweet, gorgeous Molly did so not deserve to be beaten. Not that she'd said anything to suggest it'd happened, but he knew. The sudden grief that had filled her eyes as the shock of what she'd done to Kath's husband had worn off told him there was a story behind her usually withdrawn manner.

'Glad that's over.' The woman in his head handed a file to one of the incoming shift nurses. 'I'm ready for my bed.'

Not so fast. 'I'll give you a lift home.' Nathan put on his no-nonsense voice in the hope she'd agree without an argument.

'The train will be quicker.'

He should have known it wouldn't work. 'Throw in breakfast and you'll be able to justify going the slow way.' He'd just asked her out? It might only be breakfast, but in a roundabout way it was a date. He hadn't thought before putting his mouth into gear.

So you want to withdraw the invitation?

Nathan's chest rose. No, he damned well didn't. This

wasn't only about what'd happened earlier and the reve-
lations that had come with it. He couldn't deny the need
to get to know Molly better, to learn exactly who was
behind that façade she presented to the world most of the
time. He sucked a breath. Which only showed how deep
the mire he was floundering in had become. It had happened so fast he couldn't keep up.

Molly was blinking at him like a possum caught in
headlights. 'Do you mean that?'

'About breakfast? Yes. Why wouldn't I?'

'Because you're kind and probably want to be a caring boss, making sure I'm all right. If that's the case then
believe me when I say I'm fine, and there's food in my
fridge that'll suffice for breakfast.'

That scratched at his calm. He was not playing the
boss here. He'd stepped beyond that comfortable zone—
into what, he wasn't quite sure, but knew he needed to
find out. 'Bet you haven't got eggs and hollandaise sauce.'

'Low blow.' There was a wariness creeping into her
eyes. She was worried what he'd ask about the martial
arts.

He couldn't deny he was ready to explode over what
he perceived had happened in her past, but if she didn't
want to talk about it, that was her prerogative and he'd
accept that. 'That's me. When I want something I'll try
everything in my power to get it.' *Except use my fists.*

Molly obviously had no worries on that score because
she gave him an exhausted smile. 'I'd love a ride, and
breakfast.'

'Why didn't you just say so?' He grinned and took her
elbow, wishing he could put an arm around her shoulders and tuck her in close. But they were still in the
department and already there were a couple of raised

eyebrows and knowing smiles going on. Neither were they *that* close.

'Don't like to be too obvious,' Molly retorted. Then yawned. 'Thank goodness for weekends. I'm over this week.'

'Evening shift next week, here we come.' After two days off, and hopefully a ride in his car. The Blue Mountains were looking good, and the weather was forecast to be fine and crisp. 'You been to the Blue Mountains?'

'That's a long way to go for breakfast.' Her tempting mouth gave him another smile that struck under his ribs and made his heart lift its pace.

The mountains wouldn't be too far for the morning meal if they went there the day before and stayed over in a hillside lodge, enjoying the views and a superb meal, making the most of a large, soft bed throughout the night. But that wasn't happening. *Not yet.* Nathan tripped over his own flat feet. Where the hell had that come from?

You were going to get her onside, not so close you'd get to know her so well.

He hadn't forgotten, but the rules had changed the moment she'd taken Burgess down. He had yet to figure out where he went with this now. Molly was an enigma that he was getting more than interested in. First he had to find out if he was right about her past or way off the mark. It certainly explained her edginess over mixing socially with people. Until yesterday, when she'd participated in Vicki's celebration, when she'd come out of her shell in a hurry, even singing 'Happy Birthday' in front of everyone. Not that Molly had realised what she was doing at first.

Nathan followed her to the lift, and when the door closed, he tapped the button for the basement and the car park. 'You know people will talk about what happened?'

'Fingers crossed, come Monday something else will have happened that'll take everyone's attention.' She leaned against the wall, looking so tired he wanted to wrap her up and take her home for a few uninterrupted hours' sleep. Followed by...

'How about we go to Coogee for that breakfast?'

Her eyes widened. 'That's a fair way past my apartment.'

'So it is.' What would Rosie have thought of Molly? Would she have liked her? Yes, he thought, she would. Rosie had insisted he had to move on when she'd gone, wasn't to sit around feeling sorry for himself. She'd gone as far as saying bluntly, 'Find another woman to love, have that family you've always wanted. Don't live in regret for what we've lost. That would make our time together worthless.'

But should he really take Molly to his home, show her the vacant flat? Should he start thinking ahead, instead of always looking over his shoulder at the past?

CHAPTER FIVE

WHY GO TO Coogee when there were plenty of cafés near the hospital? Or in Bondi Junction. Molly watched Nathan's firm hands with their easy movements as he drove through the morning rush hour traffic. Hands that she now knew could be gentle. Shuffling further down into the luxurious leather seat, she stifled a yawn. Which was rude when Nathan was taking her out, but the night had caught up with her.

'Have you always lived in Coogee?' she asked, in need of a distraction to stay awake. Not that Nathan wasn't one, but he might leave her on the side of the road if she stared at him all the way to the well-known beach.

'Only since I bought the house. I like being near the sea, and Coogee appealed. Before that I lived on the north shore.' His voice hitched on that last sentence.

'The surfing?' He'd told her he used to surf.

'It wasn't a priority, as I rarely rode the board at the time. Though that's turned out to be a bonus, like a lot of things about the property. I do hit the waves these days. Besides, the house ticked a lot of boxes and had that wow factor, so I bought it.'

She'd like to see the place sometime. It would tell her a lot about Nathan. Her head nodded forward, and her eyelids drooped shut. Sitting up straighter, she forced her eyelids up and stared out at the road ahead. She'd buy her own home sometime. A small, warm house that would wrap around her; not a sterile mansion that showed off to her friends how wealthy she was. That particular house hadn't been her choice. It'd had Paul written all over the grand frontage, the sweeping staircase, the expansive rooms. The place had felt more like a mausoleum than a home, and as though she as much as the house was on display to all and sundry. 'Not your first property?'

'No. The one I owned first was cosier and more family orientated.' He paused.

Molly waited, hoping she stayed awake long enough to hear what else he had to say.

'I was married. We were hoping to raise our children there. But four years ago it went horribly wrong.'

Wide awake now, she touched Nathan's arm. 'I'm sorry. Life can play nasty when it chooses.'

'You're not wrong there.' Nathan flicked the indicator and pulled into the outside lane, keeping a safe distance from the truck in front, his fingers tapping impatiently on the steering wheel.

She knew the grief of losing the chance of having a family. It undermined everything she wanted for her future. Unlike her, Nathan could have children if he chose to. Molly returned to watching those fingers as they played a silent, sharp rhythm on the wheel.

'Rosie got ALL.'

Acute lymphatic leukaemia. Molly's heart dropped for Nathan, and his wife. What could she say? No words could help. But a hug might—except hugging Nathan while he was driving along the city highway wasn't conducive to safety. Like her dream? She squeezed his arm softly, and remained quiet for the rest of the ride out to the beach.

Had Nathan told her about his wife in a bid to soften the blow when he asked her about her past? Or were they getting a little closer and he wanted to put it out there straight-up? Yesterday's argument and breakfast seemed a lifetime ago. They'd been scratchy with each other, then friendly to the point he'd had a cup of tea in her apartment. At the time it had seemed a vast improvement in their relationship, and since then she'd exposed the results of her darker side, and he was still happy to spend time alone with her.

Having spent the past two years running solo, to have now shared time talking with a man was hard to take in. It excited her about the future. Seemed she was still capable of mixing and mingling, of having a laugh, of doing things outside her four walls.

'Wakey-wakey.'

A gentle shaking of her arm had Molly sitting up and staring around. 'Sorry.' She never went to sleep in the company of anyone, let alone a man. Another point in Nathan's favour. 'This is Coogee?' The sweeping beach with its golden sand sang to her, reminding her of beach holidays with Gran. Lowering the window, she listened to the waves smacking down on the beach beyond the steps leading down from the street.

'Yes, it sure is.' He glanced along the street, then back at her. 'And, Molly?'

Uh-oh. What had she done? She'd been asleep, couldn't be too serious. 'Yes?'

'Stop saying sorry all the time. Falling asleep isn't a crime. It'd been coming ever since you dropped Burgess in ED. Shock or an adrenaline high does that.'

'I won't get into trouble for throwing him on the floor, will I?' It had only just occurred to her it might be seen as a bad move, she could have endangered others. Not that there'd been any chance of stopping her reaction.

'I'd like to see anyone try to make you out to be the villain. If you hadn't stopped him, Hazel would now have a badly beaten face, at the very least. Believe me, everyone's on your side. The word was going round the hospital within minutes that you stepped up and the question's being asked—where was Security at the time he walked through the doors into the department?'

'He could've gained access by asking to see his wife. He didn't need to get all uptight and angry.' That still would have upset Kath, though.

'Unfortunately you're right. Kath hadn't said she wouldn't see him, and I doubt she would've if asked.' He pushed open his door and unwound his long body to stand upright.

Before Molly had gathered her bag, or her wits, Nathan was opening her door. 'Come on. Let's go and eat.'

She grinned. 'Now you mention it, I'm starving.'

'There's a surprise.' Nathan laughed, and held out a hand to take hers, which he didn't drop as they began walking along the footpath.

For once she didn't try and pull away, or start filling in the sudden shyness swamping her by talking a load of drivel. Instead she looked around at the massive hotel built against the hill, and the row of small shops lining the street heading up the valley. She enjoyed the sense of freedom at being able to hold a man's hand without being frightened, or wary. A warm, strong hand belonging to a caring, exciting guy who was starting to get under her skin in ways she'd long believed wouldn't happen in this lifetime.

Then she let out a sigh. There was no getting away from telling him the bare facts about her past. Nathan had guessed the basics so to go all quiet on him when he was being so darned kind and friendly wasn't right, even when she hadn't told anyone the sordid details since she'd left Perth two years ago. She'd give him an abridged version. Bare facts, and move on.

After they'd eaten.

'Hello, Nathan.' The waitress placed menus before them. 'How's your week been?'

'Hectic, as per usual. Eva, let me introduce Molly O'Keefe. She's a nurse in the department.'

'Hey, Molly, nice to meet you. Are you living around here?'

The girl looked vaguely familiar, which didn't make sense. Unless she lived in the same apartment block as Molly did, but what were the odds? 'Over in Bondi Junction, unfortunately.' She'd love to have an apartment with those views to wake up to every day. It wasn't happening any time soon. Her bank balance couldn't cope. The money from her half of the marital property was locked in an investment, where it was staying until she decided what to do with it. The money was tainted, as far as she was concerned. Though there was her inheritance from Gran. Hmm. Possibilities started popping up. Her mother would be quick to offer assistance to make up for letting her down in the past, but she'd never ask.

'I know what you mean. It's beautiful around here.' Eva looked at Nathan. 'The usual?'

'You've got steak on the menu?' Molly laughed.

Eva gaped at her. 'Steak? No. The full Aussie breakfast.'

Molly's laugh got louder. 'Do you ever cook your own breakfast?'

'Cook it? Hell, no. Do I tip something out of a cardboard box into a bowl and add milk? Yes, more often than you seem to think.' He grinned before nodding to the waitress. 'Definitely, the works. Molly might take time deciding so can we have a flat white and a long black in the meantime?'

'Coming up.'

As Eva headed across to the barista coffee machine, Molly began scanning the menu. 'I feel I know Eva from somewhere.'

'ED. She came in with burns to her legs after a cook knocked boiling water off the stovetop and onto her.'

'She was in agony. The head chef came with her, and was so upset you had to calm him down as well.' It had happened during her first week in the department, and she'd been impressed with Nathan's handling of the chef's stress when it was Eva who had needed his attention. 'You helped them both.'

'Later, when the chef had gone, Eva told me the restaurant had a bad safety record and she wasn't going back. I put her in touch with Henri, who owns this place.'

'You did me a huge favour.' Eva placed two coffees before them. 'Molly?'

'Mushrooms on toast, and lots of crispy bacon.'

'Good choice.'

It was. The creamy sauce the mushrooms came in was divine, and the bacon done to perfection. 'I might have to reserve my own table after this.' Molly grinned as she pushed her plate aside and dabbed her lips with a paper napkin. Coogee wasn't so far from Bondi Junction that she couldn't make the trip occasionally to eat scrumptious food, check out those shops and dabble her toes in the sea.

'Help yourself to mine.' Nathan smiled, those questions back in his eyes now that breakfast was over.

Even knowing how unlikely it was, she'd been hoping he'd let it go. Yet she also thought that by telling him about Paul she'd be testing the water to see how he reacted. It'd be a barometer for the future and how she went about revealing her past to any man she might get serious about. Draining her water, she set the glass down. 'Feel like walking along the beach?' She could not sit here revealing everything, not with him directly opposite and she firmly in his line of vision.

'You read my mind.'

'Oh, no, I didn't.' She could no more read what he was thinking than ride a wave like two surfers were doing out there.

Only three other individuals were on the beach, two in a hurry to get their walk done, probably to head back indoors where it was warmer. Molly zipped her jacket up to her chin.

Beside her, Nathan slipped his hands into his pockets and matched her pace. They were halfway along the beach before she said, 'My divorce came through last Monday. I got the paperwork on Thursday.'

'Was that why you had a toast to yourself at Vicki's breakfast?'

'You noticed?' Was there anything she could keep from this man? Was that good? Or bad? She'd go for good, with a wary eye.

'I've started observing lots of things about you.' Then Nathan stopped. 'If that sounds creepy, I apologise. It's not meant to. It's only that my opinion of you has changed since yesterday morning.'

She glanced across, and couldn't resist smiling. 'We didn't exactly get off to a great start, did we?' Could be that deep down she'd sensed how he could affect her if she let him near, and so subconsciously she'd been protecting herself by pushing him away. 'Of course we might go back to being grumpy with each other next time we're at work.' Fingers crossed that didn't happen. She liked the man, more than liked, but that emotion was for another day further down the track—if they spent more time together outside the hospital. Nathan had mentioned a car trip. Should she go? It meant making herself vulnerable, if only because he was so considerate towards her, something that still had her defence mechanisms coming to the fore.

'How long were you married?' Nathan brought her back to reality with a bump.

'Two years.' Her voice had taken on an emotionless tone, designed not to give anything away she didn't choose to. 'At first it was wonderful.' Deep breath, stare at the sand ahead. 'And then it wasn't.'

'I'm sorry to hear that.'

She was sorry she had reason to say it. 'He hit me. Often, towards the end. There was no pleasing him when he was in a mood.'

'I figured that out when you talked about Kath's problem. You understand what she's dealing with.' Nathan came closer, his arm touching hers, his hand now between them—relaxed and there for her. Or so she hoped.

'Every last emotion,' she admitted.

'I hoped I was wrong.' Then he asked, 'Can I hold you?'

She didn't know whether to laugh or cry. Nathan was asking if it was all right to hold her. Pausing in her mad dash along the beach, she faced him square on. 'Yes, please.'

As his arms wrapped around her she became aware of the tension gripping his torso. It didn't frighten her. Again unusual. It only went to show how much she instinctively trusted this man. 'Nathan?'

His forehead rested against hers. 'I am spitting mad. No man has the right to hurt a woman physically. It's appalling.'

'And degrading, and terrifying, and soul destroying,' she whispered.

'Yet you were brave and left him.'

That sounded so simple. Pack a bag and walk out the front door, never to return. Don't look over her shoulder— except she'd been doing that ever since, though not any more. Other than on bad days when she was feeling down.

Nathan continued. 'You're still looking out in case he turns up. At one stage I saw you checking every male that came into the café yesterday.'

She pulled back in his arms to watch the expressions crossing his face. He was angry. For her. The tension eased. No one had done that for her since this appalling situation had begun. Not even the people who should've been there for her. 'He can't. He's locked up for years to come.'

'At least that's good.'

She could get to like this man a lot. Like? Or love? Why not? She was allowed to love again, she just had to get it right next time. 'He escaped once and came after me in Adelaide where I'd moved to get away from the people who thought I'd made it all up. They changed their attitude after the trial, but for me it was too late.' Except for her mum, and that was still a work in progress. 'I tried staying on in Adelaide but there were too many shadows at the corners so I moved here.'

'I'm surprised you can get through a day without checking behind every door in the department and studying each male patient who comes in.' So far Nathan had accepted everything she'd told him without criticism. He'd never understand just how much that meant.

'I used to when I began working at the medical centre in Bondi Junction, but it's exhausting so one day I made up my mind to stop. Not that it happened instantly, but I'm heaps better than I used to be.'

'That says you're comfortable here. Am I right?'

'I'm getting there, and, yes, I want to make a life for myself in Sydney. I will never return to Perth.' Her mother had finally accepted that, right about when she'd acknowledged she'd let her daughter down by not believing her about Paul in the beginning.

Nathan leaned in and his lips touched her forehead, brushed over her skin, before he straightened. 'Good answer. You're one tough lady, Molly O'Keefe.'

The wind gusted sharply, flicking sand at them, and Molly shuddered. From the cold or the memories she wasn't sure. Both, most likely. 'I'm starting to believe that.'

'So you should. I'll say this once, and then I'll keep quiet unless you ever want to talk about it again.' Nathan's hand entwined with hers, and she had no compulsion to pull away. 'You are so brave.' Then he kissed both her cheeks and straightened. 'Let's go find somewhere warmer.'

Molly hadn't told him everything. Nothing about the real possibility she'd never get pregnant again. That was just too close, too painful, to reveal. A huge negative when she was trying to be positive. When they reached his car, she asked, 'Where shall we go now?' She wasn't ready for this to end. She hadn't felt so at ease in years, and it was addictive. She wanted more time with Nathan. Plain and simple. Complicated and interesting.

Nathan looked at her over the roof of his car, a look of disbelief darkening his features as he said, 'I want to show you something.'

Was he sure about that? From the way he was looking at her she thought he was more inclined to take her to the bus station and buy her a ticket out of town. 'What?'

'Wait and see.'

Quick, think of somewhere to take her to. Avoid going home. Because once you show her the self-contained flat you're sunk. There'll be no backing out.

Nathan sucked in chilly air and drove through town, berating himself silently for giving in to the horror with which Molly's story had filled him. Rosie would understand how he had to make sure she was always safe, to protect her from those shadows that haunted her and probably would for a long time to come despite her courageous words. Only then would that beautiful, heart-wrenching smile return more and more readily. A smile that rocked him off his steady stride and woke up parts of him that had been asleep for way too long. Not only his libido, but emotions of longing, caring and wanting to nurture.

Because of that smile he felt as though he'd stepped off the edge of a cliff and had no idea how far below he'd land, or in what condition. Neither did he care.

'No one's said that to me since Gran died. Wait and see,' Molly mimicked in a funny voice. 'Don't be impatient, girl.'

Despite the mire in his head, he laughed. Because Molly made him forget what he'd survived and had him wanting to do whatever it took to get her life back. And his. 'You were close to your grandmother?'

'She was my rock, especially as a child. Believed in me, and taught me a lot about being strong, and not taking for granted everything my mother provided.' Molly hiccupped and turned to stare out the window at the passing scenery. 'If only I'd listened harder before I got married.'

Anger rose in Nathan. Give him ten minutes with the man who'd done this to her. But it wasn't happening, which was probably just as well. He had to accept she was recovering—without any input from him. He swallowed, flicked the music on, and pointed out some landmarks as he drove.

Molly stared out the window. 'It's a beautiful spot.' A gasp erupted from that soft mouth as he turned onto his street. 'You're taking me to your house.'

No fooling her. 'Yes. If I'm keeping you from getting some sleep then I'm sorry. We don't have to stay long and then I'll run you home.'

If I haven't found another reason for bringing you here apart from the real one.

'I stopped wanting to go to sleep before the mushrooms arrived at the table.'

'Good to know I haven't been boring you the whole morning.' He laughed. Again. See? Molly did that to him. It was scary. Yes, and a little bit fun—exciting, even. Could Rosie have been right when she'd said he would love again? Pulling into his drive, he slowed, braked, and breathed deeply. Who'd have known lungs could ache so sharply when deprived of oxygen? 'This is the back. Come around the front.'

She was quiet as they walked along the pebbled pathway to the fenced edge of his property and looked over the public walkway to the grass area and the ocean beyond. Her silence continued for a good five minutes, making Nathan nervous, though he had no idea why. About to ask her what she was thinking, he hesitated, and was rewarded with a big smile. One of those ones that warmed him from his heart to the tips of his toes, and all places in between.

'It's stunning,' she said with a spark in her eyes he hadn't seen before. 'Truly fabulous.'

Then she might be open to his suggestion. If it was the right thing to offer. Hell, he was nervous. Strange. It wasn't as if he was putting his heart on the line—he was merely helping Molly out. No, he'd been lucky in love once. No one got a second crack at that. Spinning around, he began striding back towards the house. There was no denying, though, that to have Molly in his space meant never getting her out of his head. Did he want to? So much for a challenge. Now he had another one. To love or to walk away while he still could. He stumbled. Damn, but he needed to get a new pair of shoes. These ones were tripping him left and right.

'Nathan? Are you all right?' Molly called from a little way behind him.

'I'm fine,' he replied tersely. 'Come inside.' His alter ego wasn't letting him away with not saying why he'd brought her home. Pressing the numbers to the security system a little too hard, he ground his teeth in frustration. He didn't know if he was coming or going, but helping Molly out was suddenly top of his list. Spontaneity was not one of his strong characteristics, and yet…

At the entrance Molly hesitated, making him feel uncomfortable. His fault. He should have told her straight away why he'd brought her here. 'You mentioned looking for somewhere bigger than your apartment. I have a self-contained flat you might be interested in renting.' There. He couldn't retract it. Heading down the hall, he held his breath. Would she follow? Or would she run out of the house screaming he'd gone too far? No, she wasn't running. Neither was she saying anything. Walking into the flat's living area, he turned to face her. Stunned was the only way to describe her expression. 'Molly?'

'Why would you offer me somewhere to live?'

I have no idea. Except for this strange sensation poking me in the belly—and the chest.

'If you want somewhere temporary, that's fine. Your call.'

Stunned turned to irritated. 'Thanks.' Sarcasm dripped between them. She wasn't looking around, that fierce look he'd only got to know yesterday was back. Worse, her hands were on her hips, fingers tight.

Obviously he wasn't going to be let off the question swinging between them. 'This is going to waste, and if you can use it, why not?' Totally true, just not all the truth.

Her hands dropped away, the fierceness softened.

A return to her good books? He hoped so. He believed more than he could have imagined that he needed her to accept he had her back.

'Thank you,' Molly said. He'd have missed the lifting of her lips if he hadn't been so focused on her. 'I'm a bit surprised. Actually, forget a bit. I'm shocked. I mean, we haven't exactly been the best of friends—until now—yet you're saying I should move into your house?'

'Take a look around, Molly. That's all I'm suggesting.'

And don't ask me anything I'm not prepared to answer—because I don't actually have the answers.

Relief spiralled through him as she wandered away to peek into the double bedroom and then the bathroom, and back to the living room with the kitchen in the corner. At least she was looking. That had to be a good sign. She wasn't about to chop his head off with one of those fast judo moves. He opened the glass doors leading onto the small deck overlooking the sweeping front lawn, which gave the flat a sense of more space than was real. He knew the instant she came to stand beside him, his whole body being on Molly alert.

'It's lovely. And private.'

That had to be a plus, surely? Or maybe not, given her need for security. 'Like I said, I fell in love with this place the moment I set eyes on it and have no regrets.' Nathan looked around and felt happiness swelling in his chest. He'd got it right, and could picture his children running around the lawn one day in the future, when his heart got back to being more than a pump. Something else Rosie had been right about.

'I can see why.' Molly was stalling.

His gut tightened. He *wanted* her to move in. Why? As she'd pointed out, they'd hardly got on until yesterday, their norm not having been overly friendly. Yet in little more than twenty-four hours they had done a complete flip. He'd held her in his arms, caressed her with his lips, held her hand as they'd walked to the café, breathed her scent. And found none of that was nearly enough.

'Come on. You need to see the water up close.' Once again her hand was in his as he strode out, heading back towards the grass strip and sea beyond. Now who was stalling? He did not want to hear her say, no, thanks, and that she'd find somewhere else more suitable to live in her own time.

Damn. He should be grateful if she came out with that. What was wrong with him? A few hours in Molly's company and he acted crazy, inviting her to live in his house and holding her hand like they had something going on. His fingers relaxed their grip on hers and he put a bit of space between them. Tried for sane and sensible. Boring.

'Nathan, do you honestly think it would work with me

living here when we're usually on the same shifts in the ED? We'll never get away from each other.'

Go for ordinary, light and friendly. 'You don't think two breakfasts makes us best friends now?'

She stared up at him, those hands back on her hips, this time a hold that didn't indicate her life depended on it, fingers still pink. 'I'm not sure that's what I want.'

'You prefer us being aloof with each other?'

The riotous curls flicked all over her scalp as she shook her head. 'I know you better than that now.' Her mouth lifted, those lips curving seductively. The green in her eyes gleamed like sun on an emerald.

His heart skittered. What the hell? Reaching for her, he brought his mouth to rest on hers, waited in case she didn't want this. When she didn't move away, the need clawing throughout his body won out, and he pressed his lips against hers, and proceeded to kiss her as he'd been thinking of doing since yesterday. Apparently since the day she'd arrived in the ED, if his sense of finally getting somewhere, of the future opening up, was to be believed.

Molly O'Keefe had done a number on him, good and proper. Funny thing was, he didn't give a damn.

CHAPTER SIX

MOLLY FELL AGAINST Nathan, her breasts pressing into him, her hands wound around his back to feel those muscles tighten under her palms as the kiss deepened. This was Nathan Lupton, and they were kissing. Not any old kiss either, but something that turned her on and made her knees weak and her heart rate go off the scale. She should stop, pull away.

She didn't want to. Couldn't. It was as though they'd been building towards this moment once they'd found themselves sitting together at breakfast yesterday. It was like being stuck in the path of a tornado with nowhere to hide. Not that she wanted to. So much for not trusting people. Except, not once had Nathan made her think he'd ever hurt her. Instead he'd indicated he'd go after anyone who tried to get to her.

This was starting over, getting on with a new life, and if it involved getting closer to a man then she had to take the chance. She was done with stagnating. Why wouldn't she want an exciting man in her life? It wasn't as though she'd been neutered. Everything might have been on hold, yet now the barriers were falling fast, not one at a time, as she'd expected, but crashing at her feet in a pile. Leaning closer, she increased the pressure of her mouth on his and went with the wonderful moment, let the exquisite sensations his kiss created have their way and tease her with yearnings long forgotten.

Now? With Nathan? But was she truly ready for this? She jerked, tugged her mouth free. And didn't know what to say. Words, cohesive thoughts, were as hard to catch as a handful of air.

Nathan's eyes flew open, intense with desire. For her.

Forget trying to think what she might say. Instead, she shivered; a delicious shiver that warmed her skin as it raised soft goose bumps on it. Her arms tightened around him. Why had she stopped kissing him?

'Molly?'

Don't say sorry. 'It's good. I didn't want to stop.' She'd had to, though, or lose control.

'Which, I suspect, is why you did.' His mouth twitched.

'It's too soon.' Regret had her tongue lapping at her lips, and his eyes followed, causing a knot to form in her stomach.

His nod was slow. 'You're right. It's the same for me.'

'I'd better get going.'

Nathan shook his head. 'Come inside.'

Not to continue kissing. No, he'd agreed they'd moved too quickly, wouldn't expect a rerun of that kiss. She was coming down to earth now. It was unlikely to be comfortable when the kissing was done and they were back to being professional with each other in the department. Though he was fast becoming a friend, if not something more.

You don't kiss friends like that.

Being in Nathan's arms felt safe. Exciting. Nothing like friendship. Also—and this was big—how certain was she that she wanted this after so long denying her needs?

She tramped along beside Nathan, trying to straighten

her thinking, getting nowhere except inside his house, where he led her to a sitting room overlooking the lawn and beyond. A large-screen TV dominated one wall, an enormous couch placed strategically in front.

'Take a seat,' he instructed in a voice that said he was about to get serious. Over what? Their kiss?

Please don't. She'd hate that. It would spoil the moment and hurt, when she'd enjoyed it so much. She didn't need to hear it hadn't been wonderful for Nathan. He could keep that to himself. Talk about out of practice. Gone was the confident girl prior to Paul who used to kiss and leave, or occasionally kiss and stay for the night and then leave. Look at her. She was a blithering wreck because of a kiss. She so wanted to follow up with another, and wasn't going to. She needed to be circumspect. Parking her backside on the edge of the couch, she crossed her legs, folded her arms and waited.

'Whoa, relax, Molly. I'm not about to bite your head off.' He took the opposite end of the couch, and stretched his legs out for ever. Turning in her direction, he eyeballed her. 'Neither am I going to say I regret kissing you.'

Her arms loosened and her hands splayed over her thighs. 'Go on.'

He laughed. 'What more can I say? Other than I'd like to do it again.'

So would she. But—

'But I'm not sure where we're going with this,' Nathan continued. 'I don't know what you expect from men after what's happened to you in the past.'

That makes two of us.

Or did it? Her lungs expanded as she drew a long breath. 'If I hadn't felt comfortable with you it wouldn't have happened.' She'd have backed away, run more like, not leaned in and made the most of Nathan's mouth on hers. 'What happened in the past has to stay there, not taint anyone I get close to in the future. That might sound naïve, but I firmly believe it's the only way to get back a normal, happy life, hopefully with some loving in it eventually.'

'Gutsy comes to mind. How do you do it?'

Fake it till you make it.

'Dig deep for smiles, start trusting those around me, and have fun.'

'Honest too. Though I'm sure there's a lot you haven't told me.' Nathan held his hand up, palm out. 'It's all right. I don't expect you to. All I ask is that you take me seriously, and don't treat me as an experiment to see how you're managing.'

Nathan had been hurt in the past too and wouldn't be rushing to fall in love again. Her eyes widened. 'Now who's being honest?'

'Would you want it any other way?'

This in-depth conversation with a man was foreign—and interesting. 'No. I've never tried to hurt anyone or, to my knowledge, been so thoughtless as to do so. You've got things that upset you too, and I don't want to be the one who reminds you of what you've lost.' A tremor shook Molly. So much for relaxed.

'We've learned a lot about each other in a short time.' Nathan was studying her, and she felt completely comfortable.

'Which is one reason why I can't move into your flat.' She'd like to get to know Nathan a whole lot better, bit by bit, and that would be best if they weren't living in each other's breathing space. If they were to have a relationship she needed a place to be alone at times while she got used to someone else in her life. Knowing he was on the other side of the wall could encroach on her solitude.

She'd become fiercely independent over the time she'd been alone, and it would take a lot to give up even a little of that. Not even sensational kisses suggesting sensational lovemaking would do the trick. Not yet. Nathan was kind and sincere, or so she believed. While Paul had fooled her with his charm, she doubted Nathan would ever be anything but up-front and caring. But she'd got it wrong once, and that niggled a little.

'Any other reasons for not moving into my flat?'

'We work together.'

'People share living arrangements with work colleagues all the time.' His smile nearly undid her resolve not to give in.

It would take a nanosecond to lean forward and wrap her hand around his arm and bring them closer. Nathan was that damned gorgeous. The air stuck in her throat. The knot tightened in her belly. She could do this—far too easily. But she hadn't thought it through. She needed to do that first. She was considering it? After the arguments she'd put up moments ago? 'I'm not ready.'

'I'd have your back.'

'I know.' Molly sighed her gratitude. It was true. 'And no one's out there trying to track me down any more. I don't need to check every person who comes within spitting distance.' She believed it, which had to be an improvement on her previous attitude to getting out and about.

Nathan nodded. 'Fair enough. I'm not pushing you to do something you don't want to.'

Settling back into the comfortable, soft, cosy couch, she looked around. A computer sat on a desk in the corner, an up-to-date stereo system in another. 'You've made yourself quite the den, haven't you?' There was a maleness to the sharp white décor with dashes of black in the curtains and the furniture. There was also a loneliness she recognised from her own apartment. The room here was on a far grander scale, but the emptiness felt the same.

'I spend most of my down time in here.' He picked up a remote and pressed some buttons, then music filled the air, a low female voice that lifted the hairs on the back of her neck.

Molly swallowed the urge to sing along. 'Not often, then.' She'd keep digging for info while he was so relaxed with her.

'More than you'd credit me with. I put in a fair amount of time studying and keeping up-to-date with medical programmes and the latest drugs and procedures, even though emergency medicine doesn't change a lot.'

'Why that particular field, instead of, say, surgery or paediatrics?'

'It's when people are most vulnerable. I rise to that. It brings out the best in me.'

'You'd be the same in any area of medicine.'

'True.' He shrugged those eloquent shoulders that she'd held while being kissed. 'There's also a lot of variety in an ED. A bit like a GP practice, I imagine, only lots more cases where there's an urgency about the situation. Sometimes I regret not having the follow-up and knowing how a patient fared long term. At the same time, I don't get to see it all go bad and watch someone I've got to know a little go downhill and have to face the families trying to cope.'

That wouldn't be his thing. Not that it was anybody's. 'You've suffered loss. You'd feel for those patients and their families.' To think this was the man she'd thought irritating and infuriating. He still could be, but now she'd seen behind that mask she'd never accept it at face value again. She might get cross with him but from now on it would take longer to really wind her up. She didn't need to be on guard with Nathan or protective of herself over every word he spoke.

'Yes,' he muttered. 'But then I'm not alone in that.' He stood up, walked to the glass sliding doors leading outside and stared out, his hands on his hips, legs slightly splayed.

She'd gone too far, shouldn't have mentioned his loss. But there was no taking it back. She went to join him, shoulder to shoulder, gazing outward. 'I'm sorry.'

'Do you realise how often you apologise for something?'

'One habit yet to be annihilated.' Sorry hadn't stopped the fists, but she'd always tried.

Pushing a hand through his thick hair, Nathan shook his head. 'Don't be apologetic for what you said. I prefer people don't dodge the issue. I did enough of that all by myself for the first couple of years. Rosie was my life. I cannot deny that, or how what happened has altered the way I go about things now. But I think I'm leading a balanced life again.'

He was ahead of her there, but she was working on catching up fast. 'Receiving my divorce papers knocked down the final block preventing me from getting back on track. I'd been taking baby steps, now I'm ready to take some leaps.'

'Finding somewhere new to live might be one.' He remained staring outside as he continued. 'The offer to move into my flat stands. Despite your arguments, I believe we could make it work just fine. We can talk terms and conditions any time you like.' He was serious, in control of things, but she could do control too.

'The next place I live in will be where I'd like to spend the next few years at least. Permanent, rather than a stopgap.'

'Buy or rent?'

'I haven't given it much thought. I could afford to buy a small house or a bigger apartment in a similar area to where I am now.' That'd mean using the money she'd sworn not to touch, but maybe it was time to let go of that gremlin too. 'I'm not sure where I want to live. There's no hurry.'

'Feel free to run any ideas past me. I've spent all my life in and around Sydney and know where not to buy.'

'Thanks.' Glad he'd dropped the subject of renting his flat for now, Molly headed back to the couch and sank down onto it, smothering a surprised yawn on the way. That was the answer to all this nonsense going on in her head. She was tired from working all night and tossing a man on the floor. She grinned.

I did it. Cool.

Tipping her head back, she stared up at the ceiling and thought, *I really must get going.* She couldn't hang around with Nathan all day. He'd want to catch up on sleep, and probably had plans for the afternoon when he woke up. But it was so comfortable here. She'd take another minute before calling a taxi to take her home.

Nathan woke and raised his hands behind his head on the pillow, stretched his feet towards the bottom of the bed. He'd slept like a baby. His watch showed he'd had nearly four hours. More than enough if he was to get back into his regular pattern tonight.

Was Molly still asleep? She hadn't budged when he'd

tucked the blanket around her. It had taken all his self-control not to swing her up into his arms and carry her down to his bedroom so he could lie spooned behind her while they slept. Except there probably wouldn't have been much sleep going on—for him anyway. She flicked every switch he had, and then some.

Who'd have thought it after the way they'd started out? But there was no denying he wanted Molly. She was sexy, sweet, strong, and still recovering from an appalling past. He wouldn't have kissed her for so long but she hadn't stopped, and how was a man supposed to ignore that when the woman fitted perfectly in his arms? Pressed those soft breasts against his chest?

He sat up, swinging his legs over the edge of the bed and leaning his elbows on his knees, then dropped his head into his hands. It had to be a case of wanting what he couldn't have. There hadn't been a woman who'd rattled him like Molly was doing. Not since Rosie. Strange how different they were. Rosie tall, tough, focused; Molly small, soft, trying to be focused on the future and not the past.

A fact that should have him running for the waves. Hadn't seen that coming. All he'd intended was to make her like him. Like? Or desire him? He did want to love again. 'I what?' The question roared across his tongue. 'Yes, I want to love another woman.' Molly?

Leaping to his feet, he crossed to the mirror in the en suite bathroom and stared at the face glaring back at him. Nothing looked any different from what he'd seen last night while shaving before work. He'd been tracking along nicely, and now look at him. Toast. Over a woman he hadn't even liked let alone wanted to kiss at the beginning of the week. Or had he? Had he been in denial all along? Afraid he might actually want to start looking for a future that involved more than himself? Was love possible a second time?

Spinning away from the mirror, he reached into the shower and turned the knob to hot. Cold would be better for what ailed him, but he was a wuss when it came to freezing temperatures; he far preferred the warmth. Even the extreme heat of the outback made him happier than in winter, and Sydney wasn't exactly freezing.

Standing under the water, he knuckled his head. Molly was in there, teasing, taunting with that sassy way she'd used before she'd realised what she was doing. As for her kisses—man, could the woman kiss. His groin tightened just thinking about Molly's mouth on his.

Molly had mentioned baby steps. That's how he needed to approach this. For both their sakes. She might say she was on the road to recovery, but now he knew what to look for he'd seen the sadness, anger and pain in her face and darkening those beautiful eyes at moments when she thought no one was watching. That might go on for a long time even after she found someone to trust and love again.

Like the nights when he still woke to a sodden pillow. Those were rare occurrences now, but they did happen. Rosie would never leave him completely. Likewise, that monster would always be a part of Molly, of who she'd become and where she went from here. But it seemed she was ready to reach out with *him*. He'd better not let her down.

Once dressed in jeans and a navy shirt, he went to see if Molly had woken up.

She was standing in the middle of the kitchen, looking lost. 'So much for calling a taxi. I fell asleep.'

'You needed it.'

'Blame the couch. It's so comfortable.'

When he'd taken the blanket in, Molly had been on her side, her knees drawn up and her hands crossed over her breasts, accentuating their curves and making him wish they knew each better so he could've wrapped her in his arms instead of the blanket. Her face had been relaxed, without the caution that was her everyday approach to people. 'Now you know why I often spend my sleep time there and not in my bedroom.'

'You got any tea?' she asked, then blushed. 'Sorry. I'll get out of here.'

Bet asking that was one of those steps she'd mentioned. 'Tea, coffee, hot chocolate. I've got the works.' He stepped round her and reached inside the pantry.

'Tea, thanks.' Her soft laugh hit him in the gut. 'Cake?'

He winced. 'There's some in here.' He handed her the box of tea bags and reached for a plastic container. 'This has been in here for a while.' Left by his sister when she'd visited last weekend, the banana cake might be a little the worse for not being eaten.

'You have cake lying around?' She shook her head at him.

'I haven't got a sweet tooth.' Which Allie knew, but still insisted on making him cakes every time she visited, a habit started in the bleak days of Rosie's illness as a way to cheer everyone up. Not that it had worked.

'What a waste.' Molly had the container in her hand. 'The icing's got a distinct blue tinge.'

The disappointment on her face made him chuckle as he slid out the bin so she could dump the cake. 'I've got frozen sausage rolls that won't take too long to heat, if you're starving.' Breakfast had been a long time ago. His stomach was growling quietly, and it wouldn't be long before it got really noisy. He flicked the oven on and opened the freezer.

Again her laughter got to him, tightening one telltale part of his body while softening others. 'How do you keep in such good shape if you're eating things like that?'

'Obviously I don't eat them or that lemon icing would never have had time to change colour.' Molly thought he was in good shape? 'I go for a run most days.' Which paid off in dividends, but he was lucky to have a metabolism that let him get away with quite a variety of delicious foods. Then he looked at her and saw the deep pink shade of her cheeks.

'Yes, right. You know I run too.' She busied herself with tea bags and mugs and getting the milk out of the fridge.

'As well as being into those martial arts.' A picture of Molly dropping that irate man flashed across his mind, tightened his jaw. So much for Security. She should never have been put in that position. She could've been hurt. So could Hazel. 'Your moves looked so easy, as though the man was lighter than a bag of spuds.' His heart had been trying to beat a way out of his chest. Not even seeing Molly had been unharmed had slowed the rate. That'd taken minutes of deep breathing, and pretending all was right in the department once Security finally turned up and removed the guy.

She grinned. 'It was pretty cool, wasn't it? I've worked hard at being able to protect myself, but never has that instinctive reaction taken over to make me do what was necessary. Until now I've only ever thrown a judo partner on the mat, where I get to think about the best throw to make and how to execute it properly.' Her grin slipped. 'It makes me wonder what I'd do if someone on the train or in the street raised an arm to reach for something and I reacted without thinking.'

'I bet it was the atmosphere as much as the man's actions that made you react. We were all tense, him in particular.' Nathan hoped he was right, or Molly would get a complex about something she'd learned for her own protection. Placing the pastries on a tray, he slid them into the oven and slammed the door. 'Ten minutes and we'll be into those.'

'Afterwards, I'll get out of your hair and go home.'

It wasn't his hair she was messing with; it was his mind. 'I'll drop you off. I've got to go to the supermarket anyway.'

Handing him a mug of tea in a steady hand, she nodded. 'Thanks.'

No argument? There was a first. He found the tomato sauce and placed it on the bench alongside some plates. 'Need anything else with your sausage rolls?'

'No.' She sipped her tea while moving to the counter and sitting on a stool, plonking her elbows on the bench with her mug gripped in both hands. Looking around the kitchen made for a large family with its counters and eight-seater table, intrigue filled her gaze. 'Did you furnish the house?'

Darn. One of them was behaving sensibly, and it wasn't him. Guess she wasn't feeling the vibes hitting him. He got serious, put aside the hot sensations ramping up his temperature. 'The people I bought it off were moving into an apartment in Rose Bay and wanted to start over with decorating and furnishings so I bought some pieces from them, mainly for the bedrooms and in here. While the table's massive, it gets put to good use when my sister and her lot come to stay.'

'Big family?'

'Allie's got four kids, and a very patient partner. She's like an Energizer battery, no stopping her. She wears everyone out.'

Molly was smiling. 'She sounds like fun.'

'I think you'd like her. And the other two and their broods.' He was getting ahead of himself. Molly did not need to meet any of his family. Not yet, anyway.

'You've got three sisters?'

'Yep.' He jerked the oven door open. 'Let's eat.'

Then he'd take her home before going for a run to work out the kinks in his body put there by being too close to Molly. Nathan muttered an oath under his breath. He had this bad. 'You got plans for the afternoon?'

'Not a lot. Groceries, washing, a run, do the cross-word, wash my hair.' She grinned.

'Sounds action packed.' He grinned back. 'Phone me if you're stuck for a word.'

Then her eyes lit up. 'Actually, I think I'll go watch a game of basketball.'

CHAPTER SEVEN

After a quick shower Molly dressed in fitted black jeans and a pink jersey that deliberately did not match the red curls she attacked with a hairbrush, then followed up with styling gel that did nothing to tame the wildest of them. With a shrug she selected a black leather jacket from the array in her wardrobe. It had been years since she'd worn anything bright pink, and she felt great. Never again would anyone tell her to get changed into something that toned down her complexion. No one.

Halfway out the door she turned back and snatched up the sports bag at the back of her wardrobe. Chances were it would languish in her car, but she was feeling lucky so she might as well go prepared. Humming was another first as she made her way down and outside to where her car sat in a massive puddle by the kerb. Thank goodness for her red, thick-heeled, soft-as-down leather ankle boots. Not only did they look gorgeous but they could keep water at bay without tarnishing the leather.

Grr, grr. The engine gave a metallic groan. Molly turned the ignition off, counted to four, tried again. Bingo. The motor coughed but kept going. She had power. Perfect. She really needed to start it at least every second day if she was going to leave the car out in the weather. Where else could she park it? The apartment didn't come with an internal garage. Or any designated place for vehicles.

Wind rocked the car as she drove away. Hunching her shoulders so her chin was snug against her turtleneck jersey, her humming turned to singing a cheerful song she'd sung often back in the days she'd been truly happy, getting louder with every corner she turned. By the time she reached the indoor sports arena her jaws were aching and a smile was reaching from ear to ear. Hot damn. That was the first time she'd sung her favourite song in years.

Going to watch the Roos team she'd been a part of until two months ago had been a brainwave. They were playing against one of the strongest teams in the local competition, the odds slightly in their favour. She began to hurry. The game had started ten minutes ago and she hated to miss any more. The idea to come here had arrived out of the blue, but with every passing moment it seemed better and better. Catching up with the women she'd played with, and hopefully making up for being so remote whenever they'd tried to get her to join in the after-match sessions in a nearby bar, had become imperative if she was to keep getting up to speed with her new life.

Inside the stadium she searched out the coach and reserves sitting on the benches, watching the game. 'Hello, Coach. Mind if I sit with you to watch the game?'

Georgia flipped her intent gaze from the team to her, and tapped the chair beside her with her notebook. 'Get your butt down here, girl. Where've you been?'

'Hey, Molly, how are you?'

'Molly, I tried to get hold of you to come to a party last month.'

'Hi, how's that new job going?'

'I'm great. I'll give you my number. The job's wonderful.' Wow. No knots of anxiety needed loosening. Everyone was friendlier than she deserved. Sinking onto the seat, she looked around. 'I see you trashed the Blue Heelers last week.' It was the one team everyone had believed might knock them off the top of the leader board.

'Annihilated them.' Coach laughed. 'Glad you're keeping up with us.'

'First thing I look for in the local news on Monday mornings. I miss you guys.' More than she'd realised. When she'd played for the team she'd focused on not letting anyone close, afraid they'd let her down if she needed them in any way, as her friends back in Perth had when it had come out about what had been happening. In the end, staying with the team, not going out for drinks after a game or attending the barbecues that they had once a month, not getting involved as everyone else did, had got hard to face, which in turn had exhausted her, so she'd left.

'You chose to leave.' Coach never minced her words.

'I did.' Molly turned to watch the game on the court. 'How's Sarah doing?' The girl who'd replaced her had spent four weeks on the bench after breaking a wrist in a particularly tough match but had resumed playing a fortnight ago.

'Back to her usual Rottweiler attitude and earning us points to boot. I think the wrist still gives her grief, but I'm the last person she'll admit that to.'

'No one likes telling you anything that might give cause to be sat on the bench for a game.'

'That why you left?' Georgia was watching the game, writing shorthand notes in the notebook, but she wouldn't miss a breath, word or a movement Molly made.

'I felt crowded.'

'Being part of a good, functioning team means being in each other's pockets at times.'

'I wasn't ready for that.'

'You kept to yourself a lot.'

Modus operandi. It had worked. It had kept her safe and—lonely. 'Can't deny that.' Her eyes were on the ball as Emma threw it to Sarah, who lobbed it into the net. 'Go, Roos. Good one, Sarah.' Molly leapt to her feet, stabbing the air with her fists, left, right, left, right. 'You beauty.'

Georgia was calmly making notes. 'Never seen you fly out of your skin before.'

Molly sat back down, a grin on her face. How had she not got all excited over being a part of this team? When she'd played for the under eighteens in Perth she'd been the loudest, most enthusiastic member of the team. Today it seemed she really might be getting her life back. Her grin widened as relief soared.

'Guess you didn't know me very well.' Hell, she hadn't realised how far down the ladder she'd dropped. Yet all of a sudden she was here, getting out and *looking* for fun, not just hoping it might come her way if someone had time to spare for her. When she'd determined to get out and start living she hadn't expected it to happen so fast. It was Nathan. By believing in her, he'd pushed her boundaries and helped her open up some more. 'I'm adept at keeping hidden in plain sight.'

Past tense, Mol. You're over that now.

Georgia's gaze was on every move happening on the court. 'I figured.'

Coach was the second person she'd opened up to, though only briefly. There'd been no in-depth talk about Paul and the abuse, but just admitting she had problems had been huge and had felt good in a way she'd never have believed.

It was good the barriers were dropping here too, but there were some she wouldn't let go. The likelihood of infertility for one. Today Nathan had learned more than she was prepared to share with just anyone. She'd spent so long trying to make people believe she was being abused it was hard to let go of the reticence to talk about it now. What if she woke up tomorrow to find it was all a load of bulldust and she wasn't any further on? That people thought what happened was her own fault?

Then you'll try again, and again, until you get it right. Until people accept you for who you are.

Nathan hadn't laughed or told her she was attention-seeking. No, he'd believed her from the get-go. Her grin had slipped, so she dug deep for another and found it wasn't as hard to do as it used to be.

Molly focused on the game.

The score was twenty-seven all.

The opposing team called for a substitute.

Coach stood up. 'Eloise on. Carmen off.'

At half-time the team swilled water from bottles, wiped faces with towels, crowded around Coach for instructions, and said hi to Molly as though she'd never been away.

The third quarter got under way, and the score continued to climb, each team matching the other, the Roos getting ahead only to have the Snakes catch up and pass them, before they took back the lead.

Sarah snatched the ball, blocked an opposition player and swung around to throw for a goal, and tripped over the other player's foot. Down she went, hard, her elbow cracking on the floor, reaching out with her other hand to prevent hitting the deck with her head. Pain contorted her face as she cried out, pulling her wrist against her midriff.

The coach's expletives were the more damning for being spoken quietly. 'That's the last thing Sarah needs. To do her wrist in again.'

Molly rushed on court with Georgia and knelt down beside Sarah. 'Tell me where the pain is.'

'Same place as last time.'

'Where you fractured it?'

Sarah nodded abruptly, her lips white. 'Yeah.'

'Can I take a look?'

Another nod, and Sarah pushed her arm towards her. 'It feels just the same as before. It's broken again.'

Molly carefully touched the rapidly swelling wrist, then felt up Sarah's arm and over the hand. 'Okay, I agree with you. We need to get you to the emergency department.'

A first-aider sank down on his knees beside them. 'Let me look at that.'

Georgia glared at the young man. 'Molly here's an emergency nurse, and she thinks Sarah has broken her wrist. I'll take her word on it.'

'All right, then. We need to get her to hospital.'

Molly stood up. 'I'll take her.'

Sarah glared at them. 'I'm not going anywhere until the game's finished. I want to watch the last quarter.'

'That's not a great idea. You're in pain,' Molly said.

'You're telling me?' The woman's eyes widened. 'I know what the damage is, know how the pain works, and I can deal with it for a little while longer. Now, help me off the court so the game can resume.'

Molly smiled at her courage as she took an elbow and Georgia put an arm around her waist. 'You're one tough cookie.'

'Better believe it,' Sarah said, then gasped with pain. Locking eyes on Molly, she growled, 'Don't say a word.'

'Okay.' But she wanted to bundle her up and rush her to an ED to get painkillers on board.

Once they had Sarah settled on the bench, and the game was under way again, Georgia leaned close to Molly. 'I don't suppose you've got some sports shoes with you?'

Her heart thumped once, loud and hard. 'Yes. But I'm out of practice.'

'You still run every day?'

'Yes. What about the other players?' The ones who turned up every week all season.

Standing up, Georgia growled, 'Don't you want us to win this game?'

That was one mighty compliment. 'Back in a minute.'

Shorts and a shirt in the bright yellow team colour were shoved into her hands. 'Put these on while you're at it.'

'Bottoms up.' Eloise raised her glass and tipped the contents down her throat, and most of the other team members followed suit.

Molly sipped her sparkling water. It tasted like the best champagne out there. They'd won. She'd scored eight points. Unreal.

'Glad you dropped by,' Georgia muttered beside her. 'But don't think you're getting out of Wednesday night practice from now on.'

So she was back on the team, whether she liked it or not. Thing was, she *loved* it. *And* this getting together with everyone. Once, she'd gone out of her way to avoid it; now she felt like she belonged with these women.

'One problem. I'm on shift this Wednesday night from three to eleven.'

'Some of the girls are working out here tomorrow at nine. Don't be late.'

'Yes, boss.'

'Better believe it.' Georgia winked. Then pulled her phone from her pocket. 'Sarah's texted. She's having surgery tomorrow. That'll put an end to her playing for the rest of the season.'

'Unfortunately you're probably right.' A second fracture on top of the previous one was not good. Molly felt her phone vibrate in her pocket. 'Nathan' showed up on the screen. Her heart went flip-flop. He was the last person she'd expected to hear from, despite their harmonious morning. 'Hi. How's things?'

'I saw your car parked downtown and thought I'd see what you were up to, if you'd like some company. But...' and he chuckled '...it sounds as though you're in the middle of a party.'

'I'm at the Lane Bar with the Roos basketball team. I used to play for them.'

Played for them today and made some points. Yeeha.

'Feel free to join me. Us.' He wouldn't come. She'd been rash suggesting it. 'Some of the others' partners are here.'

'Two minutes.' Gone.

She stared at the phone. Had that really just happened? Nathan was coming to have a drink with her? Her heart raced.

You did kiss him this morning. Maybe he wants another.

He could get as many kisses as he wanted from most single females he crossed paths with. He was drop-dead gorgeous and damned nice with it. Nice? Okay, kind, considerate, opinionated and bumptious. But if he made to kiss her again then she wasn't saying no. Yeah, well. She sighed. The kiss had been pretty darned awesome. Her knees still knocked thinking about it.

That might be exhaustion from charging around the court, not desire, Mol.

Sipping her drink, she stifled a yawn. It had been a long, emotional roller-coaster of a day and suddenly she felt shattered. Just when Nathan was about to join her.

One good thing about Molly's red hair was she was easy to find in a crowd. Another—maybe not so good?—she drove him wild with need, but that was on hold as he tried to slow down his pursuit of her. Yeah, right. If that was so, why was he here? The challenge had got out of hand fast, to the point he didn't know who was challenging who. Hopefully Molly was unaware she rocked him off his usually steady feet.

He stood watching her for a moment as she chatted with the women surrounding the table they stood at, her finger running down her cheek as she laughed over something someone said. This was a whole new Molly from the one he thought he knew in the ED. Yet the vulnerability was still there in the guarded way she stood, one shoulder slightly turned, ready to spin around if she sensed trouble approaching.

'Hey, Molly,' he called, a little louder than necessary, not wanting to disturb her comfort zone.

The curls flicked left then right as her head shot up and around. The smile spreading across her mouth hit him hard in the belly. 'Hey, you, too.' She shuffled sideways to make room for him.

Nathan stepped up beside her, happy when she leaned his way so that their arms touched. 'Looks like you're all celebrating.' He nodded at the array of glasses on the table.

Her smile extended into a grin. 'We won. Against the hardest team we have to play all season.'

'We? You played?' Hadn't she said she was going to *watch* a game?

'Since Coach knew me she asked if I'd fill in for the last ten minutes after one of the girls broke her wrist. Re-broke it.'

'Why did you leave in the first place?'

Molly's look told him to shut up, so he did, for now.

'What Molly's not telling you is that she scored eight points,' one of the women said in a very loud voice.

Molly shook her head. 'It was a team effort. Nathan, let me introduce everyone.' She went around the table, stumbling when it came to naming the men and laughing when they teased her about her memory. 'This is Nathan Lupton, a—a friend of mine.' Colour filled her cheeks. 'We work together.'

She didn't have a definite slot to fit him into. Friend, colleague. What else? He had no answer either. 'Can I get you a drink?' He needed a beer, fast, before he came up with some whack-a-doo ideas and put them out there.

Molly shook her head. 'No, thanks. I'm good.'

'Be right back.' *Don't go anywhere.* Luck was on his side. The bar was momentarily quiet, no doubt a hiatus in a busy night. 'Thanks, mate.' He took his beer and handed over some cash before returning to his reason for being there.

She was toying with her glass. 'I was struggling with fitting into the group. On court, fine. Off court, not so good.'

Nathan nodded. 'Same as you've been with your work-mates. I'm picking same reasons too.'

'Yes. At least I'm doing something about it now.' Her eyes met his. 'Were you headed somewhere in particular when you saw my car? How did you recognise it, by the way? It's so ordinary even I have trouble finding it in a parking garage.'

'I wasn't a hundred percent certain. That's why I gave you a buzz instead of checking out the bars first. How long have you been here?' Molly looked tired, and her eyes were a little glassy. Too many of those bubbly wines that she seemed to be enjoying? That on top of last night's shift, and only a few hours' sleep today, would knock anyone off their perch.

She glanced at her watch, and gasped. 'It's after ten? I think we got here around five thirty. No wonder I'm zonked.' Then she glanced at him, and guilt filled those eyes. 'Sorry. That's rude when you've just arrived. We had a celebratory drink, then a meal and some more drinks. Everyone's stoked to have won. I'm going to the training session tomorrow morning since I can't make Wednesday night practice. I'll probably ache in places I don't know I've got afterwards.' She drained her glass and dropped it back on the table with a thud. 'Damn, I'm talking too much.'

'Yes, but it beats the cold shoulder routine.' He smiled to show he wasn't looking for trouble. 'I like the Molly I'm getting to know.'

She stared at him.

'What? Have I grown a wart on my nose?'

'Not quite.' Finally she dropped her eyes to focus on her hands clasped together in front of her.

'Molly?'

She blinked, sighed, looked at him again, this time with remorse clouding her expression. 'Thank you for not running a mile when I told you everything this morning.'

Oh, Mol. 'As if I'd do that.' Nathan lifted one of her hands and wrapped his fingers around it.

'I knew you wouldn't before I told you or I wouldn't have said a word. It was blatantly clear you'd have my back right from the moment I tossed that creep onto the floor. Actually, I think I'd already reached that conclusion before then.'

'So what's the problem?'

'I probably haven't got one that a good night's sleep won't fix.'

'Then let's go.'

Her curls flicked. 'You just got here.'

'I can leave just as quickly. Come on.'

A tight smile flitted across her mouth. 'Okay. Sorry, everyone, but I'm heading home. I'm knackered.'

'Yeah, yeah.' Someone laughed. 'Your man turns up and suddenly you're tired. We get it.'

Heat spilled into Molly's cheeks, but she didn't give one of her sharp retorts. Instead she managed a quiet, 'Whatever,' and slung her bag over her shoulder to walk out of the bar, her hand still firmly in Nathan's.

On the footpath Molly turned right.

Nathan tugged her gently to the left. 'My car's this way.'

Pulling her hand free, she nodded. 'Mine's the opposite way, as you must know if you saw it parked.'

'I'll give you a lift.'

Those curls moved sharply. 'I'm fine. I need my car in the morning.'

Okay, now he had to be brutal. 'Molly, you've been drinking. You cannot drive.'

Her mouth fell open. Her eyes widened. Then she found her voice. 'You think I'm drunk?' she screeched.

'Yes, I do. You said you've been in the bar for hours.

Drinking was mentioned.' No way was she getting behind the wheel of her car. 'Your eyes are glassy and you were talking the hind leg off a rabbit in there.' He jerked a thumb over his shoulder in the direction of the bar. 'Which is unlike you.' Unless she was nervous, but he didn't believe her nerves had anything to do with this.

'You're wrong.' She spun away to storm down the road.

'Molly.' He caught up with her. 'Please be sensible and let me take you home. It would be safer for everyone.'

She stopped so abruptly he had to duck sideways to avoid knocking into her. 'I had one alcoholic drink when we first arrived. Since then I have been downing sparkling water by the litre. I am not a danger to anyone.'

'Right.' Even to him his sarcasm was a bit heavy as he stepped in front of her.

Stabbing his chest with her forefinger, she glared at him, the anger ramping up fast in those wide eyes. 'I am tired. Not drunk. Please get out of my way. Now.'

'Even exhaustion is a good reason not to drive.' Lame, but true. And desperate. He didn't want her driving. Giving her a lift would make him happy. Apparently not her. He should let this go, but deep inside was a clawing itch that made him try harder to win her over. Reaching for her hand, he tried to pull her in the opposite direction.

She jerked free, stretched up on her toes and said in the coldest voice he'd ever heard, 'Out of my way, Lupton. Damn, but you're so cocky and infuriating.'

When he didn't move she stomped around him and continued down to her car, head high, boots pounding the tarmac. 'I'll follow you,' he called, and headed for his vehicle so as not to lose her. He was going to make sure she got home safely, one way or another.

Cocky and infuriating. What the hell was that about?

Putting him in his place? He'd laugh if it didn't sting. Here he'd been thinking they were getting somewhere. Into a deep, murky hole at the moment.

Slamming the stick into drive, he pulled out and caught up to her at the lights. So he'd infuriated her. No surprises there.

He'd insisted she get into his car.

He hadn't listened to her when she'd said she hadn't been drinking.

He had tried to force his opinion on her.

Starting to sound like her ex.

One very big difference. He would never, ever, use his fists. Molly knew that, or she wouldn't have gone to his house with him that morning. Wouldn't have fallen asleep on his couch, leaving herself vulnerable.

She might not have kissed him either. Keeping a respectable distance, he followed Molly's car to her apartment.

He owed her an apology for being such a prat.

Even if he still thought she should've come with him, he had to say sorry. This argument was bigger than what he'd wanted her to do. It was about not believing her, not letting her make her own decisions—in other words, control. He didn't do control, unless it was about himself. People were allowed to make their own mistakes, unless they endangered someone else in the process. Unfortunately he didn't want Molly making a hideous mistake and so he'd overreacted. She'd had her share of bad deals. She didn't need any more.

Now he had to find a way back into her favour.

Molly closed her door with a firm click, leaned back against it and stared up at the ceiling. 'Damn you, Nathan. Your bossy manner had me reacting faster than a bullet train.'

Her bag slid off her shoulder and hit the tiles with a bang, making her jump. She was wired. And cold. Driving home with her window down to blast the tiredness and keep her alert had chilled her while her temper had combated some of the cold. Now both were backing off. She'd let Nathan get to her—again. Back to how it'd always been between them before birthday breakfasts and judo throws and spilling the beans about her past. It might be for the best. If she hadn't kissed him and been kissed back. Because now she wanted more. Lots more. If she could forgive him for believing she was drunk—*and* telling her what to do.

Picking up her bag, she headed to the kitchen and the kettle. A cup of tea was supposed to remedy lots of things. Hopefully her indignation was one of them.

The buzzing doorbell echoed through the apartment. 'Molly, it's me. Nathan,' he added in his don't-fool-with-me attitude. 'I want to talk to you.'

Well, guess what? She didn't want to talk to him. Filling the kettle, she pushed the 'on' button.

'I know you're in there.'

Who let him into the building this time? Seemed he charmed everyone he came across. Except her. No, even her, when she stopped trying to resist him.

Buzz. Knock, knock. 'Molly.'

Persistent. No surprise there. Back to the door, growling into the speaker, 'Go away, Nathan. I have nothing to say to you right at this moment.'

Except that you've upset me, and stirred me in ways a man hasn't in a long time.

'You want me to shout until the neighbours come out to see what's going on?'

'Go for it.' She huffed at the peephole.

'Let me in.'

Definitely louder, and he wouldn't stop there. Another huff and she wrenched the door wide. 'You're not coming in.'

'Fine.' He leaned a shoulder against the doorjamb and concentrated his entire focus on her.

The cheek of him, so damned sure of himself. She stabbed his chest before she put her brain in gear and jerked her hand away. 'You think you can say what you like to me and get away with it.'

'Wrong, Molly. I know I'll never get away with anything around you.'

Her mouth dropped open. Hurriedly closing it, she swallowed hard. What did he say?

'You don't take any bull from anyone and, for some reason, especially from me.' His mouth twitched. 'I like that.'

Again her jaw dropped. Again she slammed it shut, jarring her teeth in the process. This wasn't going according to plan. Not that she'd had one other than to keep Nathan out of her apartment. 'Right. Fine. You've had your say so kindly remove yourself from my doorway so I can close the door.'

He didn't move a centimetre. 'I haven't told you why I'm here.' His eyes were locked on her as though seeing right inside to every thought crossing her confused mind. 'Can you spare me a couple of minutes?' That couldn't be a plea. Could it? His eyes were dark, his mouth soft.

Nathan was making it hard to stay uptight and focused when he looked at her like that. This was probably the biggest mistake she'd made in a while, but she stepped back, holding the door wide, and nodded, once, abruptly.

'Thanks.'

The tenderness in his gaze made her shiver. Had he done an about-face? If so, why? No, he wouldn't have. Molly headed into her lounge, where she remained standing. To sit would give him a height advantage. The kettle whistled, clicked off. She ignored it.

Nathan stood before her, not so close as to dominate her but near enough that she was fully aware of him. Heck, she was aware of him all over the ED, so there was no way she could ignore him in her apartment even if she shut herself in the bathroom.

He reached for her hands and said, 'I'm very sorry for doubting you. I had no right to do that. Or to criticise you. If I could take those words back, Molly, they'd be gone already. Not thrashing around inside your head.'

He understood her too well. Now he'd stunned her. Nathan Lupton had said sorry—to her. The tension fell away, leaving her wobbly, with a spinning head and racing blood. Somehow her fingers had laced with Nathan's. 'Accepted,' she whispered. What else could she do? Being offside with Nathan wasn't what she wanted. Not now, not ever if possible.

His gaze remained fixed on her. The coffee shade of his eyes had lightened to tan with hints of green and black. A smile was growing on his lush mouth.

Heat expanded in her stomach, spreading tentacles of longing throughout her body, knocking at her heart, shimmering into her womanhood, weakening her knees.

'Molly?' Nathan's hands took her face to ever so gently bring her closer to his mouth. Those full lips brushed her quivering ones, apologising and teasing. Then he pulled back to again lock eyes with her. Heat sparked at her, set her blood humming, lifting her up on tiptoe.

As her mouth touched his she fell into him, winding her arms around to spread her hands over his back, pushing her awakened nipples against his solid chest. She breathed deeply. *Nathan.* His name reverberated around her skull, teasing, laughing, giving.

Oh, yes, giving. His mouth was devouring hers, his tongue plunging deeper with every lick. Hands skimmed over her arms, her waist, then held her butt tenderly while stroking, firing her up to the point of no return. Molly hesitated, her mouth stilled. Did she want this? Stupid question. Her mouth went back to kissing him hard, demanding more, sharing everything.

Then Nathan raised his head. 'Molly?' Disappointment knocked behind her ribs when he took her hands and held them tightly between his. 'I think I'd better go while I still can.'

Thump, thump went her heart. He was right. The next step would be in the direction of her bedroom, and despite feeling comfortable and safe with Nathan, she wasn't as ready as that entailed. Sure, they could make out and have fun, but the sun would rise and then she'd have plenty of misgivings to deal with. This man had got closer to her than anyone in a long time, but it had happened so fast she needed to pause, take a breath, and think about what she wanted. 'You're right. It's too soon for me.'

He squeezed her hands gently, brushed his lips across hers, and stepped back. 'Me, too.'

CHAPTER EIGHT

MOLLY WAS WHACKED. Every muscle ached, and she'd thought she was fit. Lifting the kettle to fill it took energy she didn't have. That afternoon's basketball game had been tough. She'd worked hard to justify Coach's belief in her. They'd barely won—surprising considering the opposition team was ranked seventh compared to their second slot in the competition.

Pride lifted Molly's spirits further. Not once had she failed to take a catch or run the length of the court bouncing the ball. She'd made most of her shots count, taken some intercepts without too much difficulty. Yes, it had been a good game, and now she was worn out.

Work had been busy beyond normal all week, making everyone tired and scratchy. Though Nathan had remained friendly and easygoing with her. There'd been no more kisses or time together away from work, but lots of laughs and friendship. A very normal week for most people, and she couldn't ask for more.

Her bed looked so tempting since she'd changed the sheets and straightened up her room. The washing machine was humming in the kitchen, the pantry had some new food on the shelves, and her newly washed hair was under control. Not that that would last, the curls being the unreliable nuisances they were.

Sinking on the edge of the bed, there was no holding back the smile splitting her face. Or the soft, warm feeling settling over her. Yes, it seemed she was getting up to speed with returning to a normal life, and she had Nathan to thank for some of it. That man made her feel special. She only hoped she'd given some of the excitement and wonder back.

Without thought, she sprawled over the bed, her head snug on her pillow as she kept running images of Nathan through her mind. Laughing over something silly, stitching up a cut in an old man's arm, kissing her. They were more than friends now. But were they becoming a couple? Hardly.

The ringing phone woke her. Scrabbling around the top of her bedside table, her fingers latched onto the instrument just as the ringing stopped. Damn.

Then it started again. Nathan's name blinked out at her.

'Hi.' She scrubbed the sudden moisture from her eyes. It was *only* a phone call.

'Hey, Molly. How did the game go?'

Man, she loved that voice. Over the phone it was even more gravelly. 'It was awesome. We won.'

'So you'll be out celebrating. Though it does sound rather quiet.'

'I'm at home. Some of the girls were going to a wedding and the rest of us had other things to do.' She hadn't, but she'd fallen in with the general consensus that one weekend not celebrating wouldn't hurt.

'Bet you're exhausted. But I was wondering if you're up to meeting my mob. They've descended upon me without warning, and I need some backup.'

'You didn't know your family was coming to visit?'

Nathan's laugh was a short hoot. 'The day any of my

sisters tell me they're on their way I'll buy a lotto ticket. All the nieces and nephews are here too, I might add.'

'How many?' Nathan wanted her to meet these people? Seemed they were way past being civil with each other and on to greater things.

'Eight.'

'You're pulling my leg,' she spluttered.

'Nope.' He laughed. 'Three married sisters make for eight brats to buy birthday and Christmas presents for.'

It didn't sound like he resented that. Quite the opposite. He seemed very happy he belonged to this family. 'You must have lists everywhere to keep up with what you've bought who, and what you'll get them next.'

'You have no idea. So, are you up for them? I have to be fair and warn you it won't be a quiet afternoon and you'll never have seen a meal like it. Also, dinner will be at some ridiculously early hour that's closer to lunch so that everyone can be back on the road early. Getting the ankle-biters home late causes bedlam the next morning apparently.'

'It doesn't sound as though any of this is a hardship.' Did he really want to introduce her to his family? Had he thought it through? *Grab the opportunity.* Even if they didn't go much further with whatever was happening between them, she should get out and enjoy herself while she could. 'I could come for a few minutes,' she teased. This teasing was another first. She'd forgotten how to long ago—safer that way—but apparently the ability had been hovering under the surface.

'Minutes? Oh, no, you don't. All or nothing, girl.'

She laughed. This was so different from anything she'd have expected from Nathan before Vicki's breakfast. Before V day and after V day were now her measures. 'I'm on my way. Well, I will be when I've spruced myself up a bit.'

'Don't get carried away. By the time the little horrors have finished with you you'll wish you'd saved yourself the effort.'

'This sounds like fun.'

'You have no idea.' Nathan was laughing fit to bust as he hung up.

Eight kids in one hit? Crikey. Molly stared around her cramped bedroom. What was happening to her? She'd been out more often to more places since V day than at any time throughout the last two months put together. Even better, she was happy. The only time she hadn't been was when Nathan had accused her of being drunk, and his apology more than made up for that.

Leaping off the bed, she threw the wardrobe door open. What to wear? Something to impress Nathan, even if he had warned her to downplay the outfit?

Molly settled for tight black jeans, a cream jersey, and her favourite red boots. No, cream was a magnet for grubby hands. Tossing that jersey aside, she flicked hangers from one side to the other, found the bright orange jersey and tugged it over her head, instantly feeling at ease. Orange top and red curls. Perfect. Lipstick. Red or orange? Red was the first one to land in her hand, so red it was. She had to stop singing to apply the gloss.

So much for exhaustion and muscle aches. She was going to a party of sorts. Bring it on.

Nathan's house on Saturday morning had had an air of quiet elegance about it, with the sweeping lawns and ocean view attention grabbing.

Today Molly felt as though she'd dropped into the middle of a circus. Who knew kids could make so much noise? Then there was the exuberant adult joining in all the games and flying kites and chasing balls, seemingly all at once. Gone was any vestige of Dr Lupton.

'Hey, you came.'

'You didn't think I'd turn up after saying I would?'

'I figured you'd pull into the drive, hear the racket going on and take off faster than a rocket.' Nathan wrapped an arm around her shoulders. 'I've said it before—you're one brave lady. Come and meet the tribe. I promise not to quiz you on names later.'

She felt a bit bedazzled as she was introduced to sisters, brothers-in-law and all those children, and had to pinch herself to make sure this was real. It was nothing like her family, where she was the only child, with her mother and all the expectations of grandeur and a father in New Zealand replaced by a stepdad. They loved her, but this? She looked around and swallowed. The Luptons left her speechless. It was probably just as well or she might say something so odd they'd be putting her back in her car and waving goodbye before she'd had time to relax.

'Here, get this into you.' One of the women handed her a glass of wine. Annemarie? Or Jessie? It wasn't Allie, or was it? 'I hope you like wine, because a few hours with us will turn anyone to drink. We're enough to scare off the bravest.'

Molly accepted the glass. 'I think you might be right.'

'Try and leave, and I'll wheel-clamp your car,' Nathan called over his shoulder as two young boys tried to tackle him to the ground. 'And that's Annemarie.'

She laughed. She was doing a lot of that lately. Again Nathan had seen right through her confusion. 'Thanks, Annemarie.' Colour filled her cheeks. 'I'm in the mood for a wine, which is rare.' So much had been happening, so something, someone to relax with was perfect.

Her gaze found Nathan. Having a drink made standing around talking to strangers easier, and kept her hands busy. Unless— 'You look like you need some help,' she called over to Nathan.

'Stay back, and look after those sore muscles. We have a few hours to get through yet.' When she lifted one eyebrow, he laughed. 'You're walking round like a toddler on a high.' Boys and girls fell onto Nathan, pushing him onto the lawn, tickling him as he carefully tossed one after another into the air and caught them again.

'Let's sit on the sidelines,' Annemarie said, heading for the expansive deck and some chairs, sheltered from the light, cool breeze coming off the sea. 'The men can play while the women relax with wine and nibbles. It's tiring just watching.'

Settling into a wicker chair, Molly watched Nathan and his brothers-in-law chasing kids and balls around the lawn and waited for the questions from the sisters, sipping her wine in an attempt to look the part of a friend with nothing else to do on a Saturday afternoon. That part was kind of true. When the grilling didn't come she began to enjoy herself.

'Mum, when can we eat? I'm hungry.' A little girl stood in front of them a while later, hands on hips, just like her uncle Nathan had been doing earlier.

'Ask Uncle Nathan. He's in charge of the barbecue.'

'Now,' came the call.

The women hit the kitchen, and Molly found herself taking an endless supply of salads, breads, dressings and sauces out to the huge table in the conservatory. Delicious smells wafted from the barbecue where Nathan and the guys had begun cooking steak and sausages.

'How're you doing?' Nathan came over to her. 'I've neglected you a bit.'

'It's fine. I don't need to be babysat. Anyway, I liked talking with your sisters.'

'That's a worry.' He grinned.

'You were having fun with the kids. You're just like them, getting muddy rolling around on the lawn. I half expected you to ask for a turn on the trolley.' There was a box on wheels that the men had taken turns pulling children around in.

'No one would take me on.' Another grin.

'I can see why your family descends on you.' No sign of being in control or wanting things done his way today. 'You love those kids and they love you back just as much.' She could see him with a large family of his own. Not with her—she couldn't. Her stomach squeezed a little, her mouth lost the sweet taste of the wine. 'You ever plan on having your own brood?'

Nathan turned from watching the kids arguing over a game of hopscotch to studying her a little too intently. 'Is that a loaded question?'

An important one. 'It stands to reason you might want your own family when you're so comfortable with this crowd.'

'You're right, I adore them. I fully intend on raising some kids of my own one day. What about you? You want a family some time?'

'Absolutely.' It was true. She did. People didn't always get everything they wanted, though. 'It's not something I've thought too much about lately.' Again true, because there'd never been a reason to. There hadn't been a man waiting in the wings to be a part of that life. Now there was a possibility of love happening she had to think how to go about this.

'Rosie and I had planned on starting a family as soon

as I qualified.' His gaze had left her, appeared to have gone out across the lawn somewhere.

Molly touched his arm. 'Nathan? I'm sorry. I didn't mean to upset you.'

He looked at her, placing his hand over hers on his arm. 'You said sorry again.'

'Because I spoiled the moment.' He wanted a family. A bucket of cold water couldn't have chilled her any more than that information. It was the wake-up call she hated. Of course he'd want children when he fell in love again. It's what most men and women wanted. She did. Only it wasn't going to happen for her, and she wouldn't take anyone else on that ride. It would be grossly unfair to expect Nathan to drop his dream of children for her. A weight settled over her heart—the one that wasn't supposed to be involved with this amazing man.

'Get it into your head that talking about Rosie comes as naturally to me as eating. Sure, there're moments I feel sad, but it's a whole lot worse if she's never acknowledged.' He squeezed her hand, then let it go to step aside, putting space between them. 'If it's a problem for you then there's not a lot I can do. I will never deny she was the love of my life and how hard it's been to lose her.'

Collecting a few wake-up calls today. What was next? 'I like it that you feel that way. No one should be forgotten when they've been such a special part of your life. Hearing you talk about her says a lot about you, all good.' Her smile wavered, but since he wasn't watching her she got away with it. She wasn't going to be as special to him because even if he wanted that, she couldn't allow it to happen.

Instead she had to back off in case he did start to fall for her. That's when the day would come that she'd have to tell him the very long odds of her ever getting pregnant. Already she knew a quickening of her pulse whenever she heard Nathan's voice or laugh. Felt a softening of her limbs when he touched her. This had to stop. He'd been hurt once, she wasn't giving him a second blow.

'It helps you understand.' Nathan turned back to the barbecue. 'I'd better take over before the guys burn the steaks.' He hesitated, faced her again. 'We'll have some time to ourselves later.'

'I need to head home early. Catch up on sleep. And I'm working in the charity shop tomorrow.' She needed to think all this through. Unfortunately leaving now would be awkward after she'd helped set out the food and had said she couldn't wait to sample the salads.

'If that's what you want to do.' Nathan nodded abruptly. Sensing her withdrawal?

As soon as dinner was over and the kitchen cleaned up, she'd go home and revert to the Molly he used to know. No, not that. She'd be friendly and outgoing, but no more kisses. Already, walking away wouldn't be simple. Not when she'd finally come out of a drought to find she could be aroused by a man—one in particular.

But they weren't a couple. It was presumptuous to hope there might be more to Nathan's invitations and kisses than having a good time. It was quite possible he wanted to have some uncomplicated fun, and wasn't looking for a more permanent arrangement, and that she was reading too much into his friendliness. Something she'd be better thinking about than getting her knickers in a knot because he was the one helping her step back out into the real world.

Molly shoved aside all the reasons for not spending time with Nathan and said, 'It isn't, really. I don't know what came over me.' Except she did, and it wasn't going to disappear. She should leave, now. If only it was that easy. When she finally came out of her cave she didn't want to go back into the dark, cold space that her life had become.

'Gun-shy? I'm not surprised after meeting all this lot. It's enough to scare anyone off.'

'More that I feel very comfortable with them—too comfortable, maybe.'

He ruffled her hair like she'd seen him do with his nieces. 'Nothing wrong with comfortable.'

Yes, there was, if it led to greater expectations than were reasonable. But for tonight at least she'd relax and continue enjoying herself. And Nathan.

The family didn't leave early. It was as if they knew they were frustrating him. Nathan ground his teeth. Molly had said she'd leave after dinner, then changed her mind. Finally the brothers-in-law had made sounds about heading away and he'd had the front door open with embarrassing speed. But if they hadn't gone soon Molly might have, and he didn't want that. He wanted time with her not being interrupted by one of the children asking for more ice cream or a sister quizzing him on his next holiday plans.

'At last.' He shoved his hands in his pockets before he could haul Molly into his arms and kiss her senseless.

'You don't mean that.' She smiled as she stood in front of him, looking sensational with the riotous curls and that perfect body.

'Normally I'd agree, but tonight I just wanted to be with you for a while.' Hell, he wasn't going to be able to not kiss her.

Her breasts rose on an intake of air. 'I'm still here.'

'Tell me something I don't know.' He had to touch her. Had to. Placing his hands on her shoulders, he drew her closer. And closer. Until she was up against him, those breasts nudging his chest, her mouth so near to his. Then his mouth was on hers, kissing, tasting, drinking her in. As he kissed Molly he waited to see if she'd pull back or tense even a little, but, no, her arms were winding around his neck and her hips were pressing into his. Giving up on caution, he went deeper with the kiss, savouring Molly, her softness, her scent, all of her. Everything about her woke him up.

Then her mouth was gone. 'Nathan?' she gasped, blinking rapidly, no disappointment blazing out at him this time. But hope was, and enough desire to drown in.

'Yes, Mol. I'd like to take you to bed.'

She sank back against him, and returned to kissing the minutes away, until he couldn't take any more. Swinging her up into his arms, he asked, 'Bedroom?'

'No. Right here. Now.'

As he walked her up to the wall, he said, 'I'll be gentle.' No way did he want to frighten or hurt her.

'Don't you dare.' She lifted a leg to his thigh, freed her hands from his and wound them around his neck. 'I won't break.'

The corners of his mouth lifted. 'Tell me something I don't know.' Then he claimed her mouth, and placed his hands on her butt to lift her higher. When she wound her legs around him and settled against the growing evidence of his sex he had to take a deep breath and hold onto the need trying to break free. This wasn't just about him.

'Nathan,' she growled.

He returned to kissing, drawing out the exquisite moment for as long as possible. His mouth trailed below her ear, down her throat, to the neck of her jersey. 'Damn it. This has to go.'

How she did it he had no idea, but within moments her

lace-covered breasts were before him, drying his mouth and tightening his groin to breaking point. Molly first. He pushed between them, slipped his hand under her trousers, then her underwear, and found her centre, and touched, caressed, and felt her blow apart with one hard, swift stroke.

She clung to him, hauling in gulps of air, her eyes barely open.

He waited, kissing her forehead, her breasts, her arm.

'Nathan, let me.' She wriggled in his hold, trying to unwind her legs from his torso.

'Steady,' he whispered against her feverish skin.

'Inside. I want you inside. It's your turn.'

'Shh. It's not about turns. I'm here, with you. We'll get together as soon as we remove the obstacle.' But, yes, he was more than ready.

She blinked. 'Obstacle?' Of course. 'Then let me down. I'll be quick.'

'You'd better be,' he grunted as he lowered her carefully and held her as she got rid of the rest of her clothes.

Then she was back in his arms, her legs wound around his waist. Lowering herself over his sex.

He couldn't halt the trembling throughout his body as he pushed deep inside. Molly held on tight as he withdrew and returned, winding her tighter and tighter until she exploded again. Then he let go, and rode the wave of desire, passion and need. Unbelievable.

Nathan stretched out in his bed, one hand behind his head, the other on Molly's breast as she slept. Earlier she'd been exhausted, and now after two bouts of lovemaking she'd succumbed, and had been comatose for a couple of hours.

Not that he minded. Lying here with her, listening to

the soft snuffles she made, he couldn't have felt more relaxed or happy, in a way he hadn't expected to ever feel again. Though lately he'd been open to it, he just hadn't believed it might happen. Certainly not with Molly O'Keefe. Here was a woman who'd turned out to be nothing like the face she presented to the world. It could be that he hadn't known what to look for and her feisty, strong personality had been simmering in the background all along. Or it might be that with the divorce papers in her hands she'd found the hope and courage to go in search of the life she wanted.

Whatever it was, it didn't really matter, as long as he was a part of the future she unravelled. This had started as a challenge to make her like him, to be friendly towards him, but now the challenge had changed. He thought he might want her in his life—in all ways possible. Since Rosie no other woman had made him *want*. Love, a partner, family. Molly did that. *Rosie.* His heart slowed. He still missed her, but not as severely as in the past. Was he getting over the crippling loss? Did he want to have a future with another woman? Yeah, he thought he might. The only problem was that it was happening fast. Too fast?

'I'm glad your family turned up today or this might only be wishful thinking.' Molly's sleep-filled voice sounded sexy as hell.

As his body reacted in the only way it knew, he grinned, and caressed her breast, extracting a gasp of pleasure from her. 'You have an open invitation to visit any time you like.'

The sleep was rapidly disappearing from those sensational eyes, replaced with a sparkle that warmed his heart as Molly reached for him, wrapping her hand around his obvious attraction for her. 'Knock, knock, I'm here.'

'Can't argue with that,' he muttered as he leaned in to kiss that exquisite mouth, before exploring her body with his mouth. He couldn't get enough of her.

Hours later he woke suddenly as the bed rocked sharply.

'Look at the time.' Molly sounded frantic as she tossed the covers aside, along with the arm he'd had around her waist. 'Ten past eight. I've got to be at the arena by nine.'

'There's plenty of time.'

'No, there's not. I can't be late, or Coach will send me packing permanently. I don't intend letting her down again.' She disappeared out the door, returned with last night's clothes, still yabbering. So unlike the Molly of the past. 'I have to get my gear from home and clothes to wear to the charity shop afterwards.'

Shoving the covers aside, Nathan stood up and stretched, and she didn't stop to notice. She was definitely on a mission. 'I'll put the coffee on. You want something to eat? Toast? Cereal?'

Finally she stopped and came to kiss him, a brief touch of those lips on his stubble-covered chin. Nowhere near enough. 'No, thanks. I'll grab something at home.' Then she was in the bathroom, the shower spraying out water and the extractor fan making a racket.

He knew when he was not needed. But if Molly thought he'd toe the line that easily, she was going to have to think again. In the bathroom he opened the shower door and joined her, taking the soap from her hands to wash her skin, starting at her neck, and working his way down to her feet. 'No complaints, madam?' He grinned through the water pouring over his head.

She waved a hand in the narrow space between them. 'How quick can you be?'

'Let me show you.'

When Molly dragged herself out of the shower not too much later and began drying her glistening skin, Nathan watched her while soaping himself. 'You're beautiful.'

Her head shot up, surprise widening her eyes.

He repeated himself. 'You are beautiful.'

Her hands hesitated in the process of towelling her stomach, and dropped to her thighs.

His gaze followed, then backed up to her lower belly. 'How'd you get that scar?' It was small, and stark against her pale skin.

The towel came up instantly, and the shutters came down over her eyes. 'I had an accident.' Then she was gone, out into his bedroom.

Snapping the shower off, Nathan picked up another towel and followed her. 'Molly, I'm sorry. I didn't mean anything by my question. I didn't even think before I asked.' The result of one of her ex's rages? Gritting his teeth, Nathan dried himself hard and fast.

Her face was blank. 'It's nothing, okay?'

No, it wasn't okay, but nothing would make him say so. His thoughtless question had already upset her. He was ready to murder someone.

Pausing in her rapid dressing, Molly looked at him with sadness pouring off her in waves. 'Sorry to rush off like this.'

He suspected she was apologising for something entirely different. It took all his strength not to wrap her in his arms and tell her everything would be all right. Because he didn't know for sure that it would be, and making false promises was not the way to go. Instead he placed a hand on her cheek. 'Go impress Coach. I'll see you later, though probably not today.' He needed some space while he thought through everything that had been happening between them.

Molly didn't look unhappy with that. 'It's fine. I've got stuff to do after basketball.' She was already making her way to the door, where she paused and looked directly at him. 'I had the best night.'

Steal his breath, why didn't she? 'So did I, Molly. So did I.' It was true. So true it was scary. And exciting. And something to think about.

CHAPTER NINE

'Hi, Vicki. I'm not going to ask how your weekend went. It's written all over your face.' Vicki had headed north to Darwin to spend time with Cole when he wasn't on duty.

Molly banged her locker shut and pocketed her key. When Vicki didn't reply she looked closer. 'Oh, hell. Come here.' Regretting her comment, she reached to hug her friend.

Palms out towards her, Vicki shook her head. 'Don't. I'll fall apart if you're kind to me.'

'Fair enough.' How awful to have her husband heading away so soon for who knew how long. Molly went for a complete change of subject. 'I see you've gone all out today. Love that shade of purple in your top, and as for the boots, I'm drooling.' Relief glittered out of Vicki's sad eyes. 'Took me weeks to find boots to match my outfit. Finally found them in a second-hand shop. This is not my usual style of clothes. I'm more the black on black type. Except for the shoes.'

'Except for the shoes,' Molly said at the same time, and they burst out laughing. Leaning back against her locker, she waited while Vicki changed into her uniform. 'Hope we have a quiet night.'

'I want it so busy I don't come up for air.'

'One of us should get lucky, then.' Her ears were straining for the sound of Nathan's voice out in the department. She hadn't seen him when she'd arrived, and as he was always early he had to be tied up with a patient already.

'You been for a spin in Nathan's fancy car yet?'

'I was too busy.' Doing other things with Nathan, and avoiding certain issues that weren't going to go away no matter how much she wanted them to.

'Doing what?' Disappointment blinked out at her.

Vicki wanted her to get with Nathan? Then she'd be pleased to know what had gone on between them, but Molly wasn't spilling the beans. She didn't do juicy gossip, and when it involved herself she remained especially tight-lipped. She straightened up. 'Better get cracking and start earning my living.' Away from the questions that were likely with Vicki needing a distraction from her aching heart.

'I'll be right there.'

Joining the rest of the shift waiting for change-over, Molly still couldn't see or hear Nathan. She should be relieved, not sad. Having decided to go for friendly and easy with him, disappointed wasn't an option. Saturday night had been sensational. Not a lot of sleep, though. Instead she'd had quite a workout, and still wanted more.

'Morning, everyone. Hope you had a good weekend.' Nathan strode in with a large smile and sparkling eyes as he scanned the room, pausing for a moment when he saw her. The smile brightened briefly, then he seemed to remember where he was, who he was with, and he straightened. 'Right, let's get the show on the road.' He came to stand beside Molly, though.

Her body was doing the happy dance on the inside

while externally she tried to keep her face still while listening to Mick run through the patients in the department. It wasn't easy when she was fighting the desire to curl into Nathan, struggling with the need to touch him, to feel his warm skin under her palms.

'Cubicle one, forty-two-year-old male, waiting for liver function tests to be completed. In two, fifty-six-year-old female, extreme abdo pain, query diverticulosis.' Mick continued through the list of patients, and Molly felt tired before they'd started.

'You okay?' Nathan asked quietly as everyone dispersed to get on with the shift.

Why was he asking? 'I'm good. Did you get the place cleaned up yesterday?'

'Eventually.' His smile was devastating.

'You went back to sleep.' She grinned.

'Quiet, woman, unless you want everyone knowing why I was so exhausted.' His whispered words sent a thrill of excitement down her spine.

How was she going to remain focused on not getting too close to this man who'd woken her up from her dull and cautious life?

Mick was talking to the triage nurse and now turned to Molly. 'Can you take this one? Twenty-one-year-old male, stab wounds to his face and arms. I'll send someone else to help you in a mo.'

'On my way.' She checked which cubicle to use, glad of something to keep her busy and away from Nathan, because even standing beside him made her weak at the knees.

Got it bad, Mol?

Yeah, she was beginning to think so.

'I'll check the man out with Molly, Mick. Those stab wounds might need my sewing skills.'

So much for putting space between them. But what could she say? She liked working with him, even when they hadn't been comfortable together. He was a superb emergency specialist, and she learnt from watching him. So she went to meet her patient and settle him on the bed in cubicle eleven as the triage nurse gave them the details.

'Beau Cooper, twenty-one, stabbed with a broken bottle, significant wound to his face, minor cuts on both arms.' Sally turned to the young woman who'd accompanied him. 'Gina, here, is Beau's girlfriend. She brought him in.'

'Hi, Beau. I'm Molly, one of the nurses who's going to look after you.' She turned to Nathan. 'This is Dr Lupton.'

Nathan moved up to examine the young man's face. 'Beau, tell me what happened when you were attacked. Did you fall to the ground, bang your head? Any details are important.'

'I'm not sure. Two guys attacked me when I asked for my girlfriend's bag back. They smashed a beer bottle and got me in the head, the arms and my leg. I stayed upright, didn't hit my head on anything. That's all I can tell you.'

'How's your breathing? Are you having any difficulty with that?'

'Seems all right.'

Then the glass hadn't cut through anything vital in his throat. Holding her hand up, Molly moved it from left to right. 'Follow my hand.'

Beau's eyes slid sideways, focused on her movements.

'Good, your vision checks out.'

The curtains flicked wide and Hank joined them. 'Nathan, you're wanted in three urgently.'

'On my way.' Nathan turned to her. 'I'll be back when you've cleaned him up.'

After a quick rundown on what had happened, Hank said, 'I'll remove his jeans so we can check his legs for abrasions.'

Molly nodded. 'Might as well. Though from the small amount of blood I don't think there's anything too serious in that region, but he needs to get out of the messy clothes anyway.' The wound in Beau's neck and face was deep, his neck had damaged muscles that would require surgery that couldn't happen until the morning. She began swabbing the area, careful not to cause him any more distress.

Hank got Beau to lift his hips while he tugged the jeans off.

Their patient groaned but did as asked.

'I'll get you some penicillin next,' Hank told him. 'Who knows what was on that bottle?'

'Get something to numb the pain too.' Molly had finished cleaning the man's neck and face, and dropped the swabs into a hazardous waste bin at the head of the bed. 'I'm going to talk to Dr Lupton, Beau.'

Nathan was entering notes on a patient file on the screen. 'How's your man?'

'I'll be interested to hear what you say after you take a look at the neck and face wound. I think he needs surgery.'

Nathan's chair rolled back from the desk and those long legs pushed him upward. 'Any other serious injuries?'

'Not really. Hank's getting some drugs. The guy's in a lot of pain and trying not to show it.'

'The tough type.'

'That's because he's a boxer,' Beau's girlfriend told them minutes later. 'They're expected to take the knocks without complaining.'

'Why did those men have your handbag?' Molly asked Gina as she handed Hank the painkiller drug and checked the dates with him.

'Thought they were being clever,' Beau snarled. 'They reckoned they were better than me and could help themselves to my girlfriend.'

'Don't let them get to you. You'll only upset yourself and I'd prefer you stay calm and get on with recovering.' Nathan was at the side of the bed. 'I need to look at your wound. That all right with you?'

'Yeah.' Beau nodded, then grimaced and swore.

'Tip your head sideways. That's it.'

After a thorough examination Nathan told his patient, 'You're lucky. There's no serious damage, but a plastic surgeon will have to put it back together so you're not left with an ugly scar. In the meantime I'll put in a few temporary stitches to keep the wound closed, and the bleeding to a minimum.'

'Thanks,' Beau muttered, reaching out for his girlfriend's hand, looking scared.

'You'll be fine,' Molly said. 'I'll get the gear.'

Nathan told his patient, 'This means you'll stay in overnight.'

When Molly returned, Nathan was scrubbing his hands at the sink before pulling on gloves. She placed the suture kit on the small table next to him.

Behind her Gina was saying, 'I'll phone your mum, tell her what's happened.' Out of the corner of her eye Molly saw the girlfriend tighten her grip on Beau's hand. 'Love you,' she added as his face screwed up.

'Don't call the olds.'

'They need to know where you are. What if the police ring them?'

'I suppose.'

'Right.' Nathan stepped up to the bed. 'Let's get this out of the way.'

Molly saw Gina's face whiten. 'Why don't you go out to the waiting room to make that call? You can come back any time you like, just tell them who you're with and they'll open the security door.'

'Thanks.' Gina's relief was obvious in her speed to get away before Nathan started stitching the wound.

'Have you spoken to the police yet?' Nathan asked Beau in an attempt to distract him from the tugging and snipping as he placed stitches along the edges of the wound.

'Gina did. They're going to press charges, so I suppose they'll turn up here.'

As soon as Nathan had finished, Molly went to tell Gina it was all right to come back, and then she went to see a ninety-three-year-old who'd been found wandering in the rain in the gardens of the rest home where she lived. 'How are you feeling, Mrs Grooby?'

The old lady opened her eyes and focused on Molly. Nothing wrong there. 'I'm good.'

'What about the last couple of days? Everything all right?' She was gaunt and looked very pale. According to the rest-home staff she'd become quite vague lately, yet right now she was alert and beginning to watch everything going on out in the department.

'I think so.'

The notes said Mrs Grooby had been disorientated when she'd arrived two hours ago. A medical event, or lonely and seeking attention? 'I'm going to ask you silly questions. Can you answer them for me?'

'Yes, dear.'

'What's our national animal?'

'A kangaroo.'

'What do people get from a library?'

'Books, of course.'

'Count backwards from ten for me.'

As the old lady muttered numbers in the correct order, Molly tidied up her bed cover and watched her patient. 'No problem. You slayed the test.'

'I heard all that. Nothing wrong with your mind, Mrs Grooby,' Nathan announced as he strolled into the cubicle.

Was he following her around? He couldn't be. Since it was a quiet night he could be trying to keep busy too. 'She's lonely,' Molly said quietly as she passed him.

He nodded. 'We see that often with the oldies.'

'You two talking about me?' Mrs Grooby's eyes lit up.

Molly chuckled. 'You're too sharp for your own good. Would you like a cup of tea?'

'Yes, please. And a biscuit?'

'Of course.' Molly headed down to the kitchen and sneaked a biscuit for herself while she waited for the tea bag to brew. Only an hour in and already she was hungry. It had to be a result of running around the basketball court Saturday and Sunday.

Mick stuck his head in the door. 'There are two ambulances on the way in with an elderly couple who were in a multiple car pile-up. Nothing serious, mostly cuts and bruises, and shock. You and Hank take them when they get here.'

'Onto it.'

The couple was shaken but alert as they were wheeled into adjacent cubicles and transferred from the stretchers to beds. The curtain between was pulled back and when Mrs Andrews tried to reach her husband's hand, Hank and Molly moved the beds closer. 'There you go.'

'Some date this turned out to be,' Colin Andrews

winked at his wife. 'Should've stayed home and watched the tele.'

'I don't know. It's quite exciting in here,' his wife returned.

'Where were you off to?' There was a storm raging over the city, and it was bitterly cold out. Molly had worn her puffer jacket into work.

'It's our fifty-third wedding anniversary, and we always visit the church we were married in on the day. We didn't have time earlier what with all the family dropping in and out like we run the best diner in town.'

Mrs Andrews's gruff voice made Molly glance at her. Something wasn't sitting right.

'Has anyone got in touch with a member of your family?' Molly asked as she sponged the lady's arms where small cuts from windscreen glass had caused bleeding.

'You don't want them descending on the ED,' Colin answered quickly. 'Too noisy.'

'You can't tell one without telling them all,' his wife hastened to add.

When Molly lifted her patient's arm she felt a tremor in the soft muscles. There was definitely something not quite right going on.

'We'll sort it,' Colin growled.

Glancing at Hank, Molly saw he'd also got the sense something was wrong. But what could they do? Their role was to patch people up and send them home again, or pass them on to specialists and wards, not to solve family problems. 'Right, I'm going to do a bit of stitching.'

'Bet you're not as good at it as Sylvia. She used to make wedding dresses for the nobs.'

'Is that so? Then she can sew you back together when I've finished with her.' Molly laughed. 'Can I get you both a cup of tea while I'm at it?'

'Best offer I've had all night.' Colin smiled, relief underlining his words. So getting in touch with their family was a no-no.

As it wasn't her place to interfere, Molly let it go with a heavy heart. Families were so important, and to lose one was beyond comprehension. When her mother had insisted she was wrong about Paul, that he'd never meant to hurt her, she'd felt she'd lost everything—her marriage *and* her family. Nowadays her mother was working hard at getting back onside, and as much as Molly wanted that, she was taking a cautious approach. 'Tea along with the needles and thread coming up.'

'Molly.' Mike appeared round the corner of the hub. 'Sixteen-year-old girl, overdosed on paracetamol. Resus, please. Hank, you okay in here?'

'Sure.'

'On my way.' Shuddering, she sped along to the well-equipped room and straight up to the bed where Nathan, a junior doctor and another nurse were working with the teen while an ambulance paramedic was filling them in on the scant details.

'The mother thinks she swallowed at least twenty tablets. When they found her she was unconscious, but has since woken and been throwing up.'

'Resultant liver damage will be the biggest concern,' Nathan explained to the other doctor as he listened to the medic reading out the obs she'd taken on the ride in. 'If she's been vomiting then I don't think it's necessary to pump the stomach. I'll give her some charcoal to soak up any remaining traces of drugs in her digestive system.'

Molly began wiping the girl to clean her up. Along with the other nurse, they stripped her and dressed her in a gown and got rid of the grubby clothes.

'Nathan, you're needed next door,' someone called.

'Now we're getting busy.' He looked to Molly, a wry smile lifting his mouth. 'That'll keep us on our toes and too busy for anything else.'

'Seems like it.' She smiled back. Why did he have to be so sexy even when dressed in a boring green uniform? This should be the one time her mind didn't drag up images of him looking like a centrefold, or holding her against his naked body, or sitting opposite her having breakfast in the café.

When he joined her and Hank in the café for coffee and sandwiches just after eight, she was glad they weren't alone or she might've dropped her intention of keeping him at a distance—a very short one—while at work. He was near irresistible.

'You survived my lot okay.' Nathan bit into a thick bread roll filled with meat and a dash of salad. 'They can be intimidating.'

'I enjoyed myself, so thanks for inviting me along.'

Hank's eyebrows rose, before he went back to checking his phone for messages.

'You obviously like kids,' Nathan observed.

Hadn't they done this on Saturday? Because of her scar had he guessed there might be an issue with her infertility? 'Who doesn't?'

I'm not seeing where this is going.

'Not everyone thinks children are the best thing since sliced bread.'

'Certainly everyone in your family does. I'm only surprised you're capable of walking without a limp. They used you as a trampoline half the time.'

'I'm used to it. Though as they get bigger I'm going to

have to tone down the level of bounce.' He was watching her like there was no one else in the room, and certainly had no qualms about Hank knowing they'd spent time together.

Hank put his phone down and picked up his mug. 'I've seen Nathan bruised and limping after a round of ball games with the Lupton bunch. He hurt for days, and got no sympathy from any of us.'

Nathan grinned. 'You were pathetic, not joining in to help me out.'

'A group of us were at Nathan's for a barbecue when some of his family showed up unexpectedly. Those kids took over like they owned the place, and we had a lot of laughs watching Uncle Nathan do his impersonation of an active seven-year-old for hours on end.'

'I know what you mean.' Obviously she wasn't the first he'd invited to his house. Why did she think she might've been when they were having a party there next weekend? It was his way of being friendly, and she'd thought there was more to it. Though he'd offered her the flat to live in. After kissing her. And now he'd made love to her. 'Kind of cute, I think.' She grinned at Nathan, who screwed his face up. 'Shows he's not always the boss.'

'I'm getting another coffee. You two need any?' Hank stood up.

'No, thanks,' Molly and Nathan answered simultaneously.

She watched Hank walk across the room, stopping to yarn with nurses from the general ward.

'I missed you yesterday.'

Knock me over with a feather.

'You did?' Warmth stole through her, softening all those knots that had begun tightening since she'd seen how much he adored his nieces and nephews and heard how he wanted to add to the bunch.

'Yes. I came that close...' he held up two fingers only millimetres apart '...to driving over to your apartment late yesterday but I know you were busy at the charity shop.' His smile hit her in the chest. 'Anyway, I sat down on the couch, and didn't know a thing until seven.'

'You old man, you.'

'You think?'

'Not for a minute.' This was fun, and relaxing, and she could do it for ever. Except—

Shut up, conscience. Let me have some fun before it's time to get real.

'Sorry I had to race away but that's how it is.' Now that she was getting a life.

'It wouldn't be if you moved into the flat.'

She hadn't seen that coming. Leaning back in the hard plastic chair, she tried to lift the blinkers and study Nathan as others might see him. There was much to like, to trust, to love even. And she couldn't help the way he turned her on, how she wanted to be with him more often. But, 'Everything's happening in a hurry. I need to keep my own space at the moment.'

'Fair enough.' His face lost its relaxed expression. 'I understand. But I'm an impatient brute at times.'

'The last thing you are is a brute, Nathan. Believe me, I know.'

He gulped, and sighed. 'It was a loose term. I need to learn to be careful of my words around you.'

She shook her head. 'No, you don't. I need to lighten up. Though I thought I was doing okay.'

'You know what? We've suddenly become serious.

This isn't the place to be mentioning what's happened to you so let's relax again.' There was a plea in his eyes.

She nodded, more than happy to go along with him. 'Done.'

'So how many awkward questions did the sisters ask you?'

'Not one.' She'd been as surprised as Nathan looked. 'Not usual?'

'Not at all. My sisters believe there're no rules when it comes to their brother.' He drained his coffee.

'Families know all the buttons to push.' Would Gran have liked Nathan? She had no idea why but Molly thought she probably would have, and that gave her comfort.

'I'm glad you had a good time and enjoyed being with the kids.'

'Nathan...' She swallowed. Every time he mentioned the kids and her in the same sentence the worry intensified. It was beginning to seem like she wouldn't be able to have a few weeks of fun before telling him the truth. To be fair, that would be selfish of her. Sometime in the next few days they were going to have a full and frank conversation about her fertility—or lack of.

'Hey, guys, we're needed. All hands on deck. A van full of American tourists rolled on the highway and the first ones are expected here in ten.' Mick was already moving away in search of more ED staff.

'Mondays are supposed to be quiet,' Nathan muttered before he took a last mouthful of his roll.

CHAPTER TEN

WHAT WAS MOLLY'S PROBLEM? She seemed all out of sync.
One moment happy beyond description, the next eyeing him with trepidation. Nathan watched her calming a
teenager whose friends had brought her in with numer-
ous bee stings.

'You're not having a reaction.' Molly wiped the girl's
arms. 'Yes, you copped a lot of stings, which have been
removed, and you're hurting, but your windpipe is not
about to close up.'

He stepped in. 'Hi, I'm Nathan, a doctor. What Molly's
telling you is correct. If you'd had an allergic reaction
your throat, tongue and face would be swelling by now.'
He hoped that backing Molly and playing it down would
quieten the shrieking, shaking girl. 'Just to make absolutely certain, let me have a look inside your mouth.'

Instant quiet returned to the area as Becky's mouth fell
open for him. After his examination, he told her, 'Looking healthy. Now let me touch your neck and throat.' With
gentle fingers he felt for any sign of swelling. 'Again,
all good.'

Molly smiled at her, and *his* gut twisted. He had it
bad. The week since his family had been in town had
been sensational. Lots of laughter, shared meals and unbelievable sex. There'd been tender moments too, like

when she'd made his favourite breakfast and set it out on the conservatory table with a flower in one of his beer glasses because he didn't own a vase. He did now. Molly had found him the ugliest pottery creation imaginable at the charity shop. The vase had pride of place in a hidden corner of his office. Molly had threatened to buy flowers and bring the hideous thing out for tomorrow night's party with the medical team. Who would have believed she could be such a tease? Especially with him. It was great.

'Becky, you'll soon get very itchy to go with the pain and swelling.' Molly nudged him none too gently with her elbow. 'Dr Lupton will give you something to relieve that as much as possible.'

'I'll prescribe a cream to save you having to buy one. Just apply it a couple of times until the itching stops.' Nathan nodded as he mentally ran through the available remedies, all the while trying not to laugh out loud at Molly's temerity for giving him the get-a-grip look in here. But she was right. He shouldn't get distracted by her while at work. Though how not to he had no idea. It would be better to start by staying away from patients she was involved with.

'So I'm not going to have anaphylactic shock?' Becky sounded disappointed.

'No, I'm pleased to say you're not.' Did she want attention that badly she'd risk her life? 'Have you ever seen anyone suffer one?'

'A boy at school had one once. Everyone was around him like you wouldn't believe, and he got taken away in the ambulance. He nearly died. Heaps of kids went to see him in hospital afterwards.'

Uh-huh. 'I think there are better ways of getting people to take notice of you. Like being the person who organises the others to go visiting someone who's sick. Being the sick person sucks. Apart from the pain and all the things medical staff do to you, it's boring lying around in bed all day. Especially in hospital where it's noisy and the nurses come and poke at your body any time they like.'

Molly had turned away, her sexy mouth twitching nonstop.

Becky was eyeing him warily. 'What's the food like?'

It was hard not to laugh, even though this was one mixed-up girl. 'Nothing fancy, but it passes. But you won't be finding out. You can go home shortly.' He turned away before Becky could come up with some symptom that might let her stay in overnight. 'Molly, can you get the cream for Becky when I've signed the form?'

'Sure.' She turned to their patient. 'Want your girl-friends to come in now?'

'They won't be waiting for me.'

Molly stepped closer to the bed. 'They were still there fifteen minutes ago. The triage nurse told me.'

'Really? Can they really come in?'

'I'll get them right now.' Molly headed away.

Nathan went to write up the notes on Becky. Twenty-thirty. Half an hour before he could think about heading home or to Molly's apartment. Not too long, if all went according to plan.

'Nathan.' Mick appeared in front of him. 'You're needed in Resus. Unconscious thirty-one-year-old male, fell from the third floor of an apartment, severe head in-juries, punctured left lung, fractured femur both legs, and that's only the obvious.'

He moved fast, heading for Resus right on Mick's heels. So much for plans. But if he had to be waylaid then this was what he wanted to be doing more than anything.

Except it wasn't.

They worked their butts off trying to save Mason Haverstock, every staff member in Resus giving their best and more. To no avail. Mason's heart gave out due to blood loss and trauma from fractured ribs.

Nathan went into withdrawal, automatically closing everything down and signing off the case. Only when he talked to the man's wife and parents did he drag himself out of the funk the death had brought on—because he understood the pain he was inflicting by telling the crying woman what had happened. His words were intractable, and were stealing her dreams, her love, her future. These moments had always been hard, but for him they'd become almost personal since Rosie's death.

Next he went for a brisk walk around town, barely noticing the drizzle and cool breeze. What was a bit of weather when your heart was breaking?

Nearly two hours later he texted Molly from outside her apartment block. You awake? There was light behind the blinds of her bedroom so he wasn't waking her. He hoped. Anyway, if she was asleep she wouldn't hear the text land in her phone. He'd given up on the walk, had headed for home, and instead ended up here. Molly would know what he wanted. She also understood pain.

Come up. The door into the building clicked open.

'I need a hug,' Nathan said the moment he reached the third floor and found her standing in her doorway, dressed in a thick white robe.

Molly nudged the door shut with her hip and reached for him, wrapped her arms around his waist and pulled him close to nestle her face against his neck. 'That bad?'

'That bad.' He nodded against her. The guy had only been thirty-one, for Pete's sake. All his life ahead of him. A wife and two little girls left behind. Life was a bitch at times. A real ugly bitch. Nathan's arms tightened around Molly's warmth, and he absorbed her strength, the understanding, like a man starved.

Time disappeared as they stood there, Molly's soft hands beneath his shirt, caressing his back, slowly, tenderly. All he knew was that this was where he had to be, who he had to be with while the darkness roiled, then began to fade.

Finally Molly lifted her head enough to look at him. 'Tea? Or something stronger?'

He knew too well from the past that something stronger wouldn't fix his pain over losing a patient. It might blank out things if he drank enough, but those sights would return when he woke up with a mighty hangover and nothing solved. Then he'd feel a failure for being weak. 'Tea. Lots of it.'

Her smile was filled with understanding and care. Love? No, it couldn't be. Not this soon. That had to be wishful thinking. He wanted Molly to love him? Possibly. They had been having an amazing time, and he couldn't see it slowing down any time soon. But was that love? Or was he reacting to the aftermath of a gruelling night in the ED? Her smile had gone right to the tips of his toes, filling every space in his body, and his mind. His arms tightened around her again. 'In a minute.'

They drank tea, Molly's legs curled under her curvy butt on the small couch, while Nathan half lay in one of the chairs, stretching his legs across the room, his mug held in both hands as he talked out the gremlins. She asked no questions, made no comments about what he'd done for his patient, just listened, and accepted, and understood.

He hadn't had that before. Not even from Rosie. She'd hated hearing anything about his work except when they'd saved someone and even then she'd only wanted the bare, happy facts. It was the only area of his life she hadn't understood as much as he'd wanted. Yet here Molly was, totally getting his mood. As a nurse, she knew what it was like to face hell in the department.

They went to bed, holding each other like they'd never let go. Then in the early hours they made love, slowly, tenderly, and filled with so much care and—and love. Afterwards Nathan lay on his back, his hand on Molly's butt as she lay sprawled on her stomach, sound asleep, and he stared upwards into the dark.

Love. Was that what this was? This sense of coming home, of belonging to another person in a way not even his family could give him? Love. Yes, that's what these feelings and sensations were about. Love. That softening in his belly whenever he touched Molly, listened to her sharp voice and her light laughter, smelled her scent, saw that lithe body move sometimes as though on hot coals and at others as though she was dancing through the air.

It had happened in a flash, their relationship doing a one-eighty in weeks. Who'd have believed it could happen to him again? Not again. This was different. With Rosie they'd always been in each other's lives, had grown up falling in love. With Molly, a snap of his fingers and, *voilà*, he was a goner.

Rolling onto his side, Nathan scooped Molly against the length of his body and closed his eyes.

Molly woke instantly. No slow stretching, opening her eyes one at a time. Just ping. It was Saturday morning and tonight was the work barbecue.

Nathan held her against him as though he never wanted to let her go. Soft snores told her he was out to it. Good. He needed to move on from last night's tragedy. Not that it would vanish from his mind easily. They never did. The downside to working in medicine was the toll it could take. Snuggling harder against him, she thought about last night's lovemaking. It had been very different from the other times. Slow, and caring. She'd given everything in her to Nathan, hoping to ease his pain. It must've worked, judging by his comatose state. He'd never before slept beyond sunrise with her.

Reaching for her phone, she sat up in a hurry when '08.05' blinked at her. There was a dessert to make and get into the freezer before she got ready for basketball, and then she'd promised to go round to Nathan's house straight after to help with anything he hadn't got done.

'Morning,' came a sleepy voice beside her. Then an arm began pulling her back under the covers.

'Oh, no, you don't. We've got things to do.' She pushed away.

Nathan tugged her again, causing her to sprawl across his frame. 'Starting with this.'

She gave in. How could she not?

It was the perfect way to start the day. Followed by Nathan poaching eggs and frying bacon while she made a lemon dessert. When she felt his gaze on her, she turned from whipping the cream cheese. 'What?'

'You're singing. I like it.'

'I was?' Definitely getting back to normal.

Next she hit the court with the Roos, and they stole the game fifty-eight to thirty-five.

Bypassing the after-match celebrations again, Molly headed home for a shower and to get dressed in red and white for the evening. Then she drove to Nathan's and found Vicki already there, running around with a vacuum cleaner and duster.

'I don't know why she's bothering. By the time everyone leaves tonight the place will be a lot messier than it is now.' Nathan scratched his head.

'She needs the distraction,' Molly muttered. Vicki had been valiantly trying to be cheerful all week since returning from Darwin, but everyone saw through her attempts. 'It must be hard, saying goodbye to her man so often.' She'd hate that, couldn't imagine being married to someone who was often away for long stints.

'It gets to Cole too,' Nathan admitted. 'I don't know why he went and signed up in the first place. I get wanting to do something for your country, but it's hard on family and friends, and yourself. I doubt I could do it. In a way I admire him.'

Molly's sympathy lay with Vicki, but she kept that to herself. Holding up the plastic container she'd brought, she said, 'I'll put this in the freezer and find something useful to do.'

'I hate to tell you this but everything's pretty much ready. We can kick back and relax once madam's finished making a racket with the sucky motor machine.'

'You've been spending too much time with your nephews. Sucky motor. I'll give you sucky.'

'I wish, but we're not alone.'

Molly headed for the kitchen, swallowing her laughter. Nathan was so relaxed it was hard to believe he was the same man she'd known only a couple of weeks ago.

'You two have come a long way in a short time,' Vicki said with a grin minutes later as she packed the cleaner into its cupboard.

She couldn't have overheard their banter. 'True. We're not about to kill each other any more.'

'It's great. He needs someone like you in his life. Make that he needs *you*.'

Molly looked around for Nathan. Having him overhear Vicki was the last thing she wanted.

'Relax. He's out in the conservatory, making sure there's enough gas for the barbecue. It should've been the first thing he checked. But that's Nathan.'

'What do you mean by that?'

'He can be the most disorganised male you've ever met when he's not at work. It used to drive Cole bonkers when they were flatting together.' Vicki headed for the kitchen. 'Ready for a drink? I'm not talking coffee or tea.'

'Why not? Everyone will be turning up soon.' As long as Vicki didn't start going on about Nathan she was happy to relax. Relax. A new word in her vocabulary. Suddenly relaxing had become part of her routine, along with having fun and mixing with people without looking over her shoulder. And starting to trust a man. 'I'll have a beer.'

'Coming up.'

She sank down onto the cane couch in the little nook off the kitchen where she could see out across the lawn to the sea, and if she turned her head slightly to the left Nathan out in the conservatory filled her sight, rubbing the stainless-steel lid of the state-of-the-art barbecue, bringing out the shine.

'Here.'

She took the bottle and settled down further into the thick cushions. 'This is the life.' Then she sat up straight. That might sound like she was trying to weave her way into Nathan's home for her own gain. 'I mean, how better to spend a Saturday afternoon than with friends?'

'Take it easy. You're more than a friend to Nathan.' Vicki was eyeing her over the top of her own bottle. 'I meant what I said before. You're good for him, and I think he's good for you. I don't know anything about your life before you came to work with us, but you've changed since my birthday. I'm putting some of that down to Nathan. Am I right?'

This was what good friends did. They talked, and then she'd have to give some answers back. She wasn't ready for that. Or was she? 'Yes, you're right.' Looking outside again, she sighed with happiness. Then an image of Nathan chasing his nephews across the lawn out there swiped her, and the warmth that had started filling her slowed, chilled. Children. He'd made no bones about wanting a family. He'd been honest, whereas she'd lied—if only by omission.

'Molly? What's wrong?'

Her gaze drifted back to the man tipping her world upside down. She wanted to tell Vicki nothing was wrong, but she couldn't. 'It's early days. We don't know each other very well yet.' She knew he liked having his inner thighs stroked, that it hurt deeply when he lost a patient, that he adored his nieces and nephews. Family. She stood up. 'Let's see what else needs doing.'

'Molly, sit down, and I promise to shut up.'

Because she wanted friends in her life and not just as numbers on her phone, she plonked her backside back on the couch. Anyway, she liked Vicki and didn't want to upset her. 'Here's to a great night.'

'I'm going to put some music on. I never could understand why Nathan doesn't have it playing all the time.'

'Because I like to hear myself think.' The man himself lounged against the central kitchen bench, a beer between his fingers and a lopsided smile on his face.

Molly sucked in her stomach. It was so unfair. He was gorgeous. He was everything she wanted in a man when she moved forward.

Hey, you are moving forward.

Yes, but there was some way to go before she'd allow

permanence into the picture. Even though things were beginning to stack up as she wanted, it was early days.

While the other two gave each other cheek and talked about people and events she knew nothing about, Molly did some serious thinking. She had begun falling for Nathan too quickly. She trusted him as she'd once trusted Paul. He was fun, and caring, and sharing. Paul had once been fun, and caring, but sharing had been replaced by selfishness. She needed to step back, get to know Nathan better, if he hung around—and he acted as though he intended to.

Which brought her to the real problem. She had to tell him the truth. Because if she did fall in love with him, that was far too late.

'You going to daydream all afternoon?' Nathan tapped her shoulder.

If only that's what she was doing. Forcing a smile, she said, 'Got any better suggestions?'

He laughed, which went some way to lightening her mood again. But the clock was ticking. She had to tell him she couldn't have children.

'I didn't think they'd ever leave.' Nathan locked the door behind Hank and Myra before trailing into the kitchen where Molly was putting the last of the dirty glasses in the dishwasher.

'They've really gone?' Her knuckles were white as she gripped a dirty beer mug. She'd become more distant as the night had progressed.

What's up, Mol?

'The place is quiet, isn't it? Apart from the music, and I've lowered the decibels considerably. I might have to drop leftover desserts in to the neighbours in the morning as an apology.'

'Good luck with that. I don't think there's much left.' Glasses rattled against the wire rack as she put the mug in the washer.

'Want a nightcap?' They could sit and talk in the nook, where it was warm and cosy.

'No, thanks.'

'Tea?'

'No.'

'Bed?'

Shaking her head, she shut the washer and flicked the dials. Then she leaned back against the bench, her hands gripping the edge of the counter at her sides. Apart from the low hum of water swirling inside the dishwasher the house was quiet. Too quiet. Filling with foreboding.

Nathan rushed to fill the eerie silence before Molly could ruin the warm fuzzy feeling he got when he was with her. 'Thanks for all you did tonight.' She'd been a trouper, setting out food, clearing up after everyone, making sure no one went without a drink while barely touching one herself. 'You were taught how to be the hostess with the mostest?'

Her chin jerked down once. 'Yes. Part of being my mother's daughter was the social training that went on every day, no matter what else was happening.'

Had Molly ever been herself, doing what she wanted, how she wanted? Or had the basketball, the nursing degree and whatever other things she'd achieved been done because she'd been put under pressure? Had she spent all her life trying to please others? He wouldn't expect that of her. Ever. 'Now you can do whatever you want. You could even have tipped Carry's drink over his face when he started making rude suggestions to you and Myra.'

'I came close, believe me.' She shrugged. 'It's all right.

He'd had too much to drink and will probably fall over backwards apologising on Monday.'

'True. It's not the first time, and won't be the last. I'd like to not invite him to these dos, but he's one of the team, one of the best, and everyone has their issues.'

So what's yours tonight, Molly?

'He'll pay you back for the taxi you organised. You're right, he is one of the best—when he's sober.' Worry was in her gaze, making her nibble her lip and turning those knuckles whiter than ever.

'Talk to me.'

Her eyebrows lifted, fell back into place. 'Too clever for your own good, you are.'

The foreboding increased. This was about him. He'd swear on his next breakfast Molly was about to dump on him. Or walk away for ever. His gut tightened as nausea rose. They weren't an item so how could she drop him? This called for something stronger than a beer that had gone flat over the hour since he'd opened the bottle. Standing, he reached around Molly for the wine bottle.

She flinched.

Slowly withdrawing his hand without touching the bottle, he backed off two steps. 'I'd never hurt you,' he ground out through clenched jaws. 'Never.' It hurt for her to think differently.

'I know.'

'So what was that about?' They'd come far, or so he'd thought. Guess it wasn't easy to get over what had been done to her.

'I'm sorry.'

He hated that word coming from Molly. It came loaded with the need to please, to be safe, and she did not have to do that around him. 'You don't owe me an apology for anything. But I would like an explanation.'

Her breath intake was ragged. 'You're right. You're owed one.' She was being too compliant.

He wanted to shake her gently, make her stop being that person and return to being the Molly he was getting to know, but instead he poured a small wine and returned to sit down, giving her space, wishing he could wrap her in a big hug and hold her until she never, ever felt afraid again. He should be able to without worrying he was making her uncomfortable. 'I thought we were getting close enough to talk about most things.'

Especially since you told me about your ex.

'I think I will have a drink after all.'

He started to get up to get it for her but she put up a hand in the stop signal.

When she sloshed as much wine on the bench as into her glass Nathan knew he was in trouble.

Putting his drink aside, he sat straighter, needing to focus on Molly and whatever was worrying her. He waited. His gut churned. His heart thumped hard and heavy. And he waited.

Perching on a stool, she sipped her drink and put the glass aside to jam her shaking hands between her knees. Then finally she raised her head and eyeballed him.

He wished she hadn't. He would far prefer her not to say a word, to carry on with the silent treatment. There was something in her look that said his world as it had become was about to disintegrate. Rushing in, he said, 'You can trust me not to hurt you that way.'

You're repeating yourself.

'Not in any way, if I can help it.'

'Nathan. I get that. In spades. Otherwise we wouldn't have been spending as much time together as we have. Even though it's only been a short time, I trust you. It's me who hasn't been up-front about everything.' Her breasts rose and the last drop of colour drained from her face. 'I don't see me having babies any time soon. If at all. And they're important to you.'

His heart slowed, his lungs seized, his head spun, yet his eyes never left hers as he tried to figure out where this was going. 'You said you wanted kids.'

'Yes. One day, maybe. Right now I'm getting back on my feet after the horror that was my marriage. I don't know what I want for the future. I don't trust myself to get it right straight away. It's too soon.'

'I understand that.' As much as he could, because it was a bit like him falling in love with her after the wonderful relationship he'd had with Rosie. But he hadn't known fear like Molly had. Hadn't had his belief in Rosie undermined. Hadn't seen those she should've been able to trust not back her until later on, by which time her heart had already been broken. So, really, he knew nothing about where Molly was coming from.

Suddenly she was right in front of him, hands gripping hips, her eyes flashing. 'No, you don't,' she yelled.

Nathan waited, not wanting to risk upsetting her further.

She breathed deeply, said in a quieter voice, 'I know you've tried, but I'm still working at understanding myself, so how can you?'

He began to rise, to scoop her into his arms and hold her safe.

Her hand shot up in the stop sign again. 'No. Please, no.'

He stilled, waited.

'Sit down. Please,' she added quietly, and he knew she hadn't finished. In fact, she started before he'd taken a step, like it was a force that had to be set free. 'Watching you with your family brought it home to me that I'm being unfair to expect you to spend time with me when I can't guarantee I'll ever be ready to want to settle down, let alone have a family. If we could guarantee we'd have some fun and walk away happy then...'

She swallowed hard. 'I'm screwed up, Nathan, and while I might have stopped looking over my shoulder at every turn, I still have nightmares about being strong enough to cope with what's ahead.'

'You're stronger than anyone I know,' he ground out through the anger filling him for the man who'd done this to sweet, beautiful Molly.

'It's skin deep,' she whispered. 'Those steps I talk about taking—a toddler could do better.'

'You're taking them. That's all that matters.' Still he wanted to haul her into his arms and never let her go, to make her feel better, and stop the ache that was expanding in his chest. But the stop sign was still in her eyes, in the tight way she held herself, as though if she relaxed even a fraction she'd shatter. He also wanted, needed, to fight her gremlins for her, but Molly would never let him do that. She fought her own battles. All he could do was be there for her. 'You need more time. We don't have to stop seeing each other.'

'And if I still don't feel I can have a permanent relationship after we've spent a lot of time together?' Her curls shook as she talked. 'No, Nathan. You deserve better than that. You can love again, and have the life you want. You've been honest about your love of family and the children you want one day. I will not risk taking that opportunity away from you.'

Yeah, the news was starting to seep in around the edges of the haze in his mind, and making him begin to understand the full impact of what Molly was telling him. He had always wanted children. Growing up in a large, happy family, it had been a given he'd add to the clan, as his sisters had. Not once, not even when Rosie had died, had he given up on that dream completely. But did he want them at the cost of love? He was half in love with Molly already. Half? Now was not the time to think about it. He'd finally let a woman close for the first time since Rosie. Yeah, and look where that was getting him.

His heart was on the way to taking another battering. He didn't want to lose Molly, he wanted them to make this journey together. If at the end of it she still wasn't ready for him then he'd have to take it on the chin. But he wanted the opportunity to give it all he had. 'Why haven't you said any of this earlier?' It might've saved him falling for her. Except he'd thought that had begun the day she'd started in the department. 'You've told me so much about what happened, it would've been simple to finish it with this. I'd at least have been warned.' Anger was beginning to simmer. At her for not trusting him enough, at himself for falling for her, for finally letting go the restraints Rosie's death had put on his heart.

'At first I didn't see what was happening. I do want love and family. One day. If I can get past all that's happened. I'm afraid I might be reading too much into my feelings for you. You're everything Paul wasn't. I want that. What I don't want is to make you into someone you're not, and I could be unwittingly doing that. I need time, and getting out and about with people, before I'm ready for a commitment. It's essential to know I'm not making another horrendous mistake—for everyone's sake.'

Pain sifted through his tight chest muscles. This was not how he'd seen the night finishing. But life loved throwing curveballs. He already knew that, had dealt with it and had thought he was coming out the other side.

'I'll always be here for you, Molly. I care a lot about you.' Damn it. He wanted to say he'd move on and be grateful she'd thought of him when trying to sort her life out, but he couldn't. It wasn't true. Neither was telling her he was falling in love with her a wise idea. It'd be putting everything back on her, and it was obvious she already felt terrible about this. He also had to own some of it for rushing in.

'You sure we can't continue as we are, and see how it turns out?' He wouldn't get down on bended knee. Only because he already knew it wouldn't work and he had to have some pride left when she walked out.

Knuckling her eyes, she took her time answering him. 'I'm sorry. I didn't know if we were having a couple of dates and then getting back to life as it used to be, though a lot friendlier, or we'd end up disliking each other.'

'Stop saying sorry. You're being truthful.'

'And that includes being sorry.' She shook her head, those blasted curls flicking in every direction. 'I wanted another week with you before I said what was bothering me.' She swallowed. 'I once believed in love so much I thought it could overcome everything, now it's hard to accept I was wrong.'

So she'd been happy with him. That put the final wedge in the situation. Molly O'Keefe had wanted to spend more time with him and she'd just made absolutely certain it wasn't going to happen.

Molly staggered into her apartment and sank to the floor. She'd lied to Nathan—again by omission, but she'd been untruthful all the same. He deserved better. Through what Paul had done to her, she'd become someone else, a person she barely recognised at times. Honesty was of paramount importance now. On the other hand, telling

Nathan about the small chance she'd ever get pregnant wasn't ever going to happen. If he'd said he'd take the risk, she'd have to live with the hurt caused if it didn't happen. She was not prepared to do that. He'd thank her one day.

Her heart was shredding, her head throwing so many accusations at her about dumping Nathan, it was a wonder she'd managed to drive home safely from Coogee. But she had. There wasn't anywhere else for her to be. This was her home—small, lonely, but hers. She did not belong in Nathan's house, or in his flat.

How had she fallen in love so quickly? The answer didn't matter. She did love Nathan. Though what she'd told him was also true. It might only be a step in getting her life back. A temporary one, though judging by the agony in her chest that was complete and utter nonsense. With Paul she'd believed love would win the day. How wrong could she have been? That was the reason she was struggling to believe in herself now.

Yet, deep inside, a kernel of hope and longing and that love said this was for real. That Nathan was the right man for her. He'd always look out for her, come what may.

'I did the right thing. Especially for Nathan.'

Didn't I?

'Yes.'

She had to believe this was the right way to go or she'd never get up in the morning. But, hell, she hurt. Everywhere. Who'd have thought she'd feel like this after such a short time with Nathan? Truthfully? She'd never expected to fall in love again when Paul had blotted her thoughts of what love was meant to be. But she had. And thereby done the right thing by Nathan in walking away before they got in too deep. Except she'd already done that. Deep, then deeper, her heart was tied up in knots for him.

Her phone lit up as a text came in. You get home all right? Nathan. Caring to the end.

A waterfall cascaded down her cheeks. Something special and wonderful had ended. She had to be that strong woman he mistakenly believed she was. Fake it till she made it.

Tap, tap on the phone. Yes. Sorry. Molly paused. Stop saying sorry. She deleted the word, typed, Thanks, and pushed Send. *Fake it.*

Her bed was cold—and lonely.

Her head ached. The pillow was soon soaked.

Her heart went through the act of giving her life, all excitement and happiness gone, just a regular pumping.

So much for finally joining in on the work social scene. She'd been afraid of trusting people and had been the one to dump on Nathan's trust. Now she had to continue working with him because running away was not an option. She'd stand tall and take the knocks. *And* be strong, even if she had to fake it in the beginning.

Until now she'd believed of all the things Paul had done, taking away her baby and leaving her with only one damaged Fallopian tube was the hardest thing to deal with. Now she knew different. Walking away from Nathan was worse. He'd lost Rosie; he didn't need to lose his chance of having children with someone in the future. His nieces and nephews adored him, and the youngsters he dealt with in the ED were always in awe of him. He'd be an amazing father.

Snatching the box of tissues, she scrubbed her face, but still the tears flowed. Never before had the knowledge of not being able to have a child been quite so devastating. No children, no Nathan.

CHAPTER ELEVEN

'CAN YOU LOOK at two-year-old Lucy Charles?' Molly asked Nathan. 'She's got a plastic top from a small tube stuck in her ear. She's a right little cutie, even if she is screaming the place down.'

'You've tried oil to get the top out?' Nathan asked, ever the professional with her, though there were times he'd ask how she was doing at basketball or in the op shop.

Over the past month she'd become so used to the thudding in her chest whenever she was near him that she could answer without hesitation now. 'No. She's not letting anyone near her head, let alone the offending ear.' Maybe Nathan could charm the wee dot into letting him make her better.

'It's never easy with a toddler.' Nathan swung open the curtain to the cubicle from which shrieks emanated. 'Hello, Mrs Charles. I'm Nathan, a doctor.' He crouched down to be face to face with the little girl. 'Hey, Lucy. What's that on your shirt?' He pointed to the rabbit.

Lucy stared at him, hiccupping through her tears.

'Is it a cat?'

A headshake.

'Is it a horse?'

Another shake.

Nathan put his finger to his lips. 'I don't know, then. You'll have to tell me.'

'Wabbit.'

'So it is. Have you named it?'

'Wobby.'

'Can I look at his ear? It's so big.'

Lucy stared at him, then looked at her mother.

'Go on, show the doctor Robby's ear.'

Without touching her T-shirt, Nathan pointed to the rabbit's ear. 'Look, there's something stuck in there. I'm going to have to pull it out.' Clenching his hand tight, still without touching the shirt, he made a pulling motion and then looked into his palm. 'Yes, I've got it. Wobby didn't feel a thing. Now can I see your ear?'

Lucy shook her head.

'Not easily tricked, are you, little one?' To Lucy's mother, he said, 'I'm going to give her something to quieten her down enough so I can remove the obstruction. She'll be sleepy for an hour or two afterwards but there won't be any side effects.' Then he said to Molly, 'Can you get the drugs? I don't want to leave Lucy while she's comfortable with me.'

'Sure.' Nathan was so good with kids. Her heart skittered. She knew that. It was why she'd walked away from him, but it wasn't getting any easier to accept. Seeing him every day in the department, she was constantly questioning her ability to carry on working here. But she had to. She'd vowed not to weaken, to be that strong woman Nathan believed she was.

Once Lucy accepted the syrup she began to calm down almost immediately and the button was soon removed, then she was on her way home with her mother, and Molly went looking for someone else to help.

'Molly, ready for a break?' Vicki appeared around a corner.

'Is it time already?' She had no appetite for the soup she'd brought from the local deli but she'd go through the motions. Changing direction, she headed for her locker.

'Sure is. You were miles away. Or maybe only three cubicles down, where a certain doctor is about to examine an abscess.'

'You got nothing better to do than make up stuff?' Molly asked around the longing that wasn't in a hurry to go away.

'Better than thinking about my own problems.'

'You heard from Cole today?'

'Four times. They're heading back to Randwick late Saturday.'

Molly smiled as she opened her locker to retrieve her supper. 'That's good news.'

'It is.'

That's it? Not sure whether to press for more, Molly stayed quiet. As her soup heated in the microwave she threw out, 'You know where I am. Come round for coffee any time.'

'What time are we going to look at that apartment?'

'Eleven tomorrow morning.'

'I might watch your basketball game too.' Vicki wasn't getting her nails done, or sprucing up the apartment for Cole? There was definitely something wrong.

Molly shivered. She and her new friend made a right sorry pair.

Nathan held his breath. What apartment? Where? Molly was moving? His flat was still available.

Yes, but she doesn't want you in her life outside here.

He should be glad Vicki was going with her to check

out the new place, but all he could think was, *Why didn't you ask me to go along?*

Making an abrupt turn, he headed for the lift to go downstairs to the cafeteria. Sitting in the same small room with Molly, hearing her talking and laughing with others, was too much.

She didn't ignore him at work, did her best to remain friendly and approachable without expecting any special attention, which he'd had to back off from giving or risk upsetting her further. Yet it was as though she was a stranger. Wound up in plastic wrap, visible yet unavailable, nothing changing. His life was on hold. His head spun.

Life could be horrid, throw up the worst of bad deals, and Molly had had more than her fair share. He hurt with missing her. But he also had to sort out what it was he wanted in life. For all Molly had said, she was right about one thing. He did want a family. But he wanted it with her. Which it seemed was an impossibility, for now at least.

Then again, the day would probably come when Molly was ready, and then what? If he'd walked away as she was trying to make him do then they'd have missed out on the wonderful, loving relationship that he believed was possible. The question he'd been asking himself for the past weeks was, *Do I want to miss out on love so I can have children?*

The only answer that made its way into his skull was no. Yet he hesitated to try and persuade Molly to take a chance on them. Something in the pain that had bored into him from her desperate eyes when she'd told him she might be making a mistake held him back. *He* didn't want to cause *her* any more pain.

His phone rang. 'You're lucky I'm taking a break,' he told his sister. 'You working late?' It was after midnight.

'Only time it's quiet around here.'

'The joy of having those brats.'

'We're not coming up for the weekend,' Allie said. 'Russ has pulled a murder inquiry.'

'You and the kids can still come down.'

'Or you and Molly could come here for the weekend.'

It was like a punch in the gut. His sister thought Molly was a serious part of his life. 'She's got other things on.'

'Nathan, you've let her get away, haven't you?'

'You've read too much into our relationship.'

'We all think she's wonderful. She fitted in with everyone, and that's saying something.'

How true. 'You're right on that score.' Why did Allie automatically think he was at fault for Molly no longer being on the scene?

Ever consider Molly might have dumped me?

'I'm going now. I need to eat before I get hauled back to the department for someone who had nothing better to do on a Friday night than get into a scrap somewhere.'

'Nathan.'

'If I didn't know better, I'd say that was Mum talking to me.'

Allie chuckled. 'Believe it, brother. Now, tell me what's going on.'

'I'm at work, Allie.'

'Having a break. You wouldn't be worrying what Rosie would have to say about you finding someone else, by any chance?'

'Hardly. She told me to move on and not live on my own for ever.' So why the hesitation on his part? He couldn't put it all on Molly. Was trying to save her pain an excuse for his own insecurities? Talk about mixed up. At some point they both had to take a step into the unknown, whether it was together or with other people. He wanted to do it with Molly. So *was* he worried about letting Rosie's memory down?

'Are you sure?' His sister echoed his doubts.

No, he wasn't sure about any damned thing. 'Got to go. Talk later in the week.' He ended the call before Allie said anything else disruptive to his thinking. Not that it was hard to do, he thought as he bit into the chicken roll he'd bought at his favourite bakery. Today they'd failed him. The roll was tasteless, the bread dry, and there wasn't enough mayo. Tipping the lukewarm coffee down the sink, he went back to work in search of a distraction. One that didn't have red curls and sad eyes.

Saturday morning found Nathan charging up and down the lawn with the mower as if a swarm of bees was after him. How was Molly's apartment viewing going? The place was closer to Bondi Beach than Bondi Junction. She'd shown no reticence about filling him in on the scant details she'd obtained from the agency when he'd asked. He hadn't asked what had happened to the idea of purchasing a property. Could be she wasn't as ready for something permanent after all. It's what she'd said about a relationship with him.

Nathan ran out of lawn to do battle with. Now what? If there were some waves he'd go surfing, but the sea couldn't be calmer. If only the kids had turned up. He was in his happy zone with them. Family was what it was all about.

There's more to family than just the children. You need the right woman first. Not only as the mother but for you, your partner, lover, holder of your heart.

He shook his head. When he'd finally found the

woman he wanted to be with, a woman he'd started letting into his heart, it had all gone wrong.

Did I scare her off?

Nathan sank down on one of the outdoor stools and stared unseeingly out to sea. Was that why she'd pulled out? The only thing wrong with that idea was that she'd sounded so genuine about not being sure of herself, of needing more time to become comfortable with herself. A lot more comfortable. Molly didn't lie or exaggerate. She'd meant every word, so he could relax on that score. He hadn't frightened her away. But there had been more to what she'd said. He'd seen it flicker through her eyes as she'd turned to leave that night.

Could it be his need to have children that was the problem? That she was afraid of letting him down? Because she would be nervous about not getting everything right with the man she finally gave her heart to. That was a given, after what her ex had done to her.

This was getting too complicated. Overthinking everything in an attempt to find answers that only Molly could give him.

Tugging his phone from his pocket, he called Molly on speed dial, and listened to the ringing go on and on until voice mail picked up. Hearing her message to leave a number and name made his heart slow and his stomach tighten. Damn it. After Rosie had died he'd often rung her phone just to hear her voice. He hit 'end'. This was spooky. Molly was out there somewhere. He'd see her on Monday if not before. She hadn't gone away for ever. Comparing the situation with that of Rosie was desperate.

He rang Molly's number again. 'Hey, Molly, it's Nathan. Give me a buzz when you get a moment. Nothing urgent.'

She must've got that because he didn't hear back from her.

Finally, unable to focus on any of the chores that needed doing, he went for a drive. It wasn't until he was driving over the Harbour Bridge that he realised where he was going. A calm settled over him. Yes, he needed to do this, to find out if he was ready to move forward.

The house was small, tired, and didn't touch him in any way. Rosie's immaculate gardens were a riot of weeds and kids' toys, and he felt a moment of sadness for what had been. A dog lay on the front porch, too lazy to lift its head when he stopped at the front gate. He and Rosie had intended getting a dog one day when there was time to look after it properly, but seeing the setter sprawled over the spot Rosie had used to sit in the sun didn't raise any feeling other than nostalgia.

'I miss you, darling, but you've gone. As has the house with all our hopes and dreams. It's someone else's paradise now.' Like Rosie, it had morphed into something different, freeing him to get on with his life, to make a new future with Molly. He'd always miss Rosie, love her quietly, but to spend for ever mourning her was to waste the life he'd been given. As Rosie had told him in that last hideous week, 'Life's precious, Nat. Grab it and make the most of what you get. Don't spend it all thinking about what might've been. Do it for me, if not yourself.'

'Actually, Rosie, I am going to do this for me. And Molly.' There was a spring in his step as he walked away from the past.

The band was so loud her eardrums were bursting. It was also out of tune and the guy at the microphone couldn't have sung his way out of a paper bag if he'd tried.

'That's terrible.' Molly grimaced, and took a sip of her vodka. The second in one night. *Turning into a lush, girl.*

Vicki raised her glass in salute. 'At least he's still upright, unlike the drummer.'

They were at a bar in Randwick, close to the army base. Needing to be busy, Molly had offered to drive Vicki out here to meet Cole when his unit got into town early in the morning. After checking into a motel down the road, they'd come along to the pub for a meal, though Molly had barely touched her food, her stomach permanently tied in knots. Her clothes were a little looser too. Funny how once she'd have been thrilled about that, and now thought she looked better with a little weight on her hips to fill out her gorgeous trousers and skirts.

Molly looked around at the crowd and wished she'd stayed in the city. She didn't belong here. Standing up, she set her half-full glass aside. 'Let's go. I can't take any more of this.'

'Spoilsport.' But Vicki was quick to follow her. Outside they both checked their phones. Vicki scowled. 'Nothing. Where's Cole?'

Molly stared at her screen. 'One missed call.' She knew the number off by heart. 'Nathan.' They still talked, although not in a relaxed way as before. He hadn't phoned her since they'd gone their separate ways. If he hadn't said it wasn't urgent, she'd be starting to worry.

'What did he want?'

Molly shrugged. 'No idea.' She'd love to talk to him, to touch his hand, and feel his lips on her cheek. It wasn't going to happen. She'd left him. It was over.

'Here we are.' Vicki gestured to the bright neon lights flickering on and off. 'Why are we staying in a motel when I could be at home in my big comfy bed, watching TV?'

'Because Cole is about to ride into town, looking for you,' Molly said. 'Plus I don't drive after drinking.' Neither did she want to go home to her empty apartment. It echoed of Nathan. Fingers crossed, she'd be moving very soon. The owner of the place she'd inspected that morning was getting back to her tomorrow after he'd checked exactly when the current tenants were moving out. She hadn't found the strength to go looking for somewhere to buy. Seemed she wasn't as far ahead in her new life as she'd hoped.

Right then Vicki got a text. 'Cole says he'll be knocking down the door at six.'

'I'll get out of the way by a quarter to.' Molly set the alarm on her phone.

'Don't rush off on my account. Damned time of the month. The army never gets it right.'

She grinned. 'Some things we can't control. But I still don't want to be here for the reunion.' Molly stripped down to her underwear and slid under the covers of the nearest bed. 'Get some sleep so you're not dozing off on your husband.'

Molly fell asleep immediately, only to sit bolt upright some time later, her head thumping along with her heart. Time of the month. No. Not possible. Can't be. Picking up her phone, she brought up the calendar.

Closing her eyes, she drew air into her lungs, and tried again. It had been due last week. Her periods were never reliable. This would be another example of nature rubbing her loss in her face. But—what if… No. She tossed the duvet aside and clambered out of bed to sit on the hard chair, her legs tucked under her, her body trembling. Sleep would be impossible. At least until she found out if she was pregnant.

She *couldn't* be.

She showered, dressed, and crept out of the unit at five thirty, leaving a note saying, 'Have a great couple of days. See you at work.'

In the car with the engine running she blew on her cold hands. Now what? It was too early for any shops to be open to buy a test kit. But she wanted to be at home when she found out the result so headed for Bondi Junction, concentrating on driving and not what she'd do if the test was positive. Go knock on Nathan's door and apologise for walking away from him so quickly?

What had to happen was that she did not make any rushed, emotionally driven decisions that she'd come to regret.

Damn it. Her hand hurt where she'd hit the steering wheel. This was crazy. Here she was already thinking the test would be positive when in all reality there'd be no blue line. Her stomach sank. The gynaecologist had been clear about her slight chance of having a baby.

In Bondi Junction she sat outside the shopping centre, feeling ill, until it opened. With her purchase finally in her hand, she headed for home and privacy, afraid of the outcome, almost too scared to find out. Almost.

'Answer your damned phone, Molly O'Keefe,' Nathan shouted, dropping his on the bench with a clatter. 'I need to talk to you,' he added in a lower tone. 'Please.'

He paced the kitchen. Think of another way to get her attention. Climb the Harbour Bridge and threaten to jump off? Then she'd really believe he was mad. Mad for her might not work in the circumstances.

The phone rang. Hope soared. Allie's name blinked at him. Not in the mood for her wisecracks or helpful suggestions, he ignored her. She'd told him the family thought Molly was the bee's knees. His gut had been telling him the same for weeks now. If only he'd listened earlier he might not be feeling so sore and uptight.

He did need to talk to someone, just not his sister. Molly. Snatching up the keys to his four-wheel drive, he headed for the garage, where he paused. If she wasn't taking his calls then what were the chances she'd let him into her apartment? His gaze fell on the monster car, the sparkling paintwork reminding him it hadn't been out for a run in weeks. Not since the day he'd brought Molly home for the first time. The day he'd suggested a fast ride out of the city. The first time he'd seen how excitement turned her eyes to emeralds and brought tenderness to her face.

Now he knew what to do. His finger zipped across the keys on his phone.

Hey, Molly, feel up to that ride in the red machine I promised weeks ago? I'm heading for the Blue Mountains and would like some company.

He pushed Send before he had time to overthink things. Now what? Stand here waiting for a reply that most likely wasn't coming? Nope. He'd pack a picnic, find a blanket to spread on the grass, and put a bottle of wine in a chiller pack. Then he'd change into something less manky and head for Bondi Junction.

Midmorning, Molly gave up on her walk and let herself into the apartment, automatically reaching for the kettle to make tea. Her stomach told her it was not taking tea or anything else right at the moment. But she needed to eat. She had a baby on board to look out for. She also needed sleep, but that was probably asking too much when she felt wired. And with her mind throwing up so many questions and doubts—all to do with Nathan. The father of her baby. He had to be told, and soon. She wouldn't hold out on him. This new version of herself—still tinged with the old one but getting past that—would not hold back on the truth. All of it this time.

Her phone pinged. Nathan again.

Hey, Molly, feel up to that ride in the red machine I promised weeks ago? I'm heading for the Blue Mountains and would like some company.

So would I. Yours especially.

But would Nathan still be talking to her after she gave him her news? Or would he say she'd only told him to get back with him for all the wrong reasons? Only one way to find out. Shirking this was what the old Molly would've done. She was going to be a mother; she had to be tougher than she'd ever been. Starting with talking straight to Nathan.

Sinking onto a chair, she stared at the phone in her shaky hand. *Do it.*

Yes, please. Then she dug deeper. Do I get to drive?

I promised, didn't I? Ten minutes away.

Ten minutes? What was she going to wear? The most important date of her life and she had to look good. Sensational even. She was going to blow Nathan out of the water with her news and—and he wouldn't care about what she was wearing. Her shoulders dropped.

This is being tough?

The green floral dress was too loose, the black trousers and orange shirt didn't go with the new boots, the red blouse and cream trousers looked good and felt all wrong. The pile on the floor grew as her wardrobe emptied.

'What will you think of me when I tell you the rest of why I had to leave you, eh, Nathan?'

Ding-dong.

She was about to find out. Unless— No, she was not going to chicken out.

Ding-dong.

Molly ran through the apartment in her underwear and stabbed the button by the door. 'You can't come up. I'll be with you shortly.' Not waiting for his reply, she raced back to her bedroom and tugged on jeans and pulled a cream jersey over her head. But when her curls refused to be contained she stopped to stare at herself in the mirror.

What do I care about my appearance? We're going for a drive and I'm going to tell him about the baby and then he'll bring me home and life will go on as it has for the past few weeks.

Picking up a twist tie, she bundled up her hair and aimed for the door, not bothering with make-up. There'd be no drive anywhere. She couldn't sit beside Nathan pretending all was well in her world on the trip to the Blue Mountains.

Nathan was leaning against his fancy car, his arms crossed over his chest, his eyes fixed on her from the moment she stepped outside. 'Molly, I've missed you.'

She didn't bother with the rejoinder about seeing each other every day at work. They both knew that's not what he meant. Her mouth flattened. Where to start?

He continued, 'You look pale, and those shadows under your eyes are a worry.'

She stared at the man she loved, the man she was about to rock off his pedestal. 'You're not looking so perky yourself.' Then she looked harder. Wrong, Mol. There was something assured about him, a confidence— No, Nathan was always confident. Today he looked comfortable in his own skin. 'Forget I said that. You look great.' Might as well start out as she meant to go on.

'You think? I've not been sleeping very well.'

'Me neither.' Nights spent tossing and turning, trying to solve the riddle that was her life.

Come on, get this over. Before we get into the car, and then I won't have an agonising hour on the road sitting beside him as he takes in what I have to say.

The words stuck in her throat, refused to budge.

'Come on. Let's get on the road.' He held the driver's door open for her.

Finally she managed to speak. 'Nathan, I've got things to tell you first.'

'Same. But let's not do it out on the street. I'd like to take you to the mountains where we can talk all day if necessary. Please.'

The trip home afterwards might be long and cold. Or—or it might be the greatest trip she'd ever made. It might also be her last time with him. 'Okay. But you drive.' She wouldn't be focused enough.

'Now you're worrying me.'

There was a small smile coming her way and she ran with it, gave a tight one back. 'Let's go.'

They rode in silence, tension building as the kilometres flew by. At one point Molly wanted it over, then she wanted to continue driving the highway right into the night.

Nathan finally pulled into a parking area and turned off the engine. 'Want to walk a bit?'

'Yes.' It would be easier saying what was bottled up inside her if she was moving, not sitting looking directly at Nathan. But when he took her hand as they strolled along a path heading out to a bush-clad hillside, she nearly cried. She'd missed his touch. Face it, she'd missed everything that was Nathan. Even his grumpiness, though there had been some of that at intense moments in the department.

'Molly, I've screwed up big-time.'

Hello? She tried to pull her hand free, but he tightened his grip.

'Hear me out, please?'

'Nathan, there are things you need know first.' Panic started squeezing her chest. 'I haven't been entirely honest with you.'

'Stop, Molly. I could say the same.'

What? Nathan was so honest it could be brutal. Or was that wishful thinking? By hoping for the man of her dreams to push away the past, had she overlooked his faults? No. She wouldn't believe that for a moment. This was the man she trusted completely, did not expect to turn into a monster once she'd given him her heart. 'Go on.'

He stopped walking and turned to face her, reached for her other hand. 'I love you. I think I have from the first time I set eyes on you.'

Her knees sagged. This was not what she had been expecting. Not that she knew what he'd been going to say, but it sure hadn't been this. 'I—'

He shook his head. 'Let me finish. Yes, I love you with all my heart. But I don't want to rush you into anything you're not ready for. I hear your uncertainty about being ready for a relationship. I'll wait for you, Mol, for as long as it takes.' He swallowed, tightened his hold on her hands. 'And if you decide I'm not the man for you then I'll deal with that too.'

Tears spurted down her face. Nathan loved her. The

man she'd fallen for loved her. They could make this work. Be a family. She could forget the past, be happy again. Tell him first she loved him? Or about the baby? He mustn't think her love was because of the baby, and that she needed him onside for that only. 'I'm pregnant.'

'What?' He rocked forward like he'd taken a blow to the solar plexus. 'You're—*we're*—pregnant?'

'Yes.' She stepped back, tugging free of his grip. And he let her go. 'I don't know how it happened as we were always careful, and my chances of getting pregnant were slim.'

'We didn't use protection that first time. Besides, those condoms had been lying in my drawer for a while. Hang on. Why were your chances slim?' Then understanding dawned in his eyes, tightened his mouth. 'That scar on your tummy. He did that, didn't he?'

She nodded. 'I was four months along. Paul was jealous of our unborn baby. Said he wasn't sharing me with anyone, not even his own child.'

'Oh, Mol.' As Nathan wound her into his arms, he asked, 'Has that got anything to do with why you said you couldn't go on seeing me?'

Leaning back to read his expression, she nodded. 'I've only got one Fallopian tube, and even that's not in the best shape for conception. Or so the specialist thought. It seems he was wrong.' Nothing showing in Nathan's face said she shouldn't continue. 'You want a family, I couldn't guarantee you one, so in a way I lied. I didn't want to hurt you in the future when a baby didn't come along. If I'd told you, you might've felt sorry for me and pretended everything was all right.'

'I'd never do that.'

She nodded. 'Deep down I knew it, but I'm still insecure about knowing I'm right when it comes to understanding you. But I know for certain my love for you is real, and everlasting.'

'You love me?' A smile that was pure Nathan split his face, and melted the last band around her heart. For the first time in years she relaxed totally. 'You love me.' His hands were on her waist, lifting her, and then they were spinning in a circle. 'And I love you. That's all that matters.'

He believed her—he didn't think she'd said it because she needed a father for her baby. There was so much happiness in his face she knew he meant what he'd said. 'It is. You make me whole again,' she whispered, just before his mouth claimed hers.

Then he stopped. Pulled back, still holding her. 'Molly, please say you'll marry me. I promise to love you for ever and ever.'

'Yes, Nathan, I will. Because you love me. Not because of the baby.' That she'd have on her own if he didn't love her. But he did. He'd said so, and Nathan always told the truth.

'Yes, Mol, I do, with all my being and then some. And I love the baby already.'

The next kiss rolled into another and then another, and turned them towards the car and the picnic and the blanket. Especially the blanket and the thick bush not too far away.

Six weeks later

'I pronounce you man and wife,' announced the marriage celebrant. 'Nathan, you may kiss the bride.'

The house rocked with laughter and cheers as family and friends, dressed to the nines, crowded round.

'That's enough. Some of us have only got the weekend off.' Cole nudged Nathan when the kiss went on for ever.

Nathan came up for air and gave his mate a glare. 'Thank goodness for that. I couldn't put up with your crassness for any longer.'

Molly grinned as she shook her head at them. 'Boys, stop it.'

Cole hauled her in for a big hug. 'I'm so glad he found you.'

'So am I,' Molly admitted, sudden tears threatening.

'He didn't find her, I pushed them together.' Vicki grinned.

'Here, you're soaking your dress.' Nathan handed her a handkerchief.

Molly laughed. 'Who has these any more?' She carefully wiped her eyes, aware of not messing her make-up, done by a woman Vicki had hired from the cosmetic department of one of Sydney's large stores for them and Lizzie.

'You want me to produce a handful of tissues instead?' her husband asked.

Her husband. She pinched herself. No, she wasn't dreaming. This was real. She'd found love again, this time with the right man. Hadn't had to fake a thing. Looking at him as he waved to the waiter with a tray of champagne glasses, her heart swelled till it hurt. Damn, but she was so lucky.

'Molly Lupton, you lucky girl.' Lizzie swept her into a hug. 'I am so happy for you.'

'I glad you made it in time.'

Lizzie gave an awkward laugh. 'Well, you know me. Stubborn to the end.'

'You won't lose your job because you've taken these

few days off?' She'd been working on intense negotiations in Hong Kong until two days ago.

'Let them try. I might be the only person to come from Perth, but I'm the best.'

Molly hugged her friend. 'You are so right.'

'Your mum's thrilled, by the way.'

Molly looked across the lawn to where her parents and Dad's new lady stood together, watching the proceedings, as though unsure how welcome they were. 'I know, and this time when she says she likes my husband I'm going to accept that. We both made mistakes, and I don't want those to ruin the future. My babies need their grandparents to be there for them like Gran was for me.'

'Babies? As in plural?' Nathan had appeared beside her, two glasses of champagne in one hand.

She stretched up on the tips of her beautiful, pointy cream shoes and whispered, 'Twins.'

He shoved the glasses at Lizzie, reached for Molly and spun her around and up into his arms. 'Twins,' he yelled. 'We're having two little blighters, not one.'

So much for keeping the pregnancy quiet until they got through the first trimester and well into the second. Clapping and cheeky comments exploded around them, glasses were raised, and finally Molly got one of her own to take, not one or two, but three small sips from before putting it aside. No more for her until the babies were born. 'My husband, baby one and baby two. I love you all.'

And months later:

Nathan rushed through the Saturday afternoon crowd, elbowing people out of his way. Typical bloody weekend. Everyone was getting out amongst it, and in his way.

The ED had been flat out, dealing with idiots who'd

had too much food and alcohol when he'd got the call to go to the maternity unit. Molly had gone into labour at thirty-five weeks. It had been fast, almost too much so, but the babies were in good shape, tiny and absolutely beautiful. Like their mother.

Two teddy bears and one enormous bunch of irises was a lot to protect from these idiots who weren't looking where they were going, but at last the main entrance to the hospital loomed up in his line of vision. Why the hospital gift shop had to be closed today of all days he didn't know.

The lift was slow to arrive, and when it came, people surged past him to fill it to capacity. 'Typical,' he muttered as he charged up the stairs, reaching the maternity floor out of breath and having to bend over double while his lungs recovered.

Then he was racing down the corridor, out of breath for a different reason. Excitement gripped him, and his face ached as his smile knew no boundaries. 'I'm a dad, I'm a dad.' Spinning into Molly's room, he rushed up to the bed to hug her, forgetting he had his arms full. Slamming on the brakes, he swallowed. Both babies were snuggled against her breasts, eyes closed, cute little pink noses. He couldn't hug her anyway. 'I'm married to the most wonderful woman on the planet. Mrs-Beautiful-Molly-Mother-of-Two-Lupton.'

'Glad you remembered.' Molly laughed tiredly. 'Want to hold someone?'

'Yes, you.' He placed the teddies on the only chair and held out the flowers. 'I bought every last Dutch iris in the shop.'

'Did you get some vases? There's only one jar in here.' She was grinning at him now, sending his stomach into a riot of longing and happiness.

Damn, he loved this woman so much. His son and daughter were a bonus. It was Molly he woke up for every day. 'I love you, Molly Lupton.'

She nodded. 'I know. Love you back. Now, about names.'

That was an ongoing debate. Hopefully they'd have it sorted by the time everyone went home. Tomorrow.

Tomorrow.

'Joshua and Karina?'

Molly nodded, a look of glee at having won the battle on her face. 'Joshua and Karina.'

How could he refuse her anything?

* * * * *

A WEEKEND WITH HER FAKE FIANCÉ

TRACI DOUGLASS

MILLS & BOON

CHAPTER ONE

CERTIFIED NURSE-MIDWIFE Carmen Sanchez swiped the back of her wrist across her forehead, careful to avoid the blood staining her glove. "One more strong push and the baby will be out." She gave Teena, her twenty-eight-year-old patient, an encouraging smile. "You can do it."

"I can't!" Teena panted, her head lolling to one side on the pillows. "I'm too tired."

Fifteen hours of labor would do that to a person, but there was only one way out of this and it was through. Having Teena's husband there for moral support would have been ideal, but the poor man was working on a fishing boat somewhere in the Bering Sea right now and couldn't be reached.

"I know you're exhausted, Teena," she said, her Caribbean accent drawing out the name. "But you've done such a wonderful job so far. All you need is the strength to push one more time on your next contraction and you'll have your son in your arms. Don't you finally want to hold him? After all these long months? Think of your husband's face when he sees his son."

Teena bit back a sob and nodded.

"Right." Carmen used her most authoritative voice. "Then push as hard as you can when I tell you, okay?"

The patient nodded and took a deep breath.

It was Teena's first pregnancy, and she'd been a difficult case from the outset, with sickle cell anemia complicating matters. Carmen had worked in conjunction with an obstetrician and a hematologist to monitor the patient and provide a safe delivery.

Another contraction hit and time seemed to slow as Teena groaned.

"Go!" Carmen got into position. "That's it. Good. *Good.* Push!"

Teena leaned up on her elbows and bore down hard, toes curled and muscles straining. Finally the baby's head crowned, followed in short order by one shoulder, then two. At last the tiny infant slipped into Carmen's waiting hands and her patient flopped back onto the bed, exhausted.

Carmen cut the umbilical cord, then handed the baby to a waiting nurse, who wrapped the new arrival in a blanket and suctioned its tiny mouth and nose. Soon the boy's wailing filled the room and Teena cried again, this time with relief and joy.

Once the afterbirth was dealt with, Carmen took a moment to enjoy the wonder. Even after years in practice the addition of a new life into the world still amazed her.

She slipped out into the hall, walking over to the desk at the nurses' station so she could decompress and document the backlog of charts awaiting her.

Before she'd finished with the first one, she was interrupted.

"Just the woman I was looking for."

Carmen's heart tripped at the deep male voice, and she glanced up to see Zac Taylor. The zing of attraction she felt was decidedly inconvenient, given he was a paramedic and they saw each other a lot, both in the course of their work and hanging out with mutual friends. Also, they'd spent a steamy night together a few months back, after copious amounts of alcohol at the Anchorage Mercy Hospital holiday staff party, and since then things had been a bit awkward.

Flings weren't her usual MO. Actually, love—the romantic kind—wasn't even on her itinerary, so the way her heart continued to flutter whenever he was around, despite her wishes, was beyond annoying.

It wasn't that she was against hearts and fluff. It was just that she didn't have time for such nonsense. Not with her mother to care for, in the early stages of dementia. Some days her mother was fine, other days she didn't recognize her own family. It was heartbreaking, the slow loss of the person who'd been the one constant in her life. Plus, Carmen was saving to put her younger sister through nursing school at the University of Alaska this fall, after she graduated high school. Between her own busy work schedule and her responsibilities at home Carmen was lucky to have time enough to eat and sleep, let alone date.

In fact, given her past, it was probably better for her to stay alone anyway. Growing up with virtually nothing in the poorest part of Port of Spain, Trinidad, had taught her self-reliance and self-sacrifice. There had only been so much to go around, and you'd had to look after what you got.

Carmen considered herself a tough, responsible, independent woman. Prudent. She didn't need a man to make her life happy. And if she was lonely sometimes— well, that was the price she paid for safety and security. Lord knew she couldn't rely on anyone else to give her anything.

Only problem was, she needed a favor. From Zac.

She bit her lip and watched him through her lashes as she finished her documentation.

The guy was temptation on legs. Gorgeous and charming. And the very things that drove her nuts about him were the very reasons he was the perfect choice for her needs. He had a reputation as a player. Which meant he was not a man for long-term, serious relationships. But he sure fit the bill for Mr. Fix-It-Right-Now.

"Hey, Zac," said Priya Shaw, coming out of another delivery room down the hall, and Carmen tensed.

Priya was a fellow midwife and friend. She also happened to be Carmen's biggest rival for the supervisor position at a new state-of-the-art birthing clinic in California. The job paid twice what her current salary was here at Anchorage Mercy, and the extra funds would go a long way toward getting her ailing mother into an assisted-care facility for dementia patients and also help offset the tuition fees for her sister's university education.

"Hey, P," said Zac, but his focus remained on Carmen.

He leaned an elbow on the counter beside her and his scent—soap and fabric softener mixed with warm, clean male—wrapped around her, teasing her senses and making her far more aware of the man than she liked.

"Tell Lance I'll call him later about this weekend," Zac said to Priya.

"Will do," she called back, tucking her long dark hair behind her ear as she picked up a chart and headed into a delivery room.

Priya was engaged to Zac's best friend, local firefighter Lance Marranto—a fact that only made the favor Carmen needed more complicated. But she'd find a way to deal with it because she was a survivor.

First, though, she needed to finish this chart.

Carmen sighed and blinked down at her writing. Her normally crisp cursive was going a bit wonky from fatigue. Teena's long delivery had burned through what little energy she'd had left, considering she'd already been up late with her mother before coming in for the delivery.

Mama's memory had begun deteriorating faster recently, and the poor thing had a hard time remembering she was in Alaska now, and not back home on her warm tropical island. The night before last she'd wanted to go outside in her nightgown and walk along the beach, meaning Carmen had been up constantly to stop her. It was only early spring, and the wilds on the outskirts of Anchorage were hardly a place for a sixty-five-year-old woman to traipse around in the middle of the night.

Thankfully, Carmen's shift was almost done now. All she wanted to do was hand over Teena's care to the nurses on duty and go home for a shower and a long nap. Clara was on Mama-watch duty until tomorrow.

She yawned before she could stop herself.

"Long day?" Zac asked.

His stupid dimples were making him look far too adorable. Not that she noticed. Nope. Not at all.

"Long night too. Fifteen-hour labor." Carmen stretched her arms above her head. "Patient finally delivered this morning." She shuffled her sore feet, then closed the chart she'd completed and shoved it aside. "Why?"

"We just brought a patient into the ER and I've got a few minutes to kill. Thought maybe you'd like to grab a coffee. Looks like you need one. If you drive home now, you'll fall asleep at the wheel."

He smiled the sexy smile that always got her right in the feels. No man should be allowed to be that handsome. Seriously. The navy blue fabric of his paramedic uniform only made his dark skin glow more warmly beneath the overhead lights, and the material seemed to cling to all his rippling muscle and highlight his pure masculine grace.

"Does that kind of pick-up line work well for you?" Carmen frowned, reminding herself that Zac was off-limits, firmly in the friend zone. And that was where he needed to stay if her plan was going to work. "Telling women how awful they look?"

"C'mon," he teased. "You know you want some caffeine."

She wanted to refuse, but he was right, darn it. Plus, she needed to ask him her favor, and now seemed as good a time as any.

"Fine. One coffee. Let's go."

He chuckled. "You're cute when you're cranky."

She nudged him toward the elevator, their shoes squeaking on the shiny linoleum floor. While they waited her pulse kicked up a notch. Not because of his hotness—not entirely, anyway. No, it was nerves. She hated asking people for help. Especially when it was for a problem she'd brought upon herself.

If only she'd kept her mouth shut when the head of that clinic in California had mentioned Priya and Lance's engagement. If only she'd stopped herself from letting the easy lie roll off her tongue, sweet and potent, like the rum she'd used to serve to tourists when she'd bartended at that all-inclusive resort in Trinidad to make ends meet while paying her way through school.

Yes, I'm getting married too!

Ugh. The memory of her statement made during the interview still made her cringe.

Because she wasn't getting hitched. Hell, she hadn't even dated a man in months.

To her horror, the clinic owner had seized on that

information and invited her and her nonexistent fiancé to attend the upcoming national midwifery conference, where they'd announce their choice of candidate for the new job.

So here Carmen was, needing a fake fiancé for the weekend.

Unfortunately, time was running out and Carmen had only been able to come to one conclusion: Zac Taylor was the best man for the job. He was smart, funny, and not interested in forever.

Exactly what Carmen needed.

The elevator dinged and they stepped on board, the doors closing before anyone else joined them. She felt Zac's gaze on her and resisted the urge to fidget. She probably looked a mess after working all night, but it wasn't like she was trying to impress anyone—least of all him.

It wasn't as if he hadn't seen her at the end of a long shift before. They hung out together as part of a larger group of colleagues at the hospital, including doctors Jake Ryder and Molly Flynn, trauma nurse Wendy Smith and her OB doc husband Tom, plus Susan—Zac's EMT partner—and Lance and Priya, and some of the other local firefighters and their significant others. It was a large group and easygoing. Uncomplicated. The last thing she wanted to do was mess up that vibe by allowing her attraction to Zac to get any farther along than fantasy territory.

So, yeah. Zac was a friend. A friend from whom she needed a favor.

They got their drinks, then found a quiet table in the sunny atrium of the cafeteria, away from the other patrons. Sade's "Smooth Operator" was playing on the sound system overhead and Carmen couldn't contain her ironic snort. If there was a better theme song for Zac's serial dating, she didn't know it.

"What?" Zac leaned back in his chair, stretching out his long legs. He was a good foot taller than her petite five-foot-four-inch frame. "What's so funny?"

"Nothing. Just tired, I guess," she said, trying to pass off her inappropriate giggles as fatigue. "Are you off work soon too?"

"Nah. I wish… Pulling a double shift."

He sipped his iced chai tea. Zac worked almost as hard as she did, always picking up extra runs when he could. Work hard, play hard, apparently.

The favor nagged in the back of Carmen's mind, making her jittery. "Do you have plans next weekend?"

"Not sure." Zac frowned at her over the straw in his drink. "Why?"

Her cheeks flamed hotter. To distract herself, she toyed with a copper-colored curl that had escaped the ponytail at the nape of her neck. Her hair never obeyed, no matter how hard she tried to tame it into submission. She blamed her mother's Ghanaian ancestry as much as the ever-changing Alaskan weather.

"I have a thing."

"A *thing*?" Zac raised a brow at her.

"A national conference. Next weekend. I was hoping maybe you could come with me, if you're not busy."

She clutched her cup so hard the stiff cardboard threatened to collapse. She was *so* not good at this sort of thing.

Calm down. There's no reason to be nervous. This isn't a real date.

As far as their one-night stand went—well, she had no idea. But, given the fact he'd never brought it up with her, she doubted he even remembered their fling. They'd both had far too much to drink. It was water under the bridge. No reason for her pulse to race or her breath to catch. She was just another notch in his already well-scored bedpost.

An odd pain pinched her chest. Which was ridiculous. And stupid. She didn't want a relationship with Zac any more than he wanted one with her.

So why was all this causing her more stress than delivering triplets?

"Wait a minute." Zac sat forward, his dark gaze narrowed. "You're inviting me to go away with you for the weekend?"

He looked about as shocked as she felt at the proposition. Her throat tightened and she swallowed hard against the lump of unaccountable anxiety lodged there. "Yes. No. Well, not exactly." Nerves made her fumble her words. "I mean, yes. I'm inviting you to come with me for the weekend. To pretend to be my fiancé."

There. She'd done it. Asked for the favor. Now all she needed was for him to say yes.

Minutes ticked by like hours as Zac blinked at her in silence.

"Fiancé?" he said finally, his tone incredulous. "Uh… I'm going to need a few more details."

"Like what?" She frowned.

"Like *why*?"

She gave a heavy sigh and closed her eyes. "Because there's a new clinic opening in Big Sur, California, and I'm being considered for a supervisory midwife position there. If I get it, it would be a huge bump in salary. But Priya's up for the job too, and the company was really excited about her and Lance getting married. Not that being married is a requirement or anything, but I got caught up in the moment, and I didn't want to be outdone, so I told them I was getting married too."

She sighed and opened her eyes, forcing herself to keep going even as she avoided Zac's gaze.

"I realize how stupid it sounds, but the words just came out. And once I'd said them I couldn't take them back without making a fool of myself or risking being thrown out of contention for lying. So, yes. They're announcing the candidate they've chosen at the national midwifery conference and they asked me to bring along my fiancé to help me celebrate if I get the job."

She exhaled slowly and hazarded a look at Zac. He was still watching her with an unreadable expression. Her heart beat harder against her ribs as her embarrassment rose.

"If it helps, the conference is being held at a fancy resort in the Yukon called The Arctic Star. All expenses paid—even transportation. All you'd have to do is request the time off work—unless you're already scheduled to have the days free? The conference runs Thursday night through Sunday."

Zac's posture had stiffened now, she noticed, and his handsome face had gone a bit ashen. She wasn't sure if his distress had been caused by her avalanche of babbling or the fact that she'd lied to a potential employer. Both were pretty awful.

When she couldn't take the awkward silence anymore, she said, "Say something."

He shook his head and frowned. "Like what? You want me to lie for you? Pretend I'm something I'm not?"

She winced slightly at the edge in his voice. "I know this is not what you expected from me. Honestly, it's not what I expected from myself either. But now I'm stuck. Please? I never ask for favors, but I could really use your help, Zac." Feeling desperate, she added, "It's a five-star resort. They have room service, massage, a spa—the works. So you should have plenty to keep you busy while I'm in my seminars and interviews. And we'd only have to pretend to be a couple when other people are around. It's all harmless, I swear."

"Harmless? Lies are never harmless."

Zac exhaled slowly, a muscle ticking near his tense jaw. His voice was quiet, as if he was speaking more to himself than her. She'd never seen him as anything other than a smiling charmer before, and she found the change both disconcerting and far too intriguing. She wanted to ask him why the idea bothered him so much when he was used to being with a different woman every week, but now wasn't the time.

He took a deep breath and rolled his shoulders, seeming to come to terms with something inside himself. When he met her gaze again the flash of hurt and anger she'd seen there before had been replaced by a flat guardedness.

"You're inviting me to a midwifery conference for three days at The Arctic Star Resort as your fake fiancé?"

Yep. That about summed it up.

He sat there for a moment, fiddling with his coffee cup, then finally looked up at her. "I'm not sure this is a good idea."

Crap. This wasn't going well at all. Maybe she should've waited until later, when she'd had some sleep and some time to freshen up.

Carmen did her best to keep it light, regardless of the growing heaviness in her heart. "Seriously, Zac. I know this is coming out of left field, but I wouldn't ask if I wasn't in a bind. I really need your help. It's a free weekend of luxury for you. And if you're worried I'll lose my head and seduce you, don't be. You're not my type."

"I was once."

So he *did* remember.

She opened her mouth to answer, then closed it, doing her best to hide her shock over that revelation and failing miserably. Heat prickled her cheeks and she stared at the tabletop, squeezing her cardboard coffee cup tighter than necessary.

"That night was a mistake. We were both drunk and—well, things happened. But we've moved on, right? We're friends. That's all."

He shifted and his leg brushed hers under the table. Her heart rate kicked up another notch.

"Please. It's just for three days. No commitments, no strings attached."

"Right. You keep saying that." He tapped one long, tapered finger against the side of his plastic glass. Sudden images of those fingers on her body, the way he'd touched her, stroked her, made her beg for more, flashed through her mind, unbidden.

No. No, no, no.

"Isn't there someone else you can ask? What about that guy in Radiology you were dating? Jim or John or whatever his name was?"

"Jeff." Carmen cleared her throat. "No. I can't ask him. We didn't part well. I found out he was cheating on me with his department's receptionist."

"Right." He scowled down into his tea, then sighed. "Look, it's not you. It's… Don't you have men lined up around the block wanting to go out with you?"

Flattering as his compliment was, Carmen just felt more exhausted now than she had before the coffee.

"No. There's not. Trust me. I'm not exactly a party girl around here. I work too hard. Besides, I asked you because I feel comfortable with you. We know where we stand. I won't beg, though. I'm too proud and too tired.

If you say no, then I'll contact one of those online escort services to help me."

Zac gave her a look. "Arranging to spend the weekend with a guy you've never met and found on the internet? Yeah, great. Cause that's not dangerous or anything." He scrunched his nose, squinting at her. "Dammit. You really know how to put a guy on the spot, don't you? Fine. I'll go."

"Good." The relief was sudden, short-lived, as one more complication came to mind. "There is one more tiny hitch. Lance and Priya will be there too. In fact, they're flying up to the conference with us on the same private jet chartered by the Californian clinic. So we need to get our story straight ahead of time."

"Hold on. Are you nuts?" He leaned forward slightly, his voice angry. "It's bad enough we're fooling the people who might be your new bosses. Now you want me to lie to my best friend too? Because as far as Lance knows I'm not even dating anyone. I mean, we don't share all the intimate details, but he'd sure as hell have noticed if I had a fiancée sitting around somewhere."

"*Are* you dating anyone?"

"No."

"That's good, then. One less thing to worry about."

He arched a brow at her and her cheeks flushed anew.

"Darling, you've got yourself so turned around here you don't even see what you're doing."

The fact that he was probably right only served to annoy her more. "You're overthinking it. We get our stories straight, learn the basic details about each other, and keep our cool. It will be fine."

She picked at the edge of the table and kept her gaze downcast, because if she looked at him right now he'd be able to see exactly how uncomfortable she was with this, and she needed to fool him into thinking she was completely okay with it all.

She *was* completely okay with it all.

Or she would be once things got underway, because she had no choice.

"Okay. Say we do make it through this weekend. What happens if you get the job, Carmen?" Zac asked. "You get the job and you show up for work and suddenly there's no fiancé. How do you explain to the new bosses that I've disappeared from your life?"

"I'll deal with that if and when it happens."

Honestly, she didn't have the brainpower to devote to it right now. Her focus was solely on getting the job. She'd worry about the details afterward.

"We need to think of a way to get Lance and Priya to believe this has been going on for months, in secret. Maybe we could tell them we had instant chemistry and couldn't forget each other after the holiday party. That we've been seeing each other since."

Never mind that for her, at least, it was partially true. She'd never really forgotten about Zac and the way he'd made her feel that night—sexy, desired, beautiful, precious—even if it had been fueled by too much rum-spiked eggnog and fuzzy thinking.

"We need to convince them that things got serious fast and now we're ready for the next step."

Zac sat back and shook his head. "It's not going to be as easy as you think."

Carmen hid her wince—barely. "Because you're an expert in deception?"

"I've had some past experience with it, yes."

She didn't miss the flash of hurt in his dark eyes before he dropped his gaze to the floor.

"I mean, yeah, maybe your story could work. Lance has been bugging me about being off my game lately."

Her curiosity was piqued again before she could tamp it down. It was silly to think their night together had anything to do with it, but a little flare of hope still fizzed inside her anyway.

"Off your game? Since when?"

"I don't know. A couple months. I've been busy, okay? That's all." He sat forward and rubbed the spot between his brows with his fingers. "Listen, if we do this, what about all the little things couples know about each other? Birthdays, favorite colors, favorite foods, pets, personal peeves? Trust me, Lance will see right through the whole thing in two seconds flat if you don't know all that stuff about me. Hell, *he* knows all that stuff about me."

The tension inside her ratcheted higher. She'd already gotten herself neck-deep in this situation and the tide was threatening to pull her under. All she could do now was keep her head above water and roll with it.

"We'll each write it down. Create a dossier of our lives then give them to one another to memorize."

"A dossier?" Zac snorted. "What are we? Super-spies?"

"I'm serious. It's only three days. We don't need to know every detail—just the big stuff, like you said." She sighed and gave him an exasperated look. "How much of that will come up anyway? We'll be sure to avoid Lance and Priya as much as possible at the conference, just to be on the safe side. Shouldn't be hard with such a busy schedule. Okay?"

"I still think this is a mistake." After an aggrieved sigh and a flat stare, Zac said, "Okay."

Her posture sagged with relief. He wasn't making it easy, but she was glad to have it out of the way. Carmen checked her watch, then pushed to her feet and tossed her empty cup in the trash.

"Thank you. I'll text you with the flight details. And maybe you'll fill me in later about why you're so reluctant to go with me."

"Don't count on it," he said as she walked away.

Carmen glanced at him over her shoulder as she exited the cafeteria. "I never do."

Maybe you'll fill me in later about why you're so reluctant to go with me...

After Carmen had left, Zac sat alone in the cafeteria to finish his break, knowing he could never tell her the truth. His past was a secret he didn't share with anyone. For good reason.

God, he was such an idiot. He never should've accepted her offer, no matter how much he wanted to revisit the chemistry between them. There were things about him that made a return to The Arctic Star Resort reckless or insane.

Neither option made him feel better.

Never mind the fact he'd spent the last twelve years putting as much distance as possible between himself and that place. Now he was going to blow it all to smithereens in one fell swoop. All because of the chance to reconnect with the one woman he couldn't seem to forget.

Damn. The Arctic Star Resort. The conference just had to be *there*, in the one place he'd vowed never to set foot in again, owned by the one man he never wanted to lay eyes on again.

His father.

The man who'd cheated on his mother and betrayed his family's trust.

The man Zac would refuse to forgive for as long as he lived.

It was because of his father that Zac trusted no one—because of his father that he kept everyone at a distance, never letting anyone too close, never trusting anyone enough to get hurt.

It was because of him that Zac feared he was cut from the same lying, cheating cloth.

And maybe he was, considering the state of his personal life. He was a serial dater—a player, according to the local gossip mill—and he'd cultivated that reputation carefully, never letting anyone close enough to see what he feared most—that perhaps beneath the charade it was entirely too true. That perhaps he was just like his father.

He rubbed his eyes, sighing at fate, or luck, or whatever the hell had brought this mess into his life. He'd thought he'd left it all behind him for good. Started fresh, created a new future of his own making. Yet, here it was, right back on his doorstep again, and he had no one to blame but himself.

It wasn't like he could say no to Carmen. She was his friend. Never mind that he'd been secretly crushing on her since their incredible night together after that holiday party, or that what his best friend—Lance—teased him about was true. He *was* off his game. Because of her.

It didn't matter. Nothing could ever come of it.

He didn't do relationships and she was way too good for him. Had been back then—still was today.

Knowing that didn't make him want her any less, though.

Lost in thought, he didn't notice Lance walk up to his table with a half-eaten sub sandwich in one hand and a water bottle in the other until it was too late.

"Dude, shouldn't you be out cruising for trouble? You're on call today, right?"

The well-muscled firefighter plopped down uninvited in the seat across from Zac, his white T-shirt with the Anchorage Fire Department insignia embroidered on the chest pocket stretching tight over his chest, dark circles shadowing his blue eyes. All the Anchorage first responders had been pulling extra shifts lately, gearing up for tourist season in the spring.

"Your rig's still parked out in the ambulance bay."

"Susan's manning the radio. She'll text me when she needs me."

Zac stared out the window beside him, as much to get his head together as to avoid looking at his best friend, who would too easily read that something was wrong in Zac's face. He'd never had a poker face, despite the genes he shared with his father.

He sighed and squinted at the cars coming and going outside. "Let me ask you something, Lance. Did you ever do something so dumb, so out of your comfort zone, so crazy, that you ought to have your head examined for even considering it?"

Lance snorted. "You've met Priya, right? Still can't believe she said yes when I asked her to marry me. She's way out of my league, dude."

Zac chuckled. "True. Still, things have worked out okay for you guys, right?"

"Right." Lance halted, mid-bite of his sandwich. "Wait. Are we talking about women? Because I've been wondering when you're gonna get back out there again."

Sighing, Zac scrubbed a hand over his face. He'd walked right into that, dammit. He was probably over-thinking all this. Maybe Carmen was right. Maybe he should just enjoy the fact that a beautiful woman had asked him to spend the weekend with her, all expenses paid and no strings attached. Chances were his father wouldn't be at the resort anyway. He was probably off somewhere else, supervising his worldwide hotel empire. Zac hadn't kept up with the family business much since he'd left, preferring peace of mind to profit reports.

"Oh, man." Lance shoved his last bite of sandwich into his mouth, muffling his words. "The way you're all quiet, with that sad look on your face, this is definitely about a woman. Don't tell me the great Zac Taylor, player extraordinaire, has finally fallen."

Zac blinked at his good friend. No. He hadn't fallen. That was insane. Sure, he liked Carmen. And, yeah, they were friends. More than friends, if you counted that one night. But, no, he wasn't in love with her. Zac didn't *do* love. Not anymore. Keeping his boundaries intact was easier, safer. No messy emotions involved.

And if that pang of loneliness inside him nipped a bit harder when Carmen was around, well, that was just the price he paid.

This weekend wouldn't be about anything more than helping out a friend. That was all it could ever be where he was concerned.

He had too many secrets and shadows haunting him for it to be anything else.

Zac focused on the snowplow driving by, clearing the parking lot from the fresh three inches they'd just gotten.

You had to love March in Alaska.

"Well?" Lance asked, drawing Zac back to their present conversation. "You gonna tell me her name or what?"

Zac shook his head. "There is no name because there is no mystery woman."

His friend's gaze narrowed as he zeroed in on Zac's face. "Nope. Not buying it, dude. Something's up with you, and it's not just because you haven't been playing the field lately."

"Why are you so concerned about my private life anyway, man?" Zac shrugged and gave his friend an irritated glance. "Mind your own business."

"Don't even try to change the subject." Lance grinned. "I'm right, aren't I? You *are* hung up on someone. I knew it! You've been acting differently since that holiday party. Been hanging around the apartment more…keeping to yourself."

Despite knowing this would benefit his ruse about Carmen, Zac winced internally. It rankled. Zac liked his privacy. The scandal following his father's affair had been splashed all over the tabloids, and having the spotlight glaring on him had been uncomfortable, to say the least.

It didn't help that *he'd* acted out back in the day too. He'd only been sixteen when the news had broken about his father's infidelity and he hadn't handled it well. In fact, he'd crashed the new sports car his parents had bought him and injured the girl he'd been dating at the time, who'd been his unlucky passenger. She'd made a full recovery, but Zac still lived with the guilt of his recklessness.

One more reason he'd left his parents and all their money behind. The wealth had corrupted his dad. Who was to say it wouldn't do the same to Zac?

Needing to get out of his own head and away from the pain of his past, he tried to change the subject again. "You and Priya ready for the wedding?"

Thankfully, this time Lance took the bait. "I guess… She's in charge of all that. I just show up when she tells me." He tossed his empty water bottle into the recycling bin nearby. "Like this fancy conference thing we're going to next weekend. If she gets this new job it'll mean a move to California. Not sure I'm ready to leave Alaska behind, but I guess sand and surf wouldn't be a horrible change. Plus, we could always come back to Anchorage to visit."

Zac nodded, not ready to reveal that he and Carmen would be at the conference too, and Carmen would be competing for the same position.

"Well, I don't know what you got going on behind the scenes, but I'm telling you, dude, one of these days you're going to find someone who'll knock those player socks right off you," Lance said, standing. "You'll end up in wedded bliss just like the rest of us. See you later."

Sooner than you think, buddy.

Standing too, Zac checked his watch. "I should get back to the rig. Help Susan check inventory."

"I'll walk with you." Lance followed him out of the cafeteria. "Break's over."

They rode the elevator to the first floor and headed down the hall toward the ER.

"No man is an island, remember?" Lance said, apparently not about to let the matter drop.

"Maybe I am."

Zac knew he sounded defensive—but, *damn.* Soon Lance and Priya and everyone else at that stupid conference would be all up in his business, so sue him if he wanted to fly below the radar just a little bit longer.

"Islands suit me. Some tropical place with fruity drinks and beaches for miles. I like that kind of island."

They rounded the corner into the controlled chaos of the emergency room, where people were rushing around and the air was filled with the sound of babies crying and clacking gurneys. The scent of antiseptic and lemon floor wax mingled around him like a comforting blanket.

Across the way, Zac spotted Carmen talking to Wendy Smith at the nurses' station and stopped short.

Lance glanced between Zac and Carmen and then clapped him on the shoulder and chuckled. "Sounds a whole lot like Trinidad to me, dude."

Zac barely noticed his friend walk away, his attention focused on the gorgeous midwife with the warm green-gold eyes and even warmer heart. He'd agreed to help Carmen and he would. He'd go to her conference and play her besotted fiancé and keep his promise—because that was what he did. He wasn't his father. He was trustworthy, moral, strong. He'd play her perfect date, wine and dine her to within an inch of her life, fool her potential bosses, and help her get the job.

He'd keep his emotions and his past out of it.

And maybe, if he told himself that enough times, he'd start to believe it.

CHAPTER TWO

"UNITS RESPOND TO motor vehicle accident on Arctic Boulevard at West Fifty-Eighth Avenue. Thirty-seven-year-old female, eight months pregnant, complaining of chest pain. Over."

"Copy. FA14 responding," Zac said from behind the wheel. "Two minutes out."

He steered through the congested midday traffic toward the accident scene with lights blazing and sirens blaring, glad for something else to focus on besides Carmen. His weekend with her was only two days away now, and the closer the conference got the more worried he was that he'd made a horrible mistake.

What the hell had he been thinking, saying he'd pretend to be her fiancé in the last place in the world he ever wanted to set foot in again?

Besides the looming threat of being in his father's world again, there was also the fact that the connection between him and Carmen had never gone away after their one night together. It wasn't even a conscious thing, really—more an underlying thread of awareness that pulled a bit tighter each time he was around her. In truth, it was why he hadn't dated anyone since they'd slept together. Much as he hated to admit it, since their fling he hadn't wanted anyone but her.

Which scared him more than just about anything else.

Because if he did get serious with her, what was to say it wouldn't end in betrayal, just like his father had betrayed his mother? Sure, his mother had found a way to forgive his father and work things out between them, but Zac couldn't expect the same from Carmen if he screwed up. Or *when* he screwed up, since the odds weren't in his favor given his genetics.

"What's got your drawers in a twist?" said Susan, his EMT partner, from the back of the rig as she readied their medical packs for the scene. "You've got that look again."

He glanced in the rearview mirror, scowling. "What look?"

"That brooding, pained one." Susan snorted. "Either that or you're constipated."

"Funny. *Not.*"

Zac sighed and shook his head, pulling in behind one of four squad cars at the accident scene and jamming the transmission into park. He was unbuckling his seat belt as he opened the door.

"I'm fine. Why are you so nosy?"

"Not any of my business," Susan said, climbing out at the back and handing him his pack. "Just figured you'd be a lot more cheerful since you have the whole upcoming weekend off. Lord knows I would be. I'd love to have three whole days to get away somewhere."

They weaved through the crowd of onlookers and cops to where three vehicles were crunched together and blocking two lanes—a flatbed truck in front, followed by a compact car, and finally a four-door sedan. Pretty clear from the damage and the placement that it had been a rear-end accident.

"Going anywhere special?" Susan asked him as they stopped near the middle car.

Yes.

"No." Zac dropped his pack on the ground near his feet and spoke to the cop in front of him. "EMT Zac Taylor. We got a call on a pregnant woman with chest pain?"

"Over here," the cop said, leading them around the vehicles to where two women stood near the curb, one perhaps around sixty, the other holding her very pregnant belly as she leaned against a lamppost. "That's her."

"I got it," Susan said, walking over to the pregnant woman.

Zac approached the older woman, who looked pale as death and was visibly shaking. "Were you involved in the accident, ma'am?"

She nodded. "Yes."

"This car?" He pointed to the middle car.

The woman raised a shaky hand toward the last vehicle. "That one."

"Are you hurt?"

"No…"

Her voice was barely more than a whisper and her trembling worsened as shock set in. She cradled her left hand and Zac noticed blood on one of her fingers, oozing from a fairly deep laceration.

The woman swayed slightly, and Zac grasped her arm to steady her. "Ma'am, how about I take you inside the ambulance and we see about getting your finger bandaged up? You can rest there a moment, okay?"

"She's pregnant…" the woman said, her voice dazed as he guided her toward the ambulance. "I want to make sure the baby's okay. I was driving behind her and she slammed on her brakes. I didn't realize I was so close and I went right into her."

Susan was already at the rig, getting the pregnant woman loaded onto a gurney. As he helped the older woman up the stairs into the back Zac caught snippets of what the woman was telling his partner.

"I was hit from behind and then pushed into the flat-bed in front of me."

Given the damage to the vehicles, things could've been a lot worse for everyone, thought Zac.

He got the older woman situated on a bench in the rear of the rig, then climbed back out to help Susan load the gurney inside as well. Once both patients were secure, he tended to the older woman's lacerated finger while Susan checked the pregnant patient's vitals.

A bit of color had returned to the older woman's cheeks since she'd sat down and Zac handed her a cup of water. Her focus, though, remained fixated on the pregnant woman across from her, her expression anxious. "It all happened so fast. Then she got out and said the wheel had pushed into her stomach."

Zac glanced over to where Susan was hooking up a portable Doppler to the pregnant woman's stomach to monitor the fetal heart rate. A comforting *thump-thump* rhythm soon filled the interior of the ambulance. Susan looked up at him and hiked her chin to let him know everything sounded okay for now. They'd still transport the patient to the hospital, to make sure everything was fine, but it appeared she'd been lucky.

"Right," Zac said, finishing up with the bandage on the woman's finger. "This isn't as deep as I first thought, so you should be fine taking care of it at home, ma'am. Keep the wound clean and dry and change the dressing daily until it's healed. Any questions?"

The older woman shook her head.

"Okay, then." Zac stood. "You're done here. I believe the police officers outside might have a few questions for you."

"Blood pressure's one hundred and two over sixty-nine," Susan said, adjusting the cuff on the pregnant woman's arm.

"Is that good?" the other woman asked Zac.

"Fine. It's usually a bit low when you're pregnant." He helped the older woman stand, then led her toward the door. "Watch your step on the way down. I'll keep ahold of your arm until you're safely on the ground."

"Oh, wait," the woman said, stopping to turn back to the pregnant patient. "I'm so sorry about all this."

The pregnant woman nodded. "Thank you."

Once he'd gotten the older woman out of the rig and over to the cops, Zac secured the rear doors on the ambulance, then climbed behind the wheel and radioed the ER to let them know they were coming.

"Anchorage Mercy, this is Frontier Ambulance Fourteen en route to your facility with a thirty-seven-year-old female who is thirty-eight weeks pregnant, involved in an MVA. Five minutes until arrival. Over."

"Copy. We'll have OB on standby," came the voice of a trauma nurse. "Any visible injuries?"

He glanced back at Susan in the rearview mirror.

"I have a midwife there," the pregnant woman said. "Carmen Sanchez. I want her present."

Zac nodded. Of course it would have to be Carmen.

He relayed the information, then signed off. "Be there soon. Over."

Thankfully, traffic was lighter now, and they pulled into the ambulance bay at the hospital in under six minutes. Zac and Susan unloaded their patient from the back, then wheeled the gurney through the automatic doors into the brightly lit ER.

As they headed down the hall toward one of the open trauma bays Zac gave the ER team a rundown from Susan's notes, doing his best to ignore the fact that Carmen was rushing along beside him, her arm brushing his and sending all sorts of inappropriate zings through his system.

"Patient states her abdomen struck the steering wheel hard during the accident. Fetal heart rate was normal during transport, no bleeding, spotting or cramping, though patient did complain of some chest pain post-accident. Patient has a history of three previous miscarriages and one stillbirth."

"Thank you. I'm familiar with her history," Carmen said, and she nudged him aside as they pushed the patient into an empty trauma bay where the OB on call, Dr. Tom Farber, raised a hand to Zac in greeting.

"We've got it from here."

The curtain abruptly swooshed closed in his face, and Zac stood there a moment, blinking at it, while Susan chuckled beside him.

"There's that look again, buddy." Susan clapped him on the back and chuckled. "Don't worry. Carmen's too good for you anyway. I'm going back out to the rig to clean up."

Zac moved over to the nurses' station to get out of the way. He didn't usually hang around after they'd dropped off patients, but things had been slow all day and his shift was almost over. Besides, he wanted to make sure things were all right with the baby.

That was the excuse he was going with anyway.

"You're still here?" Carmen said when she emerged from behind the curtain twenty minutes later.

The words had emerged snarkier than she'd intended— but *darn it*. Bad enough that she hadn't been able to sleep well since their conversation in the cafeteria, her mind whirling with thoughts of him. Now he was distracting her at work too. The only way her plan was going to work was if she kept her wits about her and her feelings out of it. In fact, most things in life worked better that way, in her experience. Caring too much only meant trouble.

She stepped around Zac, who stood far too close for her comfort. The weekend conference was approaching fast. And, as if that weren't stressful enough, she'd just worked three twelve-hour shifts in a row and now, with this new patient's arrival, her already long night was about to become even longer.

"Figured you'd have a hot date or something."

"No dates for me. I'm off the market now, remember?"

She gave him a pointed glance. If Zac had taken offense at her snapping at him, he didn't show it. He just stood there, grinning and looking smug.

"Just getting into practice for my role this weekend. Besides, my shift's almost done. And since when do you care so much about my schedule?"

"I don't care," Carmen lied. "I just don't want any rumors starting around here about us. You know how people gossip."

Zac snorted. "You don't think they're going to hear about it from Priya and Lance anyway? The guy's my good friend, but I don't tell him anything I don't want the rest of the hospital to know. He's worse than social media when it comes to privacy."

He laughed, but she gave him a dark look. "Don't remind me."

"Hey, this was *your* idea, remember?" he said, leaning closer.

Close enough that his warm breath ghosted the shell of her ear and made her shiver.

"Speaking of remembering—I've been thinking about

that night we spent together. I remember those soft little sounds you made when I held you close. The way you gasped and sighed when I kissed that sensitive spot on your neck…the one near your collarbone where…"

The sound of a clearing throat had her jerking away from Zac. Good thing too, since her pulse was throbbing in her ears and her skin felt too tight for her body. As if the memories she had of that night weren't naughty enough, now she had to think about Zac reliving them too. Lord, help her. When had it got so hot in here?

Carmen swallowed hard and looked over her shoulder to see Tom standing outside the trauma bay as she tugged at her collar.

"Sorry," Tom said, glancing between her and Zac. "Didn't mean to interrupt."

"You weren't," Carmen answered, too fast. After smoothing her hand down the front of her pink scrubs, she raised her chin. "What's your assessment, Doctor?"

"I think she's good to go. No signs of fetal distress. Baby's heart rate is normal and strong. Mother's blood pressure is fine too." He walked over to the counter. "No spotting or cervical effacement on exam. I'd say she's fine to discharge—unless you disagree."

"Agreed. Excellent."

Carmen was doing her best to portray her usual efficient self, even though her insides were still fluttering from Zac's heated flirtation. Lord help her… If one brief encounter with him had her this riled up, she was in big trouble for the weekend ahead.

"I'll go in and talk to her for a bit…answer any questions she might have…then send her on her way. Thank you, Dr. Farber."

"My pleasure." Tom gave her and Zac one more assessing look before backing away toward the elevators. "You kids have fun."

"We will, thanks," Zac said, raising his hand.

"No, we won't." Carmen gave him a narrowed stare. "Fun is the last thing we'll be having this weekend."

"Remind me again why I'm going, then?" He raised a brow at her, then sighed. "I know… To help out a friend. Got it. Trust me. This won't be a party for me either."

It was her turn to snort now. "Really? Why not? Free stay at a luxury resort, all expenses paid? Sounds like a great time to me."

When he didn't answer right away she looked up from the paperwork she was filling out and noticed his playful expression had turned serious.

"What?"

"Nothing. It's not important."

He looked away and she saw the shadow of something cross his handsome face. Before she could ask about it though, one of the nurses came up to the desk and started talking to him.

Carmen felt a quick pinch of unaccountable jealousy before she pushed it aside. She had no claim on Zac Taylor. He was helping her out this weekend. That was all.

She sighed and returned to her documentation, doing her best to ignore Zac and failing miserably. Seeing Tom and Wendy so happy together with their new baby, plus Tom's daughter Sam from his previous marriage, had given Carmen hope that she'd find the same for herself someday—if she ever found the time to date again in her busy schedule.

Until then she was stuck with fake fiancés and imaginary lovers.

Exhaling slowly, Carmen signed off on the patient's discharge papers and handed them to the nurse, telling her to let the patient know she'd be in momentarily to answer her questions, then continued scribbling on the patient's chart.

Zac remained steadfastly beside her, and she gave him a side glance and rubbed her stiff neck. "Don't you have another EMS run to go on, or something?"

"It's Tuesday. Things are slow. Susan and I are just hanging out until the clock runs down or another call comes in."

Her stupid neck cramped again and she winced, cursing softly.

"Here." He brushed her hand aside, massaging the knots in her neck and upper shoulders with those long, strong fingers of his. Between the heat of his body behind her, penetrating her scrubs, and the heavenly feel of his talented digits easing away her tension, Carmen nearly melted into a puddle of goo at the man's feet. Good thing she had the desk there to hold her up.

"You shouldn't push yourself so hard."

She scoffed. "I push myself because that's what it takes to survive."

"Last time I checked this was Alaska, not the apocalypse."

"You never know when things could fall apart. Slack off and you could lose everything."

She closed her eyes as he worked on a particularly sore spot between her shoulder blades with his thumbs, leaving her feeling far too relaxed and vulnerable.

Reluctantly, Carmen forced herself to step away from him. "Besides, I've got more than myself to provide for."

"Hmm? Tell me more about that," Zac said, leaning against the counter once more. "I know we're exchanging fact sheets, but if we're going to pretend to be in love I'd like to hear about your family and your responsibilities from you. What's important to you should seem important to me if we want this to be believable."

The reminder of the upcoming weekend was like a glass of icy water to her face. Carmen straightened and moved out from under his touch. She had to keep her head and be cool, calm, and rational about this if she wanted to succeed.

"My mother and my sister live with me. My mother is ill and requires round-the-clock care. My sister is trying to get into the nursing program at the University of Alaska after she graduates from high school in May. Both things are expensive. This new job in California pays more money and has more responsibility. That's all you need to know for now. If you'll excuse me? I need to go back in with my patient. Unlike you, I still have several hours left on my shift."

She started to walk away, only to have him tag along next to her.

Damn. Hopefully he'd drop the subject of her private life. She didn't like talking about herself. She especially didn't like feeling such a strong attraction to a man who made her want to open up to him, made her want to confide in him and lean on him. All of that was completely unacceptable.

Men were unreliable. Her father had taught her that lesson the day he'd walked out on them, leaving her poor mother to work three jobs just to keep a roof over their heads. Because of that, Carmen had virtually raised her little sister Clara.

Forget childhood. She'd had to grow up quickly. The more self-reliant she was, the better.

Perhaps her upbringing was the reason midwifery suited her so well. Well, that and the fact that her patients needed her. Carmen liked to be needed. She was used to being needed, no matter the time involved or the personal cost. When a call for help came in she shut off her feelings and got the job done.

Which was just as well because messy emotions only got in the way.

Instead of heading back into the trauma bay she continued on around the corner, deciding to burn off a little energy before speaking with her patient again. The nurse would be busy going over the discharge papers anyway.

They reached the stairwell and Carmen stopped, pushing open the door.

"I thought you were going to see your patient?" Zac said.

"I am—in a minute." Carmen's phone buzzed in her pocket and she pulled it out. "Need to take this phone call first."

Not exactly true. But if she didn't get away from Zac soon she was liable to do something stupid—like push him up against the wall and have her wicked way with him.

He continued to stand there, staring at her, looking far too gorgeous for his own good, which annoyed her to no end. "Anything else I can do for you?"

Zac opened his mouth and then closed it, as if reconsidering his words. He backed away slightly. "It's okay to let people in sometimes."

"Seriously?" She laughed and shook her head, doing her best to sound flippant. "Maybe you should take your own advice, then, mister, instead of shutting me down each time I ask a personal question about *you*. See you later, Zac."

"Is that a challenge?" he called from behind her. "I love a challenge."

Carmen chuckled as the door closed behind her, leaving her alone in the stairwell. She leaned back against the wall, her heart still pounding and her mind still racing.

Silly. So silly. Just infatuation. That was all her reaction was.

She closed her eyes and took a deep breath to calm herself—only to have more images of their one night together flash through her head. The two of them entwined in her sheets...him bringing her to release again and again as she cried out his name in ecstasy.

No matter how drunk she'd been that night, a girl didn't forget something that good.

Weys, dat boy rel bess...

The Trinidadian slang echoed in Carmen's head. And it wasn't wrong.

Zac was really sexy. Sexy times a thousand. Sexy times infinity and beyond.

She was in trouble and the conference hadn't even started yet.

Hands shaking, Carmen pulled out her cell phone and called her sister back as she climbed the stairs to the third floor.

Clara picked up on the second ring. *"Ey, wam?"*

"I might have done something incredibly stupid. That's what's up."

Before she could stop the words, an explanation of her fake engagement and the upcoming weekend with Zac tumbled out of her. She felt like she had to tell someone or else she'd burst.

"Wait—wait!" Clara said, as the sound of their mother's favorite soap opera droned on in the background. "You did *what*?"

"I lied to my potential new employer in California. They're very pro-family, and they were so impressed with Priya and her engagement to Lance I felt like I had to make something up in order to still have a shot at the job. I *need* this promotion, sis. *We* need this promotion. The extra money would pay for Mama's care and help put you through university."

Carmen stopped on the landing between the second and third floors, trying to convince herself as much as her sister that she'd done the right thing.

"Look, it's no big deal, right? Three days of pretending and then it's over and hopefully I get the job. Easy."

"What about leaving Alaska? I thought you liked it here. *I* like it here," Clara said.

"I do like Anchorage," said Carmen.

She loved Anchorage the same as Mama and her sister did. She'd hate to leave. But that was beside the point. You did what you needed to do.

"California is pretty too, though. If I get the job it will be like we're living on the island again. Beaches and sunshine and the ocean. They have good nursing programs at their colleges too."

"Hmm…" Clara didn't sound convinced, but it was too late to back out now. "And you think taking this man you had a fling with and having him pretend to be your fiancé will get you this new job? After you two… you know…?"

Yeah, she'd told her sister about the one-night stand. Hard to hide a man staying over in your bed when you shared the same living space. *Ugh.* Clara was right. Whatever had made her think inviting Zac to be her fake fiancé was the most brilliant decision ever?

In the end, though, what choice had she had? With Priya's stellar background and experience, Carmen needed to produce someone who could seriously schmooze. Priya's family was rich, and she'd had the best education and training money could buy. Carmen had worked nights and weekends to pay for her RN degree at the University of the Southern Caribbean.

After that she'd scraped together enough money from tips at the bar and working third shift at a twenty-four-hour convenience clinic to move her family from Trinidad to Anchorage, where she'd interned at Anchorage Mercy and completed her graduate degree.

Then she'd sat for the national certification exam and applied for her Advanced Nurse Practitioner license. The whole process had taken a decade, but it had meant a more secure future for the ones she loved and she'd do it all again, if asked.

Carmen said at last, "Zac knows the score."

"Does he?" Clara said, her tone skeptical. "I don't want you to get your heart broken."

Carmen didn't want that either. Problem was, she'd never really had a Plan B when it came to this weekend. And, honestly, their mutual attraction might be a *good* thing if they could keep to the script and use it to their advantage, making their ruse more believable. Lord knew their chemistry was still sizzling hot, despite the fact months had passed since they'd done the deed.

"I'll be fine—promise," she said, to convince herself as much as Clara.

She pushed away from the wall and squared her shoulders before walking out of the stairwell again. The hallway was delightfully empty, thank goodness.

"You're all set to take care of Mama this weekend?"

Clara sighed. "Yep."

Regret pinched Carmen's chest. She hated to ask her little sister to care for their mother, but it couldn't be helped in this situation. She wanted Clara to experience all the things she'd never had at her age—parties and fun and boyfriends and dating and all of life's good things.

"What time's your flight?" Clara asked.

"We fly out Thursday morning. Zac's meeting me at the airport." Carmen picked at her nails—a bad habit that tended to recur when she was stressed. "On a private jet."

"*Weys!* Well, try to have a good time this weekend. You deserve to let loose. Just not too much, eh?"

"Don't worry. It's still a working midwifery conference." Carmen laughed. "Mama doing all right?"

"She's fine. Watching her *telenovela*."

"Good. Okay. I need to go. Tell her I love her and I'll see her later tonight."

Carmen ended the call and headed back into the busy ER. She'd hoped her little walk would help clear her mind and sort out her thoughts. Instead, it had only brought more concerns to the surface.

If she was honest, her sister had touched on something she feared herself. Not that she and Zac wouldn't be able to fool people into thinking they were a couple, but that Carmen wouldn't be able to stop fooling herself into believing they were...

CHAPTER THREE

LATE THURSDAY MORNING, Zac took a moment to collect himself as he stepped into the ticketing area of Ted Stevens Anchorage International Airport. There were, of course, dozens of people milling about, but his eyes went immediately to a petite beauty with glowing mocha skin and copper-streaked curls, standing on the other side of the security gate, checking her watch.

Dressed in jeans, an emerald-green turtleneck, a black parka and black suede boots, Carmen looked a far cry from the way she looked dressed in her usual scrubs at the hospital. Younger and way sexier, if that were possible.

Whoa, cowboy.

He took a deep breath and reminded himself why he was here. This wasn't a vacation. This wasn't about sex. This was *work*.

After going through the security checkpoint, he strode toward her, coming up on the side opposite to where she was looking.

"Sorry I'm late," he said, setting his leather carry-on bag on the floor near his feet.

She turned and looked him up and down, checked her watch again, then took off for the nearby escalators, calling to him over her shoulder as she went. "You *are* late. I hope this isn't a sign of how the rest of the weekend will go. And you're also overdressed."

"I wasn't sure what to wear. We didn't discuss that," he muttered, racing after her and catching her up near the end of the concourse, feeling uncomfortable now in his dark jeans and tweed blazer, with the open collar of his white dress shirt suddenly too confining for comfort. "You already have the gate number?"

"Don't need one," she said to him over her shoulder. "Private jet, remember?"

"Right." Zac nodded, feeling even more like an idiot. He knew that. Should've remembered from the days traveling with his father.

He forced his attention away from the seductive sway of Carmen's hips as she walked slightly in front of him and focused straight ahead instead.

Mind on the game, buddy.

A flight attendant waited for them near a side door and escorted them out onto the chilly tarmac, where Zac got his first view of the plane, which was similar to the one his father had owned when Zac was growing up. The knots in his gut tightened.

They approached the small, sleek white aircraft with the fancy logo of the California clinic painted on its tail. Whoever owned that clinic certainly had cash in the bank. These things carried a sixty-five to seventy-million-dollar price tag. Flew like a dream too.

Back in the day, before his father's betrayal had caused the world Zac knew to crash down around him, he'd logged enough flight hours to become a pilot himself. But that had been another life—a different Zac.

"Here we are," the flight attendant said, stopping at the bottom of a set of steps. "Enjoy your flight."

"Thank you."

Carmen climbed the steps in front of him and Zac did his best not to notice how her jeans cupped her cute butt perfectly. She stopped just before the top and turned to face him. Distracted, he nearly collided right into her. Good thing he had a firm grip on the railing, otherwise he might have had to grab her to keep his balance. And touching her at this point, even for safety reasons, would be a big mistake.

"Ready for this?" she asked. "Did you bring your dossier?"

He squinted up at her in the sunshine and avoided staring at the gold cross necklace nestled atop her bosom. "I am. I did. Did you?"

She inhaled deep, then nodded. "Yes. We can go over them during the flight. I was hoping you'd be on time so we could do it beforehand. I think Priya and Lance have already boarded."

Damn. He'd wanted to get here sooner too, but Susan had called him with some questions about the inventory, and then he'd gotten wrapped up in packing, and there'd been road construction, and now it seemed like everything was conspiring against him today.

If he didn't know better, he'd take it as a sign that he shouldn't be here at all. Too late now, though.

"We'll just have to bluff our way through," she said.

Bluffing he could do. He might not have a good poker face, but he could BS with the best of them. Another dubious skill he'd picked up from his father.

Zac stepped up on the next stair, putting him and Carmen level. This close, he caught a hint of her jasmine perfume and her heat penetrated his cotton shirt, making his fingertips itch to pull her closer.

To keep himself from reaching for her, he jammed his

hand into his jacket pocket instead and pulled out the ring he'd purchased and stashed there earlier.

Zac held Carmen's gaze as he took her left hand and slid it on her finger. "Need this if we're going to make it believable, eh?"

When she didn't respond, he glanced up to find her staring down at the single solitaire round-cut diamond set in platinum. He'd gone for the real thing, thinking it would fool even the most persistent of doubters at the resort. He'd return it once they got back. No big deal.

"Let's do this."

Carmen bit her bottom lip. "It's beautiful…"

"Beautiful ring for a beautiful woman."

He winked, then waited until she'd turned around again before nudging her toward the door of the plane. If they didn't get off these steps soon he'd be running the risk of sweeping her into his arms and kissing her right there. Which was bad. So, *so* bad. They hadn't even left Anchorage yet and he was already having a hard time not imagining all the naughty things he wanted to do to her…with her. Same as he'd done that long-ago night…

Damn.

The good news came as soon as they boarded the aircraft. Lance and Priya gaped at their arrival, stunned and speechless. The bad news was that their silence didn't last.

"Dude!" Lance looked at the sparkling ring on Carmen's finger, then up at Zac. "I was right! No wonder you didn't tell me what you were doing this weekend. Sly dog!"

"I wasn't sure until the last minute that I could make it. And, yes, Carmen and I are together. You were right. Congrats," Zac said, tucking his leather bag in an overhead bin, then taking a seat beside Carmen in a cushy leather chair and buckling his seat belt. "I had to do some schedule-wrangling at work, but anything to spend more time with my snuggle-bug, here. Isn't that right, sweetheart?"

At his use of the endearment a small muscle near the corner of Carmen's eye began to twitch. He reached over and clasped her icy hand in his. She covered it quickly and forced a tight smile.

"Yes, that's right, *doux-doux*."

At his raised brow, she squeezed his hand.

"Zac and I have been searching for ways to spend more time together outside of work and I thought this weekend was a perfect opportunity. What with all the stress of planning a wedding and all."

"Okay. Wait a minute. You're telling me that you two have not only been dating but that you're *engaged*? How the hell did you keep this secret from everyone?" Priya asked, her expression skeptical. "We work together. I see you more than your own family does. And I didn't have a clue. I didn't even know you were dating anyone since Jeff, let alone Zac."

Zac was pretty sure he'd lost all circulation in his fingers. Carmen was holding his hand so tight, and the stupid diamond was cutting into his skin, but he'd signed on for this and he intended to make sure the weekend was a success.

He kissed Carmen's cold hand and tucked it near his heart, milking the moment for all it was worth. "We purposely kept it under wraps. You know how brutal the rumor mill at the hospital is, and my Carmen loves her privacy. Plus, we wanted to make sure things were solid between us before announcing it to the world."

Lance watched him closely, gaze narrowed. "But you never once mentioned it to me either, and I'm your best friend. In fact, I've never even *seen* you two together, except for that crazy holiday party. Wait! Did you two hook up that night? You did, didn't you?" Lance leaned forward, his gaze darting between Zac and Carmen. "Well, I'll be damned. And you're okay with moving to California if she gets this job, huh? Never thought I'd see the day you'd leave your beloved Alaska."

Uncomfortable heat rose beneath the collar of Zac's shirt, but he resisted the urge to fidget. Lance was right—both about him and Carmen hooking up and about Zac leaving Anchorage. The thought of moving away from his beautiful home state felt like a punch in the gut. Still, he needed to play along, because that was what he'd agreed when he'd signed on for Carmen's weekend of deception.

Besides, having a grain of truth mixed in with the lies should make them more believable. And the fact that he knew *that*—again courtesy of his father—made him even more queasy. His gut cramped and disgust flooded his bloodstream.

This is not the same. I'm not like him. Not at all.

He was only pretending in order to help out a friend, to help someone he cared for.

Never mind that his father had claimed the same reasons—said he'd lied to protect Zac and his mother, said it had only happened one time.

Old memories and pain rose, threatening to overtake him if he didn't get up, get off this plane, get back home where he'd be safe.

Thankfully a flight attendant came to make sure they were prepared for takeoff and to get their drink orders. The captain announced on the PA that they were completing their preflight checks and that once they received clearance from the tower they should be airborne.

Zac took a few much-needed deep breaths and concentrated on the in-flight safety checklist a second attendant was going over with them.

By the time the first flight attendant returned with their beverages he was back to normal again. Or about as close as he was going to get on this trip. It helped that Lance and Priya had been directed to swivel their chairs forward during takeoff, giving him and Carmen a reprieve from their inquisition—at least for now.

Zac exhaled, glad the spotlight was off him for the moment. They taxied down the runway, Carmen still hanging on to his hand for dear life.

He wondered if she was a nervous traveler. They'd never really discussed it. They'd never really discussed a lot of things.

Zac turned slightly to glance her way and lowered his voice. "That seemed to go about as well as could be expected."

She released his hand at last and took a long drink of her wine. "Yeah? You looked like you were going to throw up there for a minute when Lance was grilling you."

"I'm fine. Considering we didn't prep what we were going to say ahead of time, it just threw me a bit off-kilter, that's all."

Liar.

He looked over to where Lance and Priya faced away from them, their heads together, most likely discussing their impromptu engagement.

The fact was, the prospect of heading straight back into the lion's den was shaking him more than he cared to admit. His mother might have been the bigger person and forgiven his father, but Zac hadn't been able to do the same. It had broken her heart, but he'd left out of respect for her. He loved his mother more than anything, and he hadn't wanted to disrupt her life further by constantly arguing and fighting with his father, so he'd gone.

He missed her every day, though—and, much as he liked to think he'd gotten over the hurt a long time ago, perhaps it wasn't as far behind him as he pretended.

As soon as the seat belt light went off he unbuckled and shifted in his seat. "Where's your dossier? I want to be prepared the next time those two come at us."

He stood and pulled his own dossier out of his bag in the overhead bin and handed it to her. It had seemed stupid to put his paltry list of ten things in a binder, but he didn't want Lance and Priya to see it accidentally.

"It's not much, but it's all I can share with you."

"*All* you can share?" She opened the binder and looked at the paper inside, then back at him. "Are you working for the CIA?"

"No. There are just things about me that I don't tell people."

"I'm not *people*," she whispered. "I'm supposed to be your fiancée."

"Fake fiancée," he corrected. "Look, this flight's only an hour. Maybe now would be a good time for you to fill me in on your list and anything else you think I should know."

She finished off her wine, then reached into the tote near her feet and pulled out her own folder, which she handed to him. "Unlike you, I have no secrets. Everything about me is on there."

He read her papers, then raised a brow. "You even wrote a meet-cute for us? I'd been chasing after you for years and you finally took pity on me?"

"It's better than the truth, yeah? Which Lance has already guessed, darn him." She reached into her bag again and pulled out a pair of reading glasses. He raised an eyebrow "What? Working on all those charts makes my eyes tired."

He snorted. "Sure. I like them. Makes you look like a sexy librarian."

"Don't get any ideas, mister."

"Can't help it when I'm around you."

Carmen gave an aggrieved sigh. "Save the flirting for when it counts, okay? It's wasted on me now."

"But it wasn't back then, was it?" He laughed, resting his head back against the seat. "Do you remember that night? I do. That little red dress you wore…with the neckline down to there and the split up to—"

"Stop it." She smacked his arm. "It wasn't that bad. Besides, you weren't much better, Mr. Tight-Jeans-and-T-shirt. Looking all sexy on the dance floor."

"You thought I was sexy, huh?" He waggled his brows. "You were the sexy one. Shaking your booty. And, man, when we slow-danced." He sighed and closed his eyes. "I can't hear that song now without thinking of you."

She chuckled. "What was it again? Oh, right. 'Havana' by Camila Cabello."

He shifted slightly, knowing he was treading on dangerous ground by flirting with her, but unable to stop himself. A night didn't go by when he didn't remember her at that party, looking like heaven on earth in that dress, holding her, kissing her, making love to her all night long.

"You were scorching hot, lady."

"You weren't so bad yourself, mister."

She turned her head to look at him, her full lips parted and her eyes sparkling with heat. Then the attendant stopped by to refill their drinks and the spell was broken.

Carmen faced forward and frowned down at his dossier. "Best concentrate on this right now. Like you said, the flight's only an hour."

Right.

Zac straightened and went back to memorizing the stuff on her papers. Father deserted the family when Carmen was just a kid...raised by a single mother...caregiver for her younger sister...worked her way through nursing school. No wonder they got along so well. They were very much alike. Well, except for the father leaving part. Unfortunately, his father was still right where he'd started.

Zac had been the one to do the leaving.

"So, tell me what's not on here."

She gave him a side-glance and a frown. "I told you—it's all on there."

"One thing isn't."

"What's that?"

She crossed her arms, drawing his attention to her breasts before he looked away fast. Apparently not fast enough, though, if her perturbed look was any indication.

"Why did you choose *me* to bring this weekend?" he asked around the sudden constriction in his throat.

Because *darn* if more memories of that night after the holiday party weren't shoving their way into his brain. How her soft curves had felt in his palms, the way she'd sighed and held him closer, how he'd taken her taut nipple into his mouth and licked and sucked gently...

Nope. Nope, nope, nope.

Not going there. Not now and definitely not later.

Keep it together.

Carmen was the opposite of the kind of woman he normally slept with. Usually he went for girls who liked to party. Women who weren't looking for more than a night or two and then left with a fond farewell. Carmen had *forever* written all over her, even if she denied it.

Knowing she wasn't his type should be making keeping his distance this weekend easier. Except it wasn't.

"I told you that day in the cafeteria. You're a friend. I trust you. We have chemistry, and I thought that would make this whole charade easier. Don't read more into it than is actually there." She scanned his list again. "You're a Capricorn? I would've guessed Leo, or maybe Scorpio."

"Scorpio, huh?" he said, going along with her explanation for now, even though his gut told him there was more to her reason for asking him than she was letting on. "How's that?"

"Because you obviously like your secrets."

"I don't like secrets. What I like is privacy. I've seen from experience how rash decisions can hurt people and I—"

"Aw...trouble in paradise already?" a female voice interrupted.

Zac looked over to find Priya and Lance had turned toward them again, clearly ready for a new round of questions.

Yeah. It was going to be a very long weekend.

"So, spill the beans," Lance said, focusing his laser-like attention on Carmen. "How did you two get together? How long has it been going on? Mostly, how in the hell did you manage to keep it a secret so long?"

"Oh, well—" Zac started.

But Carmen held up a hand to stop him.

"We hooked up at the hospital holiday party and we saw each other off and on after that. Things got more serious recently and we got engaged."

"Really?" Priya narrowed her gaze and crossed her arms. "That quick?"

"When the love bug bites..." Carmen said, stiffening slightly beside him.

"That's odd…because just last month you told me you had no intention of getting involved with anyone. You said your career and your family were too important to you and took up too much of your time. Did that change?"

"No." Carmen frowned down at her hands in her lap and fiddled with the zip on her down vest. "I mean, yes. I mean, perhaps I just had a change of perspective. Meeting the right person can do that to you."

"Hmm…" Priya looked completely unconvinced. "Is this about the job? Are you faking this to try and get the job at the California clinic?"

Zac coughed to cover his surprised laugh. Nothing like having your ruse ruined before it had even started. "No. Of course not."

"Don't be ridiculous. My qualifications speak for themselves—as do yours. I don't need a man to win a job." Carmen lifted her chin defiantly. "Zac is here because we're in love and because this weekend is a chance for us to spend some quality time together away from the hospital. That's it. Right, *doux-doux*? 'Every bread have a cheese,' as my mama says."

"What?" Zac scrunched his nose.

"'Every bread have a cheese'," Carmen said. "It's an old Trinidadian saying. Every person is bound to find a soul mate. And Zac is mine."

He barely had time to nod before she kissed him soundly.

Her lips were just as sweet and soft against his as he remembered. Dangerous, that, since talk of soul mates wasn't in his vocabulary anymore. Still, he'd just begun to lose himself in the moment, cupping her cheeks to keep her close, when Lance cleared his throat.

"Dude, get a room," his buddy said, breaking them apart.

"Dude, we are," Zac countered, sitting back, but keeping hold of Carmen's hand, lacing his fingers through her chilled ones, hoping to convey some strength and solidarity through the gesture.

A beep sounded through the cabin and he glanced up.

"The seat belt signs are lit up again. You two better turn around and buckle up. It could get bumpy."

Priya gave them both another pointed stare before slowly turning her chair around to face forward. Lance followed suit, giving Zac and Carmen a small modicum of privacy again.

"Okay?" he whispered, turning his head to look at her.

Her full lips were compressed into a thin line and he had the urge to kiss her again, just to get her to relax. But he thought better of it. Talking seemed like a safer option at this point, given the way his blood pounded and his heart still slammed against his chest.

"Hey, don't worry about them. We can avoid them once we get to the resort. We got this."

She didn't look convinced at all.

"Tell me some more about this job. Why now?"

She gave a small shrug, staring out the window beside her. "I've been at Anchorage Mercy for nearly a decade now. I have a chance for something bigger and I'm taking it."

"Because of the money?"

Ambition and money, he understood. He'd grown up around enough of it. Another reason his life in Anchorage suited him. Laid-back, straightforward. No fuss, no muss. No lies and betrayal. Well, present situation excluded.

He sipped his ale straight from the bottle and watched her over the rim. "You'd be a manager at this new clinic in Big Sur?"

"Yes—if I get the job. I've worked hard my entire life

and I don't want to risk losing what I've gained. That's why it's important we avoid any…complications."

"Complications?" Zac blinked, considering that a second.

He assumed she meant sex. But in his mind sex wasn't complicated. Commitment was the real complication.

Commitment couldn't be trusted. Commitment was made to be broken.

He'd learned that lesson the hard way, thanks to his father.

They sat in silence for a while, Carmen flipping through a magazine while Zac napped. Finally Carmen nudged him with her elbow and he straightened, scrubbing a hand over his face to clear his fuzzy head.

"What? Did I miss something?"

"No." She chuckled, and the sound seemed to brighten the interior of the cabin. "You were snoring."

"Was not." He frowned. "You're just saying that because it was on my sheet."

"One of the very few things on there." She set her magazine aside and turned her attention to him again. "There's nothing on there about your family or your past."

"It's not important."

"I disagree." Carmen shifted slightly, settling back into the corner of her seat to face him. "Family is everything. It shapes us, defines us—it's our beginning and our end."

"Very poetic."

Her foot bumped his and a fresh zing of awareness zipped through his system. He looked away and took a large swig of ale to get his damn fool head back on straight.

"My dad's a businessman and my mom stays home. My father runs his own company. We had a falling out.

I haven't spoken to either of them in years. My family is the last thing I want defining me. I'm my own man."

"Whatever you say. But the fact you cut them out of your life and won't speak about them is telling me a lot about you right there." Her gaze met his and held.

Zac coughed and straightened in his seat. "Drop it."

"Fine. For now." She lowered her voice. "But eventually you're going to have to tell me more, in case it comes up at the reception tonight. My potential new bosses will be there. Besides, I've laid myself bare for you."

"Bare?"

The images that word conjured were triple X. She'd leaned in, close enough for her warm breath to fan his face, and the sweet scent of her perfume surrounded him. A few millimeters more and he could kiss her again, taste her, see if she was as delicious the second time around…

The plane hit a pocket of turbulence, jarring them hard.

"Please be sure your seat belts are fastened," the flight attendant said, passing by.

Carmen sat back, pushing the curls away from her flushed face. "Dammit."

"What's wrong?"

She shook her head and gave a rueful smile, staring out the window, away from him. *"Yuh cyah play mas if yuh fraid powder."*

"Sorry?" Zac frowned as he fastened his seat belt. "Is that more Trinidadian?"

"Yes. It means don't get involved in something if you can't handle the danger."

Touché.

"Dangerous" seemed the correct word for the heat shimmering between them. Their chemistry had always been hot and volatile, ready to boil over at any second.

Which had been fine back in Anchorage, because they'd both been able to escape easily. Now, though, they were stuck on a plane, somewhere over the frozen Yukon, with no way out but through even if their choice to fake an engagement this weekend had been a bad one.

Frustrated in more ways than one, Carmen sat facing away from Zac for as long as she could—until she got a crick in her neck and her butt was numb from staying in the same spot so long.

This weekend clearly wasn't going to be as cut-and-dried as she'd planned, especially as her whole body tingled and her breath caught each time she locked eyes with the man. Yes, they were supposed to act like a couple for the next three days, but it was supposed to be *pretend*.

This connection between them felt all too real.

If the plane hadn't bumped them around earlier she would've kissed him again. Would've done a lot more too, if they'd been alone. She wanted him. Intensely. Like she'd never wanted anything *ever*.

Which made no sense. Carmen was a sensible person. She didn't go around acting on her impulses, didn't throw caution to the wind. She was the stable one, the caregiver, the person other people depended on. No matter how gorgeous Zac was, or how he made want throb through her like molten lava, she could not let him overwhelm her good sense.

She'd lived her whole life putting others before herself, always biding her time. But she wasn't a hermit. She dated. She went out with people. She socialized. But she never let things get too deep. Because all men left in the end.

Her last long-term relationship before loser Jeff had lasted two years. Until Steve had moved on to greener and less complicated pastures. He'd told her they just didn't want the same things, but deep down inside Carmen feared she knew the truth. She didn't deserve love. After all, maybe if she'd been better, smarter, more amenable and less driven, Steve would have stayed. Her father too.

She sighed and gazed out at the fluffy clouds below them. Now that the time had arrived to go after this clinic job she felt torn. Part of her didn't want to miss her shot—the ambitious part of her that always made her feel like she had to prove her worth through her accomplishments. But another part of her felt scared and sad that she was willing to lie in order to get the position.

Not that there was much she could do about it now, at thirty-thousand feet, with Zac in the seat next to her.

There was nothing to do now but make the best of it.

Never mind that he kissed like the devil and tasted like sinful desire…

"This is just pretend," she whispered aloud. "We're friends. We don't want to risk that."

"Agreed," Zac said, not looking at her.

"We have to work together at the hospital. No sense making things awkward."

"Nope."

"Okay. So…" She exhaled slowly and stared up at the cabin ceiling. "Just pretend."

He closed her folder and turned to her once more. "I'll ask again. Tell me about this job."

She looked at him, surprised. "You want to hear about the position in California? Now?"

"No." Zac gave her a flat stare. "What I actually want is to finish that kiss we started a few minutes ago. But since I can't…"

She sucked in a quick breath and forced herself to concentrate on the details of the new managerial position up for grabs at the California clinic, hoping the business talk would chill her ardor.

"The person they hire will oversee a staff of four midwives, with the possible addition of more as the practice grows. And they'll be in charge of training too."

Zac's tense shoulders relaxed a bit. "Sounds right up your alley."

"Yes. I plan to present a framework to assist midwives in developing a consistent approach to screening for perinatal mood and anxiety disorders to the owners while at the conference."

She hadn't spoken to anyone but her sister about her plan, but it might be good to practice her spiel on him before her presentation to her potential new bosses at the conference.

"I'd also like to develop interventions and strategies for referral, response to emergent situations, and following up to ensure continuity of care."

"Wow," he said, his tone impressed. "That's great."

"Thanks. Let's hope the owners think so too."

Carmen checked her watch. Less than half an hour until landing. Nervousness buzzed through her system like a swarm of restless bees.

She stared at her hands in her lap. "Listen, all reminiscing aside, I don't normally have one-night stands like we did after that party."

"I know." Zac glanced over at her.

"You do?"

He sighed. "You didn't have the confidence of a serial bed-hopper."

"Oh."

Zac handed his empty beer bottle to a passing attendant, then faced her. "It's not a bad thing."

"Right…" Heat prickled her cheeks and she quickly changed the subject. "Want to look at my magazine?"

"Sure." He laughed, staring down at the cover. "'How to pick the best lipstick based on your astrological sign'?"

"What?" She shrugged. "I didn't want anything too heavy."

"Well, you got that, then." He made a face as he flipped through the pages. "Seriously?"

She glanced at the overhead bin above their head, thinking of his lone bag. "Um… Zac?"

"Yeah?"

"Is that bag the only luggage you brought?"

"Yeah." He flipped a page. "Why?"

"Did you remember to bring a tux for the evening parties?"

Not that she didn't appreciate his current ensemble, which clung to every muscle and sinew of his chiseled torso.

"Oh, yeah. I had the rest of my stuff sent on ahead to the resort." He flipped another page. "Figured it would be easier that way."

"Huh…" She hadn't even considered doing that, and the fact *he* had gave her pause. "I didn't know that was a thing."

"People do it all the time. Business travelers, mainly, though sometimes other people too. Resorts usually have staff who will make sure the luggage gets to the right room after the guests check in."

He glanced up at her then, as if realizing he'd said too much, then looked away again fast.

"At least that's what I've heard."

"Interesting…" She watched him more closely. "What business did you say your father was in?"

"I didn't." He handed her back the magazine. "Nice try, though."

"C'mon. You'll have to trust me eventually."

"No, I won't. This is just a weekend, remember? Besides, I'm Julia Roberts here."

"I'm sorry?" She gave him a confused look.

"Julia Roberts? In *Pretty Woman*?" He grinned. "I'm your fake date. Your beck-and-call girl. Or guy, in this case. Now, give me your credit card so I can go on the shopping spree of my dreams."

She laughed. The man was full of surprises—she'd give him that. Her gaze fell to his lips again. Lord, she really liked those lips. But he was off-limits. Period. Amen.

Carmen sighed and stared out the window instead. "Sorry. No credit card. And don't expect me to climb a balcony for you either. When we part ways, I'll let you go for good."

"We'll see…" He winked, then closed his eyes again, apparently continuing his nap.

Carmen leaned her head back against the chair and did the same, though sleep evaded her. Instead her mind churned with thoughts of them getting caught and her new career and the new future she'd planned in a shambles around her.

No. She jolted awake. Time to shape up and concentrate on her goals. Get to the resort, get through her final interviews, get the job. Nothing else mattered. Not her feelings, not the hot guy beside her, not the incredible chemistry between them.

Nothing.

No matter how she might long for a real partner to share her life with someday…

CHAPTER FOUR

Half an hour later Zac sat beside Carmen in the limo they were sharing with Priya and Lance, zooming down the road. They crested a ridge and the Arctic Star Resort was still a sight to behold, even after all these years.

Zac battled a tingle of adrenaline, seeing the towering pine and glass entryway of the main lodge, and instead focused on the glow of lights from the smaller though no less impressive private chalets in the far distance, across an open plain.

That was where he'd lived, growing up.

Memories of happier times, of coming home to the wonderful smells of his mother's cooking, game nights, laughter and hugs and comfort and peace assaulted him before he shoved them away. Those days were over and best left forgotten.

Their driver pulled up under the massive portico at the front of the lodge and Zac helped Carmen out of one side of the vehicle while Lance did the same with Priya on the other. Thankfully their traveling companions had been too busy chattering about the upcoming conference and the scenery to start another round of Twenty Questions, but Zac still felt on edge.

He made an excuse to stay by the limo and make sure the bellman got all the luggage, but really he just needed a moment alone before walking into what he considered a war zone.

His father had built this resort from the ground up, after making a name for himself by running several large luxury hotels throughout the world. Taking his years of knowledge with him after breaking out on his own nearly thirty years ago, Jonathan Taylor had quickly amassed an international empire, including hotels and resorts in fourteen countries and fifteen states in America. Thirty properties total, the last Zac knew, and probably still growing.

His father had turned sixty the previous year, but showed no signs of slowing down. During his younger days Zac would've been proud of his father's accomplishments. Now, he just felt disappointed.

Once the luggage had been safely loaded onto a trolley, Zac followed the bellman into the glorious lobby of the resort. High cathedral ceilings soared above them and the glow of warm lighting glimmered off the shiny pine floors. He'd grown up here, with room service and valets and maids. He'd hung out with the cooks and the housekeepers and the security guards. They'd been like his second family.

"There you are!" Carmen linked arms with him, the copper in her curls gleaming beneath the chandeliers hanging from huge beams above. "Isn't this place gorgeous?"

He gave a curt nod. It was beautiful—but not nearly as beautiful as her.

"Wow." Priya had walked over to a round marble table near the center of the lobby. In the middle of it sat an enormous cut-crystal vase, brimming with white lilies and roses. She leaned in to sniff a bloom, then squinted at the vase. "That's Waterford. Worth thousands of dollars."

She was correct. Zac's father spared no expense when it came to the décor in his hotels.

"Smile, please," Carmen whispered.

Her warm breath sent a shiver of awareness through him, bringing him back to the present.

"We're supposed to be happy and in love."

It seemed keeping up a happy façade would be more difficult than he'd anticipated.

"Priya…" Lance said, plopping down on one of the overstuffed suede sofas that Zac knew were handmade in London. "These chairs are amazing. We should get a couple of these for our apartment."

"They wouldn't fit through the door," Priya said, snuggling up beside him. "Too big."

"C'mon, let's get checked in." Zac steered Carmen toward the reservation desk. Lance and Priya followed.

"Miss Sanchez?" A woman stepped out from behind the nearby concierge desk and walked over to meet them. "Welcome to the Arctic Star Resort and Spa. My name is Willow. And this must be Miss Shaw."

The woman shook their hands, then handed them gift bags emblazoned with the logo of the California clinic on the side.

"We're so happy to have you here. Please follow me. I've taken the liberty of booking each of you into your suites already, and the bellman has been instructed to deliver your luggage as we speak. I'll show you to your rooms. Please do let me know if there's anything you need during your stay. Miss Sanchez, you and your guest will be in the Yupik Suite. And Miss Shaw, you and your guest will be in the Aleut Suite."

They climbed a grand curving staircase to the second floor. From memory, Zac knew the wings of the hotel formed a huge square, five floors high, and surrounded a spacious courtyard in the middle, filled with flowers and blooming trees in the spring. He'd used to love playing out there as a kid. There was also a reserve near the back of the resort where the conservationists his father kept on staff cared for injured wildlife.

The group stopped to wait for the elevators to take them up to their rooms. Zac knew there were only four suites on the top floor, all named for indigenous Alaskan tribes.

Minutes later, much to Zac's relief, the concierge led Zac and Carmen to the outside door of their suite.

"Thank you, Willow," Carmen said.

"My pleasure." The concierge opened the door for them, then handed them each a keycard. "As I said, please call me if you need anything during your stay. You can reach me through the front desk from eight a.m. through eight p.m. Your evening concierge will be Dustin, and he can be reached through the front desk as well. Enjoy your stay."

"We'll talk later," Lance called as Willow led him and Priya away toward their own suite down the hall.

That was what Zac was dreading.

He held the door for Carmen, then followed her inside. The owners of the California clinic had added a few special touches to the suite, like a bottle of champagne on ice on the coffee table in the living room, and a plate of fresh strawberries covered in chocolate in the kitchenette.

The design of the suite was just as spectacular as the rest of the resort. High ceilings, huge windows overlooking the beautiful landscape, all the furniture plush and inviting. There was a large living room, a dining area with a table that seated eight, and a kitchenette with stove, fridge, and granite countertops.

He and Carmen went down a short hallway to the master suite, with an enormous king-sized bed in the center of the room, a sitting area with a love seat, chairs and table near the windows, a walk-in closet, and a private balcony with a small table and chairs outside as well. The master bath was as big as the bedroom, complete with double vanities, a whirlpool tub and an entire wall of mirrors, along with a gigantic walk-in glass shower.

If it had been anywhere but his father's resort, Zac could've happily stayed there indefinitely. As it was, he couldn't wait to get back to his small, comfy apartment back in Anchorage. His EMT salary wasn't huge, but it covered his bills, plus a few splurges. He'd walked away from his inheritance when he'd severed all ties to his family and he didn't miss it. Not too much, anyway.

They went back into the bedroom and found their luggage sitting neatly stacked atop the racks in the corner. The items he'd had delivered earlier—his tux and some additional shirts and suits—had been pressed and hung in the walk-in closet.

Money didn't buy happiness, but it did make life a bit easier sometimes.

"You're awfully quiet again." Carmen sat atop the bed, the expensive Egyptian cotton sheets rustling beneath her. "Having second thoughts?"

"No." Zac unzipped his bag. "Just tired."

"Hmm…" Carmen took off her boots, then removed her parka. "The welcome reception is at seven, which leaves us about three hours to kill."

"Good. I could use some time to relax and recharge before we deal with Lance and Priya again."

He headed for the dresser with an armload of socks and briefs, only to collide with Carmen halfway there.

"Sorry."

"My fault."

She stepped back slightly, but not before her heat penetrated his cotton shirt. Her breath caught and her wide eyes met his. Gauging her reaction, he saw he wasn't the only one feeling that flare of desire between them once more. The best thing to do would be to walk away, but he couldn't seem to get his feet to move.

"No problem."

His words emerged huskier than usual, and his gaze flickered to the bed before he could stop himself. He leaned in slightly, closing the distance between them. She was so close, so soft, so tempting… That was when he stopped. She also looked so…*nervous.*

Zac frowned and straightened. "Everything okay?"

Carmen nodded and held her hand over her heart.

Out of habit, Zac set his things aside, then took her wrist and checked her pulse—it was hard and fast.

"Listen, I would never force you to do anything you don't want—"

"I know that. It's fine. I just…" She exhaled and looked up at him. "My stomach's bothering me, that's all."

"You're not getting sick, are you?" He tilted his head slightly, concerned, and then felt her forehead. "I've got my EMT pack with me. Had it sent with my other stuff. I can get a thermometer and check if you give me a minute."

"No. I'm fine. It's just stress. With the conference and the job and this pretend engagement. Which is silly, right? I mean it was *my* idea, but now it seems a lot harder than I expected, and awkward, and…"

"No. It's not silly at all."

She was babbling—something he knew she did when she got flustered. Normally he found it endearing. But the fact it was happening now had his pulse speeding up too, with adrenaline and anticipation.

He tugged gently on her wrist, bringing her closer. "I know how you can get."

"It's crazy. I know," Carmen said. "I'm always cool, calm and collected. I shouldn't let any of this get to me. It's all pretend. It doesn't mean anything. It isn't—"

"Shh…" Zac placed a finger over her lips. "Just breathe. No pressure. Think of this as us just hanging out with the gang after work. Maybe we're at the Snaggle Tooth, having drinks after a shift. Talking, laughing, relaxing. Wendy's doing awful karaoke with Tom. Jake and Molly have the twins. It's all cool. No big deal at all…"

She nodded, inhaling deeply, her gaze locked with his.

"Good." He rubbed his thumb back and forth over the underside of the wrist to calm her pulse. "You are going to be great this weekend. You're smart and funny and the best damned midwife I've ever met." He smiled. "You've got this."

Carmen gave him another nod, her pulse slowing at last.

"That's it. Good. Relax and enjoy the weekend."

She exhaled slowly, her cheeks flushing a pretty shade of pink. "You're right. I got this."

"Yes, you do." He let her go before he couldn't, and reached for his stuff on top of the dresser. "Now, go have a nice hot bath to take the edge off. We'll talk some more when you're done."

A short while later Carmen sat in the tub with bubbles up to her neck, doing her best to forget the connection sizzling between her and Zac and failing miserably.

But indulging in fantasies about the man and their one night together was pointless. They wouldn't be repeating that here. She'd made her rules for a reason and it was high time she stuck to them.

Rules were what she lived by. Rules kept her safe.

Leaving things until the last minute and being spontaneous wasn't her thing. She liked her life all planned out.

Back in Trinidad, she'd made budgets and schedules to keep track of everything for their household, ensuring they had enough money to last each month. When she'd been in nursing school her organization skills had come in handy as well, juggling classes and jobs and internships.

Unfortunately those skills didn't translate well to love and emotion.

She'd tried to plan out her relationship with Steve, but he'd claimed she was too cold and calculating, always leading with her brain and not her heart.

The one time she'd tried leading with her heart had been the night of that party, with Zac, and, well…those results weren't exactly stellar. So, yeah. Maybe she should've just been up-front with the owners of the California clinic and told them the truth instead of a bunch of lies.

It was all just so stressful and sordid and screwed up. *Ugh.*

She reached over and hit the little button on the side of the tub to turn on the jets, then closed her eyes to shut out the world. The water hit her in all the right spots, easing the knots in the muscles of her back and shoulder blades and lulling her into a kind of half sleep.

She pictured Zac in the bedroom, standing so close to her she could see the tiny flecks of gold in his eyes, see the shadow of stubble on his jaw, hear the sharp intake of his breath as he leaned in.

Warmth spread outward from her core and moisture gathered between her legs. It had nothing to do with the bath water. She imagined his strong, capable hands taking the place of those jets. Pressure inside her built as memories of the two of them together in bed flashed into her mind. The heat of his skin beneath her fingertips, the hardness of his muscles pressed against her soft curves, the sound of his deep groans as he'd reached his ultimate pleasure…

Buzz, buzz, buzz…

The sound of her cell phone vibrating on the vanity jarred her back to reality. She shut off the jets, then quickly stood to grab a towel and wrap it around herself. Thankfully she managed to catch the caller ID and answer before they hung up.

"Carmen Sanchez," she said, taking a seat on the edge of the tub as it drained.

While the labor and delivery nurse from Anchorage Mercy on the other end of the line went over some new complications with one of her patients, Carmen pulled on a robe from the back of the door, then walked out of the bathroom—where she found Zac lying on the bed, his shirt and shoes off. Her mouth went dry as she stopped in the doorway, staring at his sculpted, toned torso.

Distracted, she lost track of the conversation on her phone. "I'm sorry. Could you repeat that, please?"

Zac looked up from the guest directory he was reading and narrowed his gaze. "Work?"

She nodded, her wicked thoughts in the tub flooding her brain again as she stared at his sleek, chiseled perfection. His dark skin glowed beneath the bedside lamp and she clenched her hand tight around the phone to keep herself from reaching for him.

"Nurse Davis? Hang on a moment, please. I need to write this down."

She covered the phone with one hand and hurried down the hall toward the front of the suite, praying Zac wouldn't follow. Because if he came after her now she wasn't sure she'd be able to resist, and resist she must. There was too much riding on this weekend to screw it up with sex and messy emotion.

Alone, Zac sank back down onto the end of the bed and scrubbed his hands over his head. What the hell had he been thinking, lounging around waiting for her to come out of the bathroom? This wasn't a couple's getaway. They were here to work. She was here to win the job of her dreams and he was here as her fake fiancé.

Still, when she'd come out in nothing but that robe, her mocha skin dewy and pink from her bath, her pretty eyes widening as she looked at him, he'd gotten so caught up in the moment it had been easy to forget all that other stuff.

Maybe it was the prospect of being stuck here in this suite with her for the next couple of days that made him start thinking about all the places on her he'd like to lick and suck. Places he remembered from their one-night stand that he definitely wouldn't mind revisiting— her lovely breasts, that spot just below her belly button that made her squirm if he teased it just right with his tongue...

Dammit.

This was ridiculous. He was a grown man—not some randy teenager.

Frustrated, he pushed to his feet and grabbed the resort directory again. There was plenty to do around here to keep him busy. It seemed his father had made plenty of upgrades in the twelve years since Zac had been gone. And if he didn't want to go out he could watch TV, order an in-room massage, check his emails and surf the internet...

Except none of those ideas appealed to him. He felt too restless to stay cooped up in here—especially with Carmen just down the hall in nothing but a robe. Besides, he wasn't one to sit around and wait. He liked *doing* things, being active.

That was why his career as an EMT suited him so well. Even when they didn't have a call he could restock the truck, take inventory, prep gear and equipment. Plus, there were always other people around. Zac didn't like to be alone. It allowed him to get in his own head too much, think about the past.

Decision made, Zac changed into jeans and a T-shirt, then pulled on socks and shoes before waving to Carmen as he passed and heading out of the room. Hoping to burn off some excess energy, he took the stairwell across the hall from the room and headed down to the lobby.

The first floor was as busy as ever when he arrived, filled with guests for the conference. That was good, because he didn't want to risk being recognized. He stuck to the outskirts of the room as he made his way over to the concierge's desk, scanning the crowds constantly for any sign of his parents, but thankfully finding none.

His father had used to be present for all major events at this resort, but perhaps that had changed. He probably had many more important jobs to do in his other hotels.

"How is your room, sir?" Willow asked as he approached the desk. "Anything I can assist you with?"

"Everything's great. Thanks." He glanced around him, then lowered his voice. "The other concierge you mentioned earlier—the one who works at night? Dustin? His last name doesn't happen to be Lewis, does it?"

She smiled. "It does. Do you know him?"

"Maybe."

Zac released a pent-up breath. Dustin Lewis had been

a good friend to him during his teens and he felt like the only person here he could trust now.

"You said he comes on duty at eight?"

"Yes, sir. But he's usually here early. Likes to socialize with the other staff before his shift." Willow chuckled. "Shall I page him for you?"

"No, no. That's fine." Zac looked around again. "If you tell me where he might be I can find him myself. Thanks."

"Try by the pool. He likes to sit out there and watch the sunset." Willow pointed to a hallway on the right. "Last door at the end."

"Great."

He headed out through the controlled chaos of the lobby and down a quieter corridor to the glass door at the end. The smell of chlorine stirred more memories of his childhood here. He'd learned to swim in this pool with his parents. His dad had taught him how to dive. He still remembered the joy on his father's face when he'd completed his first lap in under two minutes.

Good times. Until everything had gone bad.

Zac pulled open the door and walked into the heated glass atrium covering the Olympic-sized swimming pool. The air was more humid here, and his sinuses opened up as he took a deep breath.

Sure enough, he located Dustin on one of the lounge chairs on the far side of the otherwise deserted pool, staring out at the sky in the distance. It was still early, not even five yet, but this far north evening came early in March.

Not wanting to startle the older man, he stopped a short distance away and cleared his throat. "Been a while, Dustin."

"What the…?" Dustin sat forward and slowly turned,

his grin widening. "Zachary Taylor—get over here and give me a hug, boy. Where have you been keeping yourself?"

Zac embraced his friend, then took a seat on the edge of the chaise across from Dustin's. "I live in Anchorage now. Work as a paramedic."

"A paramedic? I always knew you were smart." Dustin nodded, his smile fading as his expression turned serious. "Your father know you're here?"

"No." Zac hung his head and rubbed his hand over the back of his neck. "And I'd prefer to keep it that way. Please don't say anything to him about seeing me, okay?"

"Your secret's safe with me. Besides, they don't live on this property anymore. Moved to that new place he bought in Chicago about a year ago. They stay in the penthouse suite there, from what I understand," Dustin said, narrowing his gaze on Zac as his smile returned. "So, tell me about yourself. You married? Got kids?"

"Neither." Zac's mind was still churning over the news that he might make it through this weekend without having to encounter his parents at all. He needed to make certain, though.

"Hmm…" The older man nodded slightly. "Too bad. About the kids, I mean. Always thought you'd make a great dad."

"Given the role model I had, I doubt it." Zac shrugged and peered at the darkening sky, at the streaks of gold and purple and bright red-orange fading into indigo. "How about you? How's Martha?"

A shadow of sadness passed over the older man's face. "My Martha passed away last year. Stroke. Took her fast, so for that I'm grateful."

"I'm so sorry." Zac reached over to place his hand on Dustin's shoulder. "I didn't know."

"How could you? You weren't here." Dustin exhaled slowly. "Anyway, kids and grandkids are doing well. Added another to the fold back in January. Little girl named Zoey."

"Congratulations." Zac waited while his friend brought up some pictures on his phone to show him. "Wow, she's beautiful. She's got your eyes."

"Yeah. Got my lungs too. Cries loud enough sometimes to be heard clear over in Siberia."

Zac chuckled. "Nice! Man, I miss seeing you around every day."

"Maybe you should come back more often, then."

Dustin clicked off his phone and shoved it in his pocket. That was when Zac noticed the white gauze wrapped around the older man's wrist, peeking out from beneath the cuff of his uniform dress shirt.

"Hurt yourself?" Zac asked.

"Huh?" Dustin frowned, then glanced at the bandage. "Oh, this. It's nothing. Cut myself on a knife making dinner the other day. No big deal."

From the dried blood stain on the gauze, it looked like some kind of a deal to Zac. "How's your diabetes?" he asked.

Dustin gave a dismissive wave. "Fine, fine… You trying to be my doctor now, boy?"

"No." Zac had caught the irritation in the older man's voice and he decided to keep the peace and let the matter drop—after one last thing. "But I *am* a trained medical caregiver. I'm just concerned about you, that's all. If you want me to take a look at that cut, let me know. Things heal slower because of your diabetes, remember?"

"I do. And I'm perfectly capable of taking care of myself. Been doing it long enough."

Zac shook his head and chuckled, leaning back in his

chair to gaze out the window as Dustin had been doing before. The sun had set now, and the first few stars were glimmering.

I'm perfectly capable of taking care of myself...

The fact that Carmen had said nearly those exact words to him wasn't lost on him. Neither was the fact that he needed to get back to the suite and get changed for the welcome reception soon.

"So, my parents aren't here at all this weekend, then?"

"Didn't say that. Only that they don't live here permanently anymore." Dustin reclined again in his own lounge chair and gave Zac a side-glance. "You know how your father is—doesn't like to leave anything to chance. With that big conference here this weekend, I wouldn't be surprised at all if he flies in for at least part of it. Why'd you come back, though, if not to see him and make amends? Your mother misses you terribly. Never talks about it, but I can tell."

Zac's heart nosedived a little at that. He missed his mother too. "I'm helping out a friend."

"Hmm... You always were thinking of others." Dustin shrugged. "Well, if you're trying to avoid your dad, I'd keep an eye out. Don't know his schedule, but he likes to lurk at big events."

Hopefully, with all the other attendees at the conference, he and Carmen would be able to blend into the crowd.

"How is she?" he asked.

"Your mother? Fine. They're both fine, far as I can tell. Not much changes around here, Zac—you know that." Dustin pointed out the window. "Same mountains, same snow, same glorious landscape. It's what I love about the place. Comforting to think that all places remain, regardless of what we do, constant and unchanging. Helps me not feel so lonely."

"Yeah…" Zac said, feeling a similar pang of yearning inside himself.

His self-reliance might come in handy on the job, but in his personal life it tended to isolate him. Hook-ups were easy to come by. Real intimacy that required trust and true vulnerability…? Not so much.

"Look, boy. Is this still about what happened with your father all those years ago? I know you were disappointed in him when he ran around with that other woman. I get it. I do. He's your dad. You idolized him. He made a mistake. But then we all have. He's human, Zac. Just like me. Just like you. Maybe you should—"

"I need to go."

Zac pushed to his feet, frowning down at Dustin. He loved his old friend, but the last thing he needed right now was a lecture on forgiving his father's past sins.

"I've got a reception tonight to get ready for."

"I'll come with you," Dustin said, getting up himself, ignoring Zac's offer of help.

Back in the day, the older man had used to tower over Zac. Now they were the same height, Dustin's proud shoulders bent by age.

"My shift starts soon," he said.

They walked back toward the entrance to the pool. Thankfully, Dustin let the matter of Zac's relationship with his dad drop. He held the door for Dustin, then followed him out into the hallway.

"If you change your mind about that cut, my friend and I are staying in the Yupik Suite. Come up anytime and I'll clean and dress it for you."

"Will do." Dustin shuffled along beside him on the plush carpeted floor. "And don't be a stranger this weekend. If you do run into your father let those old wounds heal, son. Life's too short. My Martha taught me that."

"Some wounds are too deep to heal," Zac said, stopping outside the door to the stairwell.

"Perhaps we just don't give them enough of a chance to get better. Things aren't always what they seem. Remember that. Nobody's perfect. Not even you, boy."

The older man looked at him a moment, before continuing on down the hall toward the lobby, speaking to Zac over his shoulder.

"See you around. Try and stay out of trouble while you're here."

"No point," he said, more to himself than anyone else, and then headed back to the room.

The truth was, Zac knew trouble had already come, right in the minute he'd agreed to come on this trip with Carmen. In hindsight, it would've been wiser to say no. But then he'd not exactly been thinking with the correct part of his anatomy when she'd asked him. Come to think of it, that happened most times when she was around.

Now they were here, and he was in too far to get out.

All he could do was keep moving forward until the weekend was done.

CHAPTER FIVE

ELLEN LANDON, SIXTY years old and the owner of the clinic in Big Sur, California, sat between Carmen and Priya at the welcome reception that night at their table for six.

Carmen had only seen photos of the woman online, and she'd always reminded her of a stately Dame Judi Dench. Despite approaching what some would consider retirement age, Ellen Landon showed no signs of slowing down. She kept as active and vibrant as many people twenty years younger, and showed no signs of selling her practice anytime soon.

Across from Ellen at the white-linen-covered table, between Zac and Lance, was Ellen's wife—an OB-GYN physician named Elizabeth Nguyen. Their progressive practice had helped pave the way for the future of midwifery in the state of California.

To work with two such pioneers in the field would be an honor—not to mention that mentorship from Ellen and her team alone would be worth more than gold. Of course the bump in pay and the promotion to clinic supervisor would be nice as well...

"I'm so glad you both made it to the conference," Ellen said, smiling at Carmen and Priya in turn on either side of her. "And it's so nice to meet your significant others as well. How long have you and your fiancé been dating, Carmen?"

"Not long, Ms. Landon," Carmen said, avoiding Priya's hawklike gaze from the other side of Ellen. "We've been seeing each other for a few months."

"Yes, it happened *so* fast," Priya said, narrowing her gaze on Carmen. "Took us all by surprise."

"Sure did," Lance said from across the table, elbowing Zac in the arm. "Man, if I'd known you two were hot and heavy after the Christmas party I would've been all over that."

"That's exactly why we didn't tell you," Zac said, giving his friend a flat stare.

"That's wonderful. I do love a whirlwind romance. And, please, call me Ellen," the older woman said, seemingly oblivious to the tension around the table. "Congratulations on your engagement, Carmen. Such an exciting time in life. I remember when Liz and I were planning our wedding. So much to do…so little time. And you, Priya. How long have you and Lance been together?"

"Almost a year." Priya kept her gaze steady on Carmen. "We're taking our time with things—not rushing. I prefer to plan, so I don't miss anything important. It must be hard for you, Carmen, having it sprung on you like that. I always thought we were alike when it came to organization. I mean, there's so much to do…so many details."

Forcing the knots in her stomach to ease, Carmen plastered on her best smile. "Yes, you're right. I do like to plan everything out. But love is what it is."

"Hmm…" Suspicion gleamed in Priya's dark eyes. "What date have you set for the wedding?"

"Oh, we haven't really gotten that far yet. Just enjoying the moment for now."

"Sure..." Priya sounded completely unconvinced. She exchanged a quick glance with Lance, then looked back at Carmen. "What about a dress? Flowers? Venue? You should start planning all that before you even set a date. What's Zac's favorite color?"

Carmen's mind raced through the facts on the sheet he'd given her. "Blue."

"Favorite food?"

"Anything Mexican."

"Favorite movie?"

"*Die Hard.*"

Carmen's stomach clenched. This was worse than the lightning round on her mother's favorite TV game show. She swallowed hard against the lump of stress in her throat. Beneath the table Zac took her hand for moral support.

"What does his favorite movie have to do with our wedding?"

"Nothing," Priya said, giving her a sly smile. "Just asking."

"How are the suites?"

Ellen switched subject and Carmen couldn't have been more relieved.

"Ours is beautiful."

"Our room is gorgeous, thanks. This whole resort is amazing—don't you think, *doux-doux*?" Carmen gave Zac's hand a squeeze.

"Yes, gorgeous," Zac said, his gaze locked on her. "Very lovely indeed."

A fresh wave of heat danced over her skin, this time nothing to do with embarrassment and everything to do with the man beside her—which was bad. Very, very bad.

She was here to impress Ellen Landon, not to flirt with Zac.

"Mr. Taylor?" Ellen said. "You're a paramedic?"

"Yes, ma'am." He sipped his Scotch. "Best EMT in Anchorage. And please call me Zac."

"Zac, then." The older woman nodded. "I bet you could swap some stories with my wife. She's always telling me horror stories from her shifts in the ER."

"I'm sure I could," he said, shifting his attention to Liz. "Do you work at a large facility?"

Grateful to have the spotlight off her, Carmen took a deep breath and smoothed her hand down the front of her simple black dress. It was far from revealing, even with its thin straps that left her shoulders bare. But with the sizzling looks Zac kept giving her tonight she felt as if he could see right through it.

Talk about making a girl feel like the belle of the ball.

She tried not to read too much into it, though. He was probably just pulling from his usual bag of tricks to get through this weekend.

Thankfully, a server arrived with the first course of their catered gourmet meal—zucchini carpaccio with salt-broiled shrimp—and saved her from a further round of Twenty Questions from Priya.

As they ate, Ellen turned the conversation to business.

"Both your résumés are quite accomplished and interesting," Ellen said. "But it was the presentations each of you submitted for the direction you'd like to take the clinic in for the future that I found most intriguing." She ate a bite of her salad before continuing. "They were the reason each of you were chosen as finalists for the position. In the end, however, there's only one position available. It's all we can allow for in the budget right now. So I'd like you each to talk more about your plans for the training program. Priya, why don't you start?"

"My concentration would be on preventing gestational

diabetes and hyperactive disorders with screening and integrative management in early pregnancy. In my experience, the pathogenesis of these conditions is multifactorial, and includes lifestyle factors such as nutrition, stress level and stress management resources, and physical activity…"

As her colleague discussed her ideas for the new California clinic, Carmen nibbled on her salad. She'd barely taken more than a few bites, though, before Zac shifted in his seat and his thigh brushed against hers. Zings of fresh electricity jolted through her system and memories of them in the suite after her bath, with her in just a robe and him naked from the waist up, filled her head before she could stop them.

"And you, Carmen?" Ellen asked. "Can you talk about your training plans, please?"

Focus, girl. Focus.

"Sure, yes," Carmen said.

She gave herself a firm mental warning to stay out of Smutty Land where Zac was concerned. It was time to dazzle with her amazing midwifery ideas, not dream about tackling Zac into bed and having her wicked way with him.

"My main focus would be on providing a framework to assist midwives in developing a consistent approach to screening for perinatal mood and anxiety disorders. I'd like to develop brief interventions and strategies for referral, response to emergent situations, and a followup to ensure continuity of care."

"Both of those ideas are excellent," Ellen said. "My plan is to have whoever takes over the management of the midwife staff at the clinic helping to design and implement the new training courses *you* discussed, Carmen, and also to develop an innovative screening and prevention planning program aiming to reduce the incidence and severity of the conditions *you* mentioned, Priya."

"I've been reading up on those conditions myself," Carmen said, congratulating herself on sounding competent and professional, instead of showing the mass of quivering nerves she felt inside.

She didn't even feel bad about elbowing her way into Priya's topic. This was, after all, a competition—even if they were friends. She wanted to show Ellen that by hiring her she'd get someone knowledgeable on both topics.

"The articles I've read suggest including standardized screenings and prevention programs based on a patient's risk level, then incorporating medical management, education and lifestyle interventions. Through my own research I've identified at least three evidence-based prevention strategies for lowering patient risk of gestational diabetes and/or hypertensive disorders. I look forward to presenting you both with a detailed, comprehensive outline at my final interview."

Not to be outshone, Priya launched into a spiel on midwife management of pelvic organ prolapse across a patient's lifespan. By the time she'd finished, their main course had arrived—braised pork with pearl onions and grapes.

Zac was being Mr. Charming, as usual, and even if the rest of the weekend went to hell in a handbasket Carmen knew that at least she'd gotten the best out of him in the schmoozing department. Every once in a while, though, she caught him scanning the crowd, as if looking for someone. Which was odd, since neither of them had been to the resort before.

Then she remembered Lance mentioning Zac had been off his game recently and that he wasn't seeing anyone at present. Was he looking to hook up with someone here?

The man was drop-dead gorgeous, and smart and funny, and any woman would be lucky to have him, and…

Ugh.

Thinking about that would get her nowhere but depressed. Which was silly, because she and Zac weren't really a couple. She had no right to be jealous of him seeing other people—even if he was supposed to pretend to be hers for the weekend.

So why does the idea of him fawning over someone else bug me so much?

Maybe because, deep down, she wanted to find someone who'd fawn over *her* that way?

Dessert was served at last—slices of hazelnut-and-chocolate meringue cake—and a small band in the corner began to play. Several couples from the surrounding tables headed for the dance floor in front of the stage, and Zac held his hand out to her.

"Carmen, dance with me."

She excused herself and let him lead her to the dance floor. He took her in his arms once they found an open spot amongst the other couples swaying to the music. It all seemed a bit surreal—him looking like he'd just stepped off the cover of a magazine in his fancy tuxedo instead of the bland EMT uniform he usually wore for work.

Then he pulled her closer and his scent surrounded her—soap, sandalwood, and a hint of vanilla. *Delicious.* Her first instinct was to bury her face in the side of his neck and inhale deeply. Then she remembered where they were, and who they were, and remained a respectable distance away.

"Dinner went pretty well, I think," he said against her temple.

"Yes. Thank goodness for those dossiers."

"Right… Even if mine *was* on the skimpy side."

His legs brushed against hers and the simmering attraction inside her boiled higher.

"I memorized yours, just in case," he said.

She laughed. "Okay. When's my birthday?"

"August twelfth."

"Favorite song?"

He tilted his head slightly and smiled. "This one, as a matter of fact. 'The Way You Look Tonight.' Though you prefer the Michael Bublé version. Why do you think I asked you to dance?"

"Smooth." She rested her forehead against his chest so he wouldn't see how much he'd touched her heart. "Favorite color?"

"Purple. Lavender, to be exact."

"Middle name?"

"Ramona. After your mother."

"Wow. You *are* good."

"That's what all the ladies say," he joked.

She leaned back and smacked his arm. "Thanks for the reminder."

That was when she noticed him nodding to an elderly African-American gentleman with white hair, standing near the service entrance.

"Who is that?" Carmen asked, curious.

"Dustin—the night concierge. I met him earlier, while you were running around the resort in your robe."

"I was not running around in my robe." Carmen gave him a look, biting back a smile at the teasing look in his eyes, happier than she cared to admit about having his full attention back on her. "I had to deal with that call about my patient. Everything's fine there, by the way."

"Never doubted it for a minute."

He chuckled, the deep, rich sound reverberating through her like honey.

"Even if you *were* working in your robe."

"What is it with you and my robe?" She shook her head and grinned. "What difference does it make anyway? They couldn't see me. As long as the patient was treated properly, that's all that matters."

"Hmm…" He steered them into a quieter corner of the dance floor and bent slightly to put his mouth near her ear. "Well, all I can say is I'm glad none of the other men from Anchorage Mercy can see you here tonight. Because you're beautiful, Carmen, and I don't want to share."

Zac held Carmen closer than was probably wise as they swayed to the music in the shadows, deep in the crowd and yet far away from the prying eyes of the rest of their table.

Honestly, at that moment Carmen could have got any man to do whatever she wanted. That dress of hers should be illegal in all fifty states. The black silky material clung to her curves enough to hint at the glory beneath without giving anything away. Tiny straps over her shoulders led to a V-shaped neckline that revealed just a tantalizing hint of her perfect cleavage. The skirt fell to mid-thigh, showing enough shapely leg to make him picture everything underneath.

She wore her hair up tonight, although a few of her curls had managed to escape and dangle around her face and throat, and her remarkable green-gold eyes sparkled with intelligence and determination. She was a woman to be reckoned with, and so lovely it almost hurt to look at her.

"Have I told you how beautiful you look tonight?"

"You did—thank you." She beamed up at him and

smoothed her hand down his tux-covered chest. "You look pretty spectacular yourself."

He smiled. This felt good—right—being here with her like this. If things had been different—if he'd been a different man, a better man—he'd have asked her to be his, and not just for the weekend either. But he was who he was, and he had a past she knew nothing about.

He managed to mumble, "Thanks."

The band finished the song and began another—one of his favorites this time. "Unforgettable" by Nat King Cole. He kept reminding himself that this was all for show, but it was getting harder to remember as they rocked gently on the dance floor. He couldn't help pulling her a bit closer, until she rested her head on his chest and the sweet jasmine fragrance of her hair tickled his nose.

"I like dancing with you," he said. Lame, considering he'd like to do a lot more than just dance with her, but it would have to do.

"I like dancing with you too," she whispered. "This is nice."

"Nice" didn't begin to cover what he felt, holding her in his arms. He wanted to pick her up and carry her back to their room, make love to her all night long, but unfortunately after the song ended, reality returned. The couples around them began to leave the dance floor and Zac forced himself to step back, away from temptation.

"We should…uh…probably get back to the table, so you can dazzle your new bosses some more."

Carmen sighed and nodded, frowning down at her shoes. "Yes, we probably should."

By the time they weaved their way back to the table it was just Ellen and Liz there, discussing their favorite vacation spots around the world. Growing up, Zac had traveled extensively with his father, to visit all of his hotel and resort holdings. He'd never thought it would come in handy, but if it helped win Carmen her dream job he'd add what he could to the conversation.

"Where are Priya and Lance?" Carmen asked as she took her seat.

"Oh, Priya wasn't feeling well all of a sudden," Ellen said. "Lance took her to the restroom. I do hope she's all right."

"Maybe I should go check on her," Carmen said.

Before she could get up, however, Lance and Priya returned, to take their seats once more. Priya looked a little pale, and Lance didn't appear much better.

"Everything all right?" Carmen asked.

"Yes, fine. Thanks." Priya kept ahold of Lance's hand. "What are we discussing?"

"Vacation destinations," Liz said.

"Awesome," Lance said. "Anyone ever been to Italy?"

"I have," Zac said. "Florence is one of my favorite places on earth—other than Barcelona."

"What about you, Carmen?" Priya asked. "Travel much?"

"Not really. Unless you count moving my family here from Trinidad after nursing school," she said, crossing her legs toward Zac and giving him another glimpse of those gorgeous legs. "I was always too busy working to go on vacation."

"Well, maybe you can plan a nice trip for your honeymoon," Ellen suggested. "Liz and I went to South America on ours. Rio, Costa Rica, Belize… Beautiful area."

"Yes, that would be nice," Carmen said. She exchanged a glance with Zac.

A buzz of conversation had started near the entrance to the banquet room and suddenly Zac caught sight of his parents entering. *Damn.* Time to leave.

He stood and helped a surprised Carmen to her feet. "We should go back to our room," he said, pushing to his feet. "Early start for you tomorrow. You need to get your rest. Ellen and Liz—it was a pleasure meeting you both, and thank you so much for everything this weekend."

Ellen stood as well and shook his hand. "Glad you're enjoying it, Zac. Be sure to take advantage of some of the amenities while you're here, since we'll be keeping Carmen busy for the next few days."

"I'll do that. I wouldn't want to distract her with such an important job on the line." Zac flashed them his most charming smile and then he slipped his arm around Carmen's shoulders and tugged her into his side, kissing the top of her head while keeping an eye on the exit. "Ready, darling?"

Carmen gave him a confused look. "What's going—"

He kissed her soundly, cutting her off. By the time he lifted his head she was blushing, he was breathless, and everyone at the table was watching them with a knowing gleam in their eye.

"You can stay here if you want," he said at last, a bit stunned himself by the heat of their kiss. "I just really want to go back to our room."

"I bet you do," Lance whispered slyly.

Zac gave his friend a withering stare. "I'm tired."

"Sure you are." Priya shook her head and took her fiancé's hand. "I think we'll head up to *our* room too. Long day tomorrow."

"I guess we'll all make an early night of it, then," Ellen said, putting her arm around Liz. "See you all in the morning."

"Good night," Zac said, and managed to steer Carmen out through a side entrance to the ballroom just as his parents drew too near for comfort.

With his hand on her lower back, Zac hurried Carmen toward the elevators.

"What's happening here?" she asked, after pushing the "Up" button. "You're acting strangely."

"Nothing. Nothing's wrong," he said, jamming his finger on the button himself, as if that would make it come faster.

His chest had constricted and he felt like he couldn't breathe, as if the walls were closing in, as memories of that final argument with his father flashed in his mind.

"Are you tired?" he asked.

"No, but I thought *you* were." She crossed her arms and stepped back as the elevator dinged and the doors opened. "That's why we're leaving, right?"

He exhaled slowly and boarded the elevator after her, hitting the number for their floor. "Actually, I could use some air. Maybe we could get out of here and check out some of the grounds of the resort before bed? Since you'll be cooped up indoors for the conference most of the time."

"Oh…" She fiddled with her small evening bag. "I suppose we could take a short walk."

"Great." They arrived on their floor and Zac shrugged out of his tux jacket as they walked to their room. "Let's change—then we'll go exploring."

CHAPTER SIX

CARMEN STILL WASN'T sure exactly where they were going when she came out of the bathroom a short while later, dressed in jeans and a blue turtleneck sweater. "Ready. Hope this is warm enough for where we're going."

"You're dressed fine. I thought we'd just walk around the grounds," Zac said.

He brushed her hands aside when she reached up to remove the pins from her hair. The backs of his fingers brushed the sensitive skin at the nape of her neck, and she shivered as he ran his hands through her curls.

"Blow off some steam...work off some energy. Relax...talk."

"Talk about what?" she asked as he helped her on with her coat and then shrugged into his own before taking her hand.

Normally she wasn't the best follower—especially with men who were far too charming for their own good. From the stories she'd heard, her father had been a smooth-talking playboy, and look how that had ended for her mother.

"Maybe we should just stay here and go to bed early. You're right. I do have an early start tomorrow."

He sighed and scrubbed a hand over his face, and she noticed faint lines of tension around his eyes that hadn't been there before. He looked as on edge as she'd felt at dinner. Maybe a bit of time away wouldn't hurt after all.

"Stay in the room if you want, Carmen," he said. "But I'm going. I need some air, like I said. And I thought you might enjoy some quiet time to reflect after the grilling you got at dinner tonight. Plus, we can to go over our fact sheets again—make sure we've got all the details memorized correctly in case Priya and Lance decide to quiz us again."

Maybe he was right. That interrogation at the dinner table had been pretty intense. Besides, her body was still humming with energy after dancing with him. There was no way she'd be able to sleep until she'd worked some of it off.

"Okay. Fine. Let's go."

Zac opened the door to their suite and led her out of the room. "Are you hungry?"

"We just ate."

"No. Everyone else at our table ate." They stood before the elevator once more. "You barely touched your food. Do you skip meals a lot?"

Surprised, she blinked up at him. Most people didn't ask about her needs at all. She was there to help *them*. "No, not often. But I was nervous, meeting Ellen face-to-face for the first time. I'm surprised you noticed."

"I notice everything about you."

He gave her a toe-curling smile, raising his hand to brush an errant curl behind her ear.

"I noticed that while you picked up your wineglass a lot you only sipped from it rarely. I've noticed that you avert your gaze when you're embarrassed or ashamed— like when you mentioned the only traveling you'd done was moving your family from Trinidad to Alaska." He traced his fingertips from her ear down her cheek, then skimmed his thumb along her jawline. "That's nothing to be embarrassed about. You worked hard to get where you are."

She swallowed hard, her heart racing. "I'm not embarrassed. I just don't like talking about myself."

"Same," he murmured as the elevator bell dinged.

They rode down to the lobby, then headed outside into the brisk, clear night. The walking trails surrounding the lodge were well lit and well maintained. The snow crunched beneath her boots as they headed off into the night, with what looked like a million stars shining above them.

After about ten minutes of walking through the silent forest, where the smell of spruce was fresh in the air, Carmen couldn't contain her curiosity anymore.

She shoved her hands into the pockets of her parka for warmth, since she'd left her gloves back in the room. "You said you wanted to talk. How about telling me why you were so cagey at dinner earlier? You kept scanning the dining room like you expected your worst enemy to walk in at any moment."

He glanced over at her, frowning. "I wasn't doing that."

"Yes, you were." Carmen stepped sideways to avoid tripping over an exposed tree root, then slowed as they approached a bubbling stream partially covered with ice. "Are you sure you know where you're going? I don't want to spend the night out here, walking in circles."

"Trust me."

The certainty in his tone made her want to do just that—which only set off those warning bells in her head again.

Zac took her hand and led her a short way down to a spot where they could both jump across the water easily.

Apparently he'd forgotten his gloves too, since his bare fingers were warm and steady around hers.

"It's not much farther. Over that next hill. Don't worry, I won't let you get lost in the wild tundra. An island girl like you wouldn't last an hour out here alone."

"Island girl?" She snorted. "I'm tougher than I look. Like I said, I can take care of myself, thanks. And there's nothing out here as scary as a drunk frat boy who won't take no for an answer."

Zac scowled over at her. "When did *that* happen?"

"When I was bartending at a hotel in Port of Spain. Rich college kids used to flock there in their droves during spring break. The resort had security, but sometimes they'd wait for us to get off work, thinking we were included in the free perks."

She shuddered, remembering the night one of those guys had approached her in the parking lot.

"But I took self-defense classes at my neighborhood youth center in Laventille when I was a teenager. A few well-placed elbow jabs and instep stomps do wonders to change a man's mind when he's amorous."

"I'm sorry that happened to you." He kept hold of her hand once they were across the stream. "Some men don't care about anyone but themselves."

His somber tone had her thinking that perhaps he wasn't only thinking about *her* past.

"Did you go to college?" she asked.

"University of Alaska at Anchorage."

She smiled. "That's where I got my graduate degree. What was your major?"

"I graduated in Pre-Med."

They continued up a small hill.

"You studied to be a doctor? Why did you end up as a paramedic?"

"I didn't 'end up' as a paramedic. I *chose* to be a para-medic. There's a difference."

She didn't miss the defensiveness in his voice.

"I love what I do and, like I said, I'm the best EMT in Anchorage. I love being on the front line, helping people in the worst times of their life. Having an MD after my name wouldn't change that. Do you feel 'less than' be-cause you're a midwife and not an OB physician?"

"No, of course not." She cringed slightly. "Sorry. I didn't mean to offend you."

He sighed. "I'm sorry too. Didn't mean to snap at you."

Silence fell as they crested the top of the hill and she looked down to see rows of pens filled with animals. A couple of large buildings were outlined near the back of the area—offices, she supposed. They were dark, obvi-ously closed this late at night. It had to be close to mid-night now.

Mournful cries from the caged wolves below filled the air and Carmen swiveled toward Zac, grinning. "A zoo? In the middle of a resort?"

"Rehab center." His breath frosted on the air as he surveyed the space below them. "All the animals here are native to the area. Some have been injured and are being rehabilitated before being released back into the wild. Some of them are permanent residents, unable to be returned to nature. The keepers here use the perma-nent residents to teach kids in the local schools. C'mon. Let's check it out."

She followed him down the trail to the pens, amazed that he knew so much about this place. It was far enough away from the main resort that it would be hard to find by chance.

They passed enclosures holding elk and moose and reindeer. The wolves were down near the end of the row.

"Tell me how you knew this was here," she said.

"Guest directory," he said, walking over to pet the snout of a curious moose near the fencing. "Figured you might enjoy it. I love being outdoors."

"Me too." She picked up some hay from a bale nearby and held it out for one of the elks to take. "When I was back home in Trinidad I used to spend every free hour I could at the beach, watching the gulls and the dolphins and the pelicans playing offshore."

"You must miss all that warmth and sunshine this far north."

"Sometimes." She laughed as the elk nuzzled her palm, looking for more food. "But as long as my family is close—that's most important."

"Yeah…" He didn't sound convinced. "Family. What about California? If you get the job you'll be moving. Will they come with you?"

"That's the plan." Carmen glanced back at him over her shoulder. "Doesn't it bother you? Not being close with your family?"

"Not really. I miss my mother sometimes." Zac dusted his hands off on his jeans. "But it's fine. I like being independent."

"Don't you get lonely, though? Twelve years is a long time to be without family."

Taking care of her mother was difficult sometimes, with her dementia, and she and Clara sometimes fought too, but Carmen couldn't imagine living without them as a part of her life.

"Not really. I mean, that's what I have friends for, right?"

They continued on down the path through the pens, with everything quiet and peaceful around them. From the way Zac was avoiding her gaze she could tell he wanted her to drop the subject, but she just couldn't. Not yet.

"Do they live in Anchorage?"

"Who?"

"Your parents."

"No." He shrugged then shook his head. "Wouldn't matter if they did. I still wouldn't talk to my father."

She took that in for a moment, along with his troubled expression, the edge of hurt in his tone. "Well, I'm sorry for whatever happened between the two of you. What about your mother? I'm sure she misses you."

"She's the reason I left. She forgave my father for his affair. I couldn't. He broke my mother's heart. She was able to get past it, but I wasn't. To keep the peace, I left." He exhaled slowly and turned around on the path. "We should get back—it's cold out here."

Carmen trailed behind him as some things about Zac began to click into place for her. His avoidance of commitment. His fierce loyalty to his friends and his patients. His serial dating to avoid anything permanent, to avoid making the same mistakes his father had made.

Not that she felt comfortable expressing those opinions to Zac at the moment. Besides, his tone at the end had effectively slammed the door on any further conversation on the topic, which was probably for the best. Honestly, she should let it go. After this weekend they'd go their separate ways again and it wouldn't matter.

But there was something…the flicker of anger and betrayal in his eyes when he'd mentioned his father's affair.

The image he portrayed in Anchorage was always so carefree and laid-back. Now she knew it masked a deep pain and it made her feel closer to him—even closer than when they'd slept together. Because he didn't share pieces of his past often. Maybe that was why she continued to be so drawn to him. He remained an enigma, and she'd always loved solving a puzzle.

In fact, her problem-solving skills were part of the reason she was so good at her job. Putting the pieces of her patients' cases and health histories together to ensure the best outcome possible. She wondered if those same skills would work as well with Zac.

Once they'd reached the top of the hill, they stopped to look down on the animals again. A shimmer of green in the sky caught her attention. She'd seen the Northern Lights several times since moving to Anchorage, but never this vividly. Soon the entire sky was awash with hypnotic waves of greens and light blues and pinks.

"Breathtaking..." she whispered, staring up into the night sky.

"Yes, it is," he said, but he was looking at her and not at the heavenly show above them.

Time seemed to slow as Zac took Carmen in his arms, his lips brushing hers once, twice, before settling on her mouth. She gasped and he took advantage, shifting closer to deepen the kiss. He tasted of Scotch and sugar and sinful fantasy.

She'd sworn not to kiss him again, to keep things strictly platonic, but this was so perfect. *Too* perfect. His kiss was as good as she remembered, and so was the hot, solid press of him against her. She slid her fingers up his chest to twine them around his neck and a low moan escaped her throat. At the rough sound, his hands slid from her waist down to her lower back, allowing her to feel the extent of his arousal.

Heat raced through her blood despite the chilly breeze and her knees trembled. If they'd been back in their suite she'd have pushed him down on the bed and had her wicked way with him, despite her vows to the contrary.

Unfortunately, they weren't in their room. They were out in the snow and the wolves were howling and her toes were numb from the cold.

Finally she forced herself to step back and gather what was left of her common sense. They'd had a fling once. She didn't want to do that again. She had too much going on as it was. Even if Zac wanted forever this time—which he didn't—given his reputation, she wasn't interested.

Am I?

No. She was not. Because that would be stupid. Ridiculous. She knew darned well what men like Zac wanted and it wasn't commitment. Then again, *she* didn't want that either, did she? That was why she'd brought him on this trip. Their fling had been nice—hot, even—but it had been just that: a fling.

She had big things ahead of her—the possibility of this new job, goals she wanted to accomplish—and getting herself locked down into a serious relationship with a man wouldn't help her reach any of those things, would it? No, it would not. Never mind that her heart yearned for more.

So, no matter how tempting Zac and the idea of being with him permanently might be, she'd let him walk away when it was over because that was what was best for everyone.

"C'mon. Let's get back to the hotel."

Zac wasn't a stupid man. He knew as soon as Carmen ended their kiss that it was a mistake. She deserved a man who could devote himself to her one hundred percent. A man with no secrets.

That wasn't him.

Dammit.

He'd agreed to come this weekend because he'd

thought it would be simple. Easy in, easy out. Easy enough to avoid his family and his past and to help her out along the way. He was finding out now that it wouldn't be.

Not that he'd come face-to-face with his father, but the man and his sins still lingered over the place and over Zac like a shroud. Carmen had been right. He *had* been on guard at dinner, waiting for an enemy—his own father. He'd managed to avoid the man for twelve years. He didn't plan to end that streak this weekend.

He knew she'd been curious about him earlier, asking all her questions. And he feared he'd been rude by not answering. But it couldn't be helped. He didn't let people close. He'd been there, done that, and had the scorch marks on his heart from getting burned by his father's deception.

Because when you let people in, allowed them into your life and your heart, you only ended up being disappointed and hurt. Never mind that he might be setting his standards too high, setting himself and everyone he cared for up to fail. He was safe, his heart was secure, and that was all that mattered. He'd made the mistake of trusting people, loving people before, with his father, and it had ripped him to shreds. So, no. He wouldn't be doing that again.

Besides, he had no business being attracted to Carmen anyway. They were friends, work colleagues. And yes, for one brilliant night they'd been lovers. But that was over. There was no point letting her in and baring his soul to her.

She was the opposite of the women he usually got involved with. She was smart. She was tough. She was proud and perfect and passionate. She'd clawed her way up from nothing to make a life for herself and her family. The thought of that frat boy attacking her back in Trinidad had him clenching his fists at his sides. If he'd been there he'd have flayed that guy alive.

But now he needed to stick to their original plan. Play his part and keep his hands to himself from here on out. He'd opened up a bit to Carmen tonight, but that would be all. It didn't matter that she was full of surprises—like the way she'd run around the hotel in nothing but a robe… Like the way she'd felt against him as they'd danced… Like the way she'd responded so passionately to his kiss.

Forget about the fact that he wanted to know what else she might do. Or say. Or if he could make her moan again like he had that night they'd spent together.

Damn.

If he wasn't careful he might lose more than his head when he was with Carmen, and that scared him most of all. Even months ago, at the party, his mind buzzing with alcohol and his blood burning with desire, he'd had an inkling that she was pretty perfect. Down-to-earth, straightforward, simple. *Real.* Everything he secretly craved.

Honestly, he was tired of superficial flings. He was tired of playing the player. He wanted more. Even though he believed deep down inside that he'd never get more. He came from bad stock. Stock that didn't measure up. Stock that couldn't be faithful if its life depended on it.

Maybe he hadn't slept with anyone since Carmen after that holiday party. And, yes, perhaps that did qualify as being monogamous. But it wasn't really a conscious choice he'd made. It was a happy accident. It didn't matter that she seemed to be the only woman he craved now. That wasn't a sign of there being something more between him and Carmen. It certainly didn't mean he'd somehow fallen for her, did it?

His heart pounded as he remembered the way his

nerves had tingled from her touch, the sweet, soft sound of her moans, the dreamy glazed look in her eyes after their kiss.

Oh, God.

The realization struck him like a brick upside the head. He needed to be on guard even more this weekend. Because in some ways Carmen could hurt him far worse than his father ever had.

He cared about her—about what she thought and felt.

His father had killed any good feelings Zac had had toward him the day he'd admitted his infidelity and wounded Zac's mother to the core. Why she'd stayed married to him after that was a mystery to him, even though it had proved her loyalties to Zac.

But if she'd been willing to stay, then he'd had to go. He hadn't been able to stand to be in the same room with the man, let alone listen to more of his apologies and excuses.

He'd grown up with people constantly comparing him to his father, saying how alike they were, how they were cut from the same cloth. For years the young Zac had considered it a compliment. Hell, he'd aspired to be just like his old man. Until the day news of his father's affair had broken in the tabloids and he'd been forced to tell the truth to his wife and son.

Zac's world had gone from heaven to hell in the span of a few hours. This man, his father, a guy he'd loved and practically worshipped, wasn't the paragon Zac had held him up to be. Turned out he was human after all—and a horrible human at that. Why else would his father have been so selfish, so deceitful, ripping his close-knit family apart and shattering the very people he'd claimed to care for most in the world?

No. Love got you nothing but pain and heartache. Best to steer well clear of all of it.

They'd reached the stream again and Zac took Carmen's hand to help her across. Her skin felt silky and smooth against his and he battled a fresh wave of desire.

But he wasn't his father. He wouldn't take what he wanted just because he could. He let her go immediately they reached the other side. And increased his pace back toward the hotel—at least until she stopped him in his tracks.

She called from behind him, "Why did you kiss me?"

Zac hesitated and closed his eyes, then swiveled to face her. "Is this a trick question?"

"No. But you're hiding something, Zac Taylor." She stood before him, gaze narrowed, as the lights from the resort glowed brighter around her. "I don't know what it is, but I'm going to find out—I promise you that. You keep too many secrets. It's not good for a man."

With that, she took off ahead of him, back up the path and into the hotel, leaving Zac to stare after her and wonder how the hell he was ever going to get out of this weekend unscathed.

CHAPTER SEVEN

BRIGHT AND EARLY the next morning, Carmen sat in her first seminar of the day, coffee in hand. The room was packed with people, including Ellen and Liz, who were sitting in the front, and Priya, who was in the chair next to Carmen's.

"Reducing cesareans is a priority for healthcare and professional organizations. And labor dystocia is the leading cause of cesareans. Delaying hospital admission until active labor is established is one evidence-based method to decrease labor dystocia diagnoses. Evidence is lacking on how best to accomplish this, but several interventions have been studied, including admission algorithms and patient and staff education. This presentation will show the results of one quality improvement project whose aim was to reduce early labor admissions and support physiologic birth through implementing evidence-based tools, and thereby decrease the nulliparous term singleton vertex cesarean rate..."

The nurse practitioner giving the talk droned on, and while Carmen found the topic interesting and informative she feared there wasn't enough caffeine in the world to keep her awake for the next two hours. After those late-night shenanigans with Zac she'd not slept well last night, tossing and turning and replaying that stupid kiss they'd shared over and over in her head.

What the hell had she been thinking, kissing him back?

It had been stupid. It had been wrong. It had been incredibly tempting.

Ugh. She had no business making out with Zac when it would never go anywhere—because it *couldn't* go anywhere. They were both established in their lives. She had her career track and he had his. Yes, they'd had sex once. Yes, it had been amazing. No, it wouldn't happen again. Even if this would be the perfect time for one last hurrah, so to speak.

You're leaving. He's available. The two of you have that whole suite to yourselves...

"So, what did you and Zac do after you left the dinner last night?" Priya whispered from beside her at the table. "Lance and I stopped by your suite, but no one answered."

"We went for a walk," Carmen said, fiddling with the notepad she'd brought with her, trying to concentrate on the speaker again. "We needed to burn off some excess energy."

"Right!" Priya chuckled. "I saw how the two of you were dancing together. I did doubt your engagement, but there's no doubting you two are hot for each other."

Heat prickled Carmen's cheeks as she scribbled unintelligible notes with her pen. "Sorry, I'm trying to hear this."

Priya gave her a side-glance and shook her head. "Right..."

"We've developed several novel tools, including an early labor triage guide, labor support checklist and early labor walking path. The triage algorithm reduced early labor admission from forty-one percent to twenty-five percent, and physiologic birth increased by two percent during the intervention. Patient experience satisfaction rates were highly positive, exceeding ninety-eight percent. The NTSV cesarean rate reduced slightly, from twenty-two percent to twenty-one percent, during this eight-week project," the presenter was saying.

Carmen did her best to catch up. And by the time she'd taken copious notes and followed along with an opportunity to explore her own clinical setting for gaps in practice and barriers to implementation, considering how to implement the new information at Anchorage Mercy, the time had passed quickly. There was a question-and-answer session at the end, followed by a break before the next session.

Priya made a beeline for Ellen and Liz, but Carmen held back a moment, wanting to collect her thoughts before approaching her potential new employers again. Besides, she needed to use the restroom.

She walked out of the bathroom to find Zac flagging her down. "Hey, what's up?" she asked as he approached.

"Do you have another seminar to get to right away?"

Carmen checked her watch. "Not for another twenty minutes. What do you need?"

"An extra set of hands." He took her by the elbow and guided her to the elevators. "I've got a friend who needs an I&D in the suite and I could use someone to help with the procedure."

"An incision and drainage?" She wrinkled her nose as the elevator dinged and Zac tugged her on board. "Here? Do you have the equipment to do that? Maybe your friend should go to the hospital to have it checked out."

"It's Dustin—the concierge you saw last night. He

refuses to go. Plus, he's diabetic." Zac punched the button for their floor.

"And you tell *me* I work too hard." She snorted. "So how is it that you class Dustin as a friend? You only met him yesterday."

Zac stared down at his shoes. "It's a long story."

"Uh-huh." Carmen crossed her arms and tapped her toe against the carpet. "I've got a long break."

"Let's just say that it's not my first time here at the Arctic Star Resort." The elevator dinged and he gestured for her to exit first. "I've been here before."

"Really?" She looked around at all the opulence. He might be the best EMT in Anchorage, but he still lived on a paramedic's salary. "When?"

"Twelve years ago."

He unlocked the door to their suite and nudged her inside before she could ask any more questions. The fact that the time period was the same as that of his estrangement from his family wasn't lost on her, though. She filed that information away for future reference.

"Carmen Sanchez, this is Dustin Lewis. Carmen and I work together in Anchorage. She's a midwife."

"Ah, nice to meet you Ms. Sanchez," Dustin said, giving her a little bow and a smile. "You must be here for the conference, then."

"I am." She set her tote bag aside. "And please, call me Carmen."

"Okay." Zac grabbed his EMT pack from the bedroom, then returned to set things out on a table: a disposable scalpel, gauze, gloves, sterile field, cotton balls and antiseptic, even a syringe and lidocaine. "Dustin, have a seat here at the table, please. Carmen's going to help me get that cut on your arm cleaned and dressed."

Dustin tried to wave him off. "Don't worry about it, boy. Told you I'm fine."

"That cut is not fine. When you came up to see me this morning and I looked at it I could clearly see it's well on its way to being infected. If you don't nip it in the bud now it could spread to your bloodstream or turn into gangrene, neither of which are pleasant. Trust me, you *want* me to take care of it for you now. After we get it cleaned and dressed, maybe Carmen can write you a script for some antibiotics as well, just to be on the safe side. Do you have any allergies?"

"No. No allergies."

Grumbling, Dustin took a seat and rolled up the sleeve of his dress shirt. Carmen saw the bandage around his lower forearm and had to agree with Zac. Dried blood caked the bandage and the skin around the gauze was red and inflamed.

"Yes, I can write a script. I always bring supplies with me, just in case. Something Zac and I have in common. Let me wash my hands, then I'll get the patient ready for you."

She scrubbed down in the kitchenette sink with the antibacterial soap packet Zac gave her, then put on a pair of gloves and laid out an absorbent pad beneath Dustin's injured arm. She cut away the soiled bandages. Yep. That cut was infected, all right. She poured antiseptic on a cotton ball and prepared to clean the wound as best she could for Zac, prior to the incision.

"Sorry, but this might hurt a bit."

"Nah. Don't feel much anymore, with the nerve damage from my diabetes," Dustin said, giving a dismissive wave with his other hand.

"I suspect that's why we're in this situation now," Zac said to Carmen, his tone low, for her ears only.

"Probably." She cleaned the cut and tossed the cotton balls away in the small red plastic portable biohazard bin from Zac's pack. "All right, Dustin—Zac, ready when you are."

"I know you said you don't feel much," Zac said, drawing lidocaine from the small vial into the syringe, then flicking it a few times with his finger to get any air bubbles out. "But this will numb the area just in case, okay?"

"Whatever, boy," Dustin said, looking the other way. "Just hurry up and get it over with. You know I don't like needles."

Zac injected the lidocaine around the cut, then scrubbed down himself before putting on fresh gloves and opening the sterile scalpel packet. "Okay. I'm going to drain the wound now. You should feel better after this, Dustin."

The procedure only took a few minutes, and soon Carmen was applying new gauze pads and bandages to Dustin's forearm while Zac finished cleaning up the area. Once the wound was bandaged, Carmen scrubbed her hands and disposed of her gloves, then went into the bedroom to dig her prescription pad out of her bag. She returned to find Zac and Dustin talking in the living room.

"Keep the wound clean and dry and I'll check it again for you tomorrow, to make sure we got all the infection out," Zac said. "You should go see your doctor in town as soon as possible. Or if not him then the traveling physician who comes to the resort, the next time he's here."

"Looks aren't the only thing you got from your daddy, boy. Got his bossiness too," Dustin said, rolling his shirtsleeve back down over the bandage. "But thank you for your help. And you too, Carmen." The older man grinned. "Never did see such a pretty nurse."

"Midwife," Carmen corrected him, then laughed as

she handed him a script for antibiotics. "Make sure you take these with food. You knew Zac's family well, then?"

Zac gave them both a pointed look that all but screamed *Shut up.*

Dustin winked at her. "I did. I *do.* But I should go. I hope you both enjoy your stay at the Arctic Star Resort."

"We will," Carmen said, following him to the door while Zac disappeared into the bedroom.

Her curiosity about his family was growing, given that Dustin knew them, but she'd hesitated to ask with Zac right there. Having him leave for a moment gave her an opportunity she couldn't pass up.

She leaned her shoulder against the doorframe and lowered her voice. "Listen, I'm not trying to pry, but Zac and I are friends and I've noticed that talking about his family really bothers him. In fact, I think being here, period, bothers him. Can you tell me why that is?"

Dustin watched her closely for a second, then glanced over at the bedroom door before answering in a whisper. "I really don't think it's my place to say anything about Zac's personal life. Those are questions you should ask *him.* I will confirm, though, that this place holds a lot of memories for him. Some good, some not so great. But, again, it's not my place to discuss them with you. Sorry."

Carmen sighed, shoulders slumped. Neither she nor Zac had slept well last night. He'd insisted she take the bedroom, and he'd taken the oversized sofa in the living room. They'd both been tired, after the busy day and their walk to the animal reserve, but judging by the number of times she'd heard him up he'd not fared any better than she had sleep-wise.

She'd asked Zac to come this weekend, and now he looked more stressed than she'd ever seen him. Feeling responsible for that, because of dredging up his past, she wanted to do something nice for him. There was no formal dinner tonight, so they had the evening free.

"I'd like to do something nice for Zac tonight. I've not been to this area before, so I'm not sure what's around besides the resort." She tilted her head slightly to catch Dustin's gaze. "You know him better than I do. What would he like?"

Dustin regarded her for a moment, then said, "Bowling."

"Bowling?" She raised a brow. That wasn't what she'd expected.

"He likes to bowl. Used to be pretty good at it too." Dustin crossed his arms, careful to avoid messing up his bandage. "There's an alley in the village not far from here. It's the weekend, so there's probably leagues in there tonight, but if you call ahead they'll take a reservation. I can handle that for you, if you like."

"Oh, yes, please."

Back home in Trinidad, Carmen had used to take Clara bowling at the alley down from their apartment on the nights when their mother had had to work late. It had been light and busy and it had made them feel safer than staying home alone in the evenings. Plus, there'd been a little greasy spoon diner inside, and the owner would slip them free food from time to time. Returning to a bowling alley now, with Zac, would be a nice change of pace. And if it was something he enjoyed, all the better.

"Thanks, Dustin."

"My pleasure. Enjoy your day. And thanks again for helping with my wound."

He left the room and Carmen checked her watch again. "Shoot. I need to get back downstairs for my next seminar," Carmen called out to Zac as she rushed to grab her tote bag from the floor, where she'd set it earlier.

"Don't make any plans tonight. I've got something in mind for us."

"Yeah?" Zac looked at her as he came out of the bedroom. "What's that?"

"A secret. One of my own this time." She grinned and headed for the door.

"Great—just what we need. More secrets."

His deep, rich laugh followed her out the door and down the hall to the elevators.

The rest of the day passed in a blur of medical information, an informal lunch interview with Ellen and more seminars with Priya. Carmen's brain ached by the time she returned to the suite at around five, to find Zac working on his computer, but she was looking forward to the night ahead.

"Hey," she said, coming through the door and dumping her heavy tote on a chair in the corner. "What's going on?"

"Not much. Catching up on some emails from work. Inventory time again. Susan's handling it alone," he said, shutting his laptop. "Always stressful."

"Yeah, I'm sure."

She toed off her comfy tennis shoes, then wiggled her toes. Clothing-wise, she was trying to dress professionally for the weekend. Skirt, blazer, white button-down shirt, name badge... But with the running around the large resort all day, from room to room, the comfy shoes were a must.

"I'm going to take a shower, then we can head out for the night. Make sure you wear something comfortable."

He narrowed his gaze on her again. "No formal dinner tonight? No interview?"

"Nope. I had another brief interview with Ellen earlier. We're on our own tonight."

She took off her blazer and tossed it on the bed in the other room, then returned to the living room. Zac's bedding from the night before was neatly stacked on the corner of the sofa. It felt a bit decadent to have that whole king-sized bed to herself, but the alternative was to share—and, well, that wasn't a good idea either, so...

She cleared her throat and forced her mind away from images of her and Zac entwined in the sheets. He was still watching her with that skeptical look of his and she finally cracked. "Fine. No more secrets from me. You took me to the animal sanctuary last night. This evening I thought we could grab some dinner then maybe go bowling."

"Wait." Zac stood and walked over to her, laughing. "You want to go *bowling*?"

"Sure—why not?"

"No reason. Just never pictured you liking that sort of thing."

"Sometimes people surprise you." She walked to the bathroom door and winked at him. "See you in a sec."

An hour later Zac held the door for Carmen at the Strike City Alley in town. He hadn't been there since high school, but it still looked the same as he remembered. To the right was an arcade. To the left was the snack bar. In the center was the counter where you paid and got your shoe rentals. Closer to the alleys were racks of balls of all colors and weights.

He still had a hard time imagining Carmen being comfortable in a place like this. But then he remembered her talking to Dustin earlier and wondered if his old friend had something to do with it. Otherwise there was no way Carmen would know about Strike City.

The bowling alley was in a nondescript building on a

side street in the middle of nowhere. In fact, he'd loved coming here as a kid because people hadn't treated him differently in this place. They hadn't cared that he was rich and black. The owners had been Inuit and they hadn't cared less what their patrons looked like or what they believed or who they slept with, only that they were respectful and paid their bill.

Carmen gave her name at the counter and was given their lane assignment along with red, white and blue rental shoes for each of them. After changing, Zac stood to watch the other bowlers in the packed alley. Most were in leagues and were very good. The scoreboards overhead listed all the teams and their rankings.

"You want to eat first?" He looked down at Carmen, who was still tying her shoes.

"Whatever you want. We've got the lane until closing, so there's time."

"Great."

Zac escorted her to the snack bar and went to the counter to order them a large plate of nachos to split and two sodas. Once the food was ready he carried the tray to the tall round table where Carmen sat. Music pulsed through the overhead speakers, adding to the fun, slightly chaotic atmosphere.

Carmen dug into the food, humming as she did so.

Zac chuckled as she bopped along in her chair while she ate, licking a drop of cheese from the corner of her mouth and giving him all sorts of naughty ideas.

Carmen looked up and caught him watching her. "What?"

"Nothing."

His gaze dropped to her mouth again before he looked away. He should *not* be remembering their kiss from last night. Especially since he'd spent most of the afternoon trying to avoid those memories and failing miserably.

He'd gone for a swim, then a run, then a massage, then gone back to the suite to fiddle with his computer and check his emails. Nothing had helped. She was in his system again, like a drug, and the chemistry between them was addictive. Maybe more so because he knew damned well he was playing with fire where she was concerned.

Carmen was a risk to his heart he shouldn't take.

And if his raging libido would get with the program he'd be all set.

She continued eating, licking more cheese off her lips, and damn if he didn't have to bite back a groan. He'd been glad to go out tonight, thinking being away from the resort and out in the open would help him relieve some of his stress and help him keep his hands to himself where Carmen was concerned. But it seemed this evening was only going to make things more difficult.

He did his best to concentrate on his own plate after that. "Have you bowled before?" he asked.

"Yep. Used to take my sister to the bowling alley by our apartment when we were growing up. I was pretty good back then. Won a lot of money off the tourists who didn't think a girl could make strikes like I did."

"Really?" He ate faster, to distract himself from the image of Carmen fleecing a bunch of unsuspecting tourists through her skill, wits and determination. Somehow, knowing she had a naughty side just made her sexier, if that were possible. "Well, I was pretty good too, in my day. Looks like we'll have a battle on our hands."

"Bring it on." She sipped her soda and gave him a sly smile, her green-gold eyes sparkling with attitude. "Ready when you are."

He shook his head and ate three chips at once. "Not yet. Finish your food first."

"Agreed." She devoured another chip, then looked around the bowling alley. "This place is a lot nicer than the one I used to go to back home. The walls there clashed with the floor and it reeked of cigarette smoke and booze."

"Doesn't sound like a good place for kids to hang out." Despite his dad's issues, Zac had grown up privileged. From what he knew about Carmen now, she hadn't. In fact, he couldn't imagine growing up in the kind of poverty Carmen had experienced. "Wouldn't you have been safer at home?"

"Nah. Our mother did the best she could, but the building we lived in had some pretty shady characters, so being out and around people was a better bet." She shrugged. "What about you? What was it like where you grew up?"

Zac forced his tense shoulders to relax. This wasn't some random person asking him about his past—this was Carmen, his friend. He wouldn't tell her everything, but he found that for the first time in a long time, he wanted to share something.

"It was great. Nice. Not much different than where we are now. My mother was kind and caring. My dad worked a lot when I was younger, so I didn't see him that much. We had a good life."

She hesitated, then asked, "But then your father had an affair?"

His instinct was to shut down, but he forced himself to continue. "Yeah. When I was sixteen. Everything changed after that."

"Oh, Zac. I'm so sorry." Carmen set her soda aside and reached over to take his hand.

He nodded. "He betrayed my trust, betrayed my mother. I couldn't forgive him for that. Still can't. He was my idol. I wanted to be like him when I grew up. Always thought I would be. Then he told us he'd made a mistake and slept with another woman. That's not a mistake. A mistake is when you forget to pick up the dry cleaning or buy the wrong kind of toothpaste. Not when you end up in bed with someone who's not your spouse. An affair is a deliberate act, a conscious choice. How do you forgive something like that?"

"I don't know," she said.

The warmth of her skin against his helped ground him.

"I don't know much about my father," she went on. "He walked out on our family when I was eight. My sister, Clara, was only two, so she barely remembers him, but I do. He was rich. South American. Turned out he had this whole other life back in Argentina we knew nothing about. Once he walked out the door my mother never heard from him again. No money, no child support. Nothing. It's like we didn't exist. Like he'd erased us from his life."

Zac entwined his fingers with hers, his throat tight. No wonder she felt the way she did about wealthy people. "I'm sorry too."

"It's fine." She sighed and sat back, pulling her hand away. "We were better off without him. If that's how he treated people, he didn't deserve us."

"Amen. You're too good for him." Zac toasted her with his soda cup.

"My mother is a saint. I owe her everything for taking care of us like she did, for the sacrifices she made on our behalf." Carmen tapped her cup against his, then exhaled slowly. "So, what about your mother? I know you don't speak with your father, but she must miss you very much. You left her behind when you left?"

He flinched slightly. "I had to. She made her choice and I made mine. Out of respect to her, I couldn't stay there. So I moved to Anchorage. Put myself through school. Like I said before, I originally planned to be a doctor, but then I volunteered with the local ambulance authority to get more experience under my belt and fell in love with it. I decided to focus on a paramedic career instead. It was the right decision for me. I've never looked back."

"Hmm… Interesting."

"What?" He frowned.

"Most people would consider forgiveness a *good* thing. Your mother was able to move past something like that and continue loving your father, strengthening her marriage to him. The mark of a solid bond, in my opinion." She shrugged. "Not that you asked for my opinion."

Her sweet smile took away a bit of the sting of her words, though tension still coiled inside him like a spitting cobra. Zac wasn't used to having his decisions analyzed and second-guessed. In his work, making clear, concise, correct decisions meant the difference between life and death. In his private life… Well, he'd never really talked to anyone about his family situation before, so all this felt more than a bit uncomfortable, to say the least.

Plus, the mental picture he had of his poor mom sitting there, pining away for him, didn't sit well with him either. She would've moved on by now, right? His father ran a multi-billion-dollar empire. There wouldn't be time for her to miss him.

Except the pinch in his heart told him maybe that wasn't the case.

Before he could dwell too long over the past, however,

Carmen broke into his thoughts, forcing him to focus on the conversation at hand.

"I feel the same way about midwifery that you do about being an EMT. I can't imagine having another career. I love being there when new life enters the world. Plus, being a midwife allows me to get involved in my patients' lives. Not to disparage the OB-GYNs, but they usually have such large patient loads, and all the extra paperwork and regulations. No, thank you. I'm happy in my niche." She smiled and snagged the last nacho from the plate. "That's why this California job seems so perfect. Aside from the money, it would give me a chance to do more of what I love and pay it forward—to help the next generation find their place in this career I love."

"Good for you. And I've signed on to teach some certification classes for EMTs at the local vocational college this spring." He leaned back in his chair, satisfied. Not just from the food, but from the company too. "I want to give back to the job that's given me so much."

They were from opposite ends of the spectrum. They shouldn't have worked. And yet he felt more connected to Carmen right now than he ever had to anyone else.

Which meant it was definitely time to start bowling.

Zac stood and disposed of their trash, then led Carmen down to their lane. There were two more days left of this conference and he didn't want to mess things up between them by taking her to bed again. Best to ignore the growing flames between them and the strengthening connection and keep to their original plan.

Carmen had selected a ball from the racks and set it in the return. Zac did the same. While she typed their names into the scoring system he picked up his own ball and eyed the pins. "Should we take a couple of practice rounds?"

"Go ahead." She gave him a cocky grin. "If you think it will help."

Considering he was practically vibrating with desire for her, it couldn't hurt. Maybe he could burn off enough of his excess energy to bowl a decent game that way.

After a deep breath to calm himself down, he sent the ball down the lane, managing to knock over all but one pin on his first try. Perhaps he hadn't lost his magic after all.

He took out that last pin on his next shot, then sat behind the screen while Carmen took her practice turn. Sure enough, she bowled a perfect strike. Pride and passion zinged through him. He did love a woman who could handle herself well.

She walked back, her expression brimming with challenge. "Let's do this."

He didn't miss the double-entendre in her words or the spark of heat in her eyes. Despite knowing better, he gave in to the attraction simmering inside him, allowing it to roll into a full boil. "Whatever you want, darling."

"Darling, huh?" she said, winking. "Just for that, I'm going to beat you even worse."

And by the end of the night she'd done just that.

Zac had honestly bowled his best game ever, but she'd still trounced him—and he'd enjoyed every minute of it. In truth, he couldn't remember having a better night.

They changed back into their street shoes, then took a cab back to the resort. Carmen was quiet during the ride, sitting closer to him in the back seat of the compact than was necessary, but Zac wasn't complaining. Her heat and the press of her soft curves against him only served to notch his pulse higher. His skin felt too tight for his body and his nerve-endings prickled with awareness.

At the hotel, they walked quickly through the lobby

and over to the elevators. The doors swished shut, leaving them alone.

Carmen turned to Zac at last, and the need in her eyes matched his own. "Look, I know we agreed not to sleep together again this weekend, but—"

He kissed her before she finished her sentence. She tasted sweet from her soda and spicy from the jalapeños on the nachos. Her hands skimmed up his chest to twine around his neck and he gripped her hips, his fingers digging into the denim of her jeans as she arched against him. Her tongue tangled with his and she ground against him, one leg looping around his waist as if she couldn't get close enough.

He was tempted to hit the stop button and have her right there, up against the mirrored wall of the elevator, but Carmen deserved better. She deserved the suite and the king-sized bed and the expensive sheets. She deserved every good and wonderful thing, and he intended to see she got it—at least for tonight.

Ding!

"C'mon," Zac growled, tugging her toward their room. "I want you, Carmen. So badly I ache."

She nodded, keeping up with him step for step. "And I want you too."

CHAPTER EIGHT

CARMEN SHED HER parka the minute she and Zac tumbled through the door in a mass of limbs and kisses. The rest of her clothes followed suit, until she was left in just her bra and panties. Her whole body burned for him.

And, yes, maybe sleeping with him again was a bad decision, but she'd denied the connection and chemistry between them for days—months. There was no more denying it now. Tomorrow she'd go back to devoting all her time to others. Tonight was just for her.

He took off his jacket as well and tossed it aside, then tugged his sweater over his head, leaving his muscled torso bare. He stalked toward her slowly, as she inched back toward the bed, and his hot, greedy gaze roamed over her.

"I didn't think it was possible to want you any more than I already did, but I was wrong."

"Same."

She gave him a slow smile. The more time she'd spent with Zac this weekend, and the more she'd learned about him, the more she'd discovered they were more alike than different. He was sexy as hell, yes. But he was also strong, smart, honest and true. Maybe he wasn't Mr. Forever, but he was hers for this weekend.

After crawling onto the bed, Carmen leaned back on

her elbows and propped one leg up, letting the other dangle over the edge of the mattress as she crooked her finger at him. "Come here…"

"Yes, ma'am."

The half-growled, half-groaned words only stoked the passion in her blood higher. Zac removed his jeans, then dropped to his knees on the floor beside the bed, taking her hips in his hands and pulling her to the end of the mattress. He leaned in, his broad shoulders forcing her thighs to part wider.

His eyes met hers over the length of her body, and the heat in his stare was brazen. Then he grinned. "This is for beating me at bowling."

The first gentle lick of his tongue across the silk of her panties made Carmen's breath catch. During their one-night stand he'd been an attentive lover. But that had been rushed and they'd both been drunk. Now he seemed more than happy to take all the time in the world. She swallowed hard and closed her eyes, clenching the covers in her hands to keep from crying out in sweet frustration.

Zac slid her panties down her legs, then licked her again, using his fingers to stroke her as well. Carmen arched beneath him, unable to hold back her soft moans of need any longer. He slid one finger inside her, then two, as his tongue nuzzled her most sensitive flesh.

"You're so ready for me," he whispered, the words reverberating through her body.

She slipped a hand down to hold him closer to her. "Zac, please…"

"Please what, darling?" he asked. "Tell me what you want."

"You. I want you."

With a soft growl he kissed his way up her body, his

fingers never leaving her slick folds, until he held himself over her. "Say it again. Tell me."

"Please, Zac. I want you."

He reached over and pulled a condom from the nightstand drawer, put it on, then removed her bra, leaving them both naked. "I want you too, Carmen. Are you sure?"

She nodded, and he lifted her hips, pulling her toward him as he thrust forward, filling her completely. Zac stilled, allowing her body to adjust to his. Moments later Carmen rocked forward, letting him know she needed more.

His expression intense, he set up a steady rhythm, his gaze locked with hers. "You feel so incredible. I thought I'd imagined it that first time. Thought it was impossible. But I was wrong. So wrong. You're amazing."

"So are you."

Carmen met him thrust for thrust, giving herself over completely to this man, this moment, this time together. Sweat sheened his forehead as they both teetered on the brink of climax all too soon. His rough groans of mounting pleasure filled the air and her blood pounded in her veins. No matter what issues they had outside of this room, in bed they fit like two pieces of the same puzzle. She wanted this night to go on forever. She wanted him to bring her to orgasm before she couldn't take it anymore.

Pressure built inside her, causing her to grind against him even harder, seeking her own fulfillment. Finally her passion crested, and her world exploded into ecstasy. Zac followed close behind her, his back arching as he thrust into her hard one last time and orgasmed.

Afterward, he collapsed on the bed, his eyes closed and his expression relaxed for the first time she'd seen all weekend. Carmen felt so limp she could barely move.

Zac's leg tangled with hers as she turned on her side and laid her hand on his chest.

The sweat on their skin chilled, and he pulled the covers over them, holding her close as she gave him a sleepy grin. "Guess that'll teach me to get more strikes than you, huh?"

He chuckled, tucking her head under his chin. "Nah. I love having a worthy opponent."

Zac wasn't an idiot. He had known as soon as Carmen snuggled atop him and gave a huge contented sigh that he'd made a mistake taking her to bed again. Not because of their stupid fake engagement, but because this was a woman he respected. A woman who was a friend and a colleague. A woman who challenged him on every level.

A woman he could love.

Dammit.

He didn't do love. Love meant trust. Love meant risk. After the disaster he'd witnessed in his parents' relationship he never wanted to leave himself open to that kind of heartache and disappointment. This weekend should've been fun. Lighthearted. Low risk. Then he'd gone and opened up to her more than he should have and they'd connected on a deeper level. Now, he'd let her into his life and his heart in a way he'd never let anyone in a long, long time.

She wanted different things. She'd be moving away soon, if she got the job in California. She had a life and responsibilities of her own. Yet he couldn't seem to stop himself from envisioning a future with them together. Working side by side at Anchorage Mercy, getting married, starting a family of their own.

Except there were still so many things she didn't know about him—his family, his past...

He should have told her the truth before they slept together again, he knew that, but the time hadn't seemed right. And then his body had taken over, and his brain had taken a back seat, and...*ugh.*

What a mess.

He stroked his fingers through Carmen's curls, savoring their silky feel against his skin. Her hair twined around his hand, as if begging him to stay.

She propped herself up on her elbow to look at him, a slight frown marring her beautiful face. "What are you thinking about?"

Zac realized he had another opportunity at that moment—to let it go or talk about it.

Letting it go would lead to more sex.

Talking about his past would guarantee she wouldn't want anything more to do with him.

She'd already made it clear she didn't trust rich people—had no use for them at all after the way her own wealthy father had behaved and the way she'd been treated by those entitled frat boys who'd expected things from her when she'd worked at that luxury resort in Trinidad. Once she found out his father owned this resort, and many more like it, any relationship they might have had would be over.

Torn, Zac rolled onto his side to see her face-to-face. Right or wrong, he wanted them to have the rest of this night together. He'd tell her the truth about himself tomorrow. He *would.* And if it all fell apart then at least he'd have these precious memories to look back on.

"I'm glad we're here together tonight."

"Me too."

She traced her finger down his chest, making him shiver.

"I feel like I can just be myself with you. I don't have

to impress you. You're real—normal. Not like some of the men I've come across before. Most guys I've been out with either expected me to take care of them or tried to impress me with their money. But I don't care about that. Wealth doesn't make a man. I learned that lesson all too well with my father."

Zac hid his wince. Yeah, he'd learned that with his father too.

"Although…" Carmen snorted and gestured to the suite around them. "All of this *doesn't* suck."

"True," he said. "But this isn't reality."

"Tonight it is." She gave him a sweet, sexy smile.

He wanted to forget—forget the lies and the past and just enjoy what time they had together here in their little private paradise of a bedroom—but he couldn't.

"Hey, why so serious?" she asked. "We're supposed to be basking in the afterglow."

She nudged him with her shoulder and Zac forced a small smile.

"Listen." She held his hand and toyed with his fingers. "I have no fantasies about money. I've seen the best and worst it can do and I'm careful. My mother and sister and I live frugally, and I don't depend on others to give me what I need. If that's a problem for you, then I'm sorry."

"No, it's not a problem, I just…" He exhaled slowly and held her closer. "Honestly, it makes me respect you even more."

"Good." She smiled. "A lot of men are threatened by an independent woman. I'm glad you're not one of them."

Zac couldn't seem to look away from her. Carmen was gorgeous, no doubt. But now he also saw her inner strength and determination, her confidence and intelligence, and that made her even more beautiful. She worked hard and she deserved the best in life.

His heart squeezed tighter in his chest, and that was when he knew he was a goner—which only scared him more. Still, he pushed past the fear, because she deserved this moment even if he couldn't give her forever. No matter how he might wish otherwise.

"Thank you."

She took a deep breath. "For what?"

"For tonight. For being my friend. For everything."

It didn't cover even half of what he needed to say, the things he needed to tell her, but it was all he could do at the moment.

"You're welcome." She gave him a surprised smile, then raised a brow, the glint in her lovely eyes positively wicked. "You ready for round two?"

Zac felt the blood in his body divert southward. Yep, his heart was definitely a goner where this woman was concerned, and he was well and truly terrified.

He was also not moving out of this bed for anything in the world—not until he had no other choice. He leaned in and kissed her deeply. "More than ready."

CHAPTER NINE

ZAC WAS UP before Carmen the next morning. Which was good, because if she'd rolled over and smiled at him he'd never have wanted to leave her side. And he needed to go. Needed to get some space and clear his mind.

The fact was, last night was messing with his head. This was supposed to be a fun weekend. No commitments. No strings attached. And while it had certainly been fun, feelings were stirring inside him. Feelings that shouldn't be there—tenderness, longing, satisfaction, sweetness. Feelings beyond like and nearing…

No. He wasn't going there.

They were friends. Good friends. Friends with benefits.

But the more he got to know Carmen, the more he wanted from her.

He went into the bathroom and pulled on his swim trunks, careful to be quiet and avoid waking her. Then he went back out into the bedroom to grab a clean pair of jeans and a T-shirt from his bag, to put on after his time in the pool. There were changing rooms downstairs and he didn't plan to come back to the suite until after she'd left for the day.

It was avoidance, plain and simple, but then "mornings-after" weren't exactly his thing.

Usually he was long gone by the time the sun rose on his flings. It was only being honest, really. He wasn't cut out for relationships—not with the example his father had set for him—and he always told his partners that up front.

He'd told Carmen that too, but something about this weekend with her had changed things. Made him think that maybe he'd been lying to himself all along. Made him wonder if perhaps settling down was what he wanted and needed, but he wasn't brave enough to try for it. Because if a man like his father had been seduced into cheating, who was to say Zac wouldn't make the same mistake? And the last thing he wanted to do was hurt Carmen. She'd been through enough in her life already.

Torn and twisted inside, he let himself out of the room and headed downstairs. Sleeping with Carmen again didn't feel like just another one-night stand. Being with her felt like champagne and breakfast in bed. Like lazy Sunday mornings reading the paper.

Like a "forever" kind of thing.

Too bad he was just a "right now" kind of guy.

Aren't I?

This early in the morning there weren't many people up and about at the resort, so he had the pool to himself. For half an hour he did laps, working out some of the tension that had been building in his muscles for days and hoping the time alone might do the same for his jumbled mind.

By the time he'd finished and pulled himself out to sit on the edge of the pool, he was out of breath and shaking from exertion—and still remembering Carmen upstairs in bed, tousled and tempting as hell. Instead of racing back there, like he wanted, he jumped back in the water to put in another twenty minutes.

But even the burn of his body as he pushed it to its

limits didn't stop the sound of her gasps as he'd brought her to climax again and again, the taste of salt from her skin, the feel of her exquisite breasts in his palms.

There was no doubt the two of them fit perfectly—in and out of bed.

She'd been a delight at the bowling alley—laughing and teasing and pushing him to do better, to be better, because she was so good. He still couldn't quite believe he'd opened up to her as much as he had about his past and his father—more than he had with anyone else in recent memory. And even with all she'd told him about herself he wanted to know more. He wanted to know what she ate for breakfast, what toothpaste she liked, how she got her hair to stay in those perfect curls, who had been her first crush and could he possibly be her last…if he was brave enough to try?

Damn.

He dunked himself underwater, then rose to swipe his hand over his face. Enough. Brave or not, all this was pointless. Because after this weekend he'd go back to his life in Anchorage and she'd most likely be moving to California. Nothing would change, because nothing *could* change.

Zac climbed out of the pool and grabbed his towel from a nearby chair. He dried off, then headed into the changing rooms to shower and pull on the clothes he'd brought.

Wishing things were different would get him exactly nowhere. He didn't like to think about his father or his upbringing often, but in this instance his father's words rang true.

Get over it, son.

Intent on doing just that, after he was dressed Zac decided to hit the resort restaurant for breakfast. Usually, when he was at home and working, he ate on the run. He never knew when a call would come in and he had to be ready in a moment's notice. Today, though, he planned to order the most elaborate thing on the menu—just to burn up some time. Whatever took the longest to cook, that was what he'd have. Then, once he'd eaten, he'd stop by the front desk, just to confirm that Carmen had gone to her seminars for the day before returning to the suite.

It wasn't that he was afraid he wouldn't be able to keep his hands to himself—though the idea of keeping her in bed all day was more than appealing. Nope. What kept him out of the room and away from her was the very real and terrifying possibility that she'd want to talk more, find out more about him. Because that was the thing about secrets. Once you opened the door even a little the whole mess had a tendency to spill out.

He berated himself again for not being honest with her up front, even though it would do him little good now. What was done was done, and the only way to move was forward.

Get over it, son.

He rounded the corner and halted at the entrance to the restaurant. It was Saturday, and he'd forgotten they only served a buffet breakfast on the weekend. *Damn.* That cut out any prep time for his food. Fine. He'd eat slowly. It was all good.

The hostess showed him to a table for two in the mainly empty dining room, then directed him to help himself at the buffet.

He was doing just that when a familiar voice said from beside him, "Morning, boy."

Dustin.

Zac glanced at the older gentleman and smiled, grateful for the distraction. "Good morning. How's the arm?"

"Better. Thanks to you and your lady friend."

Dustin let him see the bandage, then toasted him with his cup of coffee. Zac's father had always given the employees complimentary meals during their shifts. *A perk of the job,* his dad had always said. *Treat people right and they'll do the same for you.*

Too bad his good judgment hadn't carried over to his marriage or his family.

"Where is the lovely Carmen this morning?" Dustin asked, picking up several slices of bacon with a pair of tongs while Zac loaded his plate with hash browns and eggs.

He rolled his shoulders to ease the knots between his shoulder blades and forced a smile he didn't quite feel. "Carmen's not my lady friend. She's just a friend. And she's still in the room, as far as I know."

"I see… But she is lovely, though." Dustin cocked his head, as though he saw right through the BS, then headed toward a table not far from Zac's. "Why don't you join me?"

"Sure—if you don't mind?"

"If I minded I wouldn't have asked." Dustin chuckled and walked away.

Zac followed the older man to his table, where there was already a pot of coffee and a carafe of orange juice waiting. They sat down and started on their food.

"Seen your parents yet?" Dustin asked.

"Nah." Zac halted mid-bite and shook his head. "Had a near miss Thursday night, but I managed to get out of the banquet room before they saw me."

"You know you can't outrun them forever, boy?"

Yeah, Zac knew. But if he could just avoid a confrontation this weekend, that would be great. He didn't want to ruin things for Carmen. Didn't want to deal with all the pain and hurt and regret himself, either.

He stared down at his plate, his appetite plummeting. He felt like the walls were closing in on him and he didn't like it one bit.

"Maybe you should just talk to him," Dustin said, watching Zac over the rim of his coffee cup. "Get it over with."

"No." He pushed around a mound of potatoes with his fork. "I've got nothing to say to him."

"Really?" The older man remained silent for a moment, then said, "My employment anniversary here is coming up next month. Been at the Arctic Star for twenty-nine years. Almost as long as your father has owned the place."

"Congratulations." Zac didn't look up, even though he could feel Dustin's gaze on him. This wasn't a conversation he wanted to have right now.

"I still remember that night you tore out of here after talking to your dad that last time. He was devastated after you left—kept trying to get ahold of you, but you wouldn't take his calls. I think he aged a hundred years in a month back then. Hard times."

Well, at least that last part was right. "Hard" didn't begin to describe the anger and betrayal Zac had felt after learning of his dad's affair. He'd spent sixteen years idolizing the man, following in his footsteps, wanting to be just like him. To have all that demolished over one stupid, thoughtless decision had been something he just couldn't forgive and forget.

Of course the media circus that had followed the story breaking hadn't helped either. The stupid tabloids had brought it up over and over again, rubbing their family's faces in it. In fact, it had been after reading a particularly heinous smear piece about his father that Zac had wrecked his car and put his date in the hospital. He'd thought he could outrun the rage and embarrassment, but that hadn't been the case.

It was never the case. Problems had a way of following you until you dealt with them, once and for all.

"He's missed you terribly," Dustin said. "We all have."

"Yeah, well… He should've thought about that before he did what he did." Zac shook his head. "Please don't preach at me about forgiveness. What he did was wrong and now he has to live with the consequences. I know my mother was able to move past it, and I respect her decision, but I'm not there yet."

"Not disagreeing with you there, boy. Infidelity is an ugly thing. But we all stumble sometimes. It's what we do afterward that counts."

Dustin finished his coffee, then checked his watch and stood.

"Time for me to finish up back at the desk and turn things over to Willow for the day shift. I'll be around later if you need me. Think about making amends, boy. Time is precious. Don't waste new opportunities because of old tribulations."

With that, the older man walked away, leaving Zac alone to stare after him.

Frowning, he finished his food and thought over Dustin's words. As far as Zac knew, his sixty-year-old father was in fine health. Honestly, the man was stubborn enough to live to a thousand just to spite the world. Besides, Zac wasn't in much of a forgiving mood at the moment.

He had too many other things on his mind.

Like how to tell the woman he was falling for that he'd been lying to her from the start.

* * *

Carmen's day had been filled with more seminars and another lunch meeting with Ellen Landon—this time to discuss the staffing requirements of the new clinic and the newly minted outreach program for providing medical care and prenatal services to the low-income and homeless population in and around Big Sur.

When asked for her opinions, Carmen had spoken from the heart about growing up poor, and how that had given her a special insight into the problems of women living below the poverty line. It was an insight she knew Priya would not be able to share, since she'd grown up in a wealthy family near Chicago. Ellen had been impressed, and for first time Carmen had felt like she had the upper hand on the new position in California.

That alone should've made her overjoyed. It was what this weekend was all about, after all. What she'd been working so hard toward for the last two months.

But, unfortunately, all she could think about was Zac.

Waking up alone hadn't been how she'd wanted to start the day. Since then she'd kept an eye out for Zac in the halls between seminars, but so far there'd been no sign of him at all. If they'd been back in Anchorage she'd have suspected he was avoiding her. Here at the resort, however, there were plenty of fun activities to take up his time. She'd see him eventually, since the big final banquet was tonight.

The banquet where Ellen would announce her choice for the new job.

An odd mix of nervous butterflies and sad disappointment fluttered through her system. The nerves were about the job. She still wanted it. Of course she did. It was everything she'd dreamed of achieving—more prestige and more responsibility, more opportunities to help those in need, more money to help with her sister's education and her mother's medical care. It was all good.

Except...

She'd miss Anchorage, the people and the places she'd come to love, including Zac. He was her friend, her colleague, her lover.

Yes, he'd made it clear he wasn't the type of man to settle down, but the truth was she'd not been with anyone else since their one night together after the holiday party. It wasn't that she hadn't had cravings, it was just that they'd all been focused on one man, and she doubted anyone else could measure up to the incredible synergy she had with Zac.

Each time she closed her eyes it was like she was right back there with him, riding that wave of pleasure to its ultimate crest. They hadn't been able to get enough of each other and she'd loved every delicious minute of it. He was a generous lover, vocal in what he wanted and expecting the same from her. Part of her had thought maybe sleeping with him again might get him out of her system once and for all, but the opposite was true. She wanted him now more than ever. Being with Zac was addictive and she never wanted to stop.

It was like they were two halves of the same whole.

Which both thrilled and terrified her.

Mainly because she wasn't sure he'd ever admit the same, even though it was obvious he felt it in the way he touched her, held her, knew what she needed before she even knew herself.

Plus, she wasn't used to relying on another person for anything—including love.

But with Zac things seemed deeper, more permanent than in any of her previous relationships. If you could call what they had a relationship. Okay, maybe not a relationship, but the start of...*something*. Something more and special and real.

He'd finally opened up to her at the bowling alley, and later on in bed, sharing glimpses of his past, which was encouraging. And though she sensed he was still holding back secrets, the rest would come with time.

Carmen wasn't one for hearts and rainbows and flower petal romances. She was far too pragmatic. But Zac had well and truly swept her off her feet and now she needed to figure out how to proceed. They needed to talk. She needed to find out what he wanted, since before this weekend he'd made it clear that he was a player.

She wasn't naïve enough to think a night or two of great sex would change a man. Besides, it wasn't her responsibility to fix him, no matter how his broken parts might call to her. But things had moved well past the friend zone for her after last night, and she had to know if they had for him as well.

The clock on the wall said her next seminar was starting soon, so she finished up her coffee, then headed into a talk on using a physiological model for the management of the head-to-body interval during vaginal birth. It was another packed room, but Priya had saved her a seat.

"Hey." Carmen got out her notebook. "How's your day going?"

"Fine," Priya said, although her normally perky tone was flat. "And yours?"

"Good." Carmen glanced over at her and saw her friend was looking a bit green around the gills. "Everything okay?"

"Fine," Priya said. "Just tired."

Unconvinced, Carmen dug a packet of saltine crackers out of her tote. "Here. These will settle your stomach."

"Thanks."

The lights dimmed and the presentation started, but thoughts of the night before continued to distract Carmen. In terms of her career, she probably shouldn't even be looking for anything long-term right now, since she was closer than ever to landing the California job. To turn her back on all that over a man who might not even want her in his future was ludicrous.

No. They needed to talk. And as soon as she could get some alone time with him, they would. If not today, then tonight—at the banquet.

CHAPTER TEN

THE EVENING FINALLY arrived, but for Zac it felt like anything but a party. After avoiding Carmen and his parents for most of the day, and running the conversation he'd had with Dustin over and over in his head on an endless loop, he felt the burden of the secrets he was keeping weighing heavier than ever on his shoulders.

He should tell Carmen the truth.

He wanted to tell Carmen the truth.

He would tell Carmen the truth when the right time came.

Which wasn't now.

After the big announcement about who was to get the new job in California maybe.

In Zac's mind, Carmen was a shoo-in. She was more than qualified, had the practical experience, and most of all she truly cared about her patients and her coworkers. She deserved it. And he intended to do everything he could tonight to make sure she got it—even if it meant losing her forever.

Zac adjusted his black bow tie in the full-length mirror in the suite, then stared at his reflection. Elegant, refined, the designer tux would provide excellent armor for the evening ahead.

We all stumble sometimes. It's what we do afterward that counts.

Exhaling slowly, Zac walked over to the dresser to grab his cufflinks—small ovals of sterling silver engraved with his initials. They were one of the few things he'd taken with him when he'd left this place—a gift from his mother on his high school graduation. They'd cost more than some people made in a week. A reminder of everything he'd left behind.

He slid them into place, then tweaked his cuffs to be sure they were secure.

Moments later Carmen emerged from the bathroom, and he turned to face her…

"Wow," was all he managed to say, taking in the silver beaded lace evening gown that clung like a second skin to all her glorious curves.

Zac swallowed hard against the tightness in his throat. She wore her hair up again too, with a few loose curls hanging around her neck and face. All he could think about was holding her, kissing her, feeling her beneath him, surrounding him as she came apart in his arms.

Carmen put in her earrings—small, sparkling studs—then walked over and turned her back to him. She gave him a coy smile over her shoulder, the glint in her lovely eyes saying she knew exactly the effect she had on him.

"Can you zip me up please?"

Zac did as she asked, his hands far less steady than he'd like. Finished, he stepped back—away from her and her sweet jasmine scent, away from temptation. Because if he didn't keep his distance now they'd both end up back in bed and miss the dinner entirely.

"Are you ready?" She grabbed her tiny purse from the top of the dresser, then gave him a hesitant smile. "We don't want to be late."

"No." He shook his head. "I mean, yes. I'm ready. But before we go…" He took her hands, his pulse pounding in his ears and his skin prickling with heat.

Tell her.

But he couldn't. Not yet. This was her big night.

He'd wait until after the ball, when they were alone, when he would be able to suffer the humiliation and pain of her walking away in private.

She looked up at him, so beautiful, so trusting. He wanted her more than he'd ever wanted any woman in his life, but he'd never be worthy of her.

He cleared his throat. "You look amazing. You'll get that California job and take the entire state by storm. I'll be in Anchorage, cheering you on."

Something flickered in her eyes, gone before he could catch it. If he didn't know better, he'd say it was longing. But then she put on the brave, professional smile he knew so well from Anchorage Mercy and gave a decisive nod.

"Thank you. Let's get downstairs."

The event planners at the resort had certainly outdone themselves with tonight's décor. Zac took it all in as he escorted Carmen into the dining room. LED lights projected a gorgeous display of deep blue, purple and rose colors onto the vaulted ceiling, making it resemble an abstract stained-glass window. Long swathes of white tulle were draped between the columns in the room, stretching from each column to the large chandelier at the center of the space.

The tables had been arranged in semicircles before the stage, where the podium sat ready for the presentations and the big announcement later in the evening. Towering centerpieces of white lilies and roses graced each white-linen-covered table and a tasteful string quartet played in one corner. There was also DJ equipment for later, when the dance floor would open again.

Seemed his father had thought of every detail—again.

Zac's steps faltered and Carmen gave him a curious glance.

"Okay?" she asked, her expression concerned. "You seem more jittery than me tonight."

"I'm fine."

He resisted the urge to fidget with his tie again and scanned the area. Lots of the guests were milling about, talking or laughing or catching up with colleagues they saw only perhaps once a year. No sign of his parents yet, which was a relief. If he'd been here with anyone other than Carmen he would've left, but he didn't want to let her down.

Jaw set, he led Carmen to their table, near the front of the space, held her chair for her, then took the space beside her. Ellen and Liz were there already, as were Priya and Lance.

Zac greeted them all, noting that Lance wasn't acting like his usual outgoing, gregarious self. He seemed hyper-focused on Priya. Doting, even, with his head bent toward her and his arm around her protectively. Zac wanted to ask him what was going on, but the master of ceremonies for the evening had taken the podium to welcome everyone and announce that dinner was served.

While they ate, several presentations took place, and Zac kept a watchful eye out for his father. The thought of playing cat and mouse with him all night had lessened his appetite significantly, though the food was delicious—as always. Sweet potato, coconut and coriander soup for the appetizer, followed by pan-fried duck breast with black cherries and basil polenta, and finishing with raspberry mousse and homemade chocolate-dipped shortbread.

Lovely as the meal was, though, Zac could've been eating cardboard for all he tasted it.

"This resort has been lovely," Ellen said as the waiter cleared away their plates. "I'd definitely come back here for a vacation. If I can tear my wife away from her practice."

Liz laughed, finishing her last bite of raspberry mousse. "I think you could twist my arm. Besides, we should have more free time after this new position at the clinic is filled." She looked over at Carmen, then Priya, giving them each a wink. "Isn't that right?"

"Yes, ma'am," Carmen said.

Priya nodded and gave a wan smile.

Yeah, there was something definitely off with those two. Zac couldn't put his finger on it, but the shadows beneath Priya's eyes suggested that she hadn't been sleeping well. He'd have to pull his buddy aside later and ask. Maybe it would distract him from his own problems.

"Oh, look." Ellen raised her chin toward the opposite side of the dining room as some of the diners began to get up and mill around the room and the buzz of conversation filled the air. "Here comes the owner. We should tell them how much we've enjoyed the venue this year. Oh, but the MC is waving us up to the stage. If you'll excuse us?"

Both she and Liz left before Zac's parents could come over and he felt the earth disappear beneath his feet. If he could've sunk beneath the table he would have.

Instead, he stood and excused himself. "I need some air."

"You can't leave." Carmen frowned up at him. "They're going to make the announcement soon."

"I won't be long," he said, tossing his napkin on the

table and stepping back—just as his father approached their table.

Damn. Too late.

They locked eyes for the first time in twelve years and Zac saw his father's expression shift from recognition to determination in a matter of seconds. Zac opened his mouth to speak, but the words stuck in his throat. Vaguely he was aware of Priya excusing herself and heading to the restrooms with Lance following close behind her. Time seemed to slow.

His father continued to stare at him, but his mother was still speaking to a woman at another table nearby. Pulse racing, Zac fisted his hands at his sides and forced himself to stand his ground. This moment had been a long time coming and the air around their table seemed to crackle with tension.

"Son," his father said, his cool tone edged with wariness.

Fresh anger sizzled beneath Zac's skin even as he battled to keep it under control. This was not how he wanted things to go down. Not here. Not now. Not with so much on the line for him.

Carmen glanced between Zac and his father, frowning. "Son…? Zac, what's he talking about? Do you know this man?"

"I did. Once," he said, his jaw tight. "But he has no right to call me that anymore."

His mother turned at that moment, to see her son and her husband facing off across the table. Her bright smile faltered as she took Zac's father's arm. "Please, Zac. It's been so long since we've seen you. Can't we talk about this? Finally put it behind us?"

His father spoke again. "Yes. That's what I want too, son. I'm sorry about what happened all those years ago.

It was never my intention to hurt you," his father said, his voice beseeching. "But things are different now. *I'm* different. Please give me a chance to talk to you, to explain things—"

"Zac?" Carmen said, her eyes widening. "Are these your parents?"

Chest aching, Zac stepped away from her. "Yes."

Hurt flickered across her lovely face as she put the pieces together. "Your father owns this resort? Why didn't you tell me?"

"Because I don't tell anyone about my past." His sharp tone reverberated through the space between them. "Why would that be any different this weekend with you?"

Even as the words emerged he regretted them. He had opened up to her more than he had with anyone else. He had even intended to tell her the full truth about himself eventually. But it was too late to take back his statement now, if the way the color had drained from Carmen's face was any indication.

He wanted to apologize, wanted to scream to the huge pine rafters above that he loved her, that none of this mattered to him anymore. All he cared about was her. But it was too late.

Frustrated, he lashed out at his father again. "What exactly are you going to explain to me, huh? How you're a reformed liar and a cheat? How you've moved past your deception and made a new life for yourself with my mother? How you regret throwing away your family, your flesh and blood, and the love of a woman who worshipped the ground you walked on for one night of pleasure? Sorry, but I've already heard it and I can do without the replay. There was a time I worshipped you, trusted you, loved you. But no more. Because not a day goes by that I don't worry I'll turn out just like you. Does that make you proud? Is that the legacy you wanted to pass on to your son? Loneliness? Isolation? Embarrassment? If so, then congratulations. Because of you I don't trust anyone. Because of you I sleep around and never commit to anyone. Why should I when I could end up cheating on them just like you did my mother?"

The truth cut like a razor on Zac's tongue, but he'd been holding it in far too long.

His father's face had gone ashen. "Please, son…"

"Stop calling me that!" Zac pulled away when Carmen reached for his arm.

"Zac, please… Step outside with us into the hallway, where we can discuss this in private," his mother pleaded. "Your father has atoned for his mistakes. He's not the same person. Give him a chance—"

"No. No more chances. He had a chance twelve years ago. To choose to stay faithful to you and the commitment he made to you and his family. But he chose to throw all that away."

Zac glanced over at Carmen, who was watching their exchange. Dots of color had returned to her cheeks and her eyes glittered with angry heat. His heart stumbled anew. This was her special night, the whole reason he was here, and now it was ruined. Because of him. Because of his lies and his deception. He really was no better than his father.

The worst wasn't over, however, because his father had regained some composure and was not backing down.

"You want to do this here? Now? Fine," his father said, his dark eyes glittering with determination. "I've got nothing to hide. All my secrets were laid bare for the world years ago. But can you say the same, son? I've apologized for what I did. I've made amends. I've tried to live better since. People are fallible, son. We fall down.

We make mistakes. What happened back then was a horrible mistake on my part, but I've spent every day since making reparation to your mother. We put it behind us and made a new future—a better future. One I'd hoped you'd be a part of. But I can see now that the real thing you inherited from me was stubbornness. You're alone? You're afraid to commit? You don't trust people? Take a look at your own choices, son, before you go laying that on me. I talked to Dustin this evening. He told me about you and your lady friend, here, staying in the suite upstairs. You think I don't see that engagement ring on her finger? Were you planning on even inviting us to the wedding?"

"There is no wedding," Zac said, before he could think better of it. But thankfully, Lance and Priya were still gone and Ellen and Liz were up on the stage. "We faked an engagement so Carmen could get a job she wants in California. Not that it's any of your business. We're just friends. Nothing more."

He'd meant for that chilly statement to put the quick kibosh on his parents' questions about his relationship with Carmen, but he didn't miss the tiny pained gasp from the woman beside him. Zac hid his own wince and hazarded a side-glance at her.

"We'll talk about it later," he whispered. "In our room. Alone."

"Why?" Carmen asked, her arms crossed and her toe tapping against the plush carpet beneath her high-heeled sandals. "You seem to have no problem airing all your dirty laundry right here in front of everyone. Why not this too?"

"Because I'm trying to stick to our deal and keep your secret," Zac said, keeping his voice down.

"Secrets and fake engagements, eh?" his father said,

narrowing his gaze. "Looks like you've got your own issues to deal with. Can't go blaming all this on *me*, son."

"I said don't call me that," Zac growled.

"Don't talk to your parents that way," Carmen said, scowling.

"Stay out of this. It's a private matter. It doesn't concern you."

Zac's heart pinched at the way Carmen blanched, but *dammit*. This was getting out of control. He needed to keep things separate. He needed to regain his cool composure. He needed to sort through all this and find the right way forward.

Unfortunately there was no time to do any of that, because the next thing he heard was the voice of the MC, booming over the PA system in the dining hall.

"And now a special announcement from the primary sponsor of this year's conference—esteemed businesswoman and midwife, and lifelong advocate for women's health, Ellen Landon!"

The master of ceremonies stepped aside and applause filled the dining room. Carmen did her best to hide the hurricane of emotions swirling inside her—hurt, anger, regret, heartache. She took a deep breath and forced herself to smile, since all eyes were focused on her at that moment.

This whole mess was her fault. Zac was right. He was trying to stick to the deal they'd made at the beginning of this whole fiasco. He was her rent-a-fiancé for the weekend, her fake fiancé. It was her own stupid fault that she'd read more into it than she should. Last night had been special to her, but obviously to him it had been just another quick fling.

"Doh eat de bread de devil knead," as her mama would say.

This was a tough time. One of her own making, unfortunately. She'd gone ahead and opened her heart to Zac—gone ahead and fallen for him when he'd clearly shown he didn't want that.

Stupid, Carmen. So stupid.

Lance and Priya returned to the table at last, holding hands and keeping very much to themselves, as they'd done all evening. Strange, that, but Carmen had bigger problems to deal with at the moment.

Ellen smiled down from the podium. "Tonight, we're pleased to announce the candidate we've chosen to be the new head of midwife staff at our Big Sur, California, clinic. It came down to two final contenders—Ms. Priya Shaw and Ms. Carmen Sanchez. Ladies, please stand so we can give you both a round of applause."

Carmen was only vaguely aware of the cheers around her as Zac stood stiffly by her side, not looking at her at all. She wanted to shake him, and she wanted to hug him. She wanted to demand that he tell her why he'd not told her about his parents or the fact his father owned this entire resort.

He wasn't the man she thought he was. Not at all.

Stay out of this. It's a private matter. It doesn't concern you.

Gah. Why hadn't she done that? Enjoyed a nice weekend away. Stuck to her original plan. Kept her heart out of the equation. Now it was shattered on the floor, along with any hope of things continuing with Zac past this weekend, of them having more than a few nights of sex, being more to each other.

"Thank you, ladies," Ellen said. "Now for the announcement. After several rounds of interviews, and extensive face-to-face meetings this weekend, the candidate we've chosen for the job is…"

All Carmen wanted to do at that moment was to go back to her room and curl up in a ball to nurse her broken heart, to berate herself for being such an idiot. Whatever had made her think playboy Zac would settle down with *her*?

"Carmen Sanchez!" Ellen beamed down at her from the stage. "Congratulations, Carmen. We're so excited to welcome you to our California practice, and we're looking forward to all the amazing new protocols you'll put in place soon."

People rushed to congratulate her.

She responded in a fog.

Zac remained by her side, stiff as a stone, and his parents lingered as well.

Finally he leaned closer and said, "I'm going back to the room."

He started toward the side exit and his parents followed.

"We're not done here, son," his father called, racing after Zac with his wife in tow.

Carmen turned to Ellen and Liz. "If you'll excuse me? I need to check on my fiancé."

She hurried toward the exit and was almost to the door when the shaking started. Mild at first, like the vibrations of a large truck passing by on the road outside, gradually getting worse until the large chandelier at the center of the room swayed. A low, distant roar—like a freight train approaching—reached a crescendo and the world shook.

Earthquake.

They were having an earthquake.

Not a bad one, given what she'd seen following the seven point zero magnitude one in Anchorage the year prior, but still enough to send dishes crashing off carts and pictures flying off the walls. People huddled together for safety, and some even crawled under the tables. Several older attendees had been knocked to the ground, but no one seemed badly injured, thank goodness.

Earthquakes weren't uncommon in Alaska, especially smaller ones, but even so, Carmen's heart rate tripled, and she braced herself in the exit doorway until the tremor stopped and the roar of the sound waves faded away.

Legs quaking, she fumbled her way out of the exit and into the hall, only to find Zac crouched beside an older man on the floor.

It was his father, with his wife kneeling beside him, weeping softly. "Please, Zac. Don't let your father die. Please!"

"I'll do the best I can, Mom. I swear."

"What happened?" Carmen stood amongst the crumbled plaster and shattered glass on the floor, her brain taking a moment to register it all. "Was it the earthquake?"

"No. I don't know." Zac was in full EMT mode, taking the man's pulse, then ripping open his shirt to start CPR. "Call 911, Carmen. Now!"

She fumbled her phone out of her purse and did as he asked, before rushing over to his side. "ETA five minutes on the ambulance."

He didn't miss a beat in the CPR—a credit to his skill as a paramedic.

"Thank you for calling them."

"Of course," she said, kneeling and switching into nurse mode, taking over chest compressions while he gave his father life-saving breaths. "Even though it's a private matter and doesn't concern me."

At least he had the decency to look ashamed when she threw his earlier words back in his face.

"I'm sorry…"

The wail of sirens grew closer outside, matching the screeching hurt inside Carmen. He'd been clear about not wanting a commitment up front, but that was little comfort to her broken heart now. She'd fallen for Zac way too hard and way too fast, against all her wishes to the contrary.

She should've known better.

She should've done better.

Hurt almost overwhelmed her before she shoved it aside, behind a wall of professional necessity. Right now she had a patient to save. Her pain would wait until later.

Same as it always did.

CHAPTER ELEVEN

"WE'VE GOT HIM, SIR," the paramedic said as they loaded Zac's father into the back of an ambulance a short time later.

They'd had to use the defibrillator to restart his father's heart. He was breathing on his own now, though Zac knew only too well from experience how quickly a patient's status could change. His emotions were a mess—anxious, sad, pissed off and remorseful. All at the same time.

He couldn't help thinking that this was his fault, even though logically he knew that was ridiculous.

"We'll take him to the hospital in town, then I'm guessing he'll be airlifted to Anchorage as soon as he's stable."

"Thank you."

Zac helped his mother into the back of the ambulance. She looked so much smaller and more fragile than he remembered. She clung to his father's limp hand like a lifeline and Zac's troubled heart fractured a bit more. Whether he understood it or not, his mother loved his father, and she'd be devastated if anything happened to him.

"I'll come up as soon as I get things settled here at the hotel, Mom."

He stood back to let the EMTs shut the rear doors of the rig, then watched as they drove off, lights and sirens blaring in the cold, dark night. Just an hour prior he'd vowed to turn his back on his parents and never see them again. Now he was right back into the thick of it with them and he had no idea how he felt about it. It was like a case of emotional whiplash—hating his father one second, then fearing he'd lose the man forever the next.

Behind him, he felt the weight of Carmen's stare on him and knew he had another hard battle yet to fight. He'd not missed the look of shock on her face when he'd told her the truth about his parents, nor the way that shock had given way to betrayal. A feeling he was all too familiar with from his own past.

"Look, I'm sorry I didn't tell you sooner. I should have been truthful right up front." He turned slowly to see her huddled inside his tux jacket, her arms crossed beneath the expensive fabric and her green-gold eyes spitting fire at him. "I don't know what else to say except I'm sorry."

"You don't trust me." She looked anywhere but at him. "I get it. This whole weekend was about pretending. You played your part well. I guess I thought we were friends, but I shouldn't have expected that to change anything. I mean, like you said, it's not my concern. I'm not important enough for you to tell me the truth about your identity."

Not important enough?

He lowered his head to stare at his feet. Dirty icy slush covered his shiny black loafers, and if that wasn't a metaphor for this disaster of an evening then he didn't know what was.

"We are friends."

And I wanted us to be so much more...

Instead of saying those words, however, he bit them

back out of old habit. "And you are important to me, Carmen. I wanted to tell you so many times over this weekend, but the timing was never right."

He cringed, his father's words from earlier ringing in his head.

People are fallible, son. We fall down. We make mistakes.

Well, Zac sure as hell had made his share of them where Carmen was concerned.

He scrambled to keep his head above water. "If it helps, I've never told anyone in Anchorage about my true identity."

"It doesn't help."

Yeah, he hadn't thought it would. Worse, he deserved all the ire she could pour out on him after the way he'd deceived her. Deserved to lose her, same as his father had almost lost his mother, because he was no better than his old man.

A liar. A cheat. A fraud.

Just as he'd always feared.

Well, if things were going down the drain, he might as well get it all out there in the open.

"Look, at first I didn't tell you because I didn't trust you—though it's not just you… I don't trust anyone. But later I didn't tell you because I didn't want to ruin your big weekend. And I didn't want to lose what we had last night."

"I see."

The small crowd that had gathered in the parking lot after the earthquake were slowly making their way back inside now the building inspectors had deemed the structure safe.

Carmen moved closer to him, out of the line of traffic, her expression dark. "You didn't tell me so I'd keep sleeping with you?"

"No. That's not what I meant."

"Well, that's what you said."

She'd crossed her arms again and was tap, tap, tapping that toe of hers on the ground. Never a good sign.

"I always knew you were a player, but that's low even for you."

"We had an agreement. No strings. *Your* rules, not mine."

He hated bringing it up, but she had him on the defensive now, and with everything else going on he felt raw and vulnerable and way too exposed, so he lashed out.

"This whole fiasco wouldn't have even happened if you hadn't asked me here, Carmen, so don't go blaming me if things didn't turn out the way you wanted. I played my part. I acted like your doting fiancé. Based on how much you enjoyed yourself last night, I'd say you got your money's worth. Because that's all *I* was here for, right?"

Her face had paled beneath the overhead lights, but he was on a roll now.

"You don't see me as anything but your fake boy toy. Because you work too damned much and too damned hard to have time for a real relationship. All you do is sacrifice for others and never take anything for yourself. *Poor Carmen, martyring herself on the altar of everyone else's happiness and well-being.* I thought maybe a weekend away might show you the error of your thinking. But I was wrong. You're alone because you like being alone. So fine. *Be* alone. Enjoy."

"How dare you? I cared for you, Zac. Beyond friendship. Way beyond liking. I—" She stopped herself and cursed under her breath. "Fine. Whatever. As far as I remember, you enjoyed yourself as much as I did. Then again, you enjoy yourself with a lot of women. Like father like son, apparently. Who knew bed-hopping was genetic?"

Zac froze, fists clenched at his sides, livid. Her words had struck far too close for his comfort. *Dammit.* He didn't have time for this. He needed to come to terms with the fact that the entire universe he'd carefully constructed these last twelve years had crumbled at his feet. He needed to get away from Carmen before he said something else he'd regret forever.

He brushed past her, ignoring the pain in her eyes that slashed his heart into pieces. "Congratulations on your new job in California."

Tonight had been a huge mess, and now he needed to pick up the shattered pieces and get on with the rest of his life.

Or what was left of it.

Carmen went back to the suite in something of a daze, too numb to cry. This evening had not turned out like she'd planned. Not at all. She'd gotten the job of her dreams and had a bright future ahead of her—could take care of her mother and her sister as she'd always wanted. And yet it all felt hollow somehow.

Far too amped-up to sleep, despite the late hour, she began packing instead. That way when Zac returned he would see she was ready to put all this behind her and move on.

Once her bags were packed, and she'd showered and changed into her PJs, Carmen slumped down on the sofa in the living room and stared out the window at the approaching dawn. It was going on six a.m. now and there was no sign of Zac returning. Just as well, since she was in no mood to see him again at the moment anyway.

How dared he accuse her of playing the martyr, of overextending herself for selfish reasons? He knew nothing about her. Not really. He didn't know her struggles. She snorted and looked around at her lavish surroundings. Apparently *he'd* grown up in the lap of luxury.

Carmen closed her eyes and let her head fall back against the cushion. Images of the hallway after the earthquake haunted her—Zac performing CPR on his father while his mother wept at his side, the desperation on his handsome face. That hadn't been the look of a man at peace with his life. That had been the look of a man who'd made major mistakes and feared he'd never have a chance to atone.

She sighed and straightened again. Not her problem. Not her issue to deal with anymore. Like he'd said. Not her concern.

Zac Taylor was out of her life and she'd do just fine. Because she was a survivor. She didn't need Zac. She didn't need anyone.

She'd give her notice at Anchorage Mercy as soon as she got home, put their modest little house on the market, then move with her family to California and put all this ugliness behind her. She'd get her mother set up at a nice assisted-living facility. She'd get Clara enrolled in the university of her choice near Big Sur. She'd forget all about Zac and her pipe dream of the two of them having any sort of lasting relationship.

He was a player. Carmen should have known better. Going forward, Carmen would do better.

"What doh kill does fatten." What doesn't kill you makes you stronger.

Right.

Now, if she could just get her battered heart back with the program, she'd be all set.

CHAPTER TWELVE

A COUPLE OF days later Carmen was making dinner at home. She had a rare night off and hoped to make the most of it by starting to pack up some things around the house.

After returning from the conference she'd basically gone into "blinder" mode—focusing on all the tasks she needed to do to prepare for the upcoming move to California.

They'd arrived back at Ted Stevens Airport and she and Zac had gone their separate ways without another word to each other. Lance and Priya had both asked her if everything was all right and she'd explained the whole situation to them—including the fake engagement—figuring she had enough deception in her life to last her a lifetime.

Prior to leaving the resort she'd told Ellen and Liz that she and Zac had broken up. They'd felt badly for her, but had said it didn't change their decision to hire her for the new supervisor position. She was still their top choice for the job.

The truth was out there now—sort of. She and Zac weren't engaged anymore.

Funny, but she'd expected to feel better about that than she did.

For the past few days she'd kept her head down and her vision focused. She'd turned in her resignation at Anchorage Mercy, begun transitioning her current patients to other midwives on staff, and generally started the slow, sad process of pulling up her roots here in preparation for putting them down elsewhere.

And, yes, maybe in the wee small hours before dawn her mind might return to the weekend with Zac. To how blissful everything had been with him until it hadn't been anymore. To the way it had felt lying in his arms, holding him close, kissing him under the brilliant Northern Lights.

But she'd firmly remind herself that he'd lied to her about his true identity. That he probably would've continued to lie to her for the foreseeable future if he'd not gotten caught. After all, she'd been the wronged party. She'd been the one in the right.

Then images of Zac's gravely ill father would fill her head. So many times she'd started to pick up the phone to call, to ask him if he needed anything, but then she'd hung up. He'd walked away from her that night. He'd said he didn't need her, didn't want her in his life any longer. He wouldn't appreciate her intrusion now.

Ugh. She stirred the thick soup simmering on the stove and sighed. All of it was such a shame.

She'd heard through the grapevine at the hospital that Zac's father had been transferred to the Cardiac ICU after they'd returned. Rumor had it he was doing better, though stent surgery to open a couple of blocked arteries in his heart was going to be necessary. The procedure itself was a fairly routine operation these days, but that still wouldn't lessen the stress on his loved ones. Anytime a member of your family went under the knife it was hard.

Speaking of families, her mama was at the kitchen

table now, supervising Carmen's cooking as usual. She might have early-onset dementia, but that didn't stop the woman from bossing her daughters around in the kitchen.

"What's wrong, girl?" Mama looked up from the magazine she was paging through, frowning. "Time longer dan twine."

"I know…" Carmen leaned a hip against the edge of the counter while she stirred. Mama was right. Even the worst problems came to an end, if given time. She just wished it would be sooner rather than later. "I've just got a lot going on right now."

"Hmm…" Her mother flipped another page. "Wouldn't have anything to do with dat man you went to the resort with, would it?"

"No." *Yes.* Mama had always been far too observant for her own good. "I'm busy, that's all. Trying to get ready for the move and all. Plus, work's been crazy, and I'm training my replacement. It's a lot."

"But are you happy?" Mama looked up at her, eyes clear and expression lucid. "Dis what you want?"

"Of course." Carmen turned away and got things together to set the table. "It's the perfect job at the perfect clinic. I've worked hard to get the position and I'll earn enough money so we won't have to worry anymore."

"Worry?" Clara asked, dropping her backpack in the corner as she came in, then grabbing the bowls from Carmen's hands to set the table. "What are you guys talking about?"

"I asked your sister if she was happy," Mama said. "Since she been mooning around like a lost puppy after her weekend away."

"You've noticed too, eh?" Clara looked back at Carmen over her shoulder.

That was the great thing about families—you could

put on the bravest face you could and they still saw through your BS. That was also the worst thing about them. She'd never been good at fooling people, least of all her family.

Clara got silverware from the drawer beside the sink. "It's Zac, isn't it? You like him. I can tell. Is it serious?"

"No." *Yes. Ugh.* "It's not about him. Not really." Carmen turned off the burner under the soup and shook her head. "He lied to me. After what Papa did, I won't tolerate a man's lies."

Mama snorted. "Your father was a rogue and a rebel, but he never lied."

Carmen filled each of the bowls with soup, then put the pot back on the stove. "Yes, he did, Mama. He walked out on us, remember?" She took a seat at the table beside her sister and across from their mother. "He never told you about his family and fortune back in Buenos Aires. Just left us behind the first chance he got."

"That's not true. I knew who and what he was from the start." Mama blew on a spoonful of steaming hot soup before eating it. "There was no deception."

The two sisters exchanged a glance. This was new information.

Carmen sipped her soup, a savory, thick mix of split peas, corn, chicken broth, potatoes, carrots, celery, thyme and pimento peppers. It was a taste of home that always made her miss the island. "Mama, I think you're mistaken. Papa—"

"No, child. I'm not mistaken." Mama fixed her girls with a serious stare. "My mind might be going sometimes these days, but I still know what's true. I remember talking to your daddy the first night we met. Remember it as clear as day. He told me plain about his obligations to his family's business and that he might have to go home someday. But we were in love and it was a chance I was willing to take. Besides, he gave me you two beautiful girls, so I can't complain."

"He *left* us," Clara said, scowling. "What kind of man walks out on his children?"

"The kind that's told to."

"His wealthy family put pressure on him?" asked Carmen, nibbling on a hunk of corn from her soup.

"No. I insisted he leave." Mama scowled. "His father had died and it was his duty to take over the company. Your papa was torn. The fact he had two different lives was eating him up inside. I loved him too much to let that happen. So I told him I didn't need half a man. Told him to go home. Told him to take his money too. He wanted to stay, wanted to put us up in a fancy house and send money every month, but I didn't want it. Looking back, I suppose I should have taken it. But I loved my life and my independence too much."

Carmen blinked at her mother a moment. "Wait. So you're saying Papa wanted to take care of us, but you refused?"

"Yes. I thought I could do it all on my own. Stand on my own two feet. I don't regret my choices, but I can see now that I deprived you girls of the opportunity to know your father and to know the truth." Mama sighed and shook her head. "Carmen, I'm telling you this because if you care for this man perhaps you should forgive him, give him a chance to make amends. If you truly want him, don't make the same mistakes I did. You can have love and a life too."

"But Papa never tried to contact us," Clara said. "He just walked away."

"No." Mama's expression turned sad. "He kept his distance out of respect for my wishes. I hurt him badly by cutting him out of our lives. Now it's too late. He died a few years ago, during a climbing accident in the Andes. I'm sorry, girls. I never meant to hide this from you for so long. But time's short and you deserve to know."

The sight of their mother's tears had Carmen and Clara out of their seats and around the table to comfort her. The woman might have made mistakes, but she was still the strongest person Carmen had ever known.

"It's okay, Mama," Carmen said, resting her head against her mother's shoulder. "Seems this is a time for coming clean all around."

"Yeah." Clara sniffled. "Me too. I…uh…got word this afternoon that one of the scholarships I applied for came through. So I can afford to stay here and go to nursing school in Anchorage. It covers tuition, books, room and board. Everything!"

"That's amazing!" Carmen hugged Clara, fresh tears stinging her eyes—happy ones this time. "I'm so happy for you."

"And I've decided I want to move into that nice assisted-living facility down the street," Mama said after they'd finished hugging and congratulating Clara. "The one with the pretty gardens in back."

Carmen sat back on her heels. "You just said you love your independence. Assisted living would mean giving that up."

"I know." She patted Carmen's hand and smiled. "But it's time. You go off to your fancy new job in California and be free. Beat de iron while it hot."

"But, Mama…" Her chest constricted. The whole reason she'd gone for the position at the clinic in Big Sur was to support her mother and her sister. Without that, was the extra money worth the pain of leaving behind the place she now called home?

"Sis…?" Clara reached over and took Carmen's hand. "That *is* what you want, right?"

She shook her head. "I don't know anymore. I thought it was, but now I'm not so sure. For so long I've been so busy moving ahead. I never considered things might be fine as they are."

"What about this man?" Mama asked.

"What about him?" She hadn't seen Zac since they'd parted at the airport, and after the way they'd left things there was little chance he'd want anything to do with her again. "I doubt we can mend our ties."

"You never know until you try." Mama cupped Carmen's cheek and smiled. "You are such a treasure. He'd be lucky to have you, if he's what you want. But make haste while de sun shine, girl. Good men don't wait long."

Zac stood outside his father's hospital room, hesitant about going in. He'd worked the night shift the evening before and done his best to keep busy, so he wouldn't have a chance to brood about this conversation.

Talking with his mother in the waiting room during his dad's procedure had helped him see things in a different light where his father was concerned, but that didn't mean the old hurts had completely healed. They needed to have a talk, and this one had been a long time in coming.

He nodded at one of the residents who walked by in the hall, then took a deep breath for courage. Time to plunge in.

Zac opened the door and walked in to find his father looking smaller and older than he remembered. IVs and a blood pressure cuff were attached to one of his arms, and EKG wires extended out from the electrodes on his chest. The white hospital gown stood in stark contrast to his dark skin, and there was a half-eaten bowl of gelatin on the table over his bed, along with his reading glasses and a nearly completed crossword puzzle.

His mother sat in the chair beside the bed, the clack of her knitting needles keeping time with the beeps of the heart monitor.

Both his parents looked up when he walked in, making Zac halt in his tracks.

"Son!" His mom set aside her yarn and got up to give him a hug. "Come in…come in. I was hoping you'd stop by. I need a break. I'm going to take a walk down to the cafeteria and get a snack. Be back soon."

As she passed by the bed, she gave his father a stern *get your business done* look.

The door closed behind her, leaving Zac and his father to stare at each other awkwardly.

"Hey," Zac said at last, resisting the urge to fidget inside his paramedic's uniform. He'd come straight after his shift and hadn't taken time to run home and change. "Uh… How are you feeling?"

His father gave a curt nod. "Better. Thanks to you."

"I didn't do your surgery." Zac took the seat his mother had vacated, since it was the only one in the room besides the bed. "Just handled CPR until the ambulance arrived."

"Stop, son. You saved my life that night at the resort, from what I've been told." His father clasped his hands over his stomach. "I wouldn't still be here without you, so thank you. I'm sure it wasn't an easy choice."

Zac winced. Yeah, given the fight they'd had just before the quake, he'd had that coming. "I'm a professional. There was no decision to make. I save lives. That's what I do."

Silence fell between them once more, until finally Zac couldn't take it anymore. He was here to make amends, one way or another. Time to get it done.

"Listen, Dad. I'm sorry."

"For what?" his father asked, looking surprised. "I'm the one who owes you an apology, Zac. I let the bad feelings between us fester for all these years. I'm the one who's made the mistakes here, not you."

"But this…" He waved a hand toward his dad. "Your heart… I brought that on the other night."

"Don't flatter yourself. I've had high cholesterol for years. Been on medication for it. Not that you'd know, since you haven't seen me." His father sighed. "Again, my fault. Not yours. The earthquake didn't help either. All those people to keep safe. All those repairs to make."

Zac couldn't argue with that. "Mom and I talked yesterday while you had your procedure. She helped me understand some things I didn't before. I don't condone your affair, and nor will I forget it, but I have a better picture of how things are now. I thought you should know. I'm not saying we can go back to the way things were before your infidelity, but I'm different now too. I have a life and a career that I love here in Anchorage, and I'm proud of that. But…well, I wouldn't mind having you and Mom be a part of my life again. We could maybe give it a trial run…see how it goes."

"Hmm…" His dad nodded, his forehead creasing as he blinked hard. "I'd like that, son."

The last word shook slightly, as if he were holding back tears. And, oddly enough, Zac found himself battling a sting at the back of his own eyes.

"Good."

His father smiled at last, his eyes slightly watery. "I feared we'd never get to this place."

"Me too." Zac sat back in the chair, the knots of tension between his shoulder blades easing. "But I'm glad we did."

"Same."

His father scooted up in the bed slightly, setting off the heart monitor. A nurse rushed in to check, waving at Zac before she departed again.

"So, explain to me about this girl of yours," his father said.

Now it was Zac's turn to frown. "She's not my girl, remember? The whole thing was a fake. We haven't seen each other since we got back, and as far as I know she's been busy getting ready to move her life away from Alaska."

His father shook his head. "You serious about this girl?"

"Maybe..." Zac wasn't sure his newfound accord with his father extended that far yet. "Why?"

"If you like her, she must be special." His father reached over to pick up his glasses and crossword puzzle. "Where's she moving to?"

"Big Sur."

"Gorgeous place. Just opened a new hotel in that area a few years ago. Been looking for someone to run it for me." His father went back to working on his puzzle. "What's a word that starts with *f* and ends in *s*? Eleven letters? The clue's 'absolution.'"

"I don't need a job, Dad. I have one. I'm a paramedic. A great one—best in Anchorage."

Some of the knots in his stomach returned. Prior to their falling out, his father had expected Zac to follow in his footsteps. He hoped they wouldn't go right back to that again.

"I'm happy here," he said.

"Good." His father looked up at him then, his expression sincere. "That's all I ever wanted for you, son. To be happy. And if living here and saving lives is what does that for you, then I'm happy too. Truly. I just thought if you ever needed a place to stay when you came to visit your girl you'd have one at my place."

"And who says I'll be going to visit Carmen?" he asked, rolling his stiff neck.

Honestly, he would do more than visit her if she forgave him, but that was neither here nor there at the moment, until he talked to her and begged her forgiveness.

Zac sat up and blinked at his father. "That's it!"

"What?" His dad scowled.

"The answer." Zac pushed to his feet and grinned. "Eleven letters. Starts with *f* and ends in *s*. Forgiveness. Clue absolution. I need to go."

"Thanks, son!" his father shouted as Zac ran out of the room. "Now, go get that girl of yours."

CHAPTER THIRTEEN

CARMEN WAS AT work the next evening, catching up on her documentation from the last two deliveries she'd done. With spring right around the corner, it seemed everyone was going into labor these days.

Speaking of labor, there was a certain phone call she'd been putting off that she needed to make…

"Hey." Priya came up beside her at the counter. "How are you doing?"

"Fine." And perhaps if she kept repeating that word one day it would be true. Carmen glanced sideways at her friend, glad to see her color had improved. "And you?"

"Okay." Priya leaned an elbow on the counter. "Getting ready for the big move?"

Carmen exhaled slowly. She'd not shared her decision with anyone else yet, but now was the moment. The moment she admitted she wanted to try and repair things with Zac and see if he wanted to try having a real relationship. The moment when she declared to the world that the future she wanted for herself was right here in Anchorage.

"I've decided to decline the job in Big Sur."

"What?" Priya took her by the arm and led her into the nearby staff lounge, shutting the door before continuing. "*Why?* That's been our whole focus for months."

"I know, but things have changed." Carmen sank down onto the sofa against the wall and toyed with the hem of her lavender scrub shirt. "My heart's just not in it anymore."

"Does this have anything to do with a certain hot paramedic in the ER who pretended to be your fiancé?"

"No. I mean, yes. I mean…" She shook her head, sending her curls bouncing around her face. "Zac's definitely part of it, but he's not the whole reason."

"But you guys are still into each other, right?" Priya took a seat on the other end of the sofa, facing her. "I mean, I'll admit I was suspicious at first, but then I saw you guys dancing and there was no denying the chemistry. I felt like *I* needed to get a room afterward."

Carmen chuckled. "We did like each other. A lot. But we made mistakes."

"I'm sorry." Priya patted her on the arm. "Relationships are tough. Even fake ones. But what's the rest of the reason you're not taking the new job?"

"I'm happy *here*." She shrugged. "I love Anchorage Mercy and you guys and my patients. I don't want to give all this up and start over again from scratch."

"Makes sense." Priya twirled a piece of her long dark hair around her finger. "What about the money, though?"

"I make plenty here, and after talking with my mother and my sister the other night I found circumstances have changed. Some things are more important than money, you know?"

"I do know." Priya placed her hand on her stomach. "You're sticking around, then?"

"I am. I still need to call Ellen, though, and let her know. And I'm going to recommend you as my replacement." Carmen smiled.

"Oh, don't do that."

"Don't recommend you? Why?"

"My circumstances have changed as well." Priya grinned and patted her tummy. "Lance and I are expecting our first baby in December."

"Oh, my gosh!" Carmen hugged her friend tight. "That's fantastic. I'm so happy for you both! It also explains why you looked a bit green at the conference."

"Right?" Priya yawned. "Between all the naps and the morning sickness it's been a challenge. Anyway, we've decided to stick close to Anchorage too. My parents are in Sitka, and his are in Vancouver, so not that far away. Plus, we've picked out a plot of land and we're talking to the builders next week about constructing our new house."

"How wonderful!"

Carmen sighed. She really was happy for her friend. Happy for Lance too. And for her mama and Clara. Everyone seemed to have found their place in the world. Her as well, even if that place would be a bit lonelier without Zac to share it. Still, she'd gotten this far in life on her own—she could keep going.

"I'm so thrilled for you both. Really."

"Thanks." Priya narrowed her gaze. "Will you be my midwife?"

Touched beyond words, Carmen nodded. "Yes! Of course!"

"Good." Priya took her hand. "Now for some advice. Don't give up on him."

"Who?"

"Zac. Lance says he's going through some stuff right now with his parents. Who knew the guy's family was loaded, huh? He never acted like that around any of us."

"No, he didn't…"

He'd never seemed anything but real with Carmen, even when they'd been pretending to be engaged. Yes, he'd hurt her by not telling her the truth about his family and his background, but then considering the stories of his father's infidelity and Zac's estrangement from him because of it, she couldn't say she blamed him. Plus, given the conversation she'd had with her mother about her own papa and the falsehoods she'd believed about him growing up, it seemed they both had their share of daddy issues to deal with.

"He's a good man."

She closed her eyes and pictured Zac that first day at the airport, so handsome in his tweed blazer. Then later at the welcome reception in his tux, all suave and debonair. Then at the animal reserve, rugged in jeans and a T-shirt, kissing her under the stars. The bowling alley. The night they'd slept together. His scent, his taste, his voice…

God, she missed him so, so much.

Yearning squeezed at her chest before she pushed it aside.

Beat de iron while it hot…

Her mama's words echoed in her head. She was right. Carmen needed to stop wasting time and make use of the opportunities she had *now.* With her mother going into assisted living and her sister living in the dorms at college, for the first time in forever Carmen would have no one to look out for except herself. She could go where she wanted, do what she wanted, be whoever she wanted. She should stop being scared about it and instead embrace her freedom.

But first she had a phone call to make.

She pushed to her feet and walked over to the phone on the wall. "I need to call Ellen."

"Right. And I need to go check on my patients." Priya started out the door, then leaned back into the room to give her a thumbs-up. "You got this, girl."

"Thanks."

Carmen waited until she was alone to dial the number, swallowing hard as it connected.

"Big Sur Women's Health Clinic," said a receptionist in a bright tone. "How may I direct your call?"

"Ellen Landon, please. Tell her it's Carmen Sanchez calling."

"Certainly. One moment, please, Ms. Sanchez."

Generic instrumental music played in the background before Ellen picked up.

"Carmen! Great to hear from you. How are preparations going for the move? Liz and I were just talking about you last night. I planned to call you later in the week to invite you down to stay with us for the weekend. Thought we could show you around Big Sur and help you get acclimated before the big move."

"Oh, that's very sweet," said Carmen, digging the toe of her white running shoe into the tile floor. "But I'm afraid I've got some bad news. I won't be accepting the position after all."

There was a slight pause, and Carmen lived and died in those few seconds.

"I'm so disappointed to hear that, Carmen," Ellen said. "Can you tell me what changed your mind? At the conference you seemed so interested in the job."

"I was. It's a great opportunity. But after a lot of thought and introspection I've come to realize I'm happy here and I want to stay in Anchorage."

"This doesn't have anything to do with your friend Zac, does it?" Ellen asked.

"No. Not really," Carmen said. "I actually haven't even seen him since I got back home. My circumstances here have changed, though, and I've decided to go in a different direction for my future."

"I'm sorry to hear that for us, but I wish you the best of luck." Ellen sighed. "Well, I guess I need to get a hold of Ms. Shaw, then."

Carmen wanted to tell her not to, but then figured it was Priya's news to tell. "I do want to thank you again for the opportunity, Ellen. It was such an honor to meet you and I hope we can stay in touch. You never know what might change down the road."

"Absolutely." Ellen's warm smile was palpable through her tone. "It was a pleasure meeting you too, Carmen. Finding such caring and dedication is rare these days and much appreciated. I'll keep in touch."

Once the call had ended, Carmen went back down to the ER just in time for a new case.

"Anchorage Mercy, this is FA18. Stand by for arrival of suspected placental abruption. Twenty-five-year-old patient in labor, thirty-nine weeks' gestation. Bleeding vaginally. Over."

Carmen rushed to slip into a clean gown and gloves, and was ready by the ER bay doors as the ambulance pulled up. The mother was full-term, but there were any number of problems that could develop if the placenta detached before the baby was born—including death. Tom Farber, the OB on call that night, stood beside her, ready and waiting in case the worst happened.

Within seconds the automatic doors whooshed open and the EMTs raced inside with a woman on a gurney, her harried husband beside her. Carmen quickly scanned the team, but there was no sign of Zac. Even under these circumstances her heart still ached for him.

She forced the errant thoughts from her head as they wheeled the patient into Trauma Bay One. Susan, Zac's usual partner, gave her the rundown.

Carmen waited until they'd transferred the woman to

the hospital bed, then moved in beside her. "Hello, my dear. My name's Carmen Sanchez. I'm the midwife on duty in the ER tonight. Can you tell me if this is your first pregnancy?"

"No." The woman's breath caught on a sob. "My third. My daughter's five and I had another baby, but it was stillborn last year. Please save my baby. *Please.*" She cried out as another contraction hit hard.

Carmen looked down to see Tom performing the pelvic exam.

"Fresh red blood," he said. "Right. Let's get Mom hooked up to the heart monitors and see how Baby's doing."

Fresh blood wasn't good. Not good at all.

The woman clung to Carmen's arm. "Please, no surgery."

"She's terrified after her sister had a bad experience," the husband said. "She hates hospitals all around, actually. That's why we were trying to have the baby at home."

"Without any help?" Carmen gave him a side-glance. "With her history, that's very risky."

"I just wanted to make her happy," the husband said, clearly distraught. "Don't let her die, please. Save her and the baby. *Please.*"

"We'll do our best," Tom said, motioning with his head for one of the nurses to get the husband out of there. "Now, Ms....?"

"Woznichak," Susan supplied helpfully.

"Right. What's your first name, hon?" Carmen asked, holding the woman's hand.

"Lonnie," she managed to say between panting breaths. "The baby's coming!"

"Yes, it is." Carmen gave the woman her best reassuring smile. "And we'll be here with you every step of the way."

"Okay," Tom said from the end of the table. "Fetal heart rate looks good, no distress as yet, so we're going to continue in the traditional way for now." He smiled at Lonnie, then checked the nearby monitor. "On the next contraction I want you to push as hard as you can, okay?"

Lonnie nodded and gave a primal growl, bearing down hard, her back arched.

"Yes!" Carmen said, happy to take the role of cheerleader. The patient's face had turned a mottled mix of red and purple with effort. "That's it, Lonnie. Very good!"

At last the contraction subsided, only to give way to another. They were coming close together.

"Won't be long now," Carmen said, nodding to Tom.

"Nope. Almost there," he said. "I can see the head."

Lonnie screamed as another contraction hit, and gripped Carmen's hand so hard she thought her fingers might snap.

"Breathe!" Carmen said, coaching her through the pain. "That's it! That's it!"

"Head's out," Tom said. "One more push and you're done, Lonnie."

A squelching "pop" sounded and Lonnie went limp on the table, tears and sweat streaming from her face as she stared down at the newborn in Tom's hands. "Is that him?"

"Yes." He placed the baby on her chest before cutting the umbilical cord. "You have a gorgeous baby boy."

The father came around the curtain to kiss his wife and dote on his son and Carmen couldn't stop grinning. This was what she loved most about her job. Welcoming new life into the world.

After helping with the delivery of the placenta and

the clean-up, Carmen felt tired but proud. She exited the trauma bay to see Susan at the nurses' station, clearly waiting for her.

Huh? That was odd. Usually the EMTs went back to their rigs after a call.

She discarded her soiled things into the biohazard bin, then washed up in the sink in the hall. Once she'd dried her hands, she walked back to where the other woman was standing. Her first thought was to ask how Zac was doing, but she didn't want to come off as unprofessional.

"Hey," she said, feigning interest in the calendar on the wall. "How are you, Susan?"

"Okay," the EMT said. "But I'll be better if you can help my partner out."

"Huh?" Carmen glanced over her shoulder, frowning, only to stop short at the sight of Zac, standing there in the ER in his tux—the same one from the conference—looking just as handsome as she remembered.

Susan grinned. "Seems Zac, here, lost his heart a few days back, and he thinks you're the only one who can help him find it again."

"I got it from here, Susan—thanks," said Zac. Then he stepped forward and dropped to one knee in front of Carmen. "I know I screwed up, big-time. And I know I have no reason to expect you to trust me ever again. I know I lost the best thing that ever happened to me when I let you go, Carmen Sanchez, but if you can find it in your heart to forgive me, I swear I'll spend the rest of my life making it up to you."

Stunned, Carmen stared down at him, trying to take it all in. People were starting to stare, and heat crept up her cheeks. "Zac, get up. What are you doing?"

"I'm bowing before my queen." He looked up at her and winked. "Can you forgive me?"

She sighed and shook her head, laughing. "There's nothing to forgive, Zac. I'm as much to blame for what happened at the resort as you. It was my plan in the first place."

"But I went along with it. And I lied to you about who I really was."

He glanced around at the small crowd of staff who'd gathered. Word had spread like wildfire about his wealthy background once they'd gotten back to Anchorage Mercy. He knew Carmen had never said a word, but somehow the hospital rumor mill knew all.

"I should've been honest with you from the start, but back then I couldn't even be honest with myself."

"I wasn't exactly winning any awards in the honesty department myself," she said, then gestured toward a small empty supply room nearby. "How about we get some privacy?"

He nodded and followed her into the tiny room. The overhead fluorescent lights flickered on automatically, sensing their presence.

"So…" he said, his hands in his pockets and his gaze focused on his toes.

"So."

This close to him she could feel his heat through her thin scrubs and smell his cologne. She'd missed both those things more than she could say. Missed everything about him, really.

"I guess you've been busy packing for California?" he said at last.

"Actually, I turned down the job." She huffed out a breath. "I decided everything I wanted was already here in Anchorage."

Zac did look up then. "You did?"

"I did. Called Ellen earlier to tell her. I was going

to recommend Priya take my place, but then…" She stopped before spilling her friend's secret, in case Zac didn't know.

"Yeah. Lance is over the moon about the baby. It's all he talks about anymore. 'My son this' or 'my daughter that.'" He grinned. "Not that I blame him. Hope to have a couple of my own someday."

"Me too." She pursed her lips and rocked back on her heels. "Look, Zac. I'm sorry too—about the things I said to you. How you choose to live your life is none of my business. I'm afraid I let my old biases affect my life now, and for that you have my apologies. I talked with my mom after I got back, and she straightened me out on a few things."

"Like what?"

"Like the fact that my dad did want to take care of us, but she chose to refuse his help because she was stubborn and wanted to do things on her own."

"I see." He bit back a smile. "Sounds like someone else I know."

"Do you want to hear my apology or not?" she asked, needing to get it all out before she couldn't. "I shouldn't have judged you for your past any more than I would want you to judge me for mine. Neither of us had any control over what happened back then."

"Agreed."

"But I do think it might be good for you to at least talk to your father and try to reconcile. Family is one of the most important things there is in this world, Zac. It's not healthy to be alone. Especially with your father's illness. If he died and you'd never made amends that would haunt you for the rest of your days."

"Also agreed. My father's doing fine, by the way. He's had three stents put in and is being released from hospital today," Zac said. "And we did talk. My mom too. It's all good. Well, as good as can be expected for now. They're heading back to the resort."

"Wow. Okay, then…" She had to admit she was impressed. Zac was a take-charge kind of man. Another one of the things she loved most about him. "That's great."

"Know what else is great?" he asked, inching closer to her.

She shook her head, not trusting her voice as her pulse notched higher.

"The fact that for the first time in over a decade I'm finally free. Free of the guilt and the secrets and the shadow of betrayal. I feel like a new man."

"Yeah?" she squeaked.

There was only about an inch separating them now. Still, Carmen stood her ground, not willing to give up this time for anything in the world.

"Yeah. And as a new man I'm looking to settle down with the right woman."

Swallowing hard, she could only nod up at him.

"I want you to be that woman, Carmen, if you'll have me. If you can find it in your heart to forgive me and grant me another chance." He reached up slowly to take her chin between his thumb and forefinger. "I promise that if you do I will spend the rest of my life treating you like the precious treasure you are. *Can* you forgive me, Carmen?"

Mouth dry and head spinning, she gave him a trembling smile. "Yes, Zac. Yes!"

Next thing she knew she was in his arms and he was kissing her deeply—and, man, oh, man, she hadn't realized how badly she wanted this until she felt his firm lips on hers.

When he pulled away at last, they were both breathless.

"I love you, Carmen Sanchez," he said, his forehead resting against hers.

"I love you too, Zac Taylor," she said. Then she pulled back to look up at him through her lashes and give him a mischievous grin. "Although I do have one condition."

"What's that, darling?" He clasped his hands behind her lower back.

"That you take me back to that resort of yours someday and treat me to all the amenities I missed out on the first time."

"Count on it, my queen." He laughed and lifted her into his arms. "Your wish is my command."

CHAPTER FOURTEEN

One year later...

THE WEDDING DAY was gorgeous. Sunshine, blue skies and all their friends and family gathered in the gardens behind Anchorage Mercy Hospital. Considering it was where he and Carmen had first met, it seemed only right that it was where Zac and the woman he loved should start their life together as man and wife.

After they'd made their vows and sealed it with a kiss, the entire party flew over to the Arctic Star Resort for the reception. Zac's father had paid to have the whole gang flown there.

Jake and Molly and their twins. Tom and Wendy and their new baby, and Tom's daughter Sam. Carmen's mother. Even Zac's parents and Dustin. Priya was there too, with her adorable baby girl, Kaia. Lance had been his best man, of course, and Carmen's sister Clara her maid of honor.

The whole day couldn't have gone any better, and now there wasn't a dry eye in the house as Zac led his beautiful bride out onto the dance floor for their first dance. He nodded to the DJ and Michael Bublé crooned the lyrics to "The Way You Look Tonight," the song they'd danced to that first night at the conference—the night they'd both started falling in love.

"Happy, darling?" Zac whispered near Carmen's ear as they swayed gently to the music.

"So happy," she said, beaming up at him. "Though I do have something to tell you."

His pulse stuttered a bit. After all the secrets and lies they'd overcome because of his past, he wasn't sure how many more surprises he could take.

"What? If it's another horrible secret, I may jump off O'Malley's Peak."

"No, silly." She shook her head. "This is a good secret. Well, I hope it will be good."

Zac swallowed hard. "Just tell me."

"I'm pregnant," she said, her green-gold eyes shining with happiness. "I know it's earlier than we planned, but these things happen sometimes, and—"

"You're having a baby?" Zac said, cutting her off.

He blinked down at her, trying to take it in. He'd always wanted a kid of his own, but had been scared he might not be a good father. A year ago he wouldn't have been ready. But now, after putting the past to rest and forgiving his father and himself, he was beyond excited.

"We're having a baby?"

She nodded, fresh tears sparkling in her eyes. "Are you happy?"

"Yes! I'm going to be a father!"

His grin grew by the second, and then carefully he picked Carmen up and spun her around in his arms while the crowd clapped.

"We're going to be parents!"

"Yes, we are!" Carmen hugged him tight. "I love you so much, *doux-doux*."

"And I love you too, darling," Zac said, kissing her sweetly.

* * * * *

MILLS & BOON

Coming next month

CINDERELLA AND THE SURGEON
Scarlet Wilson

'You're the midwife?'

The deep voice was practically at her ear and she jumped, stumbling over her own feet.

Esther spun around. Mr Imposing was standing in her personal space, his arms folded across his chest, looking her up and down in a disapproving manner. Okay, so the NICU probably wasn't big enough for all these people, which could explain the space thing. And, the massive splatter of coffee all over her scrub trousers probably wasn't helping her appearance.

But right now she could smell his clean aftershave and see into those toffee-coloured eyes.

'Weren't you the nurse who was sleeping in the canteen?'

She could feel the blood rush to her face and all the hairs on her body prickle in indignation. Who did this guy think he was, sweeping in here with his giant entourage?

Nope. No way.

'I'm sure you know that we limit visitors to NICU. Maybe other NICUs relax rules for you and your entourage, but Queen Victoria's doesn't.'

She started to count in her head just how many people were in his little gang. She'd reached twelve when his deep voice sounded right in front of her again.

'Isn't this a teaching hospital? Famous the world over

for its training programmes?' There was a mocking tone in his voice.

Esther had been around long enough to recognise an arrogant doctor. As a nurse, and a midwife, she'd met more than her fair share—both male and female.

She hated anyone being dismissive with her. And she didn't stand for it. More than once she'd used her Scottish accent to the best of her ability to give someone short shrift.

There was something about her accent that generally made people take a step back—particularly when she was angry. If this guy didn't watch out, he'd soon find out exactly who Esther McDonald was. She'd barely had a chance to look this guy up. All she knew was he was one of a few specialist surgeons who could do the procedure that Billy needed.

She mirrored his stance and folded her arms, tilting her chin towards him as she put a fake smile on her face. 'Maybe you'd like to introduce yourself and let me know why you think your needs are more important than the needs of the very special babies we have in here?'

She could do sarcasm too.

He inhaled deeply, almost like he wanted to show her just how broad his chest was. But Esther had never been easily intimidated by anyone. 'I'm Harry Beaumont. I'm here to do the surgery on your patient.'

Continue reading
CINDERELLA AND THE SURGEON
Scarlet Wilson

Available next month
www.millsandboon.co.uk

COMING SOON!

We really hope you enjoyed reading this book. If you're looking for more romance, be sure to head to the shops when new books are available on

Thursday 23rd January

To see which titles are coming soon, please visit

millsandboon.co.uk/nextmonth

MILLS & BOON
True Love

Romance from the Heart

Celebrate true love with tender stories of
heartfelt romance, from the rush of falling
in love to the joy a new baby can bring,
and a focus on the emotional
heart of a relationship.

JOIN US ON SOCIAL MEDIA!

Stay up to date with our latest releases, author news and gossip, special offers and discounts, and all the behind-the-scenes action from Mills & Boon...

 millsandboon

 millsandboonuk

 millsandboon

It might just be true love...

MILLS & BOON

THE HEART OF ROMANCE

A ROMANCE FOR EVERY KIND OF READER

MODERN

Prepare to be swept off your feet by sophisticated, sexy and seductive heroes, in some of the world's most glamourous and romantic locations, where power and passion collide.
8 stories per month.

HISTORICAL

Escape with historical heroes from time gone by. Whether your passion is for wicked Regency Rakes, muscled Vikings or rugged Highlanders, awaken the romance of the past.
6 stories per month.

MEDICAL

Set your pulse racing with dedicated, delectable doctors in the high-pressure world of medicine, where emotions run high and passion, comfort and love are the best medicine.
6 stories per month.

True Love

Celebrate true love with tender stories of heartfelt romance, from the rush of falling in love to the joy a new baby can bring, and a focus on the emotional heart of a relationship.
8 stories per month.

Desire

Indulge in secrets and scandal, intense drama and plenty of sizzling hot action with powerful and passionate heroes who have it all: wealth, status, good looks…everything but the right woman.
6 stories per month.

HEROES

Experience all the excitement of a gripping thriller, with an intense romance at its heart. Resourceful, true-to-life women and strong, fearless men face danger and desire - a killer combination!
8 stories per month.

DARE

Sensual love stories featuring smart, sassy heroines you'd want as a best friend, and compelling intense heroes who are worthy of them.
4 stories per month.

To see which titles are coming soon, please visit

millsandboon.co.uk/nextmonth